BANJO ON MY KNEE

By
Carlton W. Truax

Senior Press

Hilton Head Island, South Carolina

Library Of Congress Catalog Number 94-074139

ISBN Number 0-9636845-5-8

Published by Senior Press

Produced by Windsor Associates, San Diego, CA

Printed in the United States of America

DEDICATION

I gratefully dedicate BANJO ON MY KNEE, in celebration of the Lord Jesus Christ who dedicated His life so that I might live eternally, to my wife, Georgianna Wilson Truax.

ACKNOWLEDGMENTS

Getting a novel into print in this high-tech age requires the wizardry of those who can unravel the confusion of Babel. The plot of BANJO ON MY KNEE came from the computer of my brain and the information in it came from education and a lifetime appetite for reading everything. Therefore, I owe a word of thanks to the those who taught me to read and write and to writers who wrote what I read.

My special thanks go to Charles Paschal of the Palmetto Computer Club and my son, Edgar M. Truax, who supervised the technical preparation of my material. Without their extraordinary help I could never have communicated the book from my brain to the brains of readers.

BONMAISON

1979

Rumors of treasures on the Gordyne plantation have floated around the South Carolina Low Country since the Civil War ended, ebbing and flowing like the tide moving through the coastal creeks and bays. They are in flood again, spreading far beyond the Santee River Basin.

Writers for several magazines and newspapers have asked citizens of St. Stephens questions about these rumors. When a reporter friend of mine from a tabloid learned that I was married to a Gordyne, he called me in Springfield, Ill. where I work for a newspaper. He said a wire service was planning a story about some missing Civil War gold shipments.

To stop the speculation, my wife's family decided I was qualified as a journalist to put into writing details of certain recent events and their connection with a legend which has been until now only oral history. I agreed though I must confess I find many of the sacraments of the "War Between the States" most tiresome. My northern blood refuses to quicken when "Dixie" is played and it matters not at all to me that bronze stars mark the spots where Sherman's shells chipped granite from the state's Capitol building in Columbia. But when I married Miss Santee Gordyne of St. Stephens, I became involved in three centuries of history which included an aristocratic antebellum tradition and the legend. The Gordyne estate wasn't much of a plantation when I first came south to meet the family of the woman who was to become my wife. The Gordyne name is found among the first settlers of old "Charlestown." A branch of the family early moved to the banks of the Santee River and built Bonmaison before the Revolution. As they prospered in cotton and tobacco the family added to the house until it became a columned mansion. The Civil War ended the years of prosperity.

Bonmaison hasn't changed much since my first visit in 1947. It is a mysterious and majestic ruin facing the river. Six massive columns stand nearly thirty feet tall on a low wall. They support beams upon which the third floor rests. The driveway between the columns and five semi-circular steps leading to the recessed front door is paved with handmade bricks. It is wide enough to unload a two-horse carriage.

In the magnificent entrance hall a flying staircase defies gravity to circle up to the third story. All of the thirty-two rooms were built on a royal scale and the whole is roofed with copper. Bonmaison had not been occupied in seventy years. Its brilliant white paint, which once reflected the bright southern sun, peeled off years ago from the wide, heart-pine siding. By the 40s the house was being used to store bales of hay, bags of fertilizer and seed and other farm supplies. Benjamin L. Gordyne IV did not greet us there. Instead Santee's grandfather met us on the porch of a neat farmhouse nearer the highway.

"Gran'pa," Santee said, "I'd like you to meet Mark Weston. He's a schoolmate of mine at Wheaton College. We're going to get married next spring."

"I've been told you're from Springfield." He sounded like a lawyer questioning a hostile witness.

"Yes, sir," I said as if I'd confessed a mortal sin.

"That's where Lincoln was from."

I thought I'd met a true son of the Confederacy who did not appreciate the fact that the great-granddaughter of the "Colonel" was going to marry a Yankee. Then he grinned and shook my

2

hand.

I misjudged the old gentleman. The fact that I went hunting with him during that brief November visit and showed I believed a good hound knows more about hunting than any living man, might have convinced Gordyne that his granddaughter had at least as much sense as a bird dog when it came to finding a man.

The old man was born three years after Lee surrendered and grew up during Reconstruction. I'll always remember him wearing a sweat-stained brown hat and blue-striped bib overalls. He was lean as rawhide and long years of hard work had bent him into a permanent stoop. However, there wasn't a room in his house that didn't have at least one bookcase filled with volumes showing the wear of use. Their margins were scribbled with his comments. I've spent time looking through some of those books and I believe he argued with everyone except the authors of his Bible. That had comments of another sort.

He took me to see Bonmaison.

"It's a shame to let it fall to ruin," I said.

"Not many in these parts have been able to afford to live in that style since the war of northern aggression," he said with a sly smile.

"Northern aggression?" I mocked, "If I remember my history, your uncle was one of The Citadel cadets who began that war when he manned a cannon on the Charleston battery to fire on Union forces in Fort Sumter."

He laughed as we turned away from Bonmaison.

"I've hoped for nigh on seventy years I could move someone into that old house again," he said sadly. "I've come to believe it won't ever happen now."

That spring, when the dogwoods were like patches of snow in the greening hardwood forests and the azaleas and redbuds were a glory around the little frame church on the edge of the swamp, Santee and I returned to Berkeley County to be married.

The night before our wedding Gran'pa and I sat on the front porch as the April moon rose over the hardwood forest. We talked late and I recall little. I do remember one thing.

3

"Hidden out there is enough gold to fight a war," he said. Then I heard the legend of Gordyne gold from the son of the man who brought the legend home from a Union prison and whose mother is part of the story. He talked until Rain, Santee's mother, came out to get him.

"I might have known," she said. "Gran'pa is telling his tall tale again. Gold. Gold. Gold. Gordyne men are all dreamers. If we'd charged people for diggin' on our land, we'd have more money than they ever could of found."

"It's a good story though," I said.

"Yes, it's a good story. It would be much better if it were true. Come on, Gran'pa, it's late and you've got to get enough rest for the wedding tomorrow."

Gordyne men may be dreamers, but they seem to have a knack for marrying practical women. Rain is no exception and not one to let yesterday's glories interfere with today's duties or pleasures. Her hair, which was black when I married her daughter, is now a white glory over and around an oval face which shows the years only in lines engraved by smiles near deep blue eyes. By holding herself tall, she masks the fact that she's rather short. I've seldom seen her when she wasn't in command. She bustles like a mother hen protecting a brood of chicks.

The next day Rain sat beside Gran'pa as Santee and I were married in the church where Gordynes have worshipped since it was built in 1823. Three months later on a steaming afternoon the funeral for Benjamin L. Gordyne IV, 78, was held in that same church. Following the service, the procession wound over a black dirt road under arching live oaks to the Gordyne cemetery on a bluff overlooking the river. The graveyard in which seven generations of Gordynes lie at rest is surrounded by a wrought iron fence which appears to be fashioned of swords with points embedded in a low, moss-grown brick wall. The top rail of the fence is formed by joining the hilts together. The monuments marking each grave are another testimony to the changing fortunes of the family during the two hundred and fifty years the plot has been used to bury its dead. The latest stones are less pretentious.

Driving home after the funeral, we passed Bonmaison, another reminder of a time when the Gordyne fortune was at its peak and I told Gran'pa that somehow I would try to move somebody back into the splendid ghost. However, Santee and I returned to Illinois and, except for trips to St. Stephens about twice a year, I seldom thought about the old house and my promise.

As we sat around the dinner table during one of those visits, Santee's father detailed a plan to expand his farm.

"That's what I want to do if I can find the money."

"There are a lot of people who would pay well for a thousand acres," I suggested.

"We'll never sell a foot of Gordyne land," he vowed.

"Why?" I asked. "You can't farm half of it and without money you can't half farm any of it."

"Out there somewhere there is enough gold to pay for a war. Some day it will be found and it will be on Gordyne Plantation."

"Like father, like son," Rain broke in angrily. "Always adreamin'. It'll never be a plantation again, but a little more reality and a lot less myth would make this place a better farm. Will we have to dig into Bart Gordyne's grave to convince you the gold is at the bottom of the Atlantic Ocean?"

"Pa wouldn't ever let anyone do that while he was alive," he said and that closed the conversation. I never brought the subject up again.

Thirty-two years after my first visit, a telephone call in the night brought us back to St. Stephens. Santee's father was in a Charleston hospital and not expected to live. A week later they buried him in the cemetery where four others who bore the same name rested. Those of us who gathered at his grave did not inherit his dream. Again we took that sad journey past Bonmaison. Nobody was making promises anymore.

The family sat late around the kitchen table, eating and visiting with friends. Rain was the first to leave for bed. She was already in the kitchen when I came downstairs the next morning.

"Good morning, Mama," I said.

"'Morning."

"Did you sleep well?"

"Exhausted, I reckon. Best night's sleep I've had since Benjamin took sick. Are you ready for breakfast?"

"We nibbled until after midnight. I don't think I'm ready for one of your breakfasts. I'll pour a cup of coffee." She had already reached for the pot.

"What have you got planned for today?" I asked.

"Well, this house is in ruin. I haven't been able to get anything done, what with running to Charleston every day. I've just got to get things back together."

"Not today, Mama," said Santee as she came down the stairs. "You've got a daughter and a daughter-in-law, both grown women, who can do that for you. This is your day to get out of the house. Relax and be good to yourself."

"But what will I do? I've got to keep busy."

"Now, Mama, for once you do what I say. Martha and I can handle the chores around here. Mark, you and Bull take Mama fishin'. Y'all will just be underfoot here."

Bull is Santee's brother, B.L. Gordyne, Jr., and Martha is his wife. Until this generation he would have spelled it all out, "Benjamin LeGare Gordyne" and put a roman numeral after it. He was the sixth in succession to have that name. Against his father's will, he laid aside the ancient history when he left the farm. In Charleston where he works he is known as just "B.L.," or "Bull," a name he earned on a high school football field.

"Well," said Rain with make-believe reluctance, "It's been a while since I was afishin'. A walk to the river would be pleasin'."

Mama can outfish most men. I consider fishing almost as essential to life as eating, and Bull, though he was making progress in the Charleston business community, never forgot his raising on the river. So we got ready. Mama is "ol' timey" enough she even wears a dress to fish and her tote bag takes the place of pockets. Picking up our rods, we headed past Bonmaison to where the amber waters of the river slipped quietly between forested

6

walls. When she reached the bluff, Rain turned and looked back over the carefully tended fields around the house below and sighed.

"How're you going to take care of all this without Daddy?" Bull asked.

"It may not be the time to bring it up, but, Benny, do you reckon we should think about selling it?"

"You may be right, Mama. I'm not a farmer and maybe it's time to bury the dream."

Bull grew up with the legend, all based on reports of Col. Benjamin L. Gordyne, CSA, and his wife, Heather. Like others who have kept the legend alive, Bull has a lot of the dreamer in him. Yet he is also his mother's son and Rain does not believe in fairy tales. He earned the name "Bull" in high school because he was dreamer enough to believe that a five-foot-seven boy could move a football against opponents six inches taller and fifty pounds heavier. Common sense told him he had to add something else to the equation. That same combination brought him out of the Army after World War II as a master sergeant and is pushing him against the big boys of business today. He still has a military crew cut. Though some muscle has changed to fat I don't want to wrestle him.

"There's a lot of space between San Francisco and New York where a gold shipment might have gone astray," he said. "It's probably at the bottom of the ocean."

"Mark, what do you think?" Rain turned to me.

"It's up to you, Bull and Santee," I said. "The legend and land are both yours. I just married into this family."

"The day is too lovely to be bothered by such things. Let's see if the fish are bitin'."

Turning to the river, she glanced at Bonmaison where a tall chimney hugged the east end of the old house. Most of the paint had peeled away revealing weathered boards. Some of those hand-hewn planks were hanging loose.

"Look at that." Rain frowned. "The woodbin door is coming off. I'd sure appreciate it if y'all would fix it before you leave."

"Tomorrow," I said. "Now, let's go fishing."

"Right." She took two or three steps towards the river, glanced back over her shoulder, stopped and said, "You two go on. I'll fish another day."

This sudden change of mind was unlike her. Bull asked, "What's the matter, Mama?"

"Nothin'. Nothin' at all. I just want to be alone to think on it for a spell."

"Think on what?" I watched her face.

"Selling the Gordyne Plantation. I've been wanting to sell part of it ever since Benjamin first brought me here. Now I can and I really don't know. Y'all go on. I'm goin' into the old house to be alone and pray for a spell. Maybe I'll join y'all later."

I looked at Bull. He shrugged. "O.K., Mama," he said. We climbed down to the river.

The fish were not biting below the house and we moved frequently looking for the right spot. About midmorning we found it. In the excitement of reeling in a half dozen good-sized rockfish, we forgot about Rain. Hunger eventually turned our minds to other things and we cut through the woods avoiding the bluff where Bonmaison stands.

"Behold the fishermen return," Bull shouted as we neared the cottage. It had been a while since we'd been on the river together and a good catch made us as excited as boys. Holding our trophies high, we crossed the yard. Santee and Martha came to the kitchen door to see what their men had caught. They were impressed, but eventually Santee asked, "Where's Mama?"

"Didn't she come home?" Bull asked.

"No."

"She decided not to go fishing with us," I said. "We left her up at the old house."

Bull and I took his five-year old Ford station wagon up the dirt road to the bluff. Rain was walking to meet us. He skidded to a stop and jumped out.

"Mama, where have you been?" he demanded.

"In Bonmaison."

"All day?"

"Yes."

"What have you been doing?'

"Readin'."

"Reading? There's nothing in that old house to read."

"It isn't the old house now. It's Bonmaison again."

"Bonmaison? Mama, what's gotten into you?"

"Readin'."

"Reading? Mama, you can be exasperating. What have you been reading?"

"Mrs. Eunice Jamison Gordyne's notes on the Civil War."

"What?"

She pulled a faded notebook out of her tote bag. Bull took it from her, looked at it briefly and handed it to me.

The book was scorched brown with age and brittle in my hand. On its ornate pasteboard cover an odd bit of verse had been lettered. This was so precise it appeared to be part of the decorations printed by the manufacturer. It read:

> "Death's words even down
> The other side.
> 'Tis won. Do rest ill.
> Three shadows meet,
> Or eat Juanitta's tone."

It made no sense. What attracted my attention were the names written around the four sides of the cover, one name to each side. "Benjamin L. Gordyne" appeared twice, on the top and right. On the left was "Bartholomew J. Gordyne" and on the bottom was "Mrs. Eunice Jamison Gordyne." Each name was followed by a date of birth. From these I guessed the two Benjamins were father and son. There was another difference. A date of death was given only for the older Benjamin -- Jan. 3, 1864.

Inside the penmanship seemed to have been done by the same hand that wrote the four names on the cover. Although time had faded the ink, all the letters were neatly formed and easy to read.

"Where did you get this?" I asked.

"There is a false bottom to the woodbin by the east fireplace," she said. "Let's go home and I'll tell you about it."

We drove back and gathered around the kitchen table to examine the book as Rain told how she had spent the day.

"Y'all know the woodbins by each fireplace have doors to the outside so they can be filled without carrying logs through the house," she said. "One door has come loose. Well, this mornin' y'all agreed to fix it. The sun was shining into the woodbin as we were talkin' and I could see the ends of the logs that have been in there for as long as I've been a member of this family. Something was sparkling in the sun underneath those logs. I thought, as we started to walk away, that whatever was shining had to be under the floor. That was strange. Well, I sent y'all fishin' so I could satisfy my curiosity."

She paused and Santee exploded. "What was it?"

"When I went to investigate, I found the door hanging by one loose screw. I noticed that the floor of the bin near the door which was exposed to the weather had rotted away."

"Mama, stop teasing and tell us," Santee cried.

"Under the floor I found this," she said and, with a flourish, pulled from her tote bag an antique gold wedding ring. Laying this on the table, she reached in her bag and came up with a jeweled comb and a silver filigree brooch. Then she extracted pearls and an assortment of other jewelry.

"All this was near the outside wall. That notebook says your great-great-grandmother hid it in there when she heard that Sherman was crossing into South Carolina to keep him from finding it if he came callin'. There was also this cache of gold United States coins. The old lady wasn't betting on the Confederacy. Up towards the front of the compartment where the weather didn't get to it, there were some other things such as a complete set of heirloom silverware like this."

She displayed a tarnished knife, fork and spoon. "Silverware is usually kept in a self-sealing box to keep it from tarnishing," she continued. "The box was there, but the silver wasn't in it. I opened the box and that's where I found the notebook and started reading." She paused to catch her breath. Excitedly she continued.

10

"This notebook was Miss Eunice's filing cabinet. Pasted in it are letters, several from her oldest son, Col. Benjamin L. Gordyne, CSA. The other boy didn't write. In one letter Benjy says he and Bart were leaving on a special mission and would not be able to write for a while. And what do you think of this?" Turning to a page towards the back, she read, "Feb. 8, 1865. A familiar visitor surprised me. Brought news of Bart and Benjy. California? No wonder I haven't heard from them. Both in good health. My visitor says Benjy may bring home a wife. Heather. A good name."

"According to the record, the 'familiar visitor' stayed three days. He attended church with Miss Eunice and left."

Rain paused and Bull put into words a thought we all had, "Something strange about that."

"More than strange, if you've read the rest of it. All the way through she calls people by name. This is a 'familiar visitor' and Gran'pa told of people seeing Bart in church. Far as I can tell, Miss Eunice never mentions that visit, unless this is it."

"But why would she write it that way?" I asked.

Rain started reading again.

"My visitor left today on a secret assignment."

Rain turned two pages and read, "Feb. 27, 1865. Sad day. Woe-be-gone darky brought Bart home this morning. Said he was killed in battle near Salkehatchie River. Put his casket in parlor. Won't open it for visitors. The darky also helped prepare Nida for burial tomorrow."

"What do you make of that?" Rain asked.

"That's all she says about her son being dead?" Santee asked. "It doesn't sound real."

"Maybe it wasn't. Look at the front cover," Rain said and handed the notebook to Bull. We gathered around to look.

"She recorded the day her husband died," I said. "But there is no death date for Bartholomew."

"Maybe Bart wasn't in that casket." Santee looked at us.

"Seems more than likely," Bull said.

"The gold!" she cried. "Let's go get it."

"It's getting dark." Martha was the cautious type.

"I'm fryin' fish and havin' a good night's sleep before I start diggin' in graveyards in the dark for treasure," said Rain.

Santee was for letting dinner wait. The rest of us were of a more practical mind. We ate, talking all the time about Eunice and her diary. By the end of the meal we were too excited to wait. Leaving the dishes on the table and taking a kerosene lantern and two shovels, we hurried to the cemetery.

Light from a quarter moon filtered through branches forming the roof of the tunnel through which the dirt path lay. Scattered clouds occasionally added to the darkness. Sometimes sighs of drifting leaves and infrequent cries of whippoorwills and hooting owls amplified the silence. Bonmaison stood to one side in ghostly stillness.

It was a twenty-minute climb to the place of the dead. The cemetery consists of two parts. Inside the wrought iron fence the Gordynes rest in graves marked by granite and marble. Outside, fenced by split rails of cypress, are the graves of numerous slaves. Few of the cypress slabs which marked these have survived. Here trees draw back from the clearing where so many lay. I pumped pressure into the lamp and lit the mantel while the others located the stone which bore the name of Bartholomew J. Gordyne. Santee held the light. Bull and I dug.

A light breeze rustled through ancient branches and moved the tall sweet grass among the tombs around us. We kept shoveling. The moon set behind the moss-shrouded trees. Darkness rose out of the swamp and with it came a damp fog, leaving us stranded on a small island of light.

Low Country earth is soft and dark. For an hour and a half the only sounds were the rhythmic swish of two shovels moving dirt and the whispered conversation of three women. Suddenly there was a hollow sound as my shovel hit something solid. Santee lifted the lantern higher. The beam showed my shovel had scarred wood. I bent down to inspect it.

"Redwood," I said.

"As grown in California?" Martha asked.

Bull and I hastily scraped away the remaining earth from the top of the casket.

"It's bolted shut," Bull observed. "They don't make coffins like that around here."

Most of the bolts seemed to have rusted away. The few which remained were easily pushed out of the wood with the point of a shovel. I straddled the head and Bull the foot and we bent to take hold of the coffin's cover.

"Ready?" he asked.

"Ready," I said and we strained. It came away and we set it aside. Santee held the lantern high. Someone screamed and I looked down into the hollow sockets of an eyeless skull. The rotted remains of a flowered dress and a tarnished silver necklace indicated the deceased had been a woman. We did not look for further identification. As we replaced the lid, I noticed a peculiarity about some of the bolts that had once secured it to the casket.

Rain interrupted my thoughts by saying, "That does it. There isn't any gold and I'm sick of speculation. Tomorrow we put this land up for sale."

"I so move," said Bull.

"I vote aye," said Santee.

"Unanimous?" I asked.

"Yes," said Martha.

The women made their way back home while Bull and I covered the grave of the woman buried under Bart Gordyne's stone.

"You know," I said to Santee the next afternoon as we sat on the porch doing more speculating, "I have a feeling those bolts were moved before."

"What do you mean?"

"We broke some of them out of the wood, but some of them weren't rusted away. They were just lying loose."

"You mean someone else thought the gold was buried there, dug it up and found what we found?"

"Could be," I said, "but who?"

13

"Gran'pa?"

"Lots of people have looked for that gold, but your grandfather had seventy-eight years to think about it."

"The old buzzard knew all that time some woman occupied his Uncle Bart's grave and never told anybody."

"He probably didn't want anyone to know what he found and that's why he never let anyone else dig there."

"If Bart isn't in that grave, where did he go?"

"That's the skeleton in your aristocratic family closet."

"What's that supposed to mean?"

"If he shipped the body of a woman home in his own coffin, he might have had good reason to permanently disappear and his brother and nephew had good reason not to tell anyone."

"You mean he killed her?"

"Can you think of a better way to hide a murder than to bury the body in your own grave?"

The only sound was the squeak of the porch swing. Then she said, "You reckon that's Rositta in Bart's grave?"

"Could be I suppose. According to the legend she and her brother tried to kill him for that gold and the three of them were last seen on that sinking ship. If they tried again, she may have ended up dead."

Inside, Bull hung up the telephone after talking to a real estate broker in Charleston.

"Well, it's on the market," he called and began reading the browned notebook.

I walked into the cottage to stand before a portrait of the Gordyne brothers. Santee says it has hung in that same spot by the fireplace since it was moved from Bonmaison more than a hundred years ago. It was painted when the brothers were cadets at The Citadel. They were in dress uniforms. Benjamin, the older, graduated two years before his brother helped start the Civil War by manning a cannon that fired on Fort Sumter. The picture shows them in the luxurious parlor of the plantation house. Benjamin is seated in a high backed chair upholstered with gold satin. Bartholomew stands beside him. Benjamin was a lean man with a sharp face and a broad forehead. His hair, the color of old honey, had enough wave in it to make it look bouncy. His eyes, under thin brows, were tea-brown like the waters of the Santee River.

The younger brother was square. He gave the impression of strength like a bull and he resembled Bull. His hair was curly with a touch more red than his brother's and his eyes, if the artist had been accurate, were a Gulf Stream blue.

It was Ben who survived the Civil War and came back to St. Stephens with the legend that kept the rumors alive.

Records show about eighteen million dollars in gold was shipped each year during the Civil War from western mines to eastern banks. There is no record of how much started across the continent but never made it. There are, however, reports of unsuccessful efforts to divert some of that gold to the Confederacy and there is this legend.

The following story of what happened to the two Gordyne brothers of St. Stephens, S.C., during the 1860s is the work of Mark Weston, based on reports passed down to his heirs by Col. Benjamin L. Gordyne III, CSA.

1
THE ASSIGNMENT

1863

Funerals for those of greatness are traumatic events. The final rites for the man known as Gen. Stonewall Jackson put an entire nation in mourning.

A premonition seemed to hang over Richmond as Col. Benjamin L. Gordyne III escorted the body of his dead commander from Chancellorsville that day in May. Gloom continued to walk with him after the sad ceremonies when he was ushered into the office of Jefferson Davis, president of the Confederacy.

There were some who knew the South could not prevail before the first shot was fired off Fort Sumter. Their numbers increased when four border states were neutralized by internal action of their own citizens or by federal strategy. Still the prospects were not impossible, although the death of Jackson after the spectacular victory at Chancellorsville was considered by a few to be an omen of the ultimate outcome. In that battle Lee's army humiliated an army half again its own size. Yet some who knew the cost began to wonder how many more victories the South could afford. Such things did not trouble Colonel Gordyne.

He had absolute confidence in Gen. Robert E. Lee and the Army of Northern Virginia. He was only puzzled that he had been ordered to report to the president.

Jefferson Davis looked up from the papers spread on the desk and saw the young man standing straight as a Carolina pine before him.

"Col. Benjamin L. Gordyne reporting as ordered, sir," the soldier said.

The president inspected the officer carefully and was impressed. Gordyne looked like a model soldier. Over six feet tall, his shoulders seemed half that wide. He had on the gray dress uniform with sword he had worn in the funeral procession. His hat was under his left arm. He appeared confident. Not arrogant.

"Sit down, Colonel Gordyne," Davis said. The young man handed him a sealed envelope and obeyed. There was silence while the president read the letter inside.

"We lost a good soldier," Davis said at last.

"We lost a lot of good soldiers, sir."

"But we won a great victory."

"Yes, sir."

There was silence again. The president stood and paced behind his desk.

"General Lee has great confidence in you," he said. "I am going to share that confidence."

"Thank you, sir."

Davis walked several steps and turned again to Gordyne.

"The North has more men than we," he said. "Our troops have demonstrated they can even that up and our generals have shown they are more than a match for Lincoln. The South will win this war if...I am going to put part of that 'if' in your hands.

"What we need is feed for our horses and supplies for our troops. We also need a commitment from the nations of Europe. To get that we have got to convince them of our victory."

Davis put his hands on his desk and leaned towards Gordyne. Lowering his voice, he said, "In a few days General Lee will move his army north. He will cross into Pennsylvania. One purpose is

18

to encourage those in the north who want Lincoln to stop the war and to convince the Europeans that we will win. We will also bring Maryland into the Confederacy. This will more than offset our losses in the west. A short range purpose is to capture the supplies we need for our army. That is well and good for short range. However, I must think of supplying this army in the field for a long war. That takes money, lots of money. Gold."

He was silent again as he sat down. Gordyne waited.

"Our informants tell us western gold is being shipped east regularly. You are to find a way to divert as much of that gold as possible to the Confederacy and return to the South with as much of it as you can bring."

The president paused and, leaning across his desk, looked intensely at Gordyne.

"I said 'you' because I assume you will volunteer for this duty. It is not an enterprise I would in clear conscience order anyone to do. You will be operating without orders, undercover, in the enemy's territory, and, because of the secrecy involved, many of your own people may think you have deserted. I will need your answer by tomorrow morning."

Gordyne stood.

"I do not need the night to know my answer, sir," he said.

Davis smiled. Standing, he walked around his desk.

"Nevertheless, I insist that you have a night to think about it. The assignment you are taking may very well be impossible. Many of my advisors think it insane. If, after a night of consideration, you think it is impossible, then you are not the man to try it no matter how willing you may be. Tomorrow morning I do not want to know if you will do it. I knew that when General Lee sent you to me. I want to know if you think you can do it."

As he said this, he ushered the younger man to the door where they shook hands, and Gordyne went out past the waiting attendants. He walked through the streets of Richmond considering the distance to San Francisco. One question repeated itself in his mind like the call of the whippoorwill back home in Carolina: "How will I do it?"

As the spring day faded into the soft grey of the evening, he found himself by the Wilson Funeral Parlor. He stopped at the street crossing to allow horses drawing an enclosed freight wagon to pass. It was driven by an emaciated white man wearing the mourning clothes of a mortician. Riding with him was a huge black man in overalls and a grey shirt. The wagon was unusually large and it had oversized windows on each side. The horses turned into the driveway of the funeral home. He watched as the driver dismounted and went into the mortuary. The Negro went to the rear of the wagon and opened the doors. Several men came out of the funeral home, pulled a luxurious casket from the hearse and carried it into the building. From the straining of the men who carried the coffin, Ben determined it was occupied.

He started to walk away, then turned suddenly back to stare at the hearse. The lettering on the side read, "Pastorman Funeral Home, Washington, D. C."

He strolled over to where the black man was releasing the horses from their harnesses.

"Beautiful," Ben said, stroking one of them.

"Yes, suh, they sho' is. Mr. Pastorman don't have nothin' but the bes'."

"Must have been a heavy man in that box?"

"Mr. Odel Cromer didn't lose no weight dyin'."

"Did Mr. Cromer live in Washington?"

"Yes, colonel."

"Was Richmond his home?"

"Yes, suh. We bringed him home to bury."

"When will you be going back?"

"Fust light."

"What's your name?"

"Adam, suh."

"Just Adam?"

"Yes, suh."

"Mighty big wagon for a hearse," he commented.

"When you buries the dead of battle, you sometimes has to carry mor'en one body en a load," said Adam.

Gordyne rubbed the face of a horse.

"Beautiful," he said again and walked once around the hearse.

"Maybe I'll see you again, Adam." He turned to continue his walk as the night settled in.

Later he took a hotel room and slept peacefully. In the morning he was waiting when the president arrived at his office.

"The dead can pass through battle lines," Ben told him. "I can get to Washington. From there, I can get to any place. If I can go anywhere, I can return. But I cannot return until I am gone, and I cannot go until I've started. I start today."

"I'm not sure I know what you are talking about," Davis said. "It is probably just as well that I don't. Here is some federal money. It will start you on your way. Your contact in San Francisco is a man who calls himself 'Bama Smith. It isn't his real name and he's probably about as honest as Judas Iscariot but he's southern. Watch him anyway."

"Sir," Ben said, "I'd like to take one man with me."

Davis hesitated.

"Because of the secrecy involved, I am reluctant to grant that request. Who do you propose to take?"

"My brother, Bart, sir."

"Is he anything like you?"

"No, sir. But as my mother says, 'One's cut from oak and the other from pine, but you can use both to get a job done.'"

"Permission granted. Colonel Gordyne, the North will not tire of this war unless we carry it to them. To do this we must have that gold. The success of our cause may very well rest in your hands. You must not fail."

"Yes, sir."

Picking up Bart's special assignment orders, Ben went out, mounted his horse and rode the post road towards Washington. He was in no great hurry and the sun had shifted to his left shoulder when he overtook the empty hearse belonging to Pastorman Funeral Home.

"So, Adam, our meeting again is sooner than we expected," he said as he drew up alongside the funeral wagon.

"Why, so we does, colonel, so we does," Adam smiled. "Is yo' travelin' to Washington, too?"

Ben laughed, "Don't think Mr. Lincoln would welcome me."

"You're right enough there, rebel," said the white man in the undertaker's suit, sitting next to Adam. "There won't ever be a rebel soldier put his foot in Washington."

Ben looked at him in silence for a moment and then said, "I don't believe we've met."

"This is Mr. Robert Barnes." Adam made the introduction.

"Glad to make your acquaintance," said Ben, "but your remark sounded suspiciously like a challenge. Would you care to make a small wager on that? It wouldn't surprise me if I didn't ride in your wagon right into Washington."

Now Barnes laughed.

"In a hearse? Yes, sir, that's the only way you'll ever get into Washington, and I'll be more than obliged to let you ride my meat wagon free."

Ben returned the laugh.

"I expect I'll be taking you up on that offer, Mr. Barnes. Thank you very much. And good day to you. Goodbye, Adam. Maybe we'll meet again."

"Yes, suh, colonel."

He rode on to a stage stop near Hanover Junction, had dinner and was in bed before Barnes and Adam drove in. Early the next morning, he was in the saddle again. He repeated the sequence that night, at another stage station.

On the third day out of Richmond, Ben went looking for Bart who was working himself into a court martial. He had already lost his lieutenancy and been demoted to the rank of private. Ben knew that one more stain on his brother's already blemished record, and Bart would probably be sent back to South Carolina.

He had heard that Bart was assigned to a regiment patrolling the front south of Washington. Early that morning he found Bart's commander and learned that Bart was on leave. He gave the major his brother's special orders and went looking for him.

Ben figured he was probably at the nearest tavern. But before he found him, he had to get a coffin and vehicle to move it. He stopped by a cluster of farm buildings and exchanged his horse and saddle for a long-faced mule and weatherworn wagon.

Entering the next town, Ben spotted the Rebel Flag, a tavern across the street from Buncombe Funeral Home. He hitched his mule near the mortuary and went in to buy the largest pine coffin in stock. When this was done and the empty casket loaded in his wagon, he started across the street. Suddenly a boisterous crowd spilled out of the tavern. Ben figured Bart was at the center of it and pushed his way through the mob. How right he was!

Bart was taking off his shirt preparing to battle a mule. Most of the men in the noisy crowd were betting on the mule and getting no takers.

"I'll cover every Yankee dollar you got," Ben shouted.

Bart looked up and grinned in his direction. Stripped to the waist and ready for action, he looked like Atlas about to pick up the world. The mule, tied to a hitching post near the tavern, was minding her own business.

A young woman stood nearby. The tint of her hair was the gold of a rose, a shifting shade like that of a flame hovering over burning logs. She was holding the wagered money. Her smile was that of an excited child and there was a sparkle in her grey-green eyes. She wore the plain blue dress of a working woman but it didn't conceal her slender figure. Her white apron indicated to Ben that she served in the Rebel Flag.

"Anybody else want to get some of the colonel's money?" she asked. "Anybody else got any Yankee dollars?"

When there was no response, Bart stepped to the center of the circle.

"Everybody stand back," he said, stepping off the distance to the mule. He untied her and handed the reins to a spectator.

"I'm going to walk off ten paces," he said. "When I count ten, you let her loose and fire a shot right close to her ear to scare the bejabbers out of her. Y'hear?"

"Yeah."

Bart counted as he walked away. At eight, the man let loose

the reins and fired a shot that took off the tip of the mule's ear. With a terrified jump, the animal leaped half way to Bart and to the spectators it appeared she would run him down. She swerved to avoid a collision. In coordinated action Bart ducked under the frightened animal's ribs and his massive right arm caught her fore legs. Straightening his back and legs, Bart lifted the mule completely off the ground. Her momentum and his quick twist flipped the huge animal over on her side. Jumping back, he avoided the kicking hooves as the mule struggled to stand.

While the crowd cheered, Bart was looking for the man who didn't wait for him to count to ten. He was trying hard not to be found by ducking into the milling crowd. Bart pulled him out by his coat collar.

"Can you count to ten?" he demanded.

"Yes, sir," said the terrified man.

"Start counting."

On the count of ten, Bart said, "I just wanted to be sure," and hit him. "That's for not counting right. And this is for taking a piece out of that poor mule's ear." He hit him again. A third blow was unnecessary.

"You can't do that," said one of the man's friends who was unhappy about the outcome of his wager. He picked up a piece of firewood. Three men moved in on Bart. That started a free-for-all with Bart's fellow soldiers battling civilians.

The brawl gave the young woman the cover she needed to try a little larceny of her own. She started to slip away with the Yankee money. It was a mistake.

"I can't believe a lady of the south would do anything dishonest," said Ben as she stepped into the Rebel Flag.

"Why, colonel," she answered, fluttering her long dark lashes and smiling. "How could you even think such a thing?"

Ben thought her accent was little too heavy for genuine northern Virginia, but those eyes, that hair, and those dimples made up for a lot of suspicion. Ushering her into the cool, dark interior of the Rebel Flag, he noticed that she was shorter by a head than he and probably weighed a scant hundred pounds, but she walked with the assurance of a well-bred southern gentlewoman.

While the brawl outside occupied the attention of most of the other patrons, they took a corner table and he offered to buy her a drink. But first he relieved her of the leather tote bag in which she had deposited his money.

"Why did you bet on Bart?" she asked handing over the bag.

"It was more an investment. I've watched my brother wrestle mules before. I doubled my money with no risk."

As he got acquainted with Heather Duncan Wanderman, the noise of street fighting gradually died away. Presently Bart strolled in, buttoning his shirt.

"It makes a man wonder if Dixie is worth fighting for. It raises serious questions about the whole matter," he grumbled and sat down.

"What's the matter?" Ben asked.

"I don't know what the South is coming to when you can't trust a southern gentleman to count to ten in a simple wager and, while you're fighting for his cause, your own brother runs off with your lady. It tends to cause disillusionment."

"Well, you did have a good fight, didn't you?" said Ben.

"Yes, that's something to think about."

"You want the fight, the money and the lady. Your greed shocks me. Aren't I entitled to some of life's pleasures? However, I'll buy you a drink."

"I fight, he gets the money, and then he's being real generous. He's going to buy me a drink with the money I won. Miss Wanderman, do you really think that's justice? How can you associate with such a scoundrel?"

"I'm trying to teach him some manners."

"I fear I shall have to postpone the lessons," Ben said. "The Confederate Army has some slight claim to our time. Will you please excuse us, Miss Wanderman?"

She stood, backed away, but slowly, and stopped.

Ben glanced at her and lowered his voice. "Brother, we have a very important job to do."

"What are you talking about?" Bart sat down.

"Special assignment. We are about to start one long journey, and I do mean long."

He opened his mouth to continue, but Bart put up his hand.

"The army has no claim on my time until midnight."

"I'm sorry, but we have an engagement with a hearse. Your pass herewith canceled."

"Is it Col. Benjamin Legare Gordyne III speaking, sir?"

"It is, and your special orders come from Jefferson Davis."

"Very well, sir."

As they left, Bart waved to Heather Wanderman and called out, "Sorry, we're off to war."

Pastorman's hearse was half an hour behind them when they left Buncombe Corner. As they rode north, Ben explained his plans.

"You were about to be cashiered out of the army anyway," he concluded. "This way you will at least save the family's honor."

"Honor? Everybody in St. Stephens will think we deserted."

"Not if we bring back that gold."

"Do you really think it can be done?"

"Somehow, Bart, we've got to do it."

"Yeah, Ben, I guess you're right. We have got to do it."

It began to rain.

26

2
THE CROSSING

Robert Barnes muttered to himself driving to Washington. It was wet and cold. He would not have chosen this day to return the hearse to the funeral home, but Mr. Pastorman had given him orders to come right back. He needed the hearse. Business was booming. A war close to his funeral home was extremely profitable.

Barnes was also upset because of the delay in Buncombe Corner. He had not expected to pick up a body there. Even if they did get to Washington before dark, he would have to spend some time unloading the hearse.

With all these things to brood over, Barnes was paying little attention to the horses slogging along or the drenched countryside. So it was that he failed to see a wagon pulled back in the woods. He did notice when a rebel soldier stuck a gun in his face and a rebel colonel ordered him to turn his horses in beside the wagon.

Bart opened the door to the hearse.

"Say, Ben," he called, "did you know there's already a coffin in here?"

Ben, holding a gun on Barnes, looked into the hearse.

"Where did you pick this up?" he asked.

"Buncombe Corner."

"Well, it complicates things a little, but we'll just have to take two bodies into Washington."

For the next few minutes Barnes and Adam were busy moving one coffin over to make room for the other and transferring the empty box from the wagon to the hearse.

"Adam," Ben said when the job was done, "what would you do with the mule and wagon if I gave them to you?"

"I'd start me a delivery service, colonel."

Ben lifted his saddlebag into the hearse. Inside where it was dry, he took out a notebook and wrote:

"Note all men that I, Col. Benjamin L. Gordyne III, CSA, of St. Stephens, S.C., do hereby and herewith grant to the man known hitherto as 'Adam' complete and total freedom. His name from this time on shall be Adam Gordyne."

"Can you read?" he said as he handed the paper to Adam.

"No, suh,"

"This paper says you are a free man. You keep it with you so nobody will bother you. The wagon and the mule are yours."

"Just a minute," interjected Barnes, "you can't do that. He isn't yours to liberate."

"As I see it, he's spoils of war, and I took him away from you and I just emancipated him," Ben answered. "You of a mind to do something about it?"

Barnes growled like an angry bear. A growl was no answer to the gun in Bart's hand.

"Adam, get on your way and don't look back," Ben said.

"Thank yo', colonel."

"Mr. Barnes, I'm going to give you a commission as a Confederate colonel," Ben said as Adam drove off.

"I beg your pardon?"

"You and I are going to exchange clothes."

"I beg your pardon?" the undertaker said again.

"Beg it as often as you like, but while you are doing it, get out of those clothes."

"Why?"

"Because Bart is holding a gun at your head."

"Oh, I see."

"Answers a lot of questions, don't it?" said Bart as Barnes hastily unbuttoned his black suit.

When the exchange of clothing had been completed, Ben and Bart tied the undertaker to a tree several hundred feet from the road.

"Somebody will come along here in a day or two," Bart said. "If you holler loud enough, they might hear you."

Bart climbed into the dry interior of the hearse and Ben, taking the driver's seat in the rain, flipped the horses into motion and steered them to the point where the post road crossed into Union territory. They rode for only about twenty minutes in the fading afternoon. Ben stopped and got into the hearse.

"Time for supper," he said, pulling a loaf of brown bread and some cheese and salt fish from his saddlebag.

"We'll be to the bridge in ten minutes," Bart said.

"I want to make the crossing before full dark and while it's still raining. The guards on both sides won't be too anxious to be searching around in the rain and there'll still be light enough for them to see without lanterns."

"How much gold do you think they're shipping east?" Bart asked as they ate.

"I hear it's about eighteen million a year. You remember the steamship Central America which went down in the hurricane off Charleston in '57?"

Bart nodded with a canteen at his lips.

"As I remember it," Bart said, "some of those poor diggers had so much gold sewed into their clothes they couldn't swim. It dragged them to the bottom."

"It's still there," Ben said.

"Seems to me it ought to be easier to get that gold out of the Atlantic right off the coast of South Carolina than to go all the way to the Pacific for it."

"It's usually easier to go three thousand miles horizontally than two hundred feet straight down."

"Does Davis really think we can do this?"

"Somewhere in a pipeline three thousand miles long there's

got to be a weak spot. It shouldn't be too hard to find that weak spot and make it leak."

They finished their meal and Ben returned to the driver's seat. Bart prepared to get inside the empty casket for the crossing. In a few minutes, however, he joined Ben on the driver's bench.

"What's wrong?" Ben asked.

"Something strange back there."

"What?"

"When did they start putting air holes in coffins?"

"What?"

"I don't think the body in that other casket is dead."

"You mean Barnes was smuggling someone into Washington?"

"That occurred to me but I don't think Barnes would have acted as he did if he knew. I think it was done back there at the funeral home."

"We're almost at the crossing now," Ben said. "It's time for you to go into hiding. It's too late to do anything about it. I'll just have to smuggle two live bodies into Washington. Then we'll find out what this is all about."

"I tell you this," Bart said, "I'm sure goin' to put a rope around the other box. I don't want a corpse comin' out until we're ready for him."

"The bridge is right around the next bend. You get in there and hide. Remember, it doesn't have any breathing holes."

"I guess I always knew some day I'd be put in one of those boxes. I just thought I'd be dead first," said Bart as he left.

On the south side of the bridge, the Confederate guards opened the door, saw two coffins and waved Ben on. On the north side the Union patrol ducked out of his tent into the rain, peered through the glassed side of the hearse and let them go.

It was late when Ben crossed into Washington where he twisted and turned through the dark streets until he found a light which shone at the right angle to illuminate the inside of the hearse. Then he joined Bart in the wagon, shutting the doors behind him.

30

"I got an idea on how we can get rid of this other coffin," Bart said loudly. "Let's take it to a graveyard, find a grave open for a funeral tomorrow and bury it."

"That'd take too much time," Ben said. "Let's take it to the city dump. They'll bury it in potter's field."

"If we dump it in the river, it'd float to the ocean."

"You're right. There's a pier over there. I'll back the wagon up so all we have to do is open the door and push this coffin into the water. One splash and we'll be shed of it."

He got out, maneuvered the wagon around a few times, backed and stopped. Once again he got into the hearse with his brother.

"You ready?"

"Yes."

They lifted one end of the casket and heard a scream.

"Don't. Please, don't. I'm in here." A woman's voice!

She was pushing against the lid which Bart had tied shut with cords from the hearse's upholstering.

Bart pulled loose the slip knot. The lid popped open and Heather Wanderman stood up, sputtering.

"You animals," she screamed, scratching and biting and kicking. "You snakes. You worms. You devils."

Bart's experience wrestling mules was of little use in trying to subdue her. Both brothers were skilled in courting southern ladies. Controlling one intent on bloody murder was a subject not covered in their military textbooks at The Citadel. They quickly discovered there are wrestling holds not proper under such circumstances and often those that could be used were of limited value when the woman appeared to be a slippery as a Santee River eel.

Ben had a gun ready when the lid popped off, but he dropped it immediately and joined his brother in getting the outraged woman under control. His first job was to clamp a hand over her mouth so that her screaming would not attract a crowd. She promptly bit him, drawing blood.

"Do that again and you'll be sitting on blisters for thirty

31

days," he promised as he replaced his hand with enough force to convince her of his sincerity. When they finally succeeded in tying her hand and foot, Ben removed his hand from her mouth. She screamed again.

"If you don't stop that noise," Ben said, "we'll put you back in the coffin and nail the lid shut."

"You wouldn't dare," she hissed.

"Bart, put her in the coffin."

"Sure." Picking her up as if she were a little child, Bart began to lower her into the box.

"I'll be quiet," she said and defiantly closed her lips.

With that promise they relaxed. She glared at them. Then she looked out the open door.

"Where's the river?" she demanded.

"River? What river?" Ben asked.

"The river you were fixin' to dump me into."

"Oh, that."

"You tricked me. You weren't going to float me out to sea."

They laughed. She clamped her lips tight and scowled angrily. The laughter died away.

"You've been in that box for a spell," Ben said. "Are you thirsty?"

"Please," she said and he removed the cork from his canteen and tipped it to her lips.

"Hungry?"

"Yes."

"It's only salt fish, cheese and bread, but you're welcome to it."

Bart fed her. She was hungry enough to enjoy the simple food.

"Why did you follow us?" Ben asked.

"It's part of my duties," she said between bites.

"Strange duties for a tavern wench," Bart said.

"Working in the tavern was just a cover to listen to the talk of rebel soldiers."

"You care to tell us about it?" Ben asked.

32

"My real name is Mrs. Warren Duncan Wanderman," she said. "I was married five days before this silly war started and my husband enlisted a week later. Your Confederate killers murdered him at the Battle of Bull Run. At my husband's funeral, I asked a friend of his how I could take Warren's place. He knew I was born in northern Virginia and told me to go back and listen."

"Why did you decide to follow us?" Ben was skeptical.

"When I was holding the money back there, I first wondered why a Confederate colonel had all that Yankee money. Then I asked myself why you wouldn't cover any Confederate notes. You said you doubled your investment. That got me real curious. I knew a hearse was coming in from Richmond and when you said you had an engagement with a hearse and orders from Jefferson Davis, I knew you were going north. I could hear everything you said back there."

She paused. Ben gave her another drink.

"The funeral director is my contact. He communicates with caskets. I could have just sent a report, but when you said you had an appointment with a hearse, I thought you were probably going to steal it. We had other reasons to report to Washington in person, so I persuaded the funeral director to let me ride along to find out what devilment you were up to."

"And did you?" Ben asked.

"It's got something to do with California gold."

"You just committed suicide," Bart said, pulling his gun.

Ben was silent, staring at her. Then he nodded.

"I don't see any alternative," he said. "I wish we could send you back to Jefferson Davis to keep you under guard until the war's over, but there isn't any way to do that. She's delayed us too long. Bart, get it over with."

"Me?" Bart protested. "Why don't you do it?"

Ben pulled his hunting knife and balanced it in his hand. Then he returned it to its scabbard.

"I've shot Yankees. I've butchered hogs. I've wrung the necks of chickens and ducks. I've hunted deer and turkey and rabbits and doves and squirrels and 'possum. But, Bart, how do you kill a woman?"

"If she were a man, I would strangle him and not think twice about it, Ben. But ain't no way I can kill Heather Wanderman."

Heather smiled. "Well," she said, "what are you going to do with me?"

"I wish I knew," Ben answered. "Here we sit a few blocks from where President Lincoln is sleeping this very minute. If they were to catch us, they'd string us up as spies before breakfast and nobody would even say grace over it. But neither of us can bring ourselves to do what we know we got to do if our mission is to succeed."

"It's a strange war," said Bart looking at the gun in his hand.

"There's a cause," said Ben. "President Davis told me the outcome of this war depends on adequate supplies for our troops. They are depending on us doing our duty. You put our entire mission in jeopardy. I regret it, Mrs. Wanderman, but I've got to sentence you to death for spying on the Confederacy. As I do this, I pass sentence on myself, because I cannot delegate this duty. Mrs. Wanderman, I give you a choice. How will you die?"

"You really mean this?" she asked.

"I'm afraid I do, madam."

She hesitated, lowered her eyes for a moment and it appeared she was going to cry. Instead, looking defiantly at him, she said, "You've got another choice."

They stared at her.

"What's that?" they asked simultaneously.

"You can take me with you as a prisoner."

"Can't be done," said Ben. "There's no way two men can stand continuous guard over a woman across the continent and back while carrying out the military assignment we've been given."

Bart grinned and said, "If she were a wife we could."

"You wouldn't dare," she gasped, her eyes opening wide.

"Or, we could put you back in the coffin and ship you across country as part of our baggage. If you don't behave yourself, we could drop you in Indian country and let the Indians have you. I

34

can think of lots of things we could do to make you mind your manners. I'm thinkin' Ben can come up with a few more."

Ben had not spoken. They both turned to him knowing the decision was his.

"There may be a way," he said. "It may get us killed, but we may get killed anyway. We'll try it. To stay alive, you've got to obey the rules, Mrs. Wanderman. There will be times when respect for you as a woman will make it impossible for us to watch you. So the first rule is you will not use those occasions to attempt escape or to pass information to our enemy. If you behave like a lady, we'll treat you like a sister. If you behave like an enemy, we'll have to treat you like a prisoner. If you provoke us too much, we may still kill you."

He moved over to Heather and, gathering her long, tawny hair in his hands over her head, stared at her profile. Then he turned her head to study her face.

"What are you thinking about?" Bart asked.

"I'll show you. But first we need some traveling clothes. You can't be seen around these parts in a Confederate uniform. You stay back here and guard our prisoner." He climbed out of the hearse.

Thank goodness it's still raining, he thought as he flipped the tired horses into motion. There isn't anyone wandering around on a night like this.

He pulled the wagon into an alley that ran behind a block of shops. Opening the door of the hearse, he said, "We're stopped at the back door of a clothing store. Untie her and come on."

The shop's door was secured with a padlock.

"Can you open it?" Ben asked.

"Easy as opening a book," said Bart. Taking hold of the lock, he gave it two quick twists. It fell apart in his hand.

"Bart," Ben said, "you go in and see if you can find a lamp. When you have a light, find yourself some clothes. We're going to travel in style, so get yourself clothing befitting your standing. Get yourself two complete outfits, shoes to hat. We'll need two good quality suitcases. Put one of your outfits on and pack the other.

"Mrs. Wanderman and I will stay out front as if we're lovers waiting for a cab. If we see anyone coming, I'll knock on the door. If I do, you blow out the light in a hurry. When you're through, you take my place at the door."

"Mrs. Wanderman," he said when Bart was gone, "you've been locked up for about four hours. Can I trust you to use the johnny house over there?"

She hesitated, then said, "Thank you, Colonel Gordyne."

When she returned he led her to the front door where they waited in the shelter of a shed roof. He kept an arm around her.

"I'm not taking any chances." He knew his motive was not altogether a desire for staying unnoticed. And she seemed perfectly content to have him holding her. What was going on here?

Nobody noticed them. Bart came out dressed in clothes that would have qualified him for a seat in Congress. He and Ben exchanged places.

"Watch her," Ben said, and Bart slipped his arm around her. She smiled in the darkness. Within a half an hour, Ben was back dressed in a new suit and a top hat.

"All right, it's your turn," he said. Taking Heather's hand he led her to the women's section.

"Get whatever you need for traveling." When she had made her selection, he pulled her away.

"How is it," she asked, "you two get two suits and I only get one dress?"

"Your other one is over here," he told her and went to a part of the shop which displayed boys' clothing.

"Pick something out that fits you," he told her.

"I won't."

"If you don't, I will and it may not fit," he said. While she did her shopping, Ben found a pair of scissors.

"What are you doing?" she demanded.

"You'll find out," he promised.

When they had finished, he called Bart in. They blew out the lamp and returned to the hearse. Several minutes later they dumped the coffins and Bart's Confederate uniform in the alley. The rain had stopped, but there was little traffic.

"I'll drive a while," Bart said. "But we can't go far. These horses need feed and rest."

"See if you can find a park where we can stay a few hours."

Before long Bart pulled up on the Mall a half mile from the United States Capitol and joined the others in the hearse.

"It's hard for me to see how a simple thing like stealing ten million in gold from the federal government can get so jammed up complicated. It beats all how everything the government does has to be scrambled up as if it were put together by lawyers," Ben said as they stretched out as best they could.

"It ain't the government that does it," Bart declared. "For turning a simple needle into a corkscrew, a woman will match a pack of lawyers seven days a week."

The sun was rising over the Potomac when Heather woke. She thought of trying to make a break for it, but realized that the brothers had carefully planted themselves between her and the door. She woke them up.

"Head for Baltimore," Ben said as Bart took the reins.

"Perhaps you can explain to me about those boy's clothes you stole for me last night?" Heather asked as she and Ben chewed on what remained of the salt fish and brown bread.

"They're our insurance, Mrs. Wanderman," Ben said.

"Insurance?"

"If you so much as look like you're trying to communicate with Union authorities, I will shave your head and dress you as a thirteen-year-old boy. As long as you act like our sister, we'll treat you like a sister. But if you try to betray us you will be treated as our younger brother. I assure you that you will never be out of sight of one of us, Mrs. Wanderman. If you succeed in passing on information to Union authorities, I will kill you."

"Colonel Gordyne, I do not like you," she said turning away from him.

He looked at her back for a long time and said, "If I could

dislike you, my duty would be much easier. We'll be together for a while and it will be more pleasant if we can become friends."

3

SEA NORTH

An intensive search was made for the two men who took Pastorman's hearse. There was also concern for the female informant who seemed to have disappeared with them.

Because the abandoned vehicle was found near the Baltimore and Ohio Railroad yard, government agents assumed the three had gone somewhere by rail. While trains heading in all directions were being searched the fugitives settled aboard a packet steamer sailing down the Chesapeake Bay.

"It's slower but you don't leave tracks on water," Ben had explained earlier as they walked from the rail yard to the docks. "Besides, nobody has yet discovered a way to telegraph to a ship at sea."

"And our prisoner'll find it harder to escape," Bart added.

He had checked into a waterfront hotel and smuggled Heather into his room. Meanwhile, Ben bought tickets for two in the name of Andrew Bartholomew on the Baltimore Queen and was assigned to cabin A-12. Inquiring about the accommodations, he learned that A-11 across the companionway was not taken.

He took the tickets to Bart and, three hours later, when another agent was on duty, Ben returned to the ticket window. This time he booked passage in the name of Josiah Benjamin. He asked specifically for Cabin A-11 and went directly on board. The crew was about to raise the gangplank when Bart and Heather arrived and went directly to Cabin A-12.

As the ship turned north from Hampton Roads, her captain found Bart on deck watching the setting sun.

"Good evening, Mr. Bartholomew," said Commodore Charles D. Penbrook. "How are you?"

"Fine."

"And how is Mrs. Bartholomew?"

"A little under the weather. She had to go to her cabin."

"Nothing serious, I hope."

"No, just one of the hazards of a sea voyage I'm afraid."

There was silence for a moment. It was obvious that the ship's officer had a delicate matter to discuss.

"Mr. Bartholomew," he ventured after a while, "I must confess I am puzzled by something."

"What might that be, sir?" Bart asked.

"You and Mrs. Bartholomew came on board as newlyweds and yet I notice that the gentleman, er...Mr. Benjamin, spends almost as much time with her as you do. Further, it has been brought to my attention that you locked your wife in her cabin last night while you shared a cabin with Mr. Benjamin."

"You are very observant," Bart said.

"I pride myself on knowing what happens on my ship."

Bart did not respond.

"I really think I am due some explanation, Mr. Bartholomew."

"Yes, commodore, I suppose it was not wise of us to try to keep this from you. But, you see it is a matter that must be kept secret. National security, you know."

"Ah, yes, I thought as much."

"I must have your assurance as a loyal citizen of the United States that you will not pass on to a single person what I am about to tell you. It must be kept a secret between us."

"Oh, certainly."

"Have I your word, commodore?"

"Most assuredly. Nothing could make me divulge something of this nature to anyone."

40

"I'm not sure I should reveal it even to you, sir."

"But, Mr. Bartholomew, as captain of this ship, I have a right and a duty to know."

Bart turned his back to the sea and leaned on the rail.

"Yes, I suppose so. But remember, sir, not only is it of utmost importance to our current war effort, but the reputation of that delicate woman is at stake, and I know that you, as a gentleman, would not wish to soil the reputation of a person who may be innocent of the terrible charges against her."

"You may depend on me, sir, as a gentleman and an officer." Penbrook looked as if he were standing at attention.

"First, please, accept my apology for not taking you into our confidence as soon as we boarded your ship. It was a mistake in judgment and not an effort to belittle your competency or integrity which, I am sure, are above reproach."

"Thank you, sir, and please, be assured there is no offense, Mr. Bartholomew."

"I hate to say this, but the woman we brought on board is accused of being a spy for the Confederacy."

"Is it possible?"

"Yes, commodore, I regret to say it is. The evidence against her is convincing," Bart said sadly. "You may be among those who are wondering why our superior Union forces have suffered so many defeats at the hands of poorly equipped and badly outnumbered rebel forces."

"Yes, this troubles many loyal citizens."

"The reason may very well be locked in Cabin A-12."

"Can it really be that a woman, so lovely, so apparently mild, could possibly have caused us so much damage?"

"We have reason to believe, commodore, that our recent defeat at Chancellorsville, among others, was directly due to the fact that Gen. Robert E. Lee had advance information of the movement of our Union troops and that this information was passed to him by your guest in Cabin A-12."

"Ah, I say, sir, the treachery of a faithless woman. Well wrote the writer of the Proverbs, 'The path to her house is the way of death, and many strong men have been destroyed by her.'"

"Yes, it is very sad, sir. Particularly sad since the woman's heart apparently betrayed the woman's mind." Bart turned again to watch the red sun drop below the horizon.

"I do not mean to pry, Mr. Bartholomew, and perhaps you have told me too much already, but..."

"The lady's name is Duncan. You may know of Mr. David Duncan. He is the civilian assistant to Maj. Gen. Daniel C. McCallum, who is chief of the War Department's Transportation Command and, therefore, knows about our troop movements. David Duncan is this woman's father."

Bart turned to stare over the ship's deck at the dark sea.

"Not only that, but she was serving as her father's private secretary. So you see, she had intimate knowledge of the most delicate nature. Our evidence is that Miss Duncan met a Confederate officer, a certain Col. LeGare Gordyne, who was in Washington to arrange for exchange of prisoners.

"You know, of course, the reputation these southern men have and how charming they are alleged to be. This scoundrel took advantage of poor Miss Duncan, compromised her hopelessly, and, whether by blackmail or by playing with her weak woman's heart, persuaded her to betray her own father's confidence. Duncan finally realized what had happened and reported his own daughter to the authorities."

"Is it possible?" gasped the horrified commodore.

"Well, of course, we do not yet know for certain, but the evidence all points in that direction. Mr. Benjamin and I are charged with escorting her to New York to stand trial."

"What will they do with her?"

"Probably hang her," said Bart with a shrug.

"Oh, how sad. How very sad. Yet she has apparently caused the death of many fine Union men."

"You will, of course, keep this in strictest confidence?" Bart spoke sternly.

"You have my word, sir."

Penbrook excused himself.

42

Heather seemed troubled the next day as she sat at lunch with the brothers.

"Something bothering you?" Ben asked.

"I don't know what it is, but everybody seems so unfriendly today," she said.

"In what way?"

"No one has said a civil word to me all morning and some have made it a point not even to respond to my greetings. There's something going on that I don't understand."

"So much for the word of a Yankee gentleman," Bart said.

"What's that supposed to mean?" Heather asked.

"Commodore Penbrook cannot respect a confidence."

"What have you been telling him?"

"He was asking some embarrassing questions and I had to provide him with some reasonable answers, that's all."

"What questions?" Ben asked.

"I'm more interested in the answers," Heather said.

"He wanted to know why we were locking the bride in her room while the bridegroom shared a cabin across the hall."

"I'm still more interested in answers."

"I simply told him you were a Confederate spy and we were escorting you to New York to hang."

"You what?" she demanded and Bart reviewed his conversation of the previous night.

"So, I'm an unscrupulous, charming scoundrel," Ben said.

Heather had laid her fork down as she listened. Now she knocked her chair over as she stood and slapped Bart's face..

"You evil-minded, filthy-tongued beast," she whispered. "How could you? You have absolutely ruined my reputation. No one will ever believe a thing I say."

"That had occurred to me," Bart admitted, still smiling. "Do you think anyone is going to believe a crazy yarn about us running after a few million in gold after they've heard my altogether reasonable story told by the ship's officer about how you were betrayed by your woman's heart? Most people would rather believe a dirty lie than the clean truth."

43

"Your behavior is...is unspeakably vile and totally unforgivable," she said. She turned and stalked away.

The brothers stood as she left. Ben stooped to set her chair upright and they sat down again.

"I sure busted the boiler on that one," Bart said sadly.

"She'll get over it."

"Oh, it won't kill her and maybe it'll keep her from giving us trouble on our mission," Bart said. "We were friendly enemies before. Now I've ruined my chances with her."

"I hadn't thought of that. Please accept my thanks."

"For what?"

"Maybe you have improved my prospects."

Bart glared at him, grinned and laughed, "You buzzard."

Heather recovered much faster that they expected. That evening she came out of her stateroom at the usual hour and joined them for dinner. She was radiant and in excellent good humor. They agreed that they had never seen her look more beautiful. Although most of the other passengers and crew continued to treat her coolly, she greeted everyone cordially and even gave one woman a friendly peck on the cheek. When the band began to play for dancing Heather whirled around the floor with all who asked her. She chatted and listened. She was the type of woman who could make most men forget which side of a conflict she was on, Ben decided. She danced most often with Petty Officer Daniel D. Lyons, the ship's signalman.

Lyons looked handsome in his dress uniform. He was slightly under six feet. His wavy black hair topped a broad forehead and he had smiling dark brown eyes. He seemed attracted to Heather and she acted as if she were very impressed with him.

That night back in their cabin the brothers discussed the evening. Neither of them liked what went on.

"She's a mystery," said Ben before they blew out the lamp, "and when it's her, the mystery has me worried. I think I'll sleep in my clothes tonight."

But nothing happened. When they unlocked Heather's door the next morning, she greeted them with a cheerful, "Good morning."

Nor did they observe anything unusual for the rest of the trip. Heather continued to be friendly with everyone on board, especially the men and Lyons in particular. The brothers took turns sleeping in their clothes.

Eventually the Baltimore Queen lay off the north shore of New Jersey waiting for dawn to enter New York harbor. About five in the morning, running feet woke Bart. He looked out in the hallway and saw nothing. He stepped over to Cabin A-12, tried the door, found it unlocked and pushed it open. No Heather.

"She's gone," he shouted, running back to wake Ben.

"Gone? Where? How did she go?"

"How should I know?" he said pulling on his shoes. "I heard a noise and checked her cabin. It's empty. Get dressed and meet me on deck."

He left Ben fumbling with his clothes and raced topside. Out in the open, Bart turned towards the stern, away from the bridge where the watch was on duty. Looking over the rail he saw a dinghy pulling away. In it were two men and what appeared in the dim light to be a woman.

"Hold it," he yelled. "Bring her back here."

"What, mate?" one of the men asked.

"I said bring that woman back here."

"Not a chance, mate," the man answered. "We got orders to pick up a package and we don't get paid unless it's delivered."

Bart mounted the rail and went over the side just as Ben ran up. He dove in too. They swam for the boat and one of the men helped them on board.

"What's this all about?" the fellow asked.

"Take that woman back to the ship," Ben insisted.

"It ain't no woman, mate. I don't know what it be. It was throwed down to us and we were told to take it back to New Jersey. It's sure enough dressed up in a woman's dress, but there ain't a woman in it."

"What?"

"Look for yourself, mates," the man said, "but don't muss it

45

up none, I'm to deliver this, and deliver it I shall."

Ben and Bart fumbled with the blue dress. In it was an empty carpetbag wrapped up in a blanket. The two boatmen continued to pull hard for the shore.

"She's still on board," said Ben. "Can you beat that?"

"Must be. We've been baited and caught like a couple of striped bass." Bart shook his head.

"Take us back to the ship," Ben said, turning to the boatmen.

"Not a chance," one of them said. "It's risky enough pullin' one trip like that. I ain't about to do it twice in one night."

"I'm an army officer," Ben said. "This is a military emergency. I order you to turn this boat about and get me back on board that ship."

The boatman pulled a gun and spat overboard.

"That, mate, is what I thinks of United States Army officers," he said, "and I think this pistol outranks you."

"My Aunt Matilda!" exclaimed Bart. "They're rebels and they think we're Yankees. Mrs. Wanderman has sure suckered us this time."

"Bye, bye," someone on the ship called with a laugh. Though they couldn't see her, they knew it was Heather. The Baltimore Queen was almost invisible. There was a long silence broken only by the squeak of oars.

"Mate," said Ben at last, "I'd like to rent your boat."

"What fer?"

"A trip to New York."

"Not tonight, mate. When we gits to New Jersey, I aim to deliver this package and git some sleep."

There was another silence.

"Could you row this boat from New Jersey to New York before that ship docks?" Ben asked.

"If this fog hangs on, it'll be late morning before the Baltimore Queen kin git to moorings. I could but I ain't."

"Would you rent us the boat at twice your rate, if my brother and I did the rowing and y'all just sleep?"

"Twice the rate?"

"Yes, mate."

"Three times the rate. That's my offer."

Ben's thoughts were interrupted by Bart.

"How long would it take you to get to the place where the Baltimore Queen will dock?" he asked.

"About three hours."

"What's your rate per hour?"

"Dollar fifty." The boatman hesitated long enough for Bart to figure he'd just doubled his fare.

"Would you like to wager my brother and I can beat three hours on the trip from New Jersey to the dock?"

"You landlubbers. What do you know about rowing?"

"Maybe not as much as you, but I'm willing to bet you ten dollars it won't take us three hours. If we beat your regular time, we'll pay your regular fee. How does that sound?"

"Matey, you got yourself a bet."

Ben grinned in the dark. He remembered times when he and Bart had pulled against the current of the Santee River in their race to get home before dark and he knew the power in his brother's arms.

The dingy docked at a makeshift ramp on the Jersey shore where a man stood holding a hurricane lantern. He reached down for the bundle and asked, "What's this?"

"I ain't been told and I ain't looked. It's what was throwed to me from the ship an' I brung it to you," said one of the boatmen.

"Who are they?"

"Two gents that fell overboard. They're anxious to git to New York, so I'd appreciate it if you'd pay me so's we kin get started." The man with the lantern handed over some coins. The two hired hands sat down in the forward seats and proceeded to divide the money. Bart moved to the stern and Ben took the bench in front of him. They spat on their hands, picked up their oars and began to pull.

For two hours and forty-seven minutes, the two in the bow watched and swore.

The next morning the Baltimore Queen berthed in New York

and those disembarking found the dock swarming with law enforcement officers. Penbrook was surrounded by newsmen demanding to know the whereabouts of the Confederate spy.

"It's a mystery," he was saying as two bedraggled men moved in the shadows around the crowd. "All three of them disappeared last night right out there off New Jersey."

Then he proceeded to embellish the story Bart had told. All eyes were on him as a young boy with an over-sized cap pulled low over his eyes came on deck. Carrying a large valise, the youth made his way down the gangplank and moved slowly around the fringes of the crowd. When he reached an alley between two warehouses, he started to run. But start was all he did. Hands caught each of his arms and the two bedraggled men fell in step beside him.

"Mind if we join you, Mrs. Wanderman?" Ben asked.

"You?" Heather said. "How did you get here?"

"Yes," Ben said. "That is one question. The other is how did you pull that one off? You answer ours and we'll answer yours. First, let's find a hiding place until the excitement dies down."

At the end of the alley they spotted a row of empty boxcars. Bart threw the suitcase into one of them. Ben lifted Heather up through the door and then both he and Bart jumped aboard. They settled in a dark corner.

"Now you can tell us how you managed your temporary escape," Ben said.

She laughed. "Y'all looked so funny jumping into the water. My heroes weren't going to let those nasty rebels run off with me."

"I ought to scalp you," Ben said. "What happened?"

"Bart spread the word that I was a southern spy, so all I had to do was play the part. I knew among all the men on that ship, there was bound to be a rebel or two. Sho' 'nuf. Petty Officer Daniel D. Lyons was born and raised in Savannah. He's the ship's signalman and the only man on board who can communicate with semaphore flags. The Confederate navy knows it and uses his services regularly."

"Oh," said Ben, remembering he had decided on the slower water route north to prevent Heather from contacting Union forces.

"Daniel set it up with his friends in New Jersey and unlocked my door. I prepared the dummy with my old dress and put on the boy's clothes you so thoughtfully provided. When I got on deck, he made a disturbance in the hall to wake you up. After you left the ship so heroically, I hid in his cabin until it was time to disembark."

"How did reporters know you were on board?" asked Ben.

"I thought I might need a diversion, so I asked Daniel if he could send word ahead with his flags. He even got Commodore Penbrook to think it was his idea. The police were there to provide security. Somehow, the newspaper reporters just accidentally found out. I didn't know southern men could be such gentlemen until I met Mr. Lyons. Isn't he just the nicest thing?"

"What are you doing with our suitcase?" asked Bart.

"Well, you see, you didn't leave me any money. I thought maybe you had departed in such a hurry to save me from those horrible people that you hadn't stopped to pick up all that cash you won wrestling a mule. You were kind enough to leave your door wide open and I didn't want a stranger to steal your things, and since you had my suitcase in the rowboat, I didn't think you would mind if I borrowed yours. I slipped back to your cabin. I was in a hurry, so I just stuffed my few things in with yours and brought the bag."

"You do think of everything, don't you?" Ben shook his head.

"Now you tell me how you got across the Hudson River."

"You used the charm of a woman. We used the charm of man."

"What's that?"

"Money," he said and told her the story of the wager.

"I had watched them row away from the ship," Bart said. "Knew Ben and I could beat their pace. It wasn't really fair."

"That took a couple of strong backs and four powerful arms, but what I say about all this is that brains are better than brawn,"

Heather said. "If you have a little wit, you can get others to do the running."

"Bart threw a boomerang and we didn't duck," Ben said.

"That ain't it at all," Bart added. "Even a Yankee woman can charm the good sense out of a good man if he don't watch out, and it don't take much charm to do it."

"Oh, I admit you have charm, Mr. Gordyne," Heather said.

"I have?"

"Yes, even a snake can be charming."

Ben started to laugh until Bart said, "I ain't the only Gordyne in this boxcar, Brother Ben."

"We've got to get some sleep," Ben said. "You sit back in that corner, Mrs. Wanderman, and don't you try anything. To get out of here, you'll have to step over two light-sleeping, South Carolina, swamp country, cottonmouth moccasins. If you don't know it, Mrs. Wanderman, they are poison."

4
TRAIN TO TOLEDO

The brothers had hardly fallen asleep when the train lurched forward. Heather screamed. Bart was on his feet before the echo of colliding cars died away. Ben opened his eyes but didn't move. The first jump was followed by several more and then the car began to roll past the rows of warehouses along the New York waterfront, slowly at first, then picking up speed.

Ben closed his eyes again and Bart walked to the open door where he stood a few minutes watching the busy city passing by. Heather joined him.

"Where are we heading?" she asked.

"If city shadows and swamp shadows lie in the same formation, I'd say we're headed north."

"West is the direction of our search," Ben said. "Let's ride this train a while and see where it's going. If it takes us out of New York City, we'll have slipped by search parties. You'll attract too much attention standing in that doorway, Mrs. Wanderman. So I'll have to ask you to take your place in the corner."

Heather stamped her foot angrily and complied. Bart and Ben stretched out on the floor and in an instant both were asleep. Heather kept watch. She had slept well while the Gordynes were rowing across the harbor. And Lyons had brought her a good breakfast.

Ben and Bart, in addition to missing a night of sleep, had had neither food or drink since the previous night. Shortly after noon, hunger and thirst woke them.

"I'm so dry I could drink vinegar," Bart said.

"Remember those fruit juice drinks Nida used to mix up for us on hot afternoons at Bonmaison?" Ben asked.

Heather laughed and said, "Maybe you should have filled up on Hudson River water when you had the chance. If you plan more entertainment like that, I may enjoy this trip after all."

"When I started smarting off back in St. Stephens, Nida would say, 'Benjamin LeGare Gordyne, you jes' shet you' mouf.' And Mrs. Heather Duncan Wanderman, that's what I'm about to say to you. You jes' shet you' mouf, y'hea'."

Heather laughed then asked, "Who's Nida?"

"She's our assistant mother," Bart said. "She raised us."

"A Negro woman?"

"Yes, but I never thought about it much."

For a few minutes they stood by the door watching the country slip by.

"We've got to eat and we can't go wandering about looking like this," Ben said looking at Bart. They were wearing clothes that had been baptized in New York harbor and after about twelve hours in a dinghy and a boxcar both were as unkempt as wharf rats. Heather looked neat enough in her boy's clothing but she was no longer wearing a cap. Her hair was loose and spread around her head like a light-gilded cloud.

Ben opened the suitcase and pointed. "You can get into your own clothes now. It should be safe."

He and Bart stood in the doorway watching the scenery while she dressed and then they changed.

"Next stop, we'll get off," Ben said.

Ten minutes later the train came to a halt in a small town near a water tower. Bart picked up the suitcase while Ben stood by the door looking up and down the track. Nobody appeared. Bart jumped and Ben handed Heather to him, then dropped down beside her. They ducked between cars just as the train began to move and then strolled down the main street to a small hotel that advertised baths and cafe.

After they filled up on steak and potatoes, Ben left Bart to watch their prisoner while he went to the station to buy tickets for the next step of their journey.

At the window he stopped and stared. Tacked to the wall behind the clerk was a map showing most of the rail lines going as far west as Missouri.

"May I be of assistance?" asked the agent.

"Where can I get a copy of that map?"

"We have them as a service for our passengers." The man reached under his counter for one.

"May I sit over there and study it a bit before I buy my ticket?"

The clerk nodded and Ben stepped to a corner table and spread the map. It took him about half an hour to plan the trip. He bought two tickets and went back to the hotel.

"The train leaves in three hours," he told Bart. "I have two tickets for Binghamton, N.Y. You buy one for Elmira, N.Y. Elmira is about thirty miles west of Binghamton, but we'll get tickets from the conductor for another stop west of that, and you can buy one at Binghamton for a stop even further west."

"Just like leap frog," Bart said.

"Yes. Those looking for us will be searching for three people. We'll always be one and a pair and we'll never buy tickets for the same destination, but we should be able to always ride the same train."

Heather stood by the window, pretending not to be listening.

"What makes you think they'll be looking for us?"

"There were more than newspaper reporters waiting at the dock. They won't give up until they find us."

Two things they did not know. Army intelligence had circulated copies of Heather's wedding picture by train before the Baltimore Queen docked. To further complicate things, Heather's parents had hired Pinkerton Detective Agency to find their daughter.

The New York Central took them to Lake Erie. From there, the route touched a corner of Pennsylvania and ran through a series of fuel stops across northern Ohio to Toledo. It was a long and wearisome trip. Heather always had the window seat spending much of the daylight hours watching the endlessly shifting scenery. Ben sat next to her during the first stage of the journey. Bart was across the aisle and one row back.

There were long times of silence, but when they talked, she learned about life on the Gordyne Plantation in St. Stephens, by the auburn waters of the Santee River near the coast. Ben told her of the quiet mystery of Low Country woods, how Spanish moss waved like grey clouds from the serpentine branches of live oaks and long leaf pines reached high to provide nesting places for eagles. He spoke of secret pools in dark swamps where deer and bear and other wild things gathered to taste the fragrant waters and alligators watched for careless drinkers.

From him she heard tales of The Citadel and Charleston and of trips to Columbia when his father served in the Assembly. She learned of Nida who raised him while his mother managed the plantation house and his father supervised the fields and how they marketed the produce of five thousand acres. He told her of Plagun, a grey-haired black man, who taught him to hunt and fish and passed along stories that had come from Africa with his mother.

"They're slaves," she reminded him.

"Yes," he admitted, "but we're friends."

"Will they leave when they are no longer forced to stay?"

He smiled. "You assume Lincoln will win this war."

"We cannot lose. Some day the slaves will be free."

Benjamin L. Gordyne III, heir to one hundred and six slaves, thought a moment before he said, "Yes, I suppose so. Freedom is a powerful thing, but I wonder."

"What's to wonder about?"

"The law of consistency."

"The law of what?"

"Consistency. The law governing all real laws is that laws to

54

be valid must be consistent with the nature of that which they are set to govern. A law that is consistent with nature cannot be stopped. A law that is inconsistent with the nature of a people cannot be enforced. Slavery is a dying institution. Steam engines and economics are ending it. The tragedy of this war is that it may stretch out a hundred years the time it takes to make the nation consistent with its own nature."

As they talked, he learned of her parents and her younger brother. She told him of growing up in the shadow of the nation's capitol. Because of her father's governmental employment she had come in contact with people of power and fame. He heard of her short marriage to Capt. Warren Wanderman.

The first night they slept not at all in the coach seats. It was too jerky, too noisy, too crowded, and they could not lie down. By the second night they were too tired for discomfort to make much difference. They stretched cramped legs by walking the length of the train and grabbed quick meals at dirty sandwich shops when stops were made for water and wood to fire the boilers.

One morning as dawn filtered through the dirty window Heather woke to find she was lying down. She had the entire seat to herself. Her head was cushioned on Ben's coat. Bart's coat was spread over her. Between her seat and the back of the seat in front of her a large suitcase provided support for her knees. Across the aisle the Gordynes seemed to be asleep.

It's hard to hate people like them, was her first thought. Then, reality set in. "If I just had some money, I could get away from them," she whispered to herself. She spent the next few minutes searching carefully in the coats and the suitcase for the horde of cash. Disappointed, she glanced across the car. Bart was watching her. His right hand was about level with his chin. Swinging on a tie cord from his thumb was a heavy canvas bag.

"Looking for this?" he asked.

She sat up and threw a coat at him.

"You disgust me." She jerked her head around to stare out the window. The brothers laughed and Bart moved over to take the seat beside her. A few minutes passed. She turned and looked at

55

him.

"Thanks for the coats and for letting me lie down."

"You're more than welcome," he said and smiled.

"You have no reason to trust me," she said, "but you have been very considerate. I do appreciate it."

They looked at each other in silence. Bart could think of nothing to say.

"Don't think I won't try again," she said.

"That, Heather, is one thing we won't forget."

Across the aisle, Ben had the map spread on his lap, studying the rail routes west. The train swayed on through the early morning mist. There was little talking among the few passengers in the car. Most of them were still trying to sleep.

"The next stop is Toledo," Ben said. "I think we may spend a few days there."

"What's in Toledo?"

"Nothing that I know of, but something which might be. Come over and see."

Bart got up and moved over. Heather started to stand.

"This is for rebel eyes only," Ben said.

"What did you find?" Bart asked.

"If you were shipping something Jefferson Davis would like mightily to get his hands on, which route would you use?" Ben handed the map to his brother.

Bart examined it intently for a few minutes.

"I'd cross the plains from California by stage and join the railroad at its farthest point west. That's the Missouri River at St. Joe. I'd bring it across Missouri to St. Louis, but then, where? I'd have several choices."

"What's been going on in southern Indiana recently?" Ben asked.

"Col. Morgan's raiders have crossed the Ohio River and given the Yankees the business. I wouldn't want to expose my shipment to him so I'd take it as far north as I could. I couldn't go any farther north than Chicago and Toledo because of the lakes."

"Right. It's true that the spring shipment may have already gone by us somewhere in New York, but I don't think they have had time since the opening of the mountain passes to get this far so the next shipment is still west of us. It's a long shot but the way I figure it Toledo is about the best spot on this route for us to catch the shipment, and then, even if we recognize it, it'll probably be moving too fast for us to smell. If there is a chance of diverting it, Toledo is the place to try."

"How long will we wait?"

"Not too long. About the middle of June. We've still got a ways to go."

Bart went back to sit by Heather. The houses of Toledo were already coming into view. Within minutes the train slowed for a breakfast break. People began to stir, getting their luggage down from the overhead racks and struggling into coats. Carrying the valise, Ben stepped down from the train while it was still in motion. Bart and Heather waited a few minutes and then followed him through the crowd. Weary people pushed to the station's cafe to grab sandwiches and coffee. Ben and Bart, with Heather between them, made their way through the station and stepped out on the street. Across from them was a three-story frame building with a sign that read, "Strange Manor, Board and Room, Mrs. H. E. Strange, Pro."

Its peeling paint and small, weed-grown yard advertised more than the name. Strange Manor looked as if it offered cheap lay-over space for railroad workers and peddlers and short-time accommodations for those with gold or Oregon fever or itinerants and immigrants getting a little rest before continuing on their way. A weary, painted face looking out of an open, upstairs window indicated that this woman's bedroom duties involved more than maid service.

"Can't think of a better place for train watching," said Bart.

"I wonder if the rooms under the eaves on the west corner are vacant. We could watch the tracks for miles from there. It has one serious flaw," Ben said glancing at Heather.

Bart noticed the direction of his look and said, "You're right.

57

It ain't hardly a fittin' place for a lady."

Heather, who had been studying the disreputable establishment with special attention to the face in the window, said, "I will not set foot inside that place."

"Don't put on airs with me," Bart said, "Any woman who worked in the Rebel Flag can't be too particular about the company she keeps."

"And a Union spy to boot," added Ben. "That's hardly an honest way to make a living."

"I wasn't making a living, I'm fighting a war against men who own and sell people and who killed my husband."

"Well, if it's war you want to fight, I can tell you from first hand experience that war is mighty dirty business. You do a lot of things fighting a war you wouldn't do in your drawing room. Strange Manor is a place where nobody is going to ask too many questions about us taking in a woman and it's a place where we can keep you safe and silent. Most of the other guests are probably traveling men and you'll have a special reason not to get friendly with them."

"Fact is, I can't think of a better place. Let's get us a suite," Bart said as he headed for the door.

"Hold it," Ben said. "Let me rent the rooms. I'll come out and get Heather and you can sneak in later. I have a notion it might be better if we're not known to be together in Toledo."

Two corner rooms on the third floor were available. There was a connecting door and the doors to the hall could be locked. Ben kept all the keys. An hour later they stood at a window surveying the railroad yards below. The building which housed the waiting room, ticket office and baggage department sat in the center of a long, roofed platform that stretched east and west. It divided two sets of tracks obviously used for passenger trains. A third set of rails seemed to serve locomotives stopping only for water and fuel. In back of that area was a sizable switching yard where they could see small engines breaking up freights into individual segments and arranging the boxcars for new trains.

Parked along the dusty street across from the boarding house were an assortment of wagons and buggies ready to transport goods and people. Some had horses hitched to them. Others had been left with shafts resting in the dust.

It was a busy place. Workmen moved around shifting barrels, boxes and bales on hand carts. Wagons hauled goods in and out. It was a time of immigration and travelers, carrying an assortment of hand luggage and wearing varied native costumes, came and went with every passenger train.

The three of them studied the scene for more than an hour, then Ben asked, "Bart, are you ready to grow a beard?"

"A beard? What for?"

"I need a vagrant. There's one down there already, but I reckon a station as busy as that one can stand two."

"Why me? Why don't you act like a bum?"

"With me it would be acting," Ben said. "You're a natural."

"You'd look like a natural drunk if I flattened your pretty nose," Bart said with a grin.

"We've got a problem," Ben said, "and her name is Mrs. Wanderman. One of us has got to guard her. I've chosen myself for that unpleasant duty."

"Unpleasant duty?" said Heather sharply. "As conceited as you are I don't suppose you find it possible to believe that I do not find it pleasant to spend a summer under constant surveillance of a couple of rotten apple scoundrels."

The brothers looked at each other. "We've been called a number of things in our time," said Bart. "Few of them complimentary, but I don't believe I've ever been called a rotten apple scoundrel before. Have you, Ben?"

"Can't say that I have. Fact is I ain't at all sure I know what a rotten apple scoundrel is."

"A rotten apple can look beautiful on the outside," Heather said, "but when you bite into one, it'll turn your stomach."

"Ben, do you get the impression she doesn't like us?"

"I can't see how that's possible, but now you know why I've assigned myself the unpleasant duty of guarding her, and I'm being very generous in asking you to be a drunk."

"Oh, you have, have you?"

"Yes, and I assure you it has nothing at all to do with the fact that she is mildly attractive. It's pure logic."

"Yeah? The devil himself can be powerfully logical."

"What we need is a vagrant looking for a job handling freight, but I don't think it wise to discuss our plans in front of a Union spy. She has ears and, brother, can she talk! So, Mrs. Wanderman, would you be so kind as to go to your room while we plot against the Union?"

Heather stamped her foot sharply and marched angrily through the door. She did not want to miss anything even if they had been extremely considerate. But she smiled thinking about what Ben had said. "Mildly attractive!"

Bart dug out the clothes he had been wearing when he jumped overboard and went to find William T. Wright, the stationmaster.

"Got enough problems without hiring on no drunk," was the response when he asked for a job. "You're so fat you'd tire yourself carrying your own weight. I need someone who can move freight."

Nearby two men were struggling to load a bulky box on a hand wagon. Bart pushed one of them aside and said, "Tell you what, if I put that crate on the wagon, will you pay me the wages of two men who can't do it?"

A small crowd began to gather and they all laughed.

"No," said Wright, "but I ain't afraid to offer you a job if you can do it, because it can't be done."

With one hand, Bart stood the crate on end, bent his knees so that his shoulder was near the balancing point of the box, tipped it to rest on his shoulder and straightened his knees, lifting the box. He carried it to the wagon and set it down. The crowd cheered.

"I'm ready to start work," said Bart, facing the stationmaster. Wright told him to report the next day.

Bart found what appeared to be an abandoned covered delivery wagon alongside a closed store. It would make a dandy sleeping place for a bum who would now start growing a beard.

One of them upstairs and one on the street. Perfect! They

could watch all traffic from two vantage points.

Several times a day, Ben locked Heather in her room and walked through the station with a notepad asking people about train movements and passengers. If someone wanted to know why, he said, "I represent a firm which believes Toledo will be the major rail center of the nation, serving as the gateway to the west. If my calculations are convincing, the largest factory in the world may be built here to manufacture a new model, coal-burning locomotive. We are getting ready for the time when there will be rails all the way to the Pacific passing through Toledo."

That kind of talk appealed to civic pride and opened many mouths. It wasn't long until he was picking up information about troop movements and military shipments. Much of this the Union high command would rather have kept secret. Several times a day he conferred with Bart. Every night he took Heather out to eat.

One evening as they left Strange Manor they found Bart, dressed in his suit, waiting for them.

"You stand watch tonight," he said. "I'm taking her to dinner."

Ben started to object. Heather smiled and said, "Isn't it customary in the South to ask a lady first?'

"Would you care to dine with me tonight?" Bart asked.

"I think Bart has earned a night on the town." She took his arm.

Ben started to turn away, then stopped and asked, "May I call you a cab?"

"No," said Heather. "I think I'd rather walk. The moon is so beautiful tonight."

When Bart returned her to the suite, she found Ben standing by the window looking out over the moon-washed railroad yards.

"Have a good time?" he asked.

"Oh, yes. It's always nice to get out of here."

"From now on, if it is all right with you, Bart and I will take turns escorting you in the evening," he said.

"Why?"

"I'm beginning to love you. I cannot let myself do that."

"Why?" Her heart jumped.

"Two reasons. I must not let you wedge yourself between me and my brother and I cannot let you interfere with our mission."

He kept his back to her as he spoke.

Heather opened her mouth to reply, but thought better of it. She went to her room disturbed by the singing in her soul, disturbed at the joy his confession had brought her, disturbed because she knew that it wasn't the possibility of success in her plan to spoil their mission that excited her, but that he had said he was beginning to love her.

5
STRANGE FREIGHT

In the bright sun of the following morning, Ben stood at the corner window watching an incoming train. It was a freight like many others he had seen arriving from the west, but there was a difference. As the train rounded a curve in its approach to the station, he saw a boxcar between two coaches in the middle of the line of freight cars.

"That's it," he exclaimed. Picking up a hand mirror, he flashed a spot of sunlight down to Bart.

"What is it?" Heather demanded.

"The shipment's in that boxcar," he said.

The light caught Bart's eye and he looked up to see Ben pointing west. For a better view he dashed across the street. From this point he could see the long, sweeping side of the train. He signaled to Ben and in a few minutes they met near the tracks.

"Must be the one," Bart said as they walked away from Heather.

"It certainly looks right. They've stopped down there, probably to take on water. That train is due at 10:30 according to the telegrapher and this is the breaking point. They'll be shifting cars around making up a new train. That ought to take them about two hours."

"While they're moving cars around the yard, we'll have time

to work out a plan to relieve them of their consignment."

"Let's get ready to leave. We've been in Toledo long enough. Even if our shipment is not on board, we'll take the noon westbound for Chicago," Ben said.

He escorted Heather back to their rooms and said, "Pack up, we're moving out and we haven't much time."

By 10:15 they were standing in the doorway of Strange Manor.

"There's another unusual thing about that train," he said. "Freight trains use the third track over next to the switch yard. This one is coming straight in between the street and the station. It's on a passenger track."

At 10:34 by the station clock the fifteen-car freight rolled in on the rails nearest the street. The heavy 4x4 locomotive belched hissing steam and bells clanged. Bart sat in the dust about six feet from the cars, leaning against a wagon's front wheel, his eyes closed, looking like someone sleeping off a binge.

As soon as the train stopped moving, a company of unarmed Union soldiers spilled on to the street and a sergeant shouted, "Fall in." The troops stood in formation. Bart counted four rows of eight soldiers. A captain descended from the rear coach and marched with military stride to stand before the men.

"At ease," said the sergeant.

"This is Toledo, Ohio," the officer announced. "It is a breaking point for the freight cars. Most of them will be diverted to other destinations and other cars will be added to ours for the trip east. This means we will have a stop here for maybe two hours. Most of you can have the time off. There are two cafes across the street. You may go to them. Other than that, you may not leave this street or at any time be out of sight of this train. If we're ready to leave early, Sergeant Miller will blow his whistle three times. That is your signal to load up immediately. We want to get out of here as fast as possible.

"Unfortunately our consignment must be guarded at all times. Johnson, Treat and Bender, front and center."

Three men stepped out of formation.

"You have a half an hour to get something to eat and report back. Be here with your rifles and full canteens. You will relieve O'Shay, Martin and Crews and it's hot in there," he told them. "Remember, I want you back here at 11:10."

"Yes, sir," they answered.

"You are dismissed until 11:10."

The three men turned and raced towards the nearest cafe.

"Company, attention. Company, dismissed," the sergeant called out and the troops broke ranks.

The captain walked to the door of the boxcar, knocked three times, paused, knocked two times, paused and knocked three times again. He waited briefly and repeated the sequence. The door slid open. Two armed men jumped to the street and took up guard positions in front of the door. Another soldier stood in the open doorway. On the floor behind him were three boxes. Other than that the car appeared to be carrying only camp equipment for the troops.

"You will be relieved for chow in thirty minutes," the officer told them. "I know it's hot in there. You've got to be inside with the door closed until you're relieved. Understand?"

"Yes, sir," the men answered.

"All right, get back in and shut the door. Make sure it's locked."

The guards vaulted back into the car and slid the door to. Bart heard the lock click. He could tell it was a special latch and figured it could not be opened from outside.

The captain stood alone carefully surveying the dusty street. It was nearly deserted. A few vehicles moved. A man on horseback rode east paying no attention to the freight train and a heavyset fellow, apparently sleeping off a drunk, sat braced against the wheel of a weatherbeaten wagon about fifteen feet away. A young couple strolled across the street. The tall man carried a heavy bag. Brakemen stepped between the cars that were to be disconnected from the train. Up and down the line switch engines backed up to the cars that were to be moved and pulled them off, leaving the two coaches and the boxcar waiting

65

to be hooked to another train. Behind him he could hear the noise of the railroad station.

The captain crossed the street to the Toledo Cafe for lunch. He didn't see the "drunk" get up or the young couple head towards the station. They met near the sandwich shop. Bart leaned against a post examining the three cars. Ben took out his notepad as though he was continuing his interviews.

"That looks like what we've been waiting for," Bart said.

"It must be," Ben said "But our assignment is in California. We'll do what we can and catch the noon train west. Can we get them to open the car?"

"Knock and it shall be opened unto you." Bart smiled. "And I think I've got the code for the knock."

He explained what the captain had done.

"Will they open the door on this side to the same knock?" Ben asked. "If we're going to get inside we've got to do it from this side while the troops are all across the street. We can't do anything until the westbound train is almost ready to pull out. Do you think we can lift those boxes?"

"Can't be heavier than a bale of cotton. I've wrestled them a time or two."

"They'll be changing guards in about twenty minutes. We've got that much time to get ready. The passenger train is due here in fifty minutes and will stay in the station about twenty minutes to let the passengers get their sandwiches. Will it take an hour and a half to put another train together?"

"Sure. Some of the switch engine crews are already breaking for lunch."

"We'll wait twenty minutes after the guard is changed. That's 11:30. It will give us ten minutes to pull this off before the crowd from the passenger train starts unloading."

"This bright sun will help us too," Bart added. "Did you notice how those Yankees squinted when they opened the door? It's dark in that place."

They went over their plan and broke up to take care of details. At 11:10 Ben watched as the captain and three men

66

emerged from the cafe and marched to the sealed boxcar. Bart, loafing against the platform side of the car, listened as the officer repeated the sequence of knocks which opened the door.

"Is everything laid out?" asked Ben as they got together again at 11:27.

"Yep. Tarp and wagon are waiting right over there."

"The only thing we don't have is our tickets for Chicago," Ben said adding the valise to the canvas on the hand cart. "I'll take care of that during the twenty minutes the passengers are eating while you get those boxes in the baggage car."

As they laid their plans a switch engine backed up five cars and hooked them to the forward coach.

"If they make up that train early, we may not have as much time as we think," Bart said. "The captain wants to move fast."

"You take the right side of the door. I'll take the left." Ben said. "Come on, Heather, we're about to rob a train."

It was lunch hour and the platform looked deserted. Inside the station, business was picking up as passengers began arriving to buy their tickets for two trains that were expected within forty-five minutes of each other. When they arrived, there would be a mob crowding the lunch counters trying to get a quick bite before the trains moved on.

"This sun is making that car an oven," Bart said as they neared the door. "Those men will be real anxious to get out."

They looked up and down the platform. A switch engine was backing a couple of cars towards them.

"Let's wait until just before it hits," Ben said. "That'll increase the confusion."

Bart leaned against the car near the west side of the door. Holding Heather's arm, Ben stepped up to the door and knocked as the captain had done and flattened himself against the siding. At the first knock, they heard footsteps inside. As soon as the second sequence was completed they heard the lock click and the door slid open. Two soldiers, their uniforms, wet with sweat, stood for a fraction of a minute in the opening, blinking in the bright sunlight. At that moment the switch engine backed two cars into the coach and the entire train lurched towards Cleveland. The shock threw the confused soldiers off balance as they jumped down. Each of the Gordyne brothers grabbed a soldier by his rifle arm, whirled them around and smashed them brutally below their ribs. Their legs sagged.

Bart caught the soldier he had knocked out before he hit the platform and hurled him with all of his strength at the third soldier still trying to recover his balance in the rocking doorway. His rifle was knocked from his hand, he stumbled back, tripped over the boxes in the middle of the floor and sprawled against the far side of the car. Bart picked up the private Ben had disabled and threw him into the car, and leaped in himself. Ben tossed the two rifles after their owners, picked Heather up and lifted her through the door. Then he jumped in after her. Bart pulled the door shut, leaped over the boxes and with one blow knocked the third soldier unconscious. It had taken less than thirty seconds.

Ben tied up and gagged the three unconscious men. He used cords from troopers' packs stacked in one end of the car. Bart examined the boxes. Each had a ring on top. They were secured by a locked chain that ran through the rings. Bart took a rifle, thrust the barrel through one of the rings, and using the gun as a crowbar, pulled the top off the box. Gold coins glistened in the dim light.

He badly bent three good U.S. Army rifles breaking the boxes loose from the chain. Then he and Ben dragged the boxes across the rough floor to the door.

"Can you lift them?" Ben asked.

"Like a baby."

Ben released the lock and slid back the door enough to look out. Across the platform, the ticket agent rushed back to his window, late from lunch. A few impatient passengers paced the boards and a half dozen men lounged on benches. Ben edged the door open a bit more and stepped down to the platform. Bart handed Heather to him. Ben took her arm and the couple strolled away. Bart jumped down and wheeled the hand truck to the door. Then, folding his massive arms around one box, he lifted it and set it on the cart. When all three boxes were on the cart, he slid the boxcar door shut and heard the lock click inside. Turning, he put their suitcase on top of the boxes and covered the load with the canvas tarp.

He had maneuvered the hand truck about half way across the platform when the stationmaster approached him.

"Whatcha got there?" Wright asked, looking at the load.

Ben steered Heather towards them.

"Some cargo for the baggage car of the noon westbound," Bart answered, and lifted a corner of the tarp to show the carpetbag. Wright bent down for a more complete inspection.

"Mr. Wright," said Ben, "could I have a word with you?"

The stationmaster turned with a smile, dropping the tarp without looking beyond the valise.

"Any time, Mr. Benjamin. What can I do for you?"

Bart pushed his load away as his brother engaged Wright by asking, "Isn't that a rather strange arrangement of cars? I don't believe I've ever seen a boxcar sandwiched between two coaches in the middle of a freight train."

"As a matter of fact it is," said the stationmaster. "It's the way the Army wanted the setup for security reasons. They have a highly secret shipment in the freight car and the two coaches carry troops to guard it."

"Interesting," said Ben. "Very interesting. Going east isn't it?"

"Yes, just as soon as the train is made up."

"I wonder what the Army is shipping east that would be that important."

Wright leaned over to confidentially whisper in Ben's ear, "I believe it's gold from California."

"You don't say," said Ben. "Did you hear that, Sarah? California gold. Must be a lot of it."

"I don't believe I've met this young lady," said Wright looking with great interest at Heather.

"Oh, pardon my thoughtlessness," Ben smiled. "This is my sister, Sarah Benjamin. Sarah, this is Mr. Bill T. Wright. He is the chief administrator of the Toledo railroad station."

69

Heather looked out from under her coal bucket bonnet and said, "It's a pleasure to meet you, Mr. Wright, but I think you're wrong."

"Wrong?"

"I don't think there is any gold in that boxcar."

"Haven't I seen you some place before?" The stationmaster studied her face.

"No, sir, I don't believe we've met," she said.

"Will you please excuse us?" asked Ben, "I've some things I need to do."

"Certainly, Mr. Benjamin."

"You are about to get yourself scalped," Ben muttered as he took Heather's arm and led her away.

Heather laughed.

At the opposite end and on the far side of the station platform, Bart parked his loaded freight wagon near the point where he thought the baggage car would stand when the passenger train came in from the east. He stacked more boxes and baggage on top of it and looked across the platform to where Ben and Heather stood. Ben checked his pocket watch. The passenger train was late.

In the east, a train whistle sounded. The freight was ready to leave. On the street, the sergeant blew his whistle three times and the troops charged in to take their places in the two coaches. Bart, leaning against his cart, watched his brother. Ben took Heather's arm, started to move towards the station to buy their tickets and stopped in mid-stride. The captain was approaching the sealed boxcar as if to check on it before the train pulled out.

Ben signaled Bart to join him.

"We've got to stop him from trying to get into that car," he told his brother. "You take Heather and buy the tickets. I'll stall him until the train starts moving."

"What'll we do with the gold?"

"Leave it there. The passenger train's late and we may still have time to load it after this freight pulls out." Ben hurried off to intercept the captain. In the distance they heard the whistle of the westbound passenger train.

"Let me congratulate you and your men," Ben said as he approached the officer.

"I beg your pardon, sir," the captain looked startled.

"Frankly, captain, I've never seen a more professional maneuver of guard and with you and your men on duty, I'm sure that shipment will be secure all the way to the New York bank."

The officer stiffened.

"Who are you, sir?" he asked.

"Oh, I beg your pardon, captain. I'm Josiah Benjamin of the United States Treasury Department out of Washington. We have received information that the rebels have assigned a detachment to intercept that shipment and I was sent west to make sure security is as it should be. I must say I am greatly impressed. What is your name, captain? I want to include it in my report to the secretary."

"I'm Capt. Andrew Hanson."

A brakeman rushed up as they talked.

"I beg your pardon, sir," he said to the captain, "but there is another passenger train coming in and we've got to clear this track. Will you please join your troops so that we can roll?"

"I'd like to check my men in that boxcar first."

"I'm afraid we don't have time, sir."

"Well, all right then."

"Good work, Captain Hanson," Ben called as officer swung into the moving coach.

With the clanging of bells, the scream of brakes and the spitting of steam, an engine pulling a string of coaches rolled to a stop on the other side of the station. While Ben was stalling the captain, Bart moved up the line of impatient passengers to buy tickets. He stood behind a soldier with a missing leg. Heather was at his side. As they waited for the clerk to issue a ticket to the veteran, she glanced around the crowded terminal and then gasped.

Tacked to the wall less then ten feet away was her picture. The legend under it read: "Heather Duncan Wanderman. If you see this woman, report immediately to the nearest police or military officer. REWARD: The Pinkerton Detective Agency offers $1,000 for the recovery of this woman."

Leaning against the wall next to the picture was an unkempt vagrant with a tangled beard and bleary eyes. She put her hand over her mouth to stifle a surprised cry. Bart looked at her.

"Just a sneeze," she said.

He turned to the counter and began negotiating to buy tickets to Chicago. She looked around. Ben was still out on the platform. The poster was around a corner of the ticket booth and out of Bart's sight. He was busy talking to the clerk.

"Three tickets for Chicago," she heard him say.

"You leavin' us, Mac?" the clerk asked.

"Yeah," he answered, "My sister here and my brother found me and have come to take me home."

"You'd better hurry, that train's late and it'll be pulling out without any delay."

Heather took him at his word. She slipped around the corner out of Bart's sight, tore the picture from the wall and handed it to the vagrant. In two steps she was back beside Bart.

"Let's go," said Bart, taking her arm.

Heather looked back and saw the man trying to hand the poster to the ticket clerk, already busy with another customer. He was obviously irritated at being interrupted by a bum. The man left the window and ran after Heather. He clutched her arm and shouted, "I want my thousand dollar reward."

Bart grabbed him by the throat.

"Quiet," he growled, "or I'll throttle you."

The man felt the power in that hand and knew there was death in it. He could not have spoken if he had wanted.

"What's this?" Bart barked. The terrified man showed him the poster.

"Where did you get this?"

The man gasped, unable to speak with that hand on his throat. Bart loosened his grip.

"She gave it to me," he said.

Bart took the man's arm and pulled both him and Heather

through the door where they found Ben.

"Take her, Ben. They've recognized her," he said pushing Heather at his brother. Ben caught her arm and hurried to the train. Bart, still holding the drunk, looked towards the freight wagon where the gold sat. The attendant had already loaded all the suitcases into the baggage car. As Bart watched, he pulled back the tarp and tossed the valise inside. Then he stooped to lift one of the boxes of gold. It didn't move. He glanced into the open box, turned away and, jerking himself around, stared as one in shock and yelled.

Bart whirled and went back through the door he had just used. It was now jammed with people attracted by the disturbance and curious to find out what was going on.

"Gold!" shouted Bart, "Gold! There's four million dollars in California gold on that freight wagon."

With that he hurled the unfortunate vagrant into the face of the crowd, turned again and raced a wild mob to the cart.

"All aboard," shouted the conductor, anxious to get his late train moving. He saw the racing crowd but did not know what was going on. He signaled the engineer to move out.

Bart reached the cart and turned to face the charging mob. With flailing arms, he drove them off long enough to pick up the first box of gold. The train began to move.

He threw the heavy box at the open door of the baggage car. It hit on the sill where it tottered, spilling some of its golden coins on the platform and the ground below. The baggage handler stooped and tried to pull the heavy box inside. He could not move it. The car lurched and, in trying to keep his feet, he spilled most of what was left in the box out on the platform in front of the screaming mob. He hurled the nearly empty box aside and leaped out to get his share. The crowd pushed him to one side. He fell against the moving car, and clutching two hands full of gold coins, he was dragged screaming underneath the moving train.

For a moment his screams stopped the mob. But the sight of the gold drove the mass forward again. Straddling the two remaining boxes, Bart laid about him with blows that sent four or five men falling to the deck giving him a few seconds to try again.

He picked up the second box and, straining every muscle, tossed it at the platform of the first coach as it rolled slowly by. It bounced off and got wedged between the car and the platform where it was chewed to pieces, sending golden coins shooting out like missiles from a cannon.

The crowd was now scrambling for the loose gold, and Bart had time to take more careful aim, but first he filled his pockets. Then he took a deep breath, squatted beside the freight wagon, laid hold of the box, heaved himself to a standing position and shoved the box at the platform of the second car. It landed right side up.

Bart caught the rear banister of the second car, swung aboard and rushed down the aisle to the forward platform. The box was there. It was empty. Passengers in the two coaches had been watching.

Picking up the crate, Bart carried it to the baggage car to see if anything was left in the box that had landed inside. About fifty Double Eagles remained. He put these in the valise along with the coins from his pockets and left both empty containers there.

He found Ben and Heather in a forward coach. She was staring out the window. Ben was studying the poster.

Bart explained what had happened inside the station.

"How did that fellow get this?" Ben asked.

"He said she gave it to him."

"Mrs. Wanderman, where did you get it?"

"Oh, you fools, it was nailed to the wall by the ticket window. I just grabbed it off the wall and handed it to the nearest man. It was just my luck that he was drunk."

Ben broke the silence that followed by saying, "The question is can that man make anybody believe his story?"

"For a thousand dollars he'll sure try," Bart said.

"They know we're on this train and they probably know the destination of our tickets. If he convinces anyone, they'll wire ahead and we can expect trouble at the next water tower. Someone will connect our prisoner here to the missing gold."

"There's another problem. If he can convince anybody that Mrs. Wanderman was in Toledo, the feds will know which way we're headed. This track points straight for California."

"What are our choices?" Bart asked.

"If nobody believes him, we're on our way none the worse for the disturbance. If they believe him, we've either got to get off this train before the next stop or we've got to make sure they don't find our prisoner when they search the train. I don't think we can take a chance on the drunk not convincing someone. Lots of people saw her at the station and some of them will remember the poster. Mr. Wright probably nailed that poster up himself."

"They're bound to put it together and that bum will throw the biggest party of his life," Bart said.

"Which brings us to another question. Do we dare tote Mrs. Wanderman around in public anymore if this poster is spread all over the country?"

Heather had been looking moodily out the window. Now she turned angrily to them and asked, "Why don't you just throw me off the train? Then you'll be permanently rid of me and you can go about your dishonest endeavor in peace."

"Ah, without you, this little assignment would have been so simple it wouldn't have been interesting at all," Bart said. "We'll try to keep you around just for the excitement you stir up every once in a while."

"What will we do? Get off the train before the next stop or hide her?" Ben interrupted. "Whatever we do had better be done before the conductor comes around checking tickets."

"I think you and I could get off the train some place where it slows down on the upgrade," Bart said. "But I'm not sure about Heather. She'd probably get hurt, maybe bad."

"You're right, so we've only one other choice. Where do we hide her?"

The train rocked through the bright summer day making enough noise to muffle their conversation.

"We won't hide her," Ben said after a brief silence. "We'll put her right out there where everybody can see her. Come on, Mrs.

Wanderman, you're going to start being our baby brother, Heath."

"I what?"

"I said in Washington we'd treat you like a sister as long as you made no effort to communicate with Union officials. Off New Jersey, you tried to escape. When you gave the poster to the drunk, you activated my promise. Let's go. Bart, in a few minutes, you follow us to the baggage car."

Because of the attendant's thirst for gold, the baggage car was unoccupied. Ben took the boy's clothes from the carpetbag and handed them to Heather.

"Put them on," he ordered. She shook her head.

"Do you want me to dress you?"

"You wouldn't?"

"Mrs. Wanderman, I could throw you out that door. Don't make me do something I don't want to do. If you refuse to dress yourself, you may be sure I will."

She took the bundle of clothes to the rear of the car.

"Don't take too long," he told her. "The conductor will be checking tickets soon and I want him to know Bart's little brother is on his train."

While she changed, Ben leaned on the frame of the open door, looking across the farmland.

I could push him out, Heather thought. At that moment Bart entered and she never knew if she would have followed through on her impulse.

When she was dressed she still did not look like a boy. Her thick hair hung over her shoulders. Ben gathered the tawny curls in his left hand. In his other hand was a pair of scissors.

"Please, Ben, don't cut my hair," Heather pleaded.

Ben lifted the scissors to her forehead and hesitated.

"I'll trim it shorter so we can hide it under your cap," he said. "You'd better keep it covered. Bart, while I'm doing this, find me something to tie up her hair."

Ben snipped until the hair was just above her collar. Heather could tell he was being careful. Once, he touched her neck lightly. I'm glad I didn't push him out the door, she thought. Taking the

76

string Bart found, Ben knotted the hair in a loop on top of her head. When he was finished, he pulled the cap over her forehead and ears.

"You still don't look right," he frowned.

"No thirteen-year-old boy ever sat ten minutes on a train without getting dirty," Bart said, and, running a finger through the heavy coating of soot on the wall, he smeared a streak across her cheek.

"Let me see your hands," Ben said. She held them out like a child standing inspection.

"Too clean," he said. "Get some dirt on them."

This she did by delicately touching the side of the car.

"That's not enough," he said and rubbed her hands roughly against the wood.

"Who ever saw a boy with his shirt tail tucked in? Pull it out some. Get a little of that dirt on your shirt. Your necktie is tied about the way a boy would tie it."

He stepped back and inspected her.

"There. Nobody will guess you aren't a boy. Now, Bart, take her to the coach behind the baggage car. She's your brother, Heath, on his first train ride. Some people, including the conductor, may remember that I got on the train with a woman. I'm going through the train to let people see I don't have anybody with me. I'll sit in the back coach until the conductor starts checking tickets. He'll punch mine first and see I don't have Mrs. Wanderman with me. After he goes the full length of the train, he'll get to you and your brother."

Bart and Heather found seats as close to the front as they could. Smoke and cinders from the wood-burning stack blew in the open window.

The conductor spent his time, when not involved in conducting, playing cards in a car reserved for "Gentlemen." This day he lost a few hands and quit. Standing, he said, "I best be earning my pay or you won't have nothing to steal."

With that he started punching tickets making his way towards the front of the train. Ben was one of his first passengers.

"Tickets, please," he said.

Ben, who was pretending to sleep, sat up.

"Certainly, sir." He fumbled in his jacket pocket.

"Where's your wife, sir?" the conductor asked.

"Wife?

"Didn't you get on board with a young lady?"

"Oh, her. I did help a young lady up the steps. She was not my wife. Wasn't she a beauty? She went forward and I came back here. I haven't seen her since. I went looking for her. Thought she might like some company."

"Enjoy your trip, sir." The conductor handed Ben his ticket.

Eventually he made his way to the front of the train.

"Ticket, please," he said to Bart who had his ready.

"I'd really rather be sitting farther back away from the smoke and cinders," he said, "but it's my kid brother's first train ride and he wanted to get as near the engine as possible. You know how boys are."

The conductor smiled and took the tickets. Heather turned away from the window. He looked at her.

"I don't remember the boy." The conductor continued to peer at Heather.

"I can understand that," Bart said with a sly smile. "Your attention was where mine was, on that very attractive young lady who got on just ahead of us. Then there was some kind of a disturbance on the platform about the time we boarded the train, so I'm not surprised you don't remember my brother."

The conductor handed him back the punched tickets and turned to the next passenger. A few minutes later Ben joined them and correlated their stories.

"I'm glad I'm not married to either of you," Heather muttered.

Ben's left eyebrow rose as he asked, "Did you offer her that option, Bart?"

"No, don't believe I did."

"Well, don't bother because it is not an option I would accept," she announced.

"Why?" Bart asked.

"You are the most proficient liars I've ever met."

"I feel real guilty about one lie," Bart said. "I never should have told the conductor you're attractive. That was a whopper."

"You're not only a liar, Bart Gordyne. You're a cad."

Ben returned to his seat in the last car.

Half an hour later the train stopped at a small town to take on water and fuel. A group of men were waiting. The conductor joined them and they talked. Then they boarded separate coaches and slowly walked through the cars carefully looking at each passenger.

The conductor accompanied the man who approached where Ben was seated.

"Something wrong, sheriff?" Ben asked noting the badge on the stranger who stopped at his seat.

"Mr. Cummins here says you helped a young lady get on the train in Toledo."

"That's right. Why?"

"Do you remember seeing her after you got on the train?"

"No, sir. She went forward and I came back here."

"Have you been in the other cars?"

"Yes. I walked the length of the train to see if I could, you know, get acquainted. She was quite attractive."

"But you didn't see her."

"No, sir. Isn't she on the train?"

"Not as far as we can tell."

"Why are you looking for her?"

"She's wanted back in Washington for something. It must be serious. They've put a thousand dollar reward out for her."

"You mean I had my hands on one thousand dollars! What could a woman have done to be worth that kind of a reward?"

"I don't know except the people back in Toledo think she got on this train and want us to send her back."

"Maybe she got on the train, walked through the car and got off again, and nobody noticed her during that disturbance across the platform."

"That must be it," the conductor said. "She's certainly not on the train now."

"What happened back there? It looked like a riot."

"A crowd discovered several million dollars in gold stolen from the government. They're not sure how much the mob got. They're saying they think that woman had something to do with it," the sheriff said.

"No? Maybe she is worth a thousand dollar reward."

"I sure wish I knew where she went," the conductor said.

Soon after the sheriff and his men got off, the crew finished filling the engine's tanks and the train moved west. Bart and Heather walked to the last car in search of Ben.

"What's our next move?" asked Bart.

"Find a place where we won't be seen together," Ben said. "We need to spend some time thinking." Turning his face to the window, he pulled his hat over his eyes and slumped as though asleep. Bart and Heather found seats four rows back.

In one way Heather was very much like a thirteen-year-old boy. Patience was not one of her virtues. An hour passed. She and Bart ran out of things to say to each other.

"Waiting kills talking," she said in irritation. "Let's go for a walk."

They went to the observation platform and stood watching the scenery until Ben found them.

6
"LEGS" PHARSON

Heather held on to the railing and tried to plot her next move. Ben and Bart, on the other side of the platform, were also figuring what to do. She could not hear them over the noise of speeding wheels crackling across uneven rail joints.

"They sure left us with us some questions," Bart said. "We'd better come up with answers soon or we won't need them."

"Yes, but they also gave us some answers so we know better what the questions are." Ben stared at Heather, admiring her profile which reminded him of the chiseled features on one of the Grecian statues in the Bonmaison gardens.

"The reward is being offered by Pinkerton, thus we know her folks are after us. And federal agents aim to find out what we're up to. They may think that shipment was all we want. Pinkerton is obviously trailing Heather and won't stop till she's found." Bart had also been watching Heather who seemed to be brooding. She had not spoken for a half hour.

"Next," Ben continued, "we know they've a good idea what we look like. They may even know your name."

"How do you figure that?"

"A lot of people have seen us and they've probably asked some of the crowd watching you wrestle that mule. It won't be long before the conductor is questioned about the man who helped

Heather onto the train. So, they'll tie me to her there."

"They don't know I was there," Bart said.

"Except the drunk."

"That's right. I'd forgotten him. And, if they describe me to the conductor, he'll remember the man with the boy."

"Yes, and then somebody will figure out who the boy is."

"My Aunt Matilda! They know almost everything except where we're going and why we're here."

"Pinkerton may figure that out as well."

Bart shook his head. "That ain't possible."

"They know we're going west," Ben said. "Some of this war is being fought in the Southwest, but not much. Not enough for the kind of action we've been givin' them. The West is providing them with only one important thing, gold. They know the South needs gold badly. If I was working on this back in Washington, I believe I would have figured that out as soon as I heard we were in Toledo. The escapade with the gold shipment there may be just enough to confirm it. We've got two empty boxes in the baggage car. By now the gold that was in them is spreading wherever trains go. Investigators may think we've still got some of it and, you can be sure, they'll be checking every rabbit trail between here and the Mason Dixon Line trying to keep us from carrying it over or getting it to General Morgan's raiders."

"What do they make of the fact that we're still headed west?" Bart asked. "That ought to confuse them some."

"That's so, Bart, if we keep going west. But what happens if we head southeast for a while?"

It didn't take Bart long to figure out what Ben had in mind.

"We let them think we've got plenty and are headed home with it," he said. "To do that, we've got to get off this train, drop out of sight for a few days, and then leave some kind of trail a couple of hundred miles towards Atlanta."

Just then Ben shifted his position and the train lurched over a siding switch, catching him off-balance. He staggered towards Heather and she caught his hand. He held on to hers.

"Still angry?" he asked. She jerked her hand away and turned from him without answering.

"There's another reason why we've got to get off this train," Ben said.

"What's that?"

"If I were a Pinkerton agent in Chicago right now, I'd be headed to meet this train before the woman I'm after vanished again. We want to be off this thing before he gets here and starts looking too carefully at our thirteen-year-old brother. She's the other reason we need to find another train."

"Why hold her anymore? If they've figured all this out, why don't we just give her some money and let her go home?"

"There are still a few things they don't know, Bart. They don't know for sure that we don't have that gold with us and that we're not headed south. They may think we plan to stick around Ohio to stop other gold shipments and play games with their railroads. Ohio has more track than any other state in the nation. It's a beautiful place to help General Johnston lick the Yankees along the Mississippi River. Besides, do you really want to get rid of her?"

"Not really, I guess."

"Neither do I. It's like a game of chess. They want our queen and I'd like to checkmate Pinkerton."

"You're sure that's the only reason you want to keep her?"

"She's quite a lady," said Ben, laughing. "That's another problem I've got to work on. For now, the main thing is to get off this train and start south."

"Since they probably know what we look like, I think it would help us move if we changed ourselves into something else," Bart said. "You and Heather have been traveling around like dudes on a sightseeing trip and I'm a bum."

"Trouble is there's not much shopping on a train."

"You wait right here. I think I know where I can find me a clothing store." Bart went back into the car. Ben moved over to Heather.

"Magnificent sunset," he said.

"Have you decided what you're going to do with me?"

"Nothing has changed, so why do you ask?"

"They'll guess before long that I'm not your brother and you won't be able to hide me anymore."

"We'll worry about that when it happens. What have you been thinking about while we've been making our plans?"

"I thought once I'd throw this silly cap off the train and then you wouldn't be able to hide my hair. I asked myself what you would do if I did, and I didn't like the answer."

"What was the answer?"

"Would you throw me after my hat?"

He rolled up his left sleeve and took out a pocketknife. Opening it, he shaved an inch of the hair on his arm. He put the knife back in his pocket and rolled down his sleeve saying, "I have more than one option. You would not like any of them. I think it best to keep you guessing, Mrs. Wanderman."

She sighed and was silent for a time.

"Why do you always call me Mrs. Wanderman? I do have another name, you know?"

"I have to keep reminding myself that you're the enemy."

She whipped off the cap covering her hair, looked angrily into his eyes and demanded, "Am I?"

For a moment he studied her face and she thought, if Bart finds him kissing me, they may leave me and this will all be over. Turning away, she jammed the cap back on her head, shivering with delight at the thought of what she had almost done.

The train echoed through a cut and burst out again into woodlands.

"Capt. Warren Wanderman was a very fortunate man," she heard him say and, enraged, turned to face him.

"How dare you?"

"A few weeks of marriage to you must have been more heaven than most men have any right to."

"Why, Colonel Gordyne..." she murmured and quickly turned back to look at the orange sky rapidly turning black.

"I thank you for not shaving my head," she said.

"It is still an option. Don't make me do it."

"Yes," she said at last. "It is a magnificent sunset, but I'm thirsty. When do we eat?"

"The train will stop for wood and water in a few miles. We'll try to get off and eat there."

When Bart returned neither of them recognized him in the fading light.

"Where did you get those clothes?" Heather asked laughing.

"There are a lot of immigrants on board who need ten dollars bad enough to exchange clothes with anyone dumb enough to make such a bargain. I traded my good suit for this outfit from Sweden. Here, I even got this for you." He held up a dress, coat and bonnet. "Ben, you'll have to find your own."

In the next half hour Ben exchanged the almost new valise for a couple of battered bags that had seen the wear of an ocean voyage. When he returned wearing an ill-fitting brown suit, he said, "Let's go to the baggage car so our little brother can be a woman again."

As the train slowed to approach a small town, they dropped the empty gold boxes from the baggage car into the brush along the right of way. Minutes later two "Swedes" and a "Dutchman" missed the train as it pulled out. They found rooms in the station inn.

Before daylight the next morning, they walked up the track and recovered the crates. Nearby was a construction yard where ties, rails, lumber and hardware were stored for building and repairing the railroad bed. They found kegs of spikes, nuts, bolts and washers. Bart filled the crates with washers and Ben fashioned rough lids for them. An hour later a stagecoach stopped on its way south. The Swedish couple and the Dutchman were waiting with two heavy boxes and their worn travel bags.

****

Pinkerton Detective Agency in Chicago was notified of Mrs.

85

Wanderman's appearance soon after the train carrying her left Toledo. An agent who signed his name P. League Pharson was dispatched immediately. Pharson was more widely known as "Legs" for two quite obvious reasons. "League" was a name the young man had endured with much displeasure. He changed it as soon as possible.

Early in life it became evident that he was to be unusually tall. This gave him an advantage over his peers as a boy, enabling the gangling youth to convince all that their good health depended on them calling him something besides "League." "Legs" was appropriate.

The black suit he wore always appeared to be too small, until an observer realized that the sleeves were actually long enough to cover his arms. "Legs" was so thin that some said he had been extruded from the machines that make railroad tracks. His head looked large because of the thinness of his frame. He had wide ears and a pointed chin, high cheekbones, deep, dark eyes and thick, dark brows under a broad forehead and straight black hair.

Legs caught the train going east. When it intercepted the one from Toledo going west, he changed over. His first job was to interview the conductor who wasn't pleased to have his card game interrupted again. Cummins told Legs what he remembered about Heather getting on the train.

"I haven't seen her since," he ended.

"Can you take me to the man who helped her up the steps?" Legs asked.

"You'll know him. He's in the last car, a tall, thin man. Almost as tall as you. Real dude. Hair's kinda light brown. Name's Benjamin, Josiah Benjamin."

Legs headed for the rear of the train. He searched the last car twice, but didn't find anyone matching the description. Then he walked the full length of the train, asking a few passengers if they were Josiah Benjamin. The man he was looking for was not on the train. He reported this to the conductor.

"What do you mean he's not on the train? He had a ticket for Chicago."

"Nevertheless, Mr. Cummins, Josiah Benjamin is not on your train. Perhaps you can tell me where he might have gotten off."

"Well, I suppose he might have gotten off at any one of the last three stops, but why?"

"It may be that he got off with Mrs. Wanderman."

"Now see here, Mr. Pharson, or whatever your name is, we searched this train at Pachee Creek. We looked it over good. I and the sheriff and his deputies. That woman was not on my train."

"You may be right, Mr. Cummins. I'll not argue the point, but would you do me a favor of walking through your train with me just once to see if I've overlooked the gentleman? I do need to ask him some questions. You know there is a one thousand dollar reward for Mrs. Wanderman?"

With that reminder, Cummins was more than willing to cooperate. As they walked along the aisles, Legs asked the conductor about his other passengers. "Do you remember a rather heavyset young man? Big shoulders. Hair has a reddish color. About average height."

"That might be the man who was takin' his kid brother for his first train ride."

"When did they get on?"

"Toledo."

"Isn't that where Mr. Benjamin and Mrs. Wanderman boarded your train?"

"Yeah. Lots of people got on at Toledo."

"Do you remember the kid brother getting on the train?"

"No. There was a mob running after that gold just as we pulled out of Toledo and I missed him."

"Is it possible, Mr. Cummins, that kid brother might have been Mrs. Wanderman?"

"No, it ain't possible. They're still sitting up near the engine."

"Are you sure?"

"Let's go see."

They soon found the empty seats. As they were walking back, Legs stopped to chat with some of the women passengers, showing them Heather's picture.

"Do you remember this woman?" he asked.

"Oh yea," muttered a robust woman wearing a babushka. "She was sitting der mit dat very fine gent'eman."

"Where did they go?"

"De vent to da front oft da car 'nd de never come back."

"Can you remember when that was?"

"Soon afte' ve lief Toledo."

"I was hoodwinked. I been cheated out of one thousand dollars," the conductor fumed as they proceeded through the cars. Suddenly he stopped and went back two or three seats. Pulling a new valise down from the rack, he almost screamed, "It's his suitcase! It's his suitcase! Where did you get this suitcase? You've got his clothes. What are you doing with his clothes?"

A terrified Dutchman told what had happened and within a few minutes, Legs discovered the Swedish couple who had supplied outfits for Heather and Bart.

Legs let Cummins get back to his card game and left the westbound train at the next stop. There he reversed his direction again and headed for one water stop west of Pachee Creek. It was late when he found the small hotel where Ben, Bart and Heather had spent the night.

"I was surprised," said the innkeeper who doubled as a ticket agent. "Why would anyone want to go by stage that far when they could get there faster by train? They paid to ride the stage to Columbus."

"Did they have any luggage?" Legs asked.

"Two real heavy boxes and a couple of beat-up suitcases."

"When's the next stage south?" Legs asked.

"A week from today. Don't have much call for it since the railroad's come through. You can get to Columbus before they do, if you take the train out this afternoon."

Legs wired the information he had gathered back to the Pinkerton Agency in Chicago and included the report on the two heavy boxes.

He continued his trip to Toledo. There he caught a train to Columbus. He wasn't too surprised when the trio he was after did not arrive with the coach.

"They insisted on getting off at Maumee Crossing," the driver told him. "It didn't make sense, but that's where I left them."

"What's Maumee Crossing?" Legs asked.

"Nothing much really since the railroad came. It used to be a stage stop with a pretty good inn. Trains only halt there now long enough for wood and water. They killed the stage business."

Pharson headed out by rail for Maumee Crossing.

7
RUBY

Rye Hunsford, the innkeeper at Maumee Crossing, was a man between. His fat fingers were always slipping like those of a falling mountain climber from the almost of yesterday and the maybe of tomorrow. His soul was starved for something of today. He cursed the railroad that had taken both his stage and river business and left him little to fill up the rooms of the rundown hostelry inherited by his wife from her immigrant father. The old man had the foresight to build it where a north-south road met an east-west river. However, he was not prophet enough to see the railroad coming.

Hunsford spent his time drinking from a crusted beer mug, chewing a black cigar and eating. Day and night his tongue vented his deep hatred by pouring out a stream of invective about railroads, Republicans and rebels who kept him from getting Cuban cigars.

His wife, Vasilisa, had made him overweight with her cooking and she was the reason he kept to himself the one hope he had.

The main business of Maumee Crossing was repair and maintenance of the railroad. The workers, almost all men, had permanent addresses elsewhere. Recently the U. S. Army had stationed a detachment of young men on the outskirts of town to guard the town's important bridge against the Confederate raiders commanded by General John Hunt Morgan. It seemed to Hunsford that the business of his inn would greatly improve if these men could be encouraged to spend more of their recreational time and money in it. However, Vasilisa put a harness to the way he planned to do this and a bit in his mouth to keep him from talking about it. Mrs. Hunsford was a woman of ashes. Twenty-four years of marriage to Rye had burned up all her yesterdays and left her no fuel for tomorrows. Her todays had been ground down by hot stoves, hot irons, hot washing and hot anger that had milled her heart to a narrow strip of ice until there was very little left of body or soul except a long stretch of bone . . . and Ruby. Then, when she had no more days, she died, victim of a massive heart attack.

Her daughter, Ruby, a vixen with black hair and eyes smoldering like dark coals, had a body that made men thirsty. From the day of her birth she had lived at the inn and seventeen years among traveling people had convinced her that she had already spent too much time at Maumee Crossing.

The recent death of his wife revived Hunsford's hope for expanding his business without increasing his labor. Reluctantly, Ruby stepped into her mother's place in the kitchen. She wasn't likely to care what her father did with the rest of the inn so long as it didn't add to her labors.

When Legs Pharson came around asking questions about the immigrant woman who had spent the night in his inn, Hunsford nodded and said, "She was some looker. I was thinking they might stay around and I could use her here, you know what I mean."

"Yes," said Rye in answer to the detective's question. "They insisted on carrying those heavy boxes to their room. Been a whole lot easier just to have left them here."

"When did they leave?" Legs asked impatiently.

"Don't know. I went to bed. They was gone when I got up."

"Do any trains stop here during the night?"

"Two. One goes west to Chicago shortly after ten. The other goes to Columbus about three."

"Is there a ticket agent in town?"

"No. Local passengers buy tickets on the train."

Legs pulled a picture of Heather out of his notebook. "Is this the woman with those two men?" he asked.

"That's her all right," said Rye. "Some beauty, I'd say even in those worn clothes she was wearin'."

"Did she seem to be in good health?"

"Far as I could see. Didn't seem to me anything wrong with her. She looked tired after that coach ride, but she ate a good meal and was spry enough when she went to her room."

"Were they talking at the table?" Legs asked.

"Sure, like three good friends, laughin' and talkin'. Only I didn't hear nothin'."

"Was the woman laughing and talking or just the men?"

"Oh, she joined right in. Wasn't nothin' shy about her."

"There's a thousand dollar reward for finding her."

"One thousand dollars! I could sure use that."

Legs rubbed the side of his large nose in thought.

"How," he asked, more to himself than to Rye, "do you move two heavy boxes around in the dark without wheels?"

"Can't say that I know."

The rubbing seemed to stimulate thought. He stopped. The faraway look left his eyes.

"They may have had someone waiting for them here," he said. "Have there been any strangers around town recently?"

"Strangers? Sure. Immigrants always goin' through and there's that military detachment camped over by the bridge."

I wonder if any of Morgan's Raiders have been this far north, the detective asked himself. Then, turning to the innkeeper, he said, "Well, if you think of anything else that might help us find this woman, wire me at this address."

"Just who is this woman that's worth a thousand dollars?"

"She's the daughter of an official in Washington. She was an undercover agent for the Union. The men she's with are Confederate agents who are holding her hostage for reasons of their own."

"What's in them boxes?"

"I'm not at liberty to say," Legs replied. Had he looked left instead of right when he turned to leave he might have seen Ruby standing in the kitchen door, listening.

The agent spent six hours questioning people until the next southbound train came through. He found no one who had seen the Gordynes leave town. There were no reports of stolen boats or wagons and the three had not bought any type of conveyance.

The trail was cold. He headed for Columbus to await further developments. South had been the direction of travel when the fugitives took the stage and he had no reason to believe they had changed directions.

The train that took Legs out of town brought in an investigative team from the War Department. Rye also answered their questions which were noticeably different from Legs'. The military men asked more about the two boxes and did not seem too interested in the missing woman. They avoided telling him what was in the two boxes. However, one of his guests had passed along a story about a gold riot in Toledo.

As the train taking Legs south picked up speed leaving Maumee Crossing, it passed a railroad service shed where work crews stored their tools. Behind it were two boxes, covered carelessly with several old planks.

In Columbus, Legs went to the station and was told no one had boarded trains in Maumee Crossing that night.

Maybe that's why General Morgan crossed the Ohio, he thought. If it is, there isn't any telling where Mrs. Wanderman is right now.

The investigative team from the War Department reached the same conclusion. Scouts sent out on all the roads around Maumee Crossing found nothing. Had they walked a mile up the railroad's right-of-way near where a track went onto a trestle over a finger of Black Water Swamp, they would have found an abandoned caboose on a weed-grown siding. Heather was locked inside.

Coming into the village on the bank of the Maumee River, Ben had noticed two things from the stagecoach window. One was the old caboose. The other was a detachment of Union troops camped nearby. The soldiers were there to guard the bridge and the water tower from possible attacks by Morgan's Raiders. He considered the situation for a few minutes and then said to Bart, "I think we got another way to throw Pinkerton off our trail."

"How's that?"

"We'll wreck a train and join the Union Army temporarily."

Though they had passage to Columbus, they got off the stage in Maumee Crossing and stayed overnight in Hunsford's Inn to leave a southbound trail. When the innkeeper woke the next morning, they were gone. The Gordynes moved into the caboose near the trestle and used it while Legs looked for them in Columbus. During the day, as they planned their next attack, it served as a place of confinement for Heather. From the brush along the right-of-way they watched a few trains speed by.

"You notice something?" Ben asked.

"What?"

"Every train, as it comes to this spot, picks up speed to carry it up the grade over yonder. If we bend the track just a wee bit at this point, a train would take a flying leap into the swamp. That's the diversion we need to requisition three uniforms from the United States Army and point our way south."

"How are we going to bend the track?"

They spent the rest of the afternoon mapping an operation.

"We've got to set our trap and leave," said Ben. "We can't wait here to make it happen because we've got to be at the camp to get our new clothes and then catch a train south."

Rye Hunsford had not been sleeping well. Those two heavy boxes and that bright-haired woman were on his mind. If the Dutchman and two Swedes did not take the train and they didn't take the stage, how did they carry that gold out of town?

Suddenly, he sat straight up in bed. It was three in the morning. He rushed to Ruby's bedroom across the hall shouting, "They didn't leave town."

"What?" she asked sleepily.

"Those immigrants who came in on the stage have got to be somewhere right around here."

94

"Oh, go to sleep."

"That gold. It's somewhere nearby. They couldn't have carried it off."

"Gold? What gold?"

"That Pinkerton man don't fool me. He's not interested in that woman. He wants that gold and I'll bet you half of it, it's right here near Maumee Crossing. And I've used every hiding place in twenty miles."

He got dressed and waited impatiently for daylight to begin his search. About the same time, Ben woke Heather.

"You've been complaining that we keep you locked up. Today we're going to take you shopping."

"Shopping? What for?"

"New clothes."

"What's it to be this time?"

"A uniform."

They approached the Army encampment by a circuitous route through the thick forest and watched soldiers getting ready for short leaves. It was a weekend and Ben knew from experience that every soldier who could get a pass would pack up a few necessary items and head for some place offering more entertainment than Maumee Crossing. They would leave military gear behind.

For some time Ben and Bart, with Heather between them, lay in the underbrush looking for three troopers whose uniforms might fit them reasonably well.

"You could get into that fat sergeant's clothes," Heather whispered to Bart, "but I don't see anybody with Ben's odd shape."

"Odd shape? There isn't anything strange about my build."

"Only your feet are too far from your head, that's all."

They laughed.

"There ain't no midgets in this outfit, so I don't know how we're goin' to fit Heather. Though with her figure, we haven't had any trouble makin' her look like a boy," Bart remarked.

"Now you're getting mean," she said.

Eventually they spotted three tents occupied by men whose

combat clothing and gear they decided to steal. Having settled this issue, they backed into the woods for the return trip to the caboose. Rye Hunsford, heading home after a fruitless afternoon looking for their hiding place, caught a glimpse of them as they dashed across the railroad right-of-way.

Look what I have got myself, he gloated. I knew it. That old woman of mine has been holdin' me back all these years. My luck changes jest es soon es she's gone. I shoulda got shuck a'her years ago.

Now he had a decision to make. He could settle for the thousand dollars reward offered by Pinkerton or he could go for the two boxes of gold. Rye was a greedy man, not foolish. He had seen Bart carry those boxes and knew there was enough strength in those arms to stretch him like taffy. He didn't know much about the other man except that he looked competent. So Rye watched as the sun went down and a ragged moon came up.

Inside the caboose the brothers rested while waiting for the afternoon passenger train to pass.

"It's liable to be a long and exciting night," Bart told Heather. "Besides a freight train will make a better fire."

"No need to endanger women and children," Ben added.

Heather sighed. "When are we going to leave here?"

"After dark," Ben said.

The sounds of the passenger train were still fading in the distance when Rye saw the Gordyne brothers leave the caboose and lock the door leaving Heather inside. Greed got the best of him. Maybe he could get both the gold, the thousand dollars and the woman too.

My luck is makin' this almost too easy, he told himself. They're leaving honey in the hands of a bear. A woman worth a thousand dollars reward oughta be some kind of woman. Besides she'd sure draw business to my inn.

He watched Ben and Bart walk along the tracks and around a bend. They were gone a long while. He waited until full dark. Then he saw the light go out in the caboose.

Heather was lying on her cot when she heard the sound of

stealthy feet approaching. She sat up as someone smashed at the hasp. The door was jerked open. She snatched the scissors Ben had left her and cowering on her bunk in a dark corner watched a man step out of the moonlight.

"Mrs. Wanderman," he said, "I've come to take you to the Union Army commander so that you can go home."

"Who are you?" she whispered.

"I'm Rye Hunsford, the innkeeper where you stayed the other night. Mr. Pharson of the Pinkerton Detective Agency came by the other day asking about you. I told him I'd help find you."

This was the opportunity Heather had been waiting for ever since the Gordyne brothers had discovered her in Washington. She laid down the scissors, found some matches and lit a candle.

"If you'll step outside, I'll get dressed, get a few of my things together and we can go," she said.

But he only turned his back. While she was dressing, she did not notice him searching the empty car. She was about ready to leave when he asked, "Where's the gold?"

Heather was instantly suspicious. "Gold? What gold?"

"You came to Maumee Crossing with two heavy boxes of gold. I saw you with the boxes and Mr. Pharson told me what was in them. I'm supposed to try to get that back too."

Heather hesitated a bit too long. "I don't know about any gold," she said. "The men hid those boxes somewhere."

As she talked she took up the small bundle of things she wanted to take with her and started towards the door. He snatched her arm, pulled her to him and growled, "Where's that gold?"

She slapped him and he twisted her arm until she screamed.

"If you do that again, I'll break your arm," he said and, wrapping his fat arms about her, he kissed her. Desperately she pushed his face away and stamped as hard as she could on his foot. In his pain, he released his hold on her and she dashed for the door, but he caught her hair and dragged her back.

"There'll be plenty of time for wrestling later, woman," he said. "Right now we've a bit of business to take care of. You're goin' to write your boyfriends a note and tell them if they want to see you alive again, I want thet gold. Sit down and write."

A quarter of a mile down the track the brothers broke into the railroad service shack near the trestle and helped themselves to a draw claw so they could pull spikes.

"Your idea," said Bart, "is to improvise a switch such as those used to turn a train from one track to another."

"Except this one will head the train into the swamp."

They started to work by the light of a misshapen moon. With the draw claw they pulled the spikes holding the right rail in place on about six railroad ties.

"Now, when the locomotive's weight hits this loose track, it'll push it out of alignment with the next length of rail," Ben said, "and the right drive wheels of the engine will shift to the right where there isn't any track. The engine should tip over, fly towards the swamp and roll down that embankment pulling all those boxcars with it."

"Should be spectacular."

"Unfortunately we won't be here to watch the fireworks. We've got to pick up Heather and our luggage and get out before the freight arrives."

Returning to the caboose, they found the door open and Heather was gone. Ben surveyed the scene and saw the note under the candle. Bart dashed for the door and searched the limited horizon. By the light of the dying moon he saw two figures moving over the railroad track about two hundred yards away.

"Heather," he bellowed. "Ben, she's on the track. There's someone with her."

Ben joined him at the door. He had read enough of the note to know what had happened. Jumping down from the caboose, the two of them started running. When they were within twenty-five feet, Hunsford shouted, "Stop! If you come one step closer, I'll cut her throat."

They saw the knife at her neck.

"All right, what is it you want?" Ben demanded.

"Gold. I want the two boxes of gold you took off that train in Toledo. Get it to me or you thieving rebels won't see this bitch alive again."

"Listen, you bloody fool, we don't have the gold," Bart yelled.

"We don't have the gold here," Ben corrected, "and I'm not at all sure we'd give it to you for a stupid Yankee spy. Kill her and you'd save us a lot of trouble."

"How would you like me to turn her over to army investigators who were snooping around asking questions about that gold you say you don't have? I could get at least a thousand dollars for her."

"Let me talk about it with my partner here." Ben turned to Bart. "We've got to convince him that she has information we cannot afford to let fall into the hands of the Yankees. Let's make him think we're having a heavy discussion."

"Hurry up. I ain't got all night," Rye shouted. "If you had wanted her dead, you could have gotten rid of her before you left Washington. Seems to me you've gone to a heap of trouble to keep her alive. You've got the gold and if you don't get it to me your little girl friend will be playing my tune before I collect my reward from Pinkerton."

Then Heather yelled, "I'd sure like to tell the U. S. Army how you're planning to get that gold across the Ohio River and where General Morgan's Raiders are right now. That would box up four thousand dirty rebels in a tight corner."

"That's tellin' them, sweetheart," Hunsford said.

"One box," Ben said. "We'll give one and we keep one."

"Nope, I'm greedy. Both of them or I leave now and take this little honey with me."

"You win. How can you argue with a Yankee sewer rat?"

"Call me names if you want, but get me that gold."

"Come on then. Let's get this over with," Bart said and the brothers turned to walk towards the railroad service shed.

Hunsford, holding the knife at Heather's back, followed them. No one spoke. Except for the sound of insects, the night was still. Then, in the far distance came the sound of a train. The moon was brushing the horizon and would almost be gone by the time they reached the boxes. A lingering beam of light lay across the misty marsh when the brothers halted about five feet from the small building. Hunsford stopped behind them.

"Well?" Rye questioned.

"Well, there they are," Ben said.

"Show them to me."

Bart moved a little away from Ben towards Heather. Eagerly, Rye pressed forward. He did not release Heather or remove the knife from her back. Ban stepped forward and lifted the boards from the two boxes.

"Open them," Hunsford commanded.

Using the draw claw, Ben smashed the lids of one box. The train sounded near. A last beam of the fading moon touched the metal disks in the box and was gone. Rye stepped forward, transfixed. Bart snatched his knife arm and pushed him towards the boxes. The innkeeper stumbled, fell to his knees near the box and began fingering the disks he could no longer see.

"Gold. I've got all this gold," he screamed as the train thundered into view, its headlight flashing across the track.

Ben and Bart clutched at Heather.

"Let's get out of here," Bart said, "'cause there's gonna be the best train wreck you ever saw."

They were running towards the woods when the headlight flashed a beam into Hunsford's hand.

"This ain't gold," he shrieked as the first wheel left the track. "It's just a bunch of washers."

Rye never said another word. The tracks spread apart and the engine's drive wheels failed to follow the fore truck. The engineer screamed as the locomotive skewed sideways. A tender full of firewood shot through the air towards Hunsford. It slammed him into the side of the iron shed. The locomotive, taking yards of the trestle with it, piled in on top. One after the other, boxcars loaded with powder and ammunition for the Union Army fighting far to the south, piled on top of the mass of wood and steel. The locomotive's firebox emptied its flame and fire began to crawl up out of the ruined heap. Kegs of gunpowder began to burn. Shells exploded and the people of Maumee Crossing were treated to Rye

Hunsford's funeral pyre, a gigantic fireworks display.

Away from the wreck in the shelter of the woods, Heather trembled. Reaction set in. She began to sob. Ben touched her shoulder and she buried her face in his chest. He wrapped an arm around her and patted the back of her head.

"It's all over now," he muttered. "You'll be all right."

Bart shuffled his feet uncomfortably. When she stopped sobbing, the brothers went over their plan.

"Shortly the Army encampment should be evacuated," Ben said. "The troops will be coming out here to fight the fire. You take Mrs. Wanderman to the caboose to get our things. I'll burglarize three tents and meet you at the Post Office. Stay out of sight until the train comes in."

Ruby Hunsford, like everyone else in Maumee Crossing, was awakened from her sleep by the sound of exploding shells. She ran to her father's room. His bed was undisturbed. He had not been home since breakfast. Ruby joined the other townspeople racing down the road that paralleled the railroad track, but she never reached the fire. Standing well away from the blaze were her father's buckboard and his horse.

Daddy? Where was he? Then it struck her. He was dead! She knew it!

Without hesitation she mounted the buckboard and rode it back to the inn. For years she had dreamed of this escape. Everything was carefully planned. Dragging an empty, domed trunk out the back door, she set it on the buckboard. The room behind the inn's desk was always locked. Ruby knocked the padlock off the door with a hammer and for the first time entered the windowless cubbyhole. She found the heavy, locked strongbox, carried it out and put it in the bottom of the trunk.

Hastily she went through the inn searching for things she thought might easily be turned into cash. Each item she wrapped in her clothing and packed in the trunk. She kept watching the clock figuring she had until 3:25 a.m. to catch the train.

When the trunk was full, she locked it. Returning to the inn she saw it was 2:15 and went through the building to make sure every door and window was secured.

Time for a quick bath, she told herself at 2:35, and took the lantern into the room where the tub stood. Twenty minutes later she was anointed with powder and perfume and attired in the gray-blue dress she wore only to weddings and funerals. Pinning a matching hat on her thick, black hair was a task that could not be hurried.

It took her another five minutes to pack toilet articles and a change of clothing in a small carpetbag. Then she went to the place under the cellar stairs where she knew her mother hid whatever money she could smuggle away from Rye. It was in a small doeskin bag. She added the key to the trunk to its contents, and hung it on a rawhide cord around her neck. The bag was tucked inconspicuously between her breasts. Finally, she sat at her father's desk and printed a message which she nailed to the front door after locking it. The paper read:

"NOTICE OF SALE: This inn is for sale. For information contact Fred Hunsford."

There followed an address in St. Louis, Missouri.

Before mounting the buckboard, Ruby dropped the inn's key down beside the stone steps and carefully covered it with the hammer and some dirt. As she slapped Rye's horse into motion, she heard the whistle of the southbound morning train in the distance.

Even if Rye happened to be alive, which she doubted, she was finally free of the place.

Ruby had not been the only one packing during those early morning hours. Hurrying through the empty army encampment Ben picked up the clothing and gear they needed. He met Bart and Heather at the Post Office. They were waiting, dressed in secondhand U.S. Army uniforms, when the train pulled in.

Ben and Heather got on board. Bart straggled behind, watching a young, dark-haired woman in a gray-blue dress as she instructed the baggage handler about the disposition of her trunk. When he got on board, he took a seat three rows back and across the aisle from Ben and Heather.

As the train rolled south, Heather stared moodily out a window. She sighed and said nothing.

"You don't seem to be in a good temper today," Ben said. "Don't you like this trip?"

"Trip's all right. I'm worried."

"What's on your mind?"

"My parents. Mother will be frantic. I just want to let her know I'm all right."

Ben sat thoughtfully, rubbed his chin and asked, "Would you like to send them a telegram?"

"Could I?"

"Yes, I think so."

"Will you let me write it?"

"No, you can read it and see if what I say meets with your approval."

"You don't trust me?"

"Yes, I do, Mrs. Wanderman. I can always trust you to be a Union spy. I'm quite sure you've got two reasons for sending a telegram. You do want to let your folks know you're all right. And you figure Pinkerton will be able to trace the telegram and it'll tell them where we are. I don't trust you any farther than the buttons on my coat, Mrs. Wanderman. You're smart enough to put something in it I don't want the Army to know and I'm not smart enough to figure out your code. That's why I won't let you write it."

They both chuckled and he continued, "However, I think I owe it to you to let you know that I also have two reasons for suggesting that you wire home."

"What might they be?"

"It's cruel to keep your folks worrying about you. I'd like them to know that you are being taken care of. Second, I'd like Pinkerton to trace the wire."

"Why?"

"It'll set them to thinkin' we're headed in one direction when actually we'll be some place else."

"So, if I send the telegram, I'll be helping you in your mission

103

against the Union?"

"Correct."

"I trust you, too," she spoke softly. "Just like you trust Satan. I can always depend on Col. Benjamin L. Gordyne III to be Col. Benjamin L. Gordyne III, who is the devil!"

Furious, she turned her head away from him. He took out a piece of paper and spent several minutes writing.

"Still angry?" he said after a spell.

"No," she muttered. "You were so nice to me back there. I'm sorry I broke down."

"You did real well. That man was mean enough to kill you. Do you want to send this telegram?"

She took the paper and read: "Mr. and Mrs. Arthur Duncan, Sr. Am well, well cared for, guarded as prisoner of war. Worry not. Love, Heather Wanderman."

"May I add something?" she asked.

"That depends on what you want to add."

"After 'prisoner of war' I'd like to add 'by two fine men.'"

"I'm not sure that would be the truth."

"It is. Really it is. It's just too bad we're enemies."

"If we weren't enemies, we'd never have met."

"True."

"May I send this telegram for you?"

"Yes, Mommy needs to know I'm all right."

"May I add one word?" he asked.

"What?"

"'Mommy' after 'worry not.' Then she'll know it's from you."

Meanwhile Bart was in a conversation of another kind. He knew the young woman he had seen earlier was alone and in the same car. Still it had been a busy night. Bart stretched out on the double seat and was soon asleep.

Ruby Hunsford was wide awake. Where had she seen that sergeant before? She got up and walked to the front of the car, turned and walked back, looking at the sleeping man. As she returned to her seat, she glanced at two soldiers on the other side of the aisle. She was sure she had seen them before. It took her a mile or two of travel time to figure it out. She moved forward again and touched Bart's shoe.

He cocked an eye up at her.

"Is this seat taken?" she asked.

Bart looked around at the other empty seats in the car and wondered what the attractive woman meant. This time he noticed her full, red lips and rounded figure. He moved his legs and stood. Bowing slightly, he said, "I would most certainly appreciate your company."

"I'm not sure you will when I tell you who I am," she said as she sat down.

"Why should that matter?"

"Because I'm Ruby Hunsford, the daughter of the innkeeper at Maumee Crossing, and I remember your visit with us. I was disappointed when you left without saying goodbye. Then I was more disappointed when you took those two heavy boxes with you. I was also there when the man from Pinkerton came by asking questions about the lady up there in the soldier's uniform. There's not much to her, but I understand she's worth one thousand dollars."

She smiled, touched his arm and said, "You are very strong. I wonder what would happen if I were to advise the conductor of her presence on his train. There are certainly enough men around to hold you for the law."

Bart was so taken by surprise that he was speechless. Now, however, as she paused, he said, "What is it you want, Miss Hunsford?"

"Not much," she said. "I'd like a small share of what's in those two boxes."

"May I discuss that with my two friends over there?"

"Oh, certainly. In case you don't know, the conductor will be coming through shortly to take your fare. It would be very kind if you would pay mine."

Bart went back to inform his brother of the new developments. Ben greeted the news in silence. Heather began giggling. The giggle burst into full-throated laughter. She could not stop. She laughed until tears rolled from her eyes.

"Oh," she sobbed at last. "I can't believe this. It's the funniest thing that's happened since you jumped into New York harbor."

Ben grinned. He too began to laugh. Then the conductor stepped into the car.

"Stop laughing," Bart ordered. "What do we do?"

"Buy her ticket," Ben said. "At least it will give us time to think this thing through."

"You're both crazy." Bart turned back to Ruby.

"What have you decided?" she asked.

"Where do you want to go?"

"Wherever you go, soldier," she said. Bart almost dropped his wallet.

"Two for Cincinnati," Bart told the conductor.

"Now let's talk about this," said Ben as the four of them gathered on the observation platform.

"Just what is it you want?"

"Gold."

"Tell her, Mrs. Wanderman. Since you are a Union spy, maybe she'll believe you."

"Miss Hunsford, there is no gold," Heather said. "All the gold was spilled on the platform and tracks in Toledo. Those boxes were filled with iron washers."

"Is that true?" Ruby asked.

"I swear to you it is true."

"You mean my daddy died for two boxes of junk?"

"I'm afraid so," Bart said, "and I'm sorry."

To their astonishment, Ruby began to laugh.

"It could not be any other way," she said. "There was never anything but junk."

"Now what do you want?" Ben asked.

"There is the thousand dollar reward," she replied. "Yet I'm not really sure I want that. What I want to know is what are you up to? Where are you going, robbing trains and wrecking them? What's next?"

The brothers looked at each other and Heather started

laughing again.

"That we can't tell you," Ben said.

"Then I'll just have to collect the reward."

"We can't let you do that either."

"How to you plan to stop me?"

"We could throw you off this moving train."

"But they won't," said Heather. "They are southern gentlemen who wouldn't think of doing such a thing. So they'll make you their second prisoner of war."

"Don't tempt me, Mrs. Wanderman," said Ben. "Don't tempt me."

They changed trains in Columbus and arrived in Cincinnati towards dusk a day later. Now they had two women to watch, but they managed.

Ben checked for trains going west.

"It'll be a while before our train leaves," Ben told them. "It isn't safe for us to be seen hanging around a depot. Let's take a walk."

They strolled down to the riverfront where the women sat on a bench. The brothers walked away and stood looking across the Ohio.

"That's the way home," Bart said.

"Yes," Ben responded. "We could turn Heather and Ruby loose and cross the river. We'd be back in St. Stephens in a week."

There was a period of silence. The dark water rustled against the stones below them. Sounds of the city rose behind them. Trails of lights twinkled across the water like an invitation. A light breeze blew in from the south. It seemed they could almost smell the fragrance of home.

"Wonder what Mama's doin'?" Bart asked.

"About now she and Nida are probably settling down the kitchen for the night. Daddy has his pint and is laying out the work for tomorrow."

"Tomorrow's Sunday. They'll all be gettin' ready for church."

"Yeah. Be good to sit on those hard pews with them and listen

107

to Pastor Craig try to keep people awake."

"Remember how we'd bet whether Harris or Culver would go to sleep first?"

"Yeah. How come you most always won?"

"The man who arrived late always went to sleep first."

"I wonder why?"

"Probably ate too much for breakfast."

Talking stopped. The murmur of the chatting women reached them. Somewhere a dog barked. A breeze rippled the water.

"We could tell Jeff Davis we tried, but it can't be done," Bart suggested.

"Probably true, too." Ben stooped down to pick up a stone. "Want to go home, Bart?"

"Wantin' and willin' is the difference between a fiancee and a wife. A gentleman knows the difference and a cad don't."

"A soldier and a mercenary, too."

"Right."

Ben tossed the stone into the darkness across the river and said, "Come on, ladies, let's catch us a St. Louis train."

8
RIVERBOAT GAMBLER

Reports of the spectacular wreck reached P. League Pharson by way of Army Intelligence.

"I thought you'd be interested in the name 'Maumee Crossing,'" the lieutenant told him. "Set us up, they did."

"While we looked all over Ohio for them, they sat within sight of the water tower," said the detective.

"For all we know they might still be there."

"Draw a circle five hundred miles wide around that wrecked train and you'd not cover all the places they could be now."

However, the detective, like a good hunting dog, returned to the last place of positive scent to try to pick up the trail.

"Everyone was at the train wreck," the constable said in answer to his questions. "We don't know what was happening in town."

"Where's Rye Hunsford?" Legs asked. "His inn is for sale."

"Nobody knows. We got back from the wreck and his buckboard and horse were standing by the track and that notice was nailed to his door. Ain't nobody seen Rye nor Ruby since."

"Who's this Fred Hunsford in St. Louis?"

"Never heard of him."

"It doesn't make sense," Legs said. "Why would a man put his business up for sale, take his daughter and leave town without telling anybody?"

"If you knew Rye, you could bet he's out looking for easy money. I'd say he's got it or he's fair certain of it."

The gold, of course, thought Pharson as he walked over to the Army encampment to talk to Captain Swayne, the detachment's commander. He's either won the pot or he's holding a full house. It may be that Mrs. Wanderman and her abductors were the losers. They may be under that pile of ashes.

He asked the usual questions and Swayne told him what he knew about the wreck.

"Do you know Rye Hunsford?" Pharson asked.

"The innkeeper? Yes, I know him."

"Do you think he might have wrecked that train?"

"He's mean enough," said Swayne, "but he isn't smart enough. Whoever engineered that wreck aimed it like a gun. Something else happened that weekend you might connect with the wreck."

"What?"

"About half my men went on leave. When they got back, three of them reported their tents were burglarized. The only time it could have happened was when all of us were over at the train wreck trying to help salvage as much as we could."

"What was taken?"

"Clothes. Camping equipment. Two Spencer carbines. Carbines were the only things worth much. Why would anyone want to steal a man's clothes? Strange thing about it was the thieves went to three different tents."

"You say they stole from three random tents?"

"Yes, like they knew exactly which tents they wanted."

"May I question those men, sir?"

"Certainly," the officer said and sent an orderly to get the soldiers. Legs laughed when the three men stood together.

"It's no laughing matter," the captain said.

"I'm laughing with relief," said Legs. "Mrs. Wanderman was not killed in that wreck. She's wearing the uniform of that short private. One of the men who took her captive is a heavy man. I figure the sergeant's uniform would fit him. The other is tall and slender. Seeing those three together convinces me that the people I'm looking for are wearing your men's uniforms. The question is where?"

When Legs got back to Columbus, he found a telegram from Chicago. Heather had wired her parents from Cincinnati across the Ohio River from Kentucky.

Cincinnati, he fumed. Where are they going?

It took him about half an minute to solve that riddle.

"By Abraham Lincoln's whiskers," he said aloud. "If I wanted to get into Dixie, I'd join the Union Army and get as close to the rebels as I could. Then I'd surrender. They sent the telegram from Cincinnati five days ago. Where are they now? If they're headed for Dixie, why take Mrs. Wanderman with them?"

It took him longer to calculate that there was more to the telegram than just a message home. It pointed south. Yet the notice on the inn door, the stolen items and the fact that the Gordynes had not released Heather pointed west.

"Leaving for St. Louis," he wired his chief.

****

Fred Hunsford sat in his barber chair and rubbed the polished dome which constituted the top of his head. It was early and the first person to need his tonsorial skills that day had not yet arrived. He held a letter in his hand. It was too short to need reading again.

Rye was dead. Fred wondered how his brother died. It was more curiosity than concern and he was uncomfortable because he felt no sorrow at the news.

"I figure Vasilisa was the only thing keeping him alive," he told his wife, Belle, who busied herself at the shelf in front of the mirror straightening the assortment of bottles and equipment which made up the tools of his trade. "Since she's gone, he had no one to fetch his beer and beans, so he just died."

111

"I'm wondering what will happen to Ruby," Belle said. "She must be seventeen or eighteen by now. Seems like she ought to come live with us."

"If she's grown to be much like Rye, I'm not so sure we could put up with her," Fred said.

The light dimmed as a figure darkened the door. Fred stood to greet a tall, thin stranger. Mrs. Hunsford slipped out. She knew a barbershop was a male sanctuary.

"Good morning, sir," said Hunsford laying the envelope on the shelf beside the hair tonic. "Shave and a haircut?"

"Yes, I could stand both if talk is part of your trade."

"It is," said Fred. "I figure most of the patrons of this establishment come as much for the conversation as the haircut."

"Good." The dark man with the thin, sharp face took his place in the barber's chair. "Are you Fred Hunsford?"

"Why, yes. How do you come to know me?"

"Your name and address are posted on an inn in Maumee Crossing, Ohio, and I've come to ask you some questions about a man named Rye Hunsford. Is he some kin of yours?"

"He was my brother and who might you be?"

"Oh, excuse me. I'm P. League Pharson, Legs to most people. I'm with the Pinkerton Detective Agency and your brother's disappearance has caused us some concern."

"Disappearance? I got word yesterday that he's dead."

"Dead? Now that is surprising. Folks back in Maumee Crossing think he just disappeared. Nobody's found a body. How do you know he's dead?"

"I got a letter from his daughter. She says he's dead and the letter gives me the authority to act on her behalf in the sale of the inn in Maumee Crossing."

"May I see the letter?"

"First, maybe you'd better tell me what this is all about?"

Legs gave him a brief account of Heather Wanderman, the train robbery in Toledo and the wreck at Maumee Crossing.

"We're hunting for Mrs. Wanderman and thought your brother might be chasing after her because of the gold."

"Well, Ruby says he's dead, otherwise I'd say you're probably right. Rye was so busy chasing the big one, he never had time to let the little ones grow."

"May I see the letter?"

"Certainly." Fred handed Legs the envelope.

"Dear Uncle Fred," he read, "Daddy is dead and so I am leaving Maumee Crossing and want to sell the inn. I want you to sell it for me and by this letter I am giving you legal authority to do so. The key is under a hammer beside the front steps. I will visit with you and Aunt Belle soon. Your niece, Miss Ruby Hunsford."

Under this was a further note. It read:

"I, Henry A. Handel, did witness the signature of Miss Ruby Hunsford on this letter."

"Appears legal," Legs commented as he continued to examine the letter. He turned it over several times looking for evidence not found in the words. Then he examined the envelope.

"Did you know this letter was mailed in St. Louis?"

"Can't be."

"The stamp was canceled at the St. Louis post office,"

"Why would she be in St. Louis to mail a letter and not come by to see us? It don't make sense."

"Maybe she couldn't spare the time. If she's anything like her father she's probably chasing the gold."

Legs looked at the letter again.

"You got any idea who this Henry A. Handel is?" he asked.

"Seems to me there's a Handel's Emporium down by the river, but I don't know who runs the place." Hunsford tipped back the barber chair and began to lather Legs' face.

Two hours later the detective was browsing through the emporium, examining the merchandise when a man of medium height and more than medium girth approached him.

"May I be of service, sir?" he asked.

"I've been looking over your stock," Legs said, "and I notice you offer the widest variety of goods I think I have ever seen under one roof. You also seem to have a rather unusual class of customers. I take it most of these are not local people."

"You are very observant, sir. I opened Handel's Emporium to serve the needs of pioneers going through St. Louis to make their homes in the wilderness. People with gold fever or Oregon fever, sod busters, prospectors, draft dodgers, people of every kind and from every place."

This man was a talker. Legs leaned on a counter to listen.

"Many of them come here with little idea of what they will need on the trail," Handel said. "They've got this far by river or by rail with their grandfather clocks, their heavy furniture, even their pianos. But there are some things you can't take in a covered wagon. St. Louis is the last place to try to talk some sense into them. My employees meet the boats and trains and try. I buy things they can't transport across the plains and the Rocky Mountains and sell them things for the trail and for settling in the wild. Then we sell their surplus to the people of St. Louis."

"Must be a very profitable business, Mr. Henry A. Handel?"

"Yes, sir, it..." began the owner of the emporium and then stopped. "How is it, sir, that you know my name?"

"I saw it on a letter you notarized a few days ago."

"Ah, yes, that is also one of the services I offer these people. They often need a witness to some legal matter."

"Do you remember witnessing a letter for a young lady named Ruby Hunsford about four days ago?"

"I'm not at all sure it is any of your business, sir."

After Legs introduced himself and explained his mission, Handel was willing to cooperate.

"Yes, I remember Miss Hunsford. A rather lovely young lady. She said her father had been killed in a train wreck in Ohio, I believe it was. She needed to authorize her uncle to sell some property and I witnessed her signature."

"So that's how he died," the detective said. "Was she alone?"

"No, there was a gentleman with her."

"Do you know his name?"

"No, I don't believe we were introduced."

"You say he was a gentleman. Was he well-dressed?"

"I'd say he looked like a riverboat gambler. Tall man."

"How was the lady dressed?"

"I'd say she was a fit companion for a riverboat gambler."

"Did they get off a boat?"

"I'm afraid I didn't notice."

"Was there a boat at the dock?"

"Yes. Missouri Belle was ready to sail for St. Joe."

"Did the couple buy anything from you?"

"As I helped the lady with her letter, the gentleman was looking at our books." Handel said pointing to a display. "He leafed through a few and then picked up one and read a few pages. After I had notarized the letter, he paid for it."

"What was the book?"

"'Wilderness Survival' by Col. Malcomb Wilcox. It's advice for people going west on what to eat, how to find water and what to do if you get lost. It's used by the Army."

"That's most interesting," said Legs and bought a copy.

"Did the couple have any other business with you?"

"Yes, sir. Some of the pilgrims passing through St. Louis are reluctant to part with their luxury items so as a service to them I keep these things in storage for a specified period. They seldom return for their goods and I add it to my merchandise. Miss Hunsford left a trunk."

"A trunk? Was it heavy?"

"If you're thinking about gold, it wasn't that heavy."

"Thank you, Mr. Handel. You have been most helpful," Legs said turning to leave. Then he looked back.

"Excuse me for taking so much of your time, but I have one more question," he said, taking Heather's picture from his coat pocket. "Have you seen this woman before?"

Handel took the picture and tipped it to better get the light from a dirty window.

"Looks familiar, but I don't believe I've ever seen her."

"If you dressed that lady in the uniform of an Army private and took off the hair, would she look more familiar?"

Handel studied the picture again.

115

"There was a couple of soldiers in here earlier that day. One was a heavy sergeant. The other was the smallest trooper I'd ever seen. Looked like a boy."

"Ah-ha," Legs shouted, "they were here. What did they buy? What did they buy?"

"Camping equipment mostly, as if they were getting ready to cross the plains. A tent. An axe. Two Colt revolvers and bullets and leather to go with them. Things like that."

"Did they get on the Missouri Belle?"

"They didn't go out the door towards the river, but then they may have circled around the outside."

Legs wired Pinkerton's Chicago office, "Leaving for St. Joe."

He plays more parts than an actor, he thought as he took a seat on the Northern Missouri Railroad. Now he's a riverboat gambler. I'll gamble this train moves faster than a boat.

****

The rail line ended at St. Joseph, Mo. This was the jumping off point for the west. From there to California it was mules, oxen, horses and feet. Legs was jammed in a crowded car filled with immigrants for the ride to St. Joe. He hurried from the station to the docks and was waiting there when the Missouri Belle tied up.

He had won his wager, but lost his prey.

"The gambler and the woman with him booked passage to St. Joe," the ship's master told him. "But I haven't seen them since Westport Landing."

"They did it again," Legs grumbled. "How do I get there?"

"If you're in a hurry, you'll go by horse. If you ain't, I'll be making a return trip shortly."

"By the time I get there, either way, they'll be long gone. But gone where?"

"Trails out of Westport Landing cover the west," the skipper

116

said.

He was right. There were routes to Santa Fe, Salt Lake City, California, Oregon and all points between and beyond. Travelers went by wagon train, horseback and stagecoach. Some walked, pulling two-wheeled wagons behind.

Legs had only questions as he leaned his chair back against the front wall of the St. Joseph Hotel and watched the ebb and flow of people. Beside him sat a U.S. marshal to whom he posed a stream of questions.

"Did they get that gold to Gen. John Hunt Morgan? He didn't have any gold when he was captured. Is it buried? Why are they taking it west? Why didn't they go south from Cincinnati? Why are they dragging those two women into the wilderness? Mrs. Wanderman tried to escape in Toledo. What's Ruby Hunsford got to do with anything? And why did they change from a train to a steamboat in St. Louis?"

"Gold seems to have something to do with it," the marshal said.

Legs slapped his hand on his leg and said, "That's it! They shipped the gold south and are headed to California for more."

"Leaving for San Francisco," Pharson wired his chief.

****

The floating palaces carrying passengers up the muddy river boasted of all the luxuries and comfort of the finest hotels of New Orleans. First class accommodations included gourmet meals and fine wines. People dressed in their best. There was dancing and music and games of chance. There was the luxury of sleeping in feather beds.

But never silence. The mechanical chorus of the steam engine followed Heather and Ruby to their cabin on the first night out of St. Louis. Even the luxury of lying down after days in railroad coaches could not block it out. So, since it was the first time they had really been alone together, they talked themselves into slumber.

"Why are they keeping you prisoner?" Ruby asked Heather as they lay in the darkness.

"I know where they are going and why. They figure if they turn me loose I'll report to military intelligence and it will spoil a Confederate plot."

"That's exciting. What's it all about?"

"I was a Union informant working in northern Virginia when it started."

"You? A Union spy?"

Heather started her account at the Rebel Flag. She remained puzzled after telling the story of her capture and the aftermath. Something about the entire situation did not make sense. The next evening as the Missouri Belle pushed toward St. Joe, she decided to question Ben. They were standing by the rail watching the flat land flow by.

"Why didn't you leave Ruby in Cincinnati?" she asked. "She didn't know what you were doing."

"We considered it."

"Well, why didn't you?"

"Don't you like her?"

"She's friendly enough. It's nice to have a woman to talk to, but that doesn't answer my question."

"Yes it does. We thought you might like a woman companion. It's a long way to San Francisco."

Heather was silent again.

"There's another reason," Ben continued. "You've told her where we're going and why."

"Of course. Now I have an ally."

"No, you don't. We do."

"Don't be silly. How can she help you?"

"She can help us watch you. You've needed a woman guard ever since we captured you. It's been hard on you and hard on us. By telling her our plans, you have created your own guard,"

"How can you possibly believe that, Colonel Gordyne?"

"Mrs. Wanderman, what do you think Ruby wants?"

"Excitement mostly. Maumee Corner hasn't given her much of that. The death of her father turned her loose to find it."

"I expect that's right," Ben agreed. "Ruby has no interest in the war. She's interested in two things...money and men."

Heather laughed.

"The reward interests her. So do Bart and the gold. Now that you've told her our plans, she's not about to let you spoil them. She's more likely to kill you than we are. Watch her."

"You insect," Heather hissed, turning from him.

"I'm sorry it's got to be this way," Ben said.

After a few minutes she turned back to him.

"I've another question, Colonel Gordyne," she said.

"What's that?"

"Why did you leave the train in St. Louis and take this steamboat? The train would get you to St. Joe much faster."

"Again, you are the answer."

"Me?"

"Yes, Mrs. Wanderman. It's a long way to San Francisco. The last few weeks have not been pleasant for you and for the next two months we'll be on horseback ten hours a day. We thought you needed a rest. A couple of days on the river will do you good."

"Was that your idea, Ben Gordyne?"

"Yes, Mrs. Wanderman."

"It's awfully hard to be your enemy," she said.

"Besides we're not going to St. Joe. We're leaving this boat at Westport Landing."

"We've got passage to St. Joe."

"I know. Maybe Pinkerton knows it too. So, we're getting off at the river's bend. That's another reason we took to the river in St. Louis. There isn't a rail line to Westport Landing yet."

9
RIVERS WEST

The Gordynes and their prisoners came by boat to the bend in the Missouri River when the settlement there -- later to become Kansas City -- was known as Westport Landing. To cross the prairies and mountains, they needed horses. Since the main business of the town was outfitting pioneers, they had no trouble finding a horse ranch.

Bart was blunt as he opened negotiations, saying,"We'll need good horses. Don't try to sell us animals that'll give out before they get half way across Kansas. We've got a long trail and need strong horses with lots of wind. If you've got four of them that can stay the trail as long as we can ride 'em, we're here to buy. If not, don't try none of your horse trading tricks on us. We can teach you a few of our own."

"They'll cost you," replied Sam Newton, the rancher.

"A good horse is cheap at any price. A poor horse is an expensive gift," said Ben.

Newton led them to a pasture where some mustangs grazed.

"Those animals ain't never won no horse races, but they was born and raised on the prairie and they know the ways of the mountains. Any one of them will get you there and back."

Heather stood on a rail of the fence and looked over the herd. Her eyes brightened as she picked out a dancing filly.

"Oh, Ben, can I have that grey?"

"She's too small," said Bart.

"I'm small and she's just my size."

"She's right, sir," said Newton. "Make her a good horse."

"I'm sorry." Ben shook his head. "We've got to put you on an animal that can carry a load."

"Why?"

"Because I weigh two hundred pounds and Bart weighs two fifty in his underwear. Horses that carry us aren't going to be carrying a whole lot more."

"Ben, please?"

"Sorry. We've got to pack a lot with us. Every horse has got to carry its share. You weigh less than a hundred pounds. If we get matching horses, yours could carry a hundred and fifty pounds more to equal Bart's carrying nothing, but Ruby's could handle about a hundred and thirty extra pounds."

Bart and Ben got in the corral and cut the four best mustangs out of the herd. Newton also sold them saddles and harnesses.

"No doubt about it," said Newton as they paid him, "you do know horses and where did you learn to handle them like that?"

"That we ain't telling," said Ben as they mounted up and rode back to Westport Landing.

The next morning they were in their saddles at first light riding west along the Kansas River. Their equipment included supplies and tools for four travelers but only one tent.

"Tents are heavy," Bart said in answer to Heather's question. "Ben and I have slept under the stars before."

The brothers each had a carbine and a handgun. The women were given no weapons.

In "Wilderness Survival," Ben read of a plains Indian mixture called "pemmican" made of dried buffalo meat and wild berries ground together and soaked in buffalo fat. According to Colonel Wilcox, cakes of this made excellent food and could be stored for months. He found an Indian woman at Westport Landing who sold them some and they added it to the normal food supplies carried by pioneers. Items that could not stand the weather were packed in buckskin bags and hung from the saddles and the straps of the horses. Extra clothes and the tent nestled in bed rolls behind their saddles. They all wore new buckskin outfits with heavy jackets.

It had been a long time since any of them had been on a horse so the first day they walked more than they rode. Still they covered twenty miles of flat Kansas country before setting up camp. Where the Republican River forked off from the Kansas, they then headed for Nebraska and where it shifted west they crossed over to the Platte River beyond Fort Kearney. The weather held and every day brought change of scenery.

Heather took it in, fascinated. She was a city girl, accustomed to riding in parks and urban woods. She knew she loved adventure, but she was also enjoying the trip for another reason. Often she found Ben staring at her as they gathered around the campfire at night.

They moved from the quiet farmlands in the more settled areas of eastern Kansas northwest into an unpopulated wilderness. The route brought them from a little used trail to one that was a major highway across the continent. They joined a long line of settlers moving to cross the mountains before snow closed the passes.

Their days quickly settled into a routine. Breakfast fires were burning before the eastern sky pearled and they were in their saddles ahead of full light. "Nooning" in the heat of the day gave the horses a chance to graze for two hours and then they moved until the sun touched the western horizon.

Heather had hours in the saddle to think about escaping, although at times she was not sure she wanted to leave Ben. Still she began telling Ruby about her life in Washington. She described in detail the lavish clothing worn by beautiful women there. Ruby was entertained with accounts of balls and theater and all the romantic gossip Heather's mind could remember or her imagination could invent. Always there were men and money.

"How I wish we were going east instead of west," said Ruby as they sat by the campfire one night.

"So do I." Heather sighed.

The next morning as they rode along the dusty trail together Heather asked, "Ruby, why didn't you take the thousand dollar reward and go? It would take you to Washington, you know."

"One thousand wouldn't last me long and there's all that gold in California. If they can get it, I might get some."

"If they can pull it off, it all goes to the Confederacy. They don't intend to keep any of it, much less give it to either of us. No one really believes they can do it."

"Well, there's Bart. I like him a lot."

"Yes," Heather agreed, "there is Bart."

One night as they settled down in the tent, Heather said, "You know, Ruby, my family might pay a great deal more than a thousand dollars to get me home."

"They would? How much?"

"That's just a reward. They might pay twenty-five thousand."

"Twenty-five thousand!"

"Yes, and they'd be thankful to have me home."

"Just suppose we wanted to get away from Ben and Bart," Ruby whispered the next day at nooning. "How do you suppose we could do it?"

"It wouldn't be too hard. Remember what they said when I wanted a smaller horse? Each horse had to be able to carry about the same load. My horse carrying about a hundred pounds could run faster and farther than Bart's horse carrying him. They'd have a time catching us if we dropped most of the baggage. Supposing won't do much good without money. It's mighty hard to travel without it."

"You're right, a woman has got to have money or a man to get any place in this country."

The new trail turned south to Denver where the river forked. But Ben led his group to the North Platte towards Fort Laramie. They crossed into land shaded from rain by the Rocky Mountains. Although the slope had not changed much, dryness set in. Except for the emerald slash along the river, it was a flat, parched country stretching away in a vista of bleached brown. A dry wind sucked moisture out of every living thing and lifted the dust from the hooves of the walking horses. From rising to setting the molten sun was a tool of torture. Every evening a red sun rested for a moment on the edge of a mesa and sank into the distant earth.

A long twilight held back the darkness as they made camp two days out of Fort Laramie. With the night, a sudden chill pressed round their little fire. Far off a wolf cried; another nearer one answered. Ben and Bart opened their bedrolls, took off their boots and for the first time slept under blankets. Heather found shelter from the wind in the tent. Ruby stayed at the fire. A thin moon was making a blurred pattern on the fabric of the tent when Heather awoke to find a hand on her mouth.

"Quiet," Ruby commanded. "Don't say a word. I've got the horses saddled. Everything except your bedroll is packed. Get your clothes on. We're leaving."

Heather dressed while Ruby rolled up her blankets in the ground cloth. Then she lifted a flap of the tent and looked out. The two men lay motionless. The wind was down. Together they went to the horses and mounted.

"Let's head west," said Heather.

"West? What for? We want a train at St. Joe."

"First, we want to get to the nearest place and report. That's Fort Laramie. After that we won't have to worry about the Gordyne brothers. We can take our time getting east. Besides, Ben and Bart will expect us to go east. This may give us just a little bit more time."

Ruby had other plans she was not yet ready to make known. They walked the horses west a quarter of a mile and spurred them into a run. When the horses began to sweat, they slowed to a canter. At daybreak they rested. Ruby slept while Heather made coffee and hoecakes.

"Where are we going to get the money for train tickets?" Heather asked as they ate.

"I got money they don't know about," Ruby said. "That's only one of the good things about a figure like mine. And when we get

124

to St. Louis, I've got things in my trunk that'll sell for enough to take us to Washington."

Meanwhile, at the camp, Ben had a fire of buffalo chips burning before the sky turned grey in the east. Bart sat up as the first light filtered across the land. He stretched and looked around.

"Ben," he shouted jumping to his feet, "two horses are gone."

"Indians have run off with the girls," Bart exclaimed, and ran towards the tent.

"Indians would have taken all the horses and left the saddles," Ben said. "Our prisoners have escaped."

"Let's get 'em," said Bart.

"You saddle the horses while I fix breakfast and think."

"Do we go after them?" Bart asked as they ate.

"If Heather gets to an Army post before we catch her, we might as well forget our trip to California and get back to the fightin'. If either of them tell what they know about where we are and where we're heading, it's the end of our mission if not the end of us. So, I don't think we've a choice."

They had camped in a concealed arroyo. Leaving most of the baggage behind, they went for their horses.

"They can't have much more than ten miles on us and we've got fresh horses," said Ben as they mounted up.

"Yes, and there's a chance they'll be so anxious to get away they won't rest their horses enough."

When they could see tracks, they started east. Bart stopped and said, "They didn't go this way."

Ben examined the trail.

"You're right. Heather is headed for Fort Laramie. Smart girl. But she may have outsmarted herself."

"How's that?'

"The trail was made for wagons. Horses can go where wagons can't. East the trail is almost as straight as a bee's flight, but ahead of us are hills. The trail will be winding and maybe we can cut off some of those loops."

Watching the tracks they saw where the women had set their mustangs into a run and where they slowed.

"They're driving them too hard," Bart observed. "If we spare our horses we should be able to cover more ground."

"Let's dismount and give these fellows a rest. A fast walk ought to do it."

"I knew we brought the moccasins for something."

All morning Heather and Ruby drove the horses. These were steady animals built for a fast sprint and a long walk. Marathon running was not one of their virtues. Their night's rest had been interrupted and by noon, though still willing, they were no longer able. Heather rode off the trail towards a small stand of trees by the river.

"The horses can't go any more," she said.

"They may be gaining on us," Ruby protested. "Their horses are carrying more weight and are running in the same sun. They've got to stop too."

The mustangs drank from the river and then stood in the shade nibbling at the short grass. The women ate without cooking and stretched out with their heads on their saddles.

At first the distant sound in the east was too faint to wake them, and so deep was their sleep, that it was almost on them before they woke. Throwing off their blankets and, on hands and knees, they stared out from the low brush along the river's edge and saw six matched horses pulling a bright red Concord coach of the Central Overland Stage Company. Heather shouted and jumped to her feet. With another shout, she started running towards the road, but Ruby gripped her buckskin skirt and jerked her back to the ground.

"What are you doing?" Heather cried. "We could have ridden into Fort Laramie on the stage."

"That's not what I planned," Ruby said. "We ain't going to let anyone know where you are until the twenty-five thousand is delivered."

On the stagecoach, Legs Pharson dozed, leaning back against padded leather. A wheel hit a hole in the road and the jolt jarred his head against the window frame. He woke just long enough to glance out at a patch of trees by the river. Then he moved his head back to its more comfortable position. Suddenly, he sat up. Feeling inside his worn black coat, he extracted a faded picture and looked out the window. The coach had already swung around a curve.The trees were no longer visible. Was he dreaming or had he seen that face?

The question bothered him all the way to Fort Laramie. It was late when the coach arrived and the detective went to bed without an answer. The next morning he rented a horse.

As soon as the sound of the stage faded away, Heather and Ruby saddled their horses. Shadows were well behind them when Ruby reached over and grabbed Heather's bridle. They were in sight of Fort Laramie.

"We stop here," she said,

"Why? That's Fort Laramie."

"I know, but that isn't where you're going. I've figured out how you are going to ask your Daddy to send us twenty-five thousand dollars and we're going to do it from right here. Then we're going to head back to St. Louis."

"What are you going to do with me?"

"We'll decide that when we find a place to hide."

Once more they went to the river and rode its shore until they found a ravine that cut into a steep bank. Here they set up camp.

"I really hate to do this, Heather," Ruby said when darkness settled on the narrow wash. "I'm gonna' have to tie you up."

"You will not tie me up!"

"Heather, I can't watch you all night, and I know you'll try to escape if you can. So I've got to tie you up."

"I'll not let you."

Ruby pulled a derringer from under her skirt saying, "This is one thing Daddy taught me to use."

"You wouldn't do it?"

"I'd do a lot of things for twenty-five thousand. Now you just do as I say and I'll see that you get home to your folks."

A root of a large cottonwood tree, exposed by years of washing, served as Heather's hitching post. She slept with her hands tied to it. Ruby spread a ground cloth under her and

127

covered her with a blanket. Then she drank what was left of the coffee and crawled under her blanket.

As she dozed off, Heather vowed vengeance.

After breakfast the next morning Ruby took a pad of paper and a pencil from her saddlebag and handed them to Heather.

"It's time to let your folks know you're all right and will be on your way home very soon," she said. "Take this down:

"'Dear Mommy and Daddy, I am being well cared for and in no immediate danger. I will be on my way home as soon as you buy the Hunsford Inn in Maumee Crossing, Ohio. The owner wants $25,000 for it. The person handling this sale is Fred Hunsford in St. Louis, Mo. I think you ought to buy this right away so that I can come home. With all my love, Heather D.Wanderman.'"

Heather swore vengeance again as she wrote the words down. Ruby took the letter, read it once, folded it and put it in an envelope. When it was sealed she handed it to Heather.

"Address it," she said.

"That inn isn't worth twenty-five thousand," Heather said as she wrote.

"You're right," Ruby said. "It's not worth one thousand, but you are and if I don't get twenty-five thousand for it, I may burn the inn down with you inside. Come on. We've got to wait for the stage going east."

"What do you plan to do?" Heather asked.

"I'm going to find a place where we can watch the fort. The next stage from the West will stop there for the night. When it comes by here the next morning, I'll be waiting for it on my horse. I'll stop it and ask the driver to put your letter in the mail pouch. After it leaves, we'll go over the river to avoid those two and head for St. Louis."

Leaving the horses and other gear in the ravine beside the river, they crossed the trail and climbed a ridge and picked a spot from which they could watch the fort.

Had Heather and Ruby been more experienced in the ways of the trail they might have observed that they were not the first to

128

use the arroyo. Among those who knew of it were a couple of highwaymen, Junk DeBris and Sonny Scythe. Some years in the past these two had started west from New Orleans. Junk had a bad case of gold fever. Sonny, tired of army life, deserted. On the way west they found gold of another sort.

Their permanent camp was on a high bluff from which they watched the caravans coming through. They robbed travelers who became careless about security and supplemented this income by visiting camp sites after wagon trains moved on. As Handel had pointed out in St. Louis, these two had learned that pioneers often began a trek west by hauling luxuries which they soon abandoned along the way. Junk and Sonny brought their salvage to St. Joe and it was not uncommon for them to sell the same things two or three times. There wasn't much overhead and almost a hundred percent profit.

They were about ready to move a load by barge down the Platte when they spotted two women riding west. Junk pointed out that two men seemed to be following them. Curiously, the women had very little baggage.

"Well, now," said Junk. He knew young and attractive females could be bartered for nuggets in some of the tougher mining camps along the eastern slopes of the Rockies where women were a scarce commodity.

"Couple of prize beauties," Junk muttered.

They followed, hiding behind rocks along the trail and sat down to watch.

Heather and Ruby first saw a lone horseman leave the post headed east.

"It's the Pinkerton agent," said Ruby as he rode by below them. "He's the one that came to the inn looking for you."

If Legs had been as good a tracker as he was a detective, he might have found the two women. As it was he had trouble figuring out where he thought he had seen Heather. Since it was a frequently used resting place, the signs he saw told him little. The dust in the road indicated two horses had been ridden west since the stage used the trail, but no one had passed him on the trail and as far as he knew the tracks could have been made during the night. He decided to return to Laramie.

Had Legs looked back one time before rounding the shoulder of a hill, he might have seen two riders coming out of the east. They saw him as he came up from the river and stopped, waiting for him to get out of sight. When he was gone they read the signs in the dust which told them the women they had followed for a day and a half had come up from the river after the coach had passed.

"Why didn't they catch the stage?" Ben asked as he examined the evidence. "It must have passed them here."

"Maybe they were asleep," Bart suggested.

"They'd have to be mighty sound sleepers. That rider in the black suit is sure interested in them. I'm going to go over the ridge and come out on the trail ahead of him. You follow along behind. Don't get too close."

Ben rode his tired mustang north and soon intercepted Pharson.

"Howdo'," he said.

"Hello," said Legs. "What're you doing out here alone?"

"Looking for some horses that run off. Ya seen 'em?"

"Can't say that I have. You going to Fort Laramie?"

"No, sir. I've got to get back to my outfit. You seem to be looking for something too. Can I help you find it?"

"You're right, I am, and maybe you can. I'm looking for this woman." Legs took the picture out of his inside coat pocket. "She might be around here some place. Probably be traveling with two men and another woman."

Ben took the picture and examined it carefully.

"I'd sure remember it if I ever saw a woman that pretty," he said handing it back. "Why do you want to find her?"

"I'm a Pinkerton agent and her family has hired us. We have reason to believe she's being held against her will."

"Is that a fact? Well, if I see her I'll sure let you know." Ben turned his horse to go.

"There's a thousand dollar reward if you find her."

130

"A thousand dollars! That's a heap of money for a woman." Ben chuckled as he rode away.

"So we know what Pinkerton looks like," said Bart when Ben told him what happened.

"Yes, and we know that he knows we're headed west. We didn't lose him in Cincinnati. He rode out from Fort Laramie to where the stage passed them, so he must have seen them from the coach. He came back, but didn't pass them and they weren't at the fort when he left. They're somewhere between here and the fort. Let's see if we can find them."

They spurred their horses across country getting ahead of the detective following the trail.

Shadows were still small on the dry, gray hills when the stage rolled out of the western mountains into Fort Laramie. From their rimrock perch, Heather and Ruby watched it arrive.

"Time to get back to our camp so we'll be ready to meet the stage in the morning," Ruby said.

They stood and walked down the slope towards the ravine. At the river's edge they knelt to wash the dust from their faces.

"I sure would like a bath," said Heather as she stood.

"Why not?" asked Ruby."Nobody can see us from the road."

"Let's." Heather started to untie her buckskin dress.

A movement across the river stopped her. For a motionless moment she stood staring at a space between bushes. Then she dropped to her knees and leaned forward as if to drink. Beside her, Ruby was taking off a shoe. Heather scooped a handful of water and brought it to her mouth. Instead of drinking she whispered, "There are horses over there. Somebody's watching us."

At that moment a shadow fell on Ruby and she turned to look behind her.

"Indians!" she screamed before a hand closed over her mouth.

131

10
INDIANS AND HIGHWAYMEN

Heather leaped into the river. Two Indians followed her. Slowed by her dress, she stumbled and fell. The Indians were on her before she could stand. They carried her to the shore where Ruby was being held by two young braves.

A tall, handsome warrior pointed to their saddles.

"Sit," he said. His tone could have been an invitation or a command. They sat and while one man watched them the others went through the camping equipment taking what they wanted and scattering everything else, including Heather's letter. In Ruby's saddlebag they found the bullets for her derringer. After they talked about the small shells for a few minutes they approached the women.

"Where are guns?" one of them demanded.

"We don't have any guns," Heather said and the Indian pulled her to her feet and began searching her for a weapon. She pushed him away and turned to run. Another man caught her arms from behind and held them. His grip was firm but not painful. She was now standing under the low branch of a tree.

"I'll give you the gun," said Ruby lifting her skirt and removing the pistol strapped to the calf of her leg.

"Why women ride without men?" one Indian demanded.

Neither of them could give an answer the Indians would have

understood, so they said nothing.

"Why white women not ride to fort?" he asked. "Why you lie on rimrock watching fort?" Another spoke up.

"We were waiting for the stagecoach," Heather said.

"Why you not ride to fort for stage?"

There was a mystery here that made the four Indians uncomfortable. One of them took a handful of Heather's hair.

"I am Hungry Wolf," he told his companions. "This one with hair like morning sun will tell Hungry Wolf. Where your man?" he barked, pulling sharply.

"Hungry Wolf is a woman," Heather taunted. "He does battle by pulling hair."

The other Indians laughed.

"This one has lightning," one of them said.

"We shall see if I am woman," Hungry Wolf said moving his hand to the collar of her dress.

Heather gripped the branch over her head, drew up her legs and kicked both feet just below Hungry Wolf's belt. The sudden action caught the Indian unprepared. He stumbled backwards, tripped and raised a spray falling into the river. Again the other Indians laughed.

Hungry Wolf came out of the river with his knife in his hand. One of the other men stepped in front of him.

"This woman is mine," he said.

"How does Running Cloud say this woman is his?" the angry man demanded. "She is mine and I will kill her."

Running Cloud drew his blade and it appeared that the issue would be settled with knives. One of the other men stepped between them and said something. There followed considerable discussion. At last an agreement was reached. The four men squatted in a rough circle and began playing some kind of game.

"What are they doing?" asked Ruby.

"I'd say they've decided there are two horses and two women and they're gambling to see who gets what."

"You mean they're putting us in the pot with horses?"

"I wouldn't be surprised if most of them wouldn't rather have the horses."

When the game was over, Hungry Wolf went to Ruby's horse and Running Cloud walked over to Ruby.

"You are woman of Running Cloud, he said.

One of the other men approached Heather.

"I am Moon of Long Nights. Woman of lightning is mine. We go now," he said.

The men who had won the horses mounted and the band started to ford the river to where the Indians had left their ponies. About ten feet from the bank, Hungry Wolf raised his right hand. The party stopped. Hungry Wolf started to turn his horse back. He was too late. The first bullet caught him in the side. Ruby screamed. The rider held to his mount which, startled by the shot, leaped back across the stream. A second shot was high as he disappeared in the brush. The other mounted warrior jerked his horse to follow. Two guns sounded and the rider jerked as one of the slugs dug into his back.

Moon of Long Nights knocked Heather into the water as though trying to shield her with his body. The bullet that hit him tore through his side. The weight of his body on her told Heather he was dead. She pushed him away and he floated face down, the slow current carrying him into the reeds along the shore and spreading a bloody streak around a bend in the river.

The first bullet to hit Running Cloud knocked him to his knees. He tried to crawl back across the river. A second shot let his life leak out through a hole at the base of his skull.

The echoes died away. Ruby began to sob and covered her face with her hands. Heather got her feet under herself and stood. Junk DuBris and Sonny Scythe stepped out of hiding.

"Howdy, ladies," said Junk, lifting his ragged hat.

The women looked from the floating bodies to the disreputable white men walking towards them. The one who had spoken was slightly taller than a freight wagon's wheel. He looked shorter than he was because of the shoulders that would have been wide on a taller man. He had so much black hair on his chin and cheeks that little of his face was visible except for small, dark eyes, a red bulb of a nose and lips that were twisted into a frightening leer. His clothing looked as if it had never known either soap or water.

Filth was about the only outward trait Junk shared with Scythe. Sonny's shaved face sat on a thin neck. He was a good foot taller than DuBris. Hair, the color and texture of straw left on the barn floor too long, straggled out from under a shapeless black hat. His eyes were a light blue. They seemed a total washout in contrast with the burnt tan of his skin. A Bowie knife was on his belt, but he also wore a gun. As he walked towards them he slapped a coiled lariat across his left hand.

"The luck of an Injun," said Scythe. "They got away with two horses."

"Yeah, but we got the women," DuBris observed, "and 'cause Injuns ride with spare mounts we picked us up eight good ponies. I'd say it's a fair day's work."

"I still say women ain't nothin' but trouble."

"I know a madam in Denver who supplies this kind of trouble to mining camps all along the eastern slope. She'll pay plenty for these heifers."

Hearing this Heather muttered, "Run, Ruby, run," and turned towards the opposite shore. She was struggling through the stream in her waterlogged clothes when Scythe's rope settled over her shoulders. In spite of her efforts to throw it off, it burned as he pulled it tight and jerked her backwards into Ruby. For the third time that afternoon, she tumbled into the river bringing Ruby down with her.

On the bank the two men rocked with laughter. Heather tried to stand and Sonny jerked her down again. Ruby got to her feet and took one step away. He flipped his rope over her and, with a tug, tripped her back into the stream.

"I ain't never caught me two prettier heifers in all my whole life," he growled.

Ruby tried again. This time she heard a gun bark and felt the bullet tug at her skirt.

"The next slug'll break your leg," Junk said. She turned and saw him standing with a gun in his hand.

"Come on. Let's go," DuBris commanded. "We got to get outa here before the two yahoos on their trail catches up with us."

Sonny reeled Heather in. Under Junk's gun, Ruby followed. Sonny succeeded in getting two stubborn Indian ponies to stand still long enough so he could harness them. The women were tied in their saddles. DuBris took the lead. The bridles of Heather and Ruby's ponies were joined with a length of rope to the back of his saddle so they rode side by side. Sonny was behind them. A string of six Indian ponies roped to his saddle, brought up the rear as they headed south.

Eventually Ruby stopped crying. For an hour they rode in silence.

"I'm sorry," Heather said.

"Why should you be sorry?"

"It was my idea to tell you about the twenty-five thousand dollars so that you would help me get away from Ben and Bart."

"I don't understand."

"Well, Ruby, I thought that as long as you had any notion of getting a part of the gold in California you would never help me. So I invented the money to get your mind off the gold. It was a trick and now we're both in trouble because of it."

"What are they going to do to us, Heather?"

"Seems like they intend to sell us in Denver."

"Sell us? Like slaves? What for?"

"It isn't to work in cotton fields, I can tell you that."

"You mean...?"

"Yes, I mean."

"What are we going to do, Heather?"

"Do you know how to pray?"

"No. Never done much of that."

"Well, I haven't prayed since Warren was killed, but I think that's what I'm going to do now. Aesop in his fables said, 'The gods help those who help themselves.' But I learned in church that isn't what the Bible says. It says God helps the helpless. That's pretty much the whole difference between religion and faith, and right now religion is not what we need. It's time to try believing. I aim to pray."

"I'll try," Ruby muttered uncertainly.

DuBris wanted to put space between himself and the two men. Switching horses every two hours, they rode all night and, with only a few breaks for food and water, all the next day. Once Ruby glanced over her shoulder and saw Sonny watching her. She knew what the look meant and she began thinking how to use it. Each time they stopped she made it a point to get close to Sonny and exchange friendly words. Towards noon when they found a stream to water their horses Ruby arranged it so that she was standing with him between two mustangs.

"Would you like to share fifty thousand dollars with me?"

"Fifty thousand? Where would you get that much money?"

"Mrs. Wanderman is the daughter of a very rich family in Washington, D.C. They've got the Pinkerton people out looking for her. They'll pay fifty thousand for her. Think about it."

Sonny spent considerable time doing that. While he did, Heather was surprised to discover that she could sleep in her saddle. It was easy after she discovered the answer to a riddle that had perplexed her ever since she was a little girl sitting in church. There she had observed that, when women fall asleep during tedious sermons, if they didn't snore, no one would notice. Most men, however, unless they were very fat, could not hide their sleeping while sitting upright in a hard pew.

The discovery came some time after they left the Platte River. She jerked herself up as she sat her pony and was amazed to find that she had been asleep. She also realized that it hadn't been a short nap because the moon was up.

"Have you been asleep?" she asked Ruby.

"How can I sleep riding a horse?"

"I did."

"It ain't possible."

But it was because Heather had done it. She spent the next hour figuring out how. She tried first by comparing herself with Ruby, then with Junk riding ahead of them. She and Junk were about the same size. Yet as she watched him in the moonlight she noticed that he'd sag in his saddle and then jerk himself awake as he started to fall. She deduced the reason for this when they next stopped to water the horses and Sonny rode up where she could see him. The contrast between his tall stature and her diminutive figure was the clue. Sonny was broad in the shoulders. Everything else about him was rake-handle thin. He sat his horse on narrow hips like a pyramid up-side down. The only reason he could keep his balance at all was due to the counterbalancing weight of long legs and huge feet.

She realized she had three advantages over the men. First,she was short. Next her hips were broader than her shoulders so the center of her weight was just above the saddle. Broadshouldered Sonny was top heavy. Then she noticed Junk was even less stable. His short legs under narrow hips did not balance broad shoulders. To add to her stability, Heather's hands were tied to the pommel. She soon figured out that her ability to sleep in the saddle was an advantage which might help her escape. When the men had to doze off she would be ready.

"I'm going to sleep. You can too, if you'll relax," she told Ruby. To her amazement, Ruby found she could do it.

****

Light was fading from the sky when the Gordynes found the ravine. They saw the moccasin tracks of the Indians and they read Heather's letter. It was almost dark when they picked out the tracks the horses had made carrying the escaping Indians west. Neither of them thought to look across the river and they did not see two bodies floating under a cottonwood tree. It was too dark to follow the trail, so they built a fire of buffalo chips in the ravine and prepared a meal of beans.

"We got to be ready to fight Indians," Bart said.

Ben nodded, wondering and fearful about what might be

happening to Heather.

As they ate, Legs Pharson rode by them along the trail back to Fort Laramie. In the darkness the detective overlooked tracks which would have told him the women had turned towards the river.

Bart broke a long silence as he finished his coffee. "At least they won't be reporting us to the authorities."

"Yes, we can ride on west and no one will ever know who we were or what happened to them."

"We can get our job done without any more interruptions."

"Yes."

They unrolled their beds, removed their boots and pulled blankets up, all in silence.

"Why? Why did they have to ride off on their own?" Ben demanded of the night sky.

"Twenty-five thousand dollars," Bart answered. "It ain't worth it."

"If they'd stayed with us, this wouldn't have happened."

Stars moved across the sky.

"We could ride into Fort Laramie and tell the Army what's happened," Bart suggested. "Maybe they could find them."

"Yes," said Ben. "But the man from Pinkerton is there. We wouldn't be able to do our job. We've got to remember why we're out here."

A piece of a moon sat over a hill. Ben threw off his covers and walked to where the tracks led west. In the moonlight, the prints were visible. Bart came and stood by him. Ben shrugged. Bart nodded. They saddled their horses and followed the trail west. Bart saw blood first and said, "One of the girls is wounded."

"Looks bad," said Ben. The trail was not hard to follow.

At Fort Laramie, sleep finally came to Legs. He could find no answers to the questions he had found along the trail. Unanswered questions always kept him awake.

Why were there only two horses? Who were the riders? What happened to the other pair? He dozed off.

****

About sunrise the brothers rode to the top of a small hill. Below them were Heather and Ruby's horses grazing by a small stream. They dismounted and crawled through the buffalo grass towards the animals. Under a cottonwood tree were the Indians. One was dead. Hungry Wolf lifted his head when he heard them and dropped it heavily to the ground. Ben and Bart moved in carefully. The Indian lay watching. Only his eyes moved.

"Hungry Wolf will die," he said.

Ben and Bart moved closer. Standing over him, Ben said, "Can we do anything for you?"

Bart stooped and, lifting the brave's head, trickled a little water from his canteen into his mouth.

"Where are the women?" Ben asked.

"Two white men with the spirit of devil shot at us as we crossed river," Hungry Wolf said. "They take women."

"Where did you cross the river?" Ben asked.

"Where women camped."

"They're with white men," Bart said. "They'll be all right."

"No," said Hungry Wolf gripping Bart's hand. "To be with those white men is to sleep with rattlesnakes. You must find woman with hair like honey. Tell her Hungry Wolf would not have killed her. Go back and follow trail at river. Now."

"What can we do for you?" Ben asked again.

"Hungry Wolf dies. Find woman. Do this for Hungry Wolf. Let me meet Great Spirit alone."

The urgency in his voice surprised the brothers.

"The woman of lightning is in much danger," he added.

The Indian coughed and closed his eyes. Blood ran from the corner of his mouth.

Bart lifted his head and poured a little more water between his parted lips.

"Go!" said Hungry Wolf.

140

They caught the horses and headed back towards the river crossing.

After breakfast Legs spent some time showing Heather's picture to everyone and asking questions without success. Heather and her companion had not come to Laramie. Yet he was sure he had seen someone from the window of the coach. He added another question to his list: Why didn't they come into the fort?

Answers were somewhere out there on the trail. Saddling up, he set out to find them.

When Ben and Bart crossed the river at the arroyo, they saw two bodies under a cottonwood tree. Buzzards were feeding. On the other bank they found the trail leading south. The tracks of ten horses were not hard to follow even in that hard and dry land. They switched mounts and rode hard.

Behind them Legs Pharson rediscovered the track he had lost in the darkness the night before. Another mystery. Why did they stop at this point and turn back? He looked around. The puzzle was answered. This was the first place on the trail from which a rider could see the fort. Whoever these riders were, and he was convinced one of them was Mrs. Wanderman, they did not want to be seen by those in the fort.

As he retraced the trail another question was answered. He found where two more horses had come out of the hills, moved around a bit in the dust of the road and then followed the first two down towards the river.

That tall man. The cowboy that met me by the trail yesterday. That must have been the Confederate colonel. They joined Heather Wanderman and Ruby Hunsford here, he decided.

In the ravine he found Indian tracks. The vultures led him to the dead. From there he saw the trail heading south.

Victorious Indians do not leave their dead on the battlefield, he reminded himself. Heather's party joined up with some others here. There was a fight with some Indians, and then they turned this way.

He followed the trail for two hours until he was certain of its direction.

South? he asked himself. What's south? Denver. What's in Denver? Gold. Gold always comes into the picture with those two and almost as much gold is shipped out of Denver as out of San Francisco these days.

He kept moving and wondered if they came this far on the Platte to throw him off their trail and then switched south. Did they join a party with a guide who knew the way to Denver?

Pharson was not prepared for the trail. He turned back to the ravine and examined more closely the remains of the women's camp. Thus it was he found the scrap of paper on which Heather had written her note. It confirmed one thing. The woman he had seen was Mrs. Wanderman. But the note also misled him.

"Twenty-five thousand," he whistled. "They're holding her for ransom."

Riding into Fort Laramie, he asked, "Is there a stage to Denver?" Assured there was, he paid the fare.

****

For a night and most of a day Junk led his party south. They stopped only for water and to change horses. Though the sun was still high when they arrived at the bank of the Lodgepole River, DuBris knew the horses could go no farther without rest and food.

"We camp here," he said and untied the women from their horses. "We've left your friends far enough behind. Sleep good 'cause in the morning me and Sonny may want to find out what kind of merchandise we're delivering to my friend in Denver." The men were drunk from lack of sleep. Sonny, after cutting lengths of rope, threw his knife at the trunk of a tree that had fallen over the river. He tied Heather and Ruby by the hands and feet and pushed them down on a sandbar.

"I'll sleep between you so's you won't try to untie each other," Junk explained.

The horses were tethered where they could graze and drink

142

and Sonny made his bed near them, "Just in case either of you get the notion to ride tonight."

He was so tired he forgot to retrieve his knife embedded in the tree trunk. Heather waited long enough for the men to sink into deep slumber. Ruby was also snoring lightly.

Carefully she rolled away from Junk towards the water. Three times these maneuvers disturbed DuBris and she lay motionless until he was fully unconscious again. Keeping an eye on him, she rolled into the shallows until she was partially afloat and let the current carry her to Sonny's knife. The same current and her buoyancy helped her stand. She hooked her hands over the blade. It took some sawing before the fibers of the rope parted.

Within a minute she untied her ankles. It took her about as long to pull the knife out of the tree. As slow and silent as a cat stalking its prey, she crept back to her place beside DuBris and held the knife at his throat.

"If you breathe aloud, you'll have trouble with your next breath," she whispered pricking him awake with the point of the knife. He opened his eyes. With her left hand she removed his guns from their holsters and tapped Ruby with one of them.

"Wake up," she whispered. Ruby stirred.

"Wake up," she repeated. "But don't say anything."

Ruby opened her eyes.

"Roll over so I can cut the rope."

Ruby obeyed. Heather sat on DuBris's chest and, holding the barrel of the Colt 44 against his throat with her right hand, she cut the ropes on Ruby's wrists.

"How....," Ruby started to ask as she sat up and began untying her feet.

"Hush!" commanded Heather. "We'll talk later. Right now we don't want to wake up that other skunk. Use that rope off your feet to tie the hands of this piece of junk. Tie them real tight."

The only sound during this process was a slight moan from DuBris as Ruby pulled the rope tight around his wrists. Quick pressure from the gun under his chin muffled that.

"Here's the rope from my feet," Heather whispered when

Junk's hands were tied. "See if it fits his."

It did.

"Since you know how to use a gun and they scare me something awful, take this over there," Heather pointed."When you've got Sonny well covered, I'll bring this knife over and we'll cut some rope for him."

Ruby kicked Scythe in the side and he jerked his hands in the direction of his own gun. "I hope you try," Ruby said, "because I'm dying for an excuse to pull this trigger."

She took his gun. Heather walked over with the knife. Sonny did a considerable amount of cursing, but Heather also knew how to tie good knots.

"Now you all can finish your nap while I keep watch," she said. "The horses need rest."

The sky was turning gray for a new day when she woke them.

"Let's have breakfast and start home," she said.

One at a time the men's hands were untied so that they could eat. During the meal, Heather explained the advantages of being a woman.

"All other things being equal, we also float better than men," she concluded. "We really ought to say thank you."

"Why? To who?" asked Ruby.

"It certainly looks like going to church and praying pays off in some rather unexpected ways sometimes."

"But you did it," growled Junk. "Prayer didn't have nothin' to do with it."

"Is that so? Who do you suppose made me think about such a silly thing as men and women sleeping in church? And who do you think made me so as I can sleep in a saddle? I haven't ever been thankful for being short before, but I sure am now. Who made Sonny forget his knife and made you have us sleep on a sandbar near the water so I could crawl and float quietly? And who made that tree fall and made me so I can float better than you?"

After each of the men had finished eating, his hands were tied again. Then their feet were untied so that they could ride.

"OK, time to move out," Heather said.

"Ain't you going to give us our shoes?" whined Sonny.

"No."

"Why?"

"For one thing, if you get down off your horses in this wilderness without shoes, I don't figure you'll go very far," Heather said. "For another, Junk's new boots have just been broken in good, and I figure, since y'all left my shoes in the river, they just might fit me. Yes, sir, they fit real good, I always did want some of these fancy western boots. Miss Hunsford, don't you think they're real handsome?"

"Certainly do, Mrs. Wanderman, and they go well with your dress, too."

"Thank you, Miss Hunsford."

"You're surely welcome, Mrs. Wanderman."

The women laughed.

"All right it's time for you owlhoots to saddle up," Heather said and, with Ruby pointing two guns at them, they obeyed.

"Which way do we go?" asked Ruby as they mounted up.

"If we don't follow the trail back the way we came, we'll probably get lost and if we asked these vultures they'd direct us towards hell. So the only way to go is back to the river."

"If we go that way, we'll run into Bart and Ben."

"After what we've been through, that wouldn't be too bad, would it?"

Ruby laughed, "It'd be pure pleasure. What're you going to do when you meet them?"

"I may ride on by them as if we did this kind of thing before breakfast every day."

"Yeah, do it every day regular as breathing."

****

Ahead of them Bart shook his brother awake. They had

145

stopped for a two-hour rest.

"Time to move on," he said. Despite exhaustion, they mounted and followed the trail south. Mile by mile, hour by hour the two parties moved closer together.

It was nearing noon when Ben jerked his head up. He had been nodding in his saddle and was so weary it took time to figure out what it was he saw. Far ahead was a dust cloud. Under it bits of darkness began to shape themselves into horses and riders. He stopped. Bart, coming up behind, almost ran into him. After watching for a moment, they turned off the trail into a small arroyo. From the dark shadow of its steep sides, they continued to watch.

Heather was riding point. One hand rested at ease on the pommel of her saddle. The other brushed the hair out of her eyes. She was wearing a gunbelt complete with pistol.

Hitched to the back of her saddle by short lengths of rope were two horses ridden by two of the most disreputable men either of the brothers had ever seen. They were both barefoot and dirty. Their hands were tied to their saddles and they looked like men anticipating their own hanging. Ruby rode behind the two men. Her long black hair was grey with dust. Her left hand held the reins and her right hand a revolver. Another gun sat on her hip. The rope from the back of her saddle was connected to a string of Indian ponies.

Bart and Ben let them ride by. Suddenly, Heather held up her hand.

"Whoa," she said and the caravan stopped. She saw fresh tracks of two horsemen who had just turned off the trail.

"Y'all goin' someplace?" Ben drawled as the brothers stepped out of the shadows.

"Oh, Ben, Bart," shouted Heather as she tumbled off her mustang and ran to them.

Ruby, gave a joyful shriek and, gun still in hand, slid off her horse.

Junk DuBris looked at Sonny Scythe.

"Don't try it," said Bart. They turned to eye him. He had a

146

gun in his hand.

The Civil War and the lure of gold was forgotten as the four embraced. Neither of the women attempted to hide tears of joy and relief.

"What y'all been doing last couple of days?" asked Bart when the greetings were over. "We kinda missed ya. I mean runnin' off that-a-way without sayin' good bye 'n all. Ain't hardly polite."

"Oh, nothing much." Heather laughed. "We took a notion to do some skunk hunting. You know you get spells like that some time. Good sport, skunk hunting. Isn't it, Ruby?"

Ruby nodded as though not quite sure what this was all about.

"Have any luck?" Ben asked.

"Oh, sure. Each of us got one. We were just takin' them in so that someone could hang them," Heather replied. "Skunk hunting ain't good without a hanging."

"What about the extra horses?" Ben asked.

"Oh, that wasn't anything. We had a little trouble with a few Indians couple of days back so we just took their horses away from them. That's all."

Junk and Sonny did not join in the laughter.

"It's nooning time," Bart noted. "Let's get us something to eat and you can tell us about all the fun you've been having."

But the brothers were asleep before the beans were warm.

"What are we going to do with DuBris and Scythe?" asked Bart when they awoke and heard the whole story.

"Take them to Fort Laramie and hang them," Heather said.

"Why are you so anxious to get 'em hung?"

"Well, for one thing they killed the only gentlemen around here who seemed interested in marriage. If you're married when an Indian calls you his woman, then they killed our husbands."

"Killing Indians isn't considered a hanging offense in these parts," Ben noted. "Some would say they should be rewarded for doing their civic duty."

"There wasn't anything civic about their intentions for Ruby and me," Heather insisted.

147

"Just what were you planning to do with these ladies?" Ben demanded, turning to Junk. Getting no answer, he turned back to the women. "Well, somebody tell me."

Heather lowered her eyes.

"They were going to sell us as slaves to somebody in Denver who supplies ladies of pleasure to the mining camps," Ruby said.

"Is that true?" Ben asked.

Heather nodded. There was a silence. Ben took a step towards Sonny.

"You want me to do it?" Bart asked.

"No," he answered and his voice was like a dry, cold wind as he untied the scavenger. "You've got too much muscle and it'll be over too fast. I aim to cut this one up in little pieces and do it real slow. He'll hurt bad and hurt for a month."

"It were Junk's idea," Scythe whined.

"Stand and fight, you pig," Ben ordered as he jammed his fist straight into the man's face.

Sonny stood and Sonny fought, but he didn't stand long and he didn't fight well. However, Ben let him stay up long enough to tear flesh from his face, pound blood from his mouth, blacken both of his eyes, mash an ear and leave bruises over most of the upper part of his body.

"What you want me to do with the little pig?" Bart asked when his brother was through with Scythe.

"He's too small to fight."

"Untie him, Bart," Ben answered. "And strip him to his waist." When this was done, he said, "Hold his arms, Bart. Slap him, Mrs. Wanderman."

"What?"

"Slap him hard."

"I..."

"That's an order."

"Colonel Gordyne, may I remind you I am not under your command."

"How is it you want him hung, but you are not of a mind to administer the sentence I have decided upon?"

148

"If you were any kind of a gentleman, you would know whose duty it is to avenge my honor," she replied.

Junk DuBris grinned and said, "Maybe the lady's honor wasn't as soiled as we thought."

He should not have said that. Heather turned and slapped him with a force that bounced his head back.

"Again," Ben barked.

She hit him again.

"Harder."

"That hurt my hand," she said.

"He's to be woman-whipped," Ben stated.

"I'll do it," Ruby announced as she picked up the piece of rope used to tie Sonny's feet. With this she went after Junk. Her first lash left a raw welt on his left cheek. Bart turned him loose. He wasn't needed. Ruby cut at him until she was out of breath and when she was through, he knew he had been whipped. He dropped to his knees.

"Stop her," he pleaded. "Stop her. I can't take no more." He toppled over and lay on the ground, sobbing, covering his face with his hands to protect it from the lashing cord. Raw welts bled where the rawhide rope had cut into his face, his arms and his body.

"Please, make her stop," he begged.

"They should still be hung," said Bart as Ruby threw down her rope.

"Hangin's too good for them," said Ben. "Besides, we can't take them to Fort Laramie and press charges."

"Why not?" Ruby asked.

"There's a Pinkerton agent there and he's showing everybody a picture of Mrs. Wanderman. Now we don't want any trouble with a Pinkerton agent do we?"

"What will we do with these two?" Ruby asked.

"They ought to be shot." Heather said, "But leaving them here for a long walk barefoot might improve their manners."

"I doubt it, though it's worth a try," said Ben.

They discussed it further and when they had agreed, Ben

turned to Junk and Sonny.

"Here's the verdict," he said. "We're taking your horses as pack animals and turning the Indian ponies loose. We'll leave you a rope and a knife. If you can catch horses and if you can do without saddles, you can ride in. Otherwise walk. You'll need food. So we'll leave you one gun by the next water hole. You can also keep your canteens. I can't say I hope you make it. You don't deserve to live. If you get what you deserve the temperature will drop so low tonight you'll die of exposure."

With that the four of them stripped the Indian ponies of all supplies and ran them off.

"Ain't you going to give us our shoes?" begged Sonny as they mounted up.

"No."

"I ain't forgetting this," DuBris vowed, "and when I catch you, you'll wish you'd gone along with my first plan. You're all gonna die and you ain't gonna die easy."

11
HARD AND HUNGRY LAND

Summer scorched the hills as they climbed towards mountains that still separated them from California. According to the rule of travel on this trail, to beat snow in the passes, pilgrims had to reach Independence Rock by the Fourth of July. That rule was for covered wagons. Traveling light on horseback could double the miles a wagon train might make on a very good day.

The Gordynes and their prisoners camped on the Sweetwater River near Independence Rock two months late. A wind with teeth in it moaned down from the Wind River Range ahead of them. It snapped at their clothing and bit into exposed skin. The night was bitter. They were wrapped in the buffalo robes salvaged from the Indians and found on Junk and Sonny's horses. Ben paced the rocky land.

"Worried?" his brother asked.

"We ought to be in California right now and we're shy a thousand miles. The question is can we make it over a desert and a half dozen mountain ranges before the snow blocks all the passes?"

He waited for an answer and got none.

"You and I could probably pull it off on foot if we had to," he continued. "But do we have a right to take women into those mountains this late in the season?"

"They're tough," Bart said. "They'll make it if we do."

"Those mountains could be a cold grave for all of us. I think it's time we let them into the council."

Heather and Ruby were preparing their tent for a cold night.

"Mrs. Wanderman, would you and Ruby like to join us for a planning session around the fire?" Ben worked a branch into the coals.

"Since when were we included in any planning?" Heather asked.

"Since we're facing a mountain that may not have a top," Bart answered.

"What's that riddle?" Ruby asked, approaching the fire.

"You feel that cold?" Ben asked.

"Everybody asks questions and nobody says anything," Heather said. "Of course, we feel that cold."

"Well you ain't felt cold yet," said Bart. "'Cause if we go into those mountains and get snowed in, it'll get so cold it'll freeze fire and we may get so hungry we'll eat our horses."

"You said, 'if.' You mean we have a choice?"

"That," said Ben, "is why we asked y'all to sit in on some planning. We're behind schedule and we've still got a winter, a pile of mountains and a desert between us and the west coast. We want you to know what's ahead and I want to know if you think you can make it."

"Here is a wondrous thing," Heather said. "You bring us two-thirds of the way across the continent to as pretty a nest of frozen rattlesnakes as you'll find between two oceans and want us to help you figure a way out."

"Let me remind you that we wouldn't be in this nest of rattlesnakes if you two..." Ben began and stopped. "No, I reckon it was my mistake to bring you along. I should have dumped you in the Potomac. Bart's right. Women always put a lot of curves in a straight road, but it's a dull journey which has no turns."

"We can't spend the winter here," she said but it was more a question than a statement.

"Nope," Bart replied. "The only thing it's got to recommend it is water and that'll freeze to solid rock before long."

"And you won't go back," observed Ruby and there was no question in her statement. Bart looked at Ben.

"That's for sure," he said.

Heather stood angrily. "Isn't a heap of planning in that if there's only one way to go."

"There are other choices," said Ben as he poked a stick deeper in the fire.

"What might they be?" Heather demanded.

"We might let you and Ruby go on back to Fort Laramie while we try the mountains."

"No, sir," Ruby said emphatically, "I've promised myself one thing. I ain't never going to travel in this part of the world again without an escort. Being captured twice in one day by Indians and cut-throats has cured me of such notions."

"Would you really let us go?" Heather asked.

"I'd sooner let you go home than kill you, Heather," Ben replied gently. He paused, looking up at her from his seat on a stone. Their eyes locked. He had not called her "Mrs. Wanderman."

"We've a job to do," he continued, standing as he spoke. "We've got to get on with it."

"Oh, you..you..You're impossible," Heather stammered.

"All this worrying is for nothing," Bart said. "The road's open. The coaches are running. If things get rough we can always go to a stage stop or an Army post. So what's the problem?"

"The problem is this book I've been using as a guide is ten years old and the main line of the overland stage doesn't go this way any more. It's shifted south of the Great Salt Lake. This is only the Oregon Trail now. There won't be much company after we turn south at Soda Springs."

"You mean that huckster in St. Louis sold you a book that's going to get us lost in the mountains?" Bart was annoyed.

"He may be a huckster, but I knew when I bought it that not many people used this trail to California today. I wanted an old map and that's what I got. If our friend from Pinkerton traces us beyond Fort Laramie, he might end up in Oregon. No, we won't get lost. The old trail is plain enough, but if we make it, we'll do it by ourselves."

He opened Col. Malcomb Wilcox's book,"Wilderness Survival," to a map of the upper Rockies and spread it on a boulder so that the light of the fire showed the winding trail cutting through the southwest corner of Oregon Territory and south in Utah, skirting the Great Salt Lake desert on its north.

"Here's where we are, Independence Rock. In a few days we'll cross the Continental Divide at South Pass. We've got until October to get to Virginia City where we'll intercept the Overland Stage Line again. There are some rough mountains beyond that and the real winter will catch up with us about then, but we should have plenty of company and a reasonable trail."

"So?" asked Heather.

"The roughest country we're likely to cross is between here and there. I want you to know what's ahead and ask if you think you and Ruby can make it. Tomorrow morning we're going to inventory all of our supplies to make sure we've got enough to get us to Virginia City. Then I'll ask you the question again."

Ruby stood.

"I'm tired and I'm cold. Let's go to bed," she said.

Clouds hung like a soggy grey tent from the peaks around them as they sat by the fire the next morning. After drinking the last of the coffee, they spread their limited supplies on a groundcloth. Most of food purchased in St. Louis and Westport Landing was gone, but they had not touched the supplies appropriated from the Indians and DuBris.

"Well, Mrs. Wanderman," Ben asked when it was all displayed, "Can you feed four people for about a month with that?"

"If hunting is good and if we don't waste any time getting to Virginia City, I think we can fix you a couple of meals a day until October. What do you think, Ruby?"

"It won't last much longer than that, but it'll stretch."

"You ready to try it?" Ben asked.

154

"Have we got a choice?" Heather glared at him.

"Not really. You've said it can be done, and I'm putting you in charge of the rations. Just watch Bart's plate. Let's load up and get on the trail. We're wasting warm weather."

At South Pass, where the trail intersected the Wind River Range, they celebrated the crossing of the Continental Divide with a group of pioneers on their way to Oregon. As they left for Soda Springs with the pioneers the next morning, Heather rode beside Ben. She was somber and scarcely spoke.

"When you aren't talkin' it's usually because you've got somethin' to say," he noted. "Care to share it?"

"You wouldn't do it."

"Try me."

"Oh, Ben," she blurted. "why don't we forget this stupid war and go to Oregon with these folks? We could be happy there."

Ben stiffened in his saddle. He looked into those eyes that sought his soul and knew the truth in what she said. He had been happy with this woman.

"That is a tempting proposition," he said.

"Ben?"

He shook his head, but lived for ten days with the temptation until they got to Soda Springs where the Oregon Trail split off from the old California Trail. The four heading south sat their horses watching new friends move north towards Fort Hall. Heather looked at Ben. She held his eye until he slowly shook his head.

"I'm sorry, Mrs. Wanderman," he said. "It's against orders."

Heather, hurt and thinking she would never find another man like Ben Gordyne, vowed to keep him for herself. She had hated a war which killed her husband. Now she hated one that kept her from her enemy. Yet she knew without the hated war, she would never have met the enemy with whom she wished to share her life.

She brushed away tears and resolved to somehow follow this man and make him her own. The war couldn't last forever. She would see Bonmaison and that river he loved, yes, she would.

They turned their mustangs towards the high desert of the

155

Great Basin and the headwaters of the Humboldt River. An early snow began to fall. Their route avoided the military post at Fort Hall, by taking them over two ridges to Lava Hot Springs and the Portneuf River. When the river turned north, they followed the twisting trail west. Ahead of them was ten thousand-foot Cache Peak.

"We don't have to go over that, do we?" Ruby gasped.

"No," Ben said. "We'll pass it by."

Raft River went below the peak and they rode over another range to Lower Goose Creek. When the water vanished in the rocks they crossed to the dry lands of the Great Salt Lake Desert.

Following the trail was not difficult. Tens of thousands had passed this way since the Gold Rush and the high, dry air retarded decay, leaving the route clearly marked with broken wagons, discarded gear, bones of oxen, mules and horses, and graves. They didn't eat much on this stretch. Water was so scarce, there was little to wash the dry food down their sandy throats. It was harder on the horses.

Their canteens had been empty for most of a cold, dry day when they topped a ridge. From the rim rock they saw early snow melting in the foothills. Water jumped among the rocks below. The horses smelled it and picked up their ears. It was a wild ride to the bottom. Heather got there first and vaulted off her mustang directly into the stream. Sitting down she let the stinging cold water break over her shoulders as she scooped hands full into her mouth between bursts of laughter. Ruby jumped in beside her followed by Ben and Bart. They laughed and rolled and played, ducking and splashing in the shallow stream until they were blue with cold.

In the privacy of buffalo robes, they stripped and washed away the grime and grit of the trail. Later, they feasted. There was still a way to go, but they had conquered the hardest part of the continent.

12
'BAMA SMITH

In the fifteen years since 1849, San Francisco had passed through centuries of municipal evolution. Though untamed in its early days, it was almost respectable by the time the travelers arrived. They had followed the Humboldt River to Virginia City and replenished supplies. Then they took the trail over the Sierra Nevada Mountains to the Golden Gate and rode into the city about mid-morning of a clear day in November, stopping to survey the scene. Wagons and horses clogged the muddy streets and wooden sidewalks teemed with people in all types of clothing.

It was nothing like Washington, Heather thought, watching some Chinese coolies working on a new building.

"Fantastic," said Bart.

Ruby became impatient.

"If women could vote," she said, "I'd vote to eat."

"You're not old enough to vote," Ben said, "However, Bart, do you think that might be a fitting place to stop?" He pointed across the busy thoroughfare.

On the other side of the intersection next to a large building was a one-story white frame structure that looked like a diner. They had passed a number of better looking eating places, but something about this one attracted Ben's attention. A small sign by the side of the front door read, "Room and Board, Mrs. Liza

Gervais, Prop." The restaurant was the Gervais Cafe.

"I'll spread a napkin there," said Bart.

They tied the horses to the hitching rail out front, mounted a couple of steps and opened the door. Inside were tables with red and white tablecloths. They sat down at one of them. A stout woman with gray hair up in a bun came from the kitchen.

"How be's you?" she asked and Bart grinned at Ben.

"We're hungry," said Ben. "You wouldn't happen to have a mess of collard greens, would you?"

The woman's radiant face glowed a little brighter.

"No, sir, cain't say thet I has. Ain't much call fer 'em in these parts."

"So, I reckon we'll have to do with lesser eatin'."

Ruby and Heather were puzzled as they ordered their meal.

"You know, Ben," Bart said after the woman returned to the kitchen, "if we're going to settle here for a spell, I think we ought to find a place where the folks have southern sympathies."

"You're right, Bart. It surely would help if we could find someone to guard our prisoners while we go about our business."

"How do you plan to do that in a city this big?" Heather asked.

"Might take us a while," said Ben, "but there's bound to be a rebel some place."

"This city isn't known for its southern sympathies," Heather said. "If I remember correctly it was the vote of the decent citizens of San Francisco that kept California in the Union. Rebels around here would be advised to keep their opinions to themselves."

"Would you care to wager a small amount that we can throw a mule here?" Bart asked.

"Careful," his brother warned. "This isn't Virginia."

Heather looked from one to the other, sensing conspiracy.

"If you'd left me any money when you searched my things in Washington, I'd bet you two South Carolina hounds can't scare up a Dixie rabbit by tomorrow at this time," she said.

"I've got ten dollars says you can't," Ruby blurted.

"Hush," Heather said.

"Shame on you, Ruby," Ben said. "You've been holding out on us. So that's how y'all planned to finance your escape. The first law of gambling is never bet more than you can afford to lose. Brother Bart, can we afford to wager ten dollars?"

"I did pocket a couple of those coins in Toledo. I guess we can spare one." Bart reached to shake Ruby's hand.

Four great smiles greeted plates heavy with country fried steaks, potatoes and green beans. It had been almost three months since they had put their feet under a table. They were too busy enjoying the food to waste much time talking. When the plates were clean, the woman in the white dress and red-checked apron brought them huge pieces of thick, juicy apple pie and refilled their coffee cups.

"Ma'am," asked Ben as he paid the bill, "are you married?"

"Yes. Why do you ask?"

"After eating that meal, I'd propose. Can you tell us where we can find the lady who operates the boarding house next door?"

"You're talkin' to her."

"You mean the people who board there eat here?" Bart said.

"That's right."

"This is their daily fare?" Bart asked.

"Right again."

"Amazing," Ben said. "Have you got two rooms we could rent?"

"Yes, sir, I do."

"Ma'am, would you mind telling me how you pronounce that name...G.E.R.V.A.I.S?" Ben asked.

"Gervais. It's French. Rhymes with 'cafe.' You don't pronounce the S."

"That's interesting. You wouldn't be kin to the Gervais family who live in South Carolina, would you?"

"Yes, sir, Mr. Gervais and I were born and raised in South Carolina. We came to California in 1851. Jack just had to try his hand at looking for gold. He's up there in the mountains now some place. The cold will bring him home shortly. I grub stake him from this boarding house every spring. He never gets tired of looking. I suppose some day he'll find it."

"Amazing," said Bart and held out his hand to Ruby. "Miss Hunsford, would you be interested in paying off your gambling debt?"

Ruby blushed saying, "It's where I can't get it in public."

"I thought so," observed Ben.

"You two have more luck than a weasel in a hen house," Heather said.

"I don't believe this," said Ruby.

Bart and Ben began chuckling, then broke out laughing. Soon all four of them were rocking with laughter.

"I'm afraid I don't understand," said Mrs. Gervais.

"I'm sorry, Mrs. Gervais," Ben said grinning. "You see my brother and I are from St. Stephens on the Santee River and these two ladies were just telling us we'd be hard-pressed to find any southerners around here. But we were fair to middlin' certain folks with a name like Gervais must come from some place in South Carolina seein' as how the street in front of the State House in Columbia is named that for one of our outstanding citizens."

"From South Carolina!" Mrs. Gervais beamed. "I declare. What in the world is y'all doin' so far from home?"

"If you let us have two rooms, we'll get settled in and answer that question where it's a little less public." Ben stood. "Come along, ladies, let us see what kind of accommodations this gracious southern lady has for us."

"Mrs. Gervais," he continued as they walked out of the cafe into the adjoining boarding house, "our business here requires quarters that are as private as possible. Would you have any such rooms in the attic?"

"Well, yes," she admitted reluctantly. "I do have three rooms up there. I haven't really tried to rent them. The steps are so narrow and steep. Mostly I just use them for storage. It'll take some doin' to get them ready for y'all."

"I'm sure they will be just exactly what we are looking for, Mrs. Gervais, and we'll help you get them ready. Won't we, ladies?"

160

Heather's look was enough to wither greenbrier. Ben just smiled.

"Do you think, Mrs. Gervais," he asked, "that if Mrs. Wanderman and Miss Hunsford do real well in the attic, you might employ them? It seems to me there is more work than one woman can comfortably handle in a house this big and a cafe like the Gervais."

"It's true, Colonel Gordyne, I do need help, but women willing to do this kind of work are in short supply in San Francisco."

"Please, Mrs. Gervais, just call me Ben. I'm sure Mrs. Wanderman and Miss Hunsford would much rather be busy around the house than cooped up in the attic. Isn't that so, ladies? In addition, it will keep you out of trouble."

There was a long pause as the two considered the options. Heather remembered endless days in a room in Toledo. Almost anything would be better than that.

"Yes, we would be delighted." she lied.

"I can't pay very well," the proprietress said.

"They'll work in exchange for our room and board. Won't you ladies?" Bart said. He got no answer.

They arrived at a narrow door. Mrs. Gervais found a key and unlocked it. On the back of the door was a small shelf with a couple of candles and matches. The landlady lit one of the candles and by its light they climbed the cramped stairs to a small, dark attic hall with three doors. Mrs. Gervais found another key and opened one of them. Bright sunlight filtered through dusty gable windows into a large cluttered room. She unlocked the other doors and showed them two rooms much like the first.

"Take your pick," Mrs. Gervais said. "We'll pile all the things in one room and you can have the other two."

"Thank you for saying 'we,' Mrs. Gervais," Heather remarked. "This room could be made very livable."

There was some furniture. Sitting on a bed, Ruby said, "It's going to be nice to sleep in one of these again."

"I must get back to the cafe," Mrs. Gervais said. "If these rooms are satisfactory, you can start arranging them."

161

She headed down the stairs.

"Pardon me," Ben said. "I wonder if we could have keys to our rooms?"

"Oh, certainly, Mr. Gordyne," she replied and took two keys off of a huge ring.

"I'd also like to have one for the door at the foot of the stairs," he said and she found another.

"This is slavery," Heather fumed after Mrs. Gervais had gone.

"Let's just call it a prisoner-of-war camp, shall we?" Ben held up the keys and grinned.

"Col. Benjamin L. Gordyne, I absolutely and totally hate you. I do," she said.

"You're not a nice man at all," said Ruby.

"Ben, if you think you can handle these Yankee wildcats," Bart said, "I'll take care of our horses and bring up our gear."

"If I don't live through it, tell Ma I died for my country."

All afternoon and into the early darkness they worked putting the rooms in order. They were almost finished when Mrs. Gervais came puffing up the stairs. She looked around scowling. Then she smiled.

"If y'all work like this all the time, I'll be more than glad to give you room and board for these two rooms," she said. "Supper's ready."

"I think we're ready too, but I'm wondering, if I get down stairs, can I get back up," said Heather. "I'm worn out."

Their day was not over yet. When they returned after supper, Ben said, "Ruby, you haven't paid your gambling debt and while you're getting it out of the hiding place I think it would be advisable if you just let me have all of your hidden treasure for safekeeping."

"I won't," she said. "You can't have my mother's money."

"I'll just keep it for you. You'll get it back when we're through here."

"No. I'll not give it to you."

"Then I'll have to take it."

162

"You wouldn't dare!"

"He will, Ruby," Heather said. "You'd better do as he says."

Ruby looked hopefully at Bart. He just nodded slowly.

The women went into their room while the brothers waited outside the door. In a few minutes the door cracked and a hand appeared holding a doeskin bag. The next morning Ben gave Ruby a receipt for fifty-six dollars.

Three days later a heavily bearded man of massive size stormed into the cafe about sundown.

"Liza," he roared, "what's to eat?"

The landlady rushed out of the kitchen shouting, "Jack! Jack! You're back."

They collided at the door and, gathering her in his arms, he lifted her off the floor and swung twice around as they laughed loudly together.

"Yeah, I'm back," he announced, "and hungry as a bear comin' out of hibernation. Ain't had a decent meal since spring."

He set her down, held her at arm's length with one hand and took off his hat. "But before I eat, let me jest look at you fer a spell."

Jack Gervais was a hurricane of a man whose bushy eyebrows met over a large red nose and blue eyes which always seemed to be anticipating a practical joke. The joke might have been his own face. What could be seen of it among the thornbush of speckled gray whiskers was battered and scarred like the tail end of an old and stubborn burro. The flat crowned hat he wore was tattered and torn, and when he removed it the pink baldness of his head revealed more evidence of many brawls. He wore frayed bib overalls, a washed-out blue flannel shirt and a sheepskin jacket. The cuffs of his canvas pants were tucked into scarred leather boots.

"Jack Gervais," said Liza, "I got work to do."

She turned back to her kitchen with her husband lumbering along behind like a great mule.

They saw no more of him until the next morning. Ruby was setting plates of hotcakes and eggs before the Gordynes when

Gervais once again entered the cafe. He surveyed the room from the door and walked to the table where they sat.

"Mind if I join you?" he asked and sat down before either of them could answer. "I'm Jack Gervais," he announced pushing out a hand big enough to make a saddle for a small horse.

"I'm Bart Gordyne." Bart took the hand and they looked into each other's eyes. No one watching could see, but Ben knew a contest was underway as those hands gripped. Gervais laughed and extracted his.

"This is my brother, Ben," said Bart.

"Glad to make your acquaintance, Ben, but I ain't too sure of this brother of yours. A man thet kin hold my grip thet long must be near as mean as me."

They laughed as Ruby approached the table.

"Coffee, sir?" she asked.

"Hot, sweet and white, if you got any milk," said Jack and turned back to the brothers.

"Liza tells me y'all is from South Carolina."

"Right," said Bart.

"I figures it must be truth because ain't too many folks out this way knows anybody by the name of Gervais unless they had connections there. What brings you to California?"

"Gold," said Bart. "We got plans..."

"Isn't that why everybody comes this way?" Ben interrupted.

Gervais got the interruption and looked from one to the other.

"There be some who come to get away from the war," he said. "Looks to me more like y'all want to bring the war with you."

Neither Gordyne responded as Ruby brought Jack's coffee and asked, "May I take your order, sir?"

Gervais turned and looked her over.

"With help as purty as you, business ought to improve considerable. Did you come in with these two rebels?" he asked.

"Yes, sir."

"Where's home to you?"

"It was Ohio, but I guess it's here for now."

"How'd you git yoked up with these two?"

164

She looked at Ben.

"May I take your order, sir?" she repeated.

"Liza knows what I want. You jest tell her I'm ready for breakfast." He turned back to Ben. "Liza tells me the other lady is from Washington. Seems to me to be a strange quartet to come three thousand miles just to beat themselves in the diggin's."

"Things aren't going too well for the Confederacy right now," Ben said and Gervais' eyes narrowed.

"If you're talkin' defeat and has run away from the fightin' 'cause you're yellow, you got no place in this house and you ain't sittin' at this table agin. I kin tolerate Yankees, but I got no use at all for Dixie turncoats. I mop the floor with 'em."

Ben laughed.

"Easy, my friend," he said. "We wouldn't have hunted out a home with the name 'Gervais' on the outside of it, if we were Dixie turncoats. We just have to be careful."

"You don't have to be careful with me," Jack assured them. "I got many of my scars teaching Yankees it ain't healthy to speak evil of the South. I take it you two got something to do in San Francisco. You don't have to tell me what it is, but I'm offerin' my services if they're needed."

"Thanks," said Ben. "I'm Col. Benjamin L. Gordyne of the Confederate Army. My brother and I are here on an orders from President Jefferson Davis. I'll hold off for now telling you what this assignment is, but you may help us."

"What kin I do?"

"President Davis said my contact in San Francisco is a man named 'Bama Smith. Do you know him?"

Gervais' blue eyes danced with laughter as if he were anticipating a rare bit of humor. He rubbed his chin briefly.

"Cain't say I remember a man by that name, but I'll put out the word. If a man with that name is in 'Frisco, he'll hear it."

Ruby brought Jack his breakfast of a half dozen fried eggs and a stack of hotcakes. He was then too busy for further talk.

The brothers excused themselves and left the cafe to explore. They were particularly interested in Wells Fargo and the western

165

terminus of the Overland Stage. They wanted to become familiar with the major streets.

It was raining and dark by the time they returned. Dripping wet, they pushed open the door and started across the lobby towards the stairs intending to change clothes before dinner. Jack Gervais was leaning on the banister as they approached.

"Someone here to see you," he said soberly, nodding towards a corner of the room near the front door.

Ben and Bart turned. They saw an attractive, well-dressed woman who looked to be in her twenties. She was seated but stood when she saw them looking at her. She was taller than she appeared to be at first. Her auburn hair was piled high. She had a pug nose and a dimpled chin at the base of cheeks that slanted flat and sharp from high cheekbones.

"Good evening," said Ben, bowing slightly as she approached.

"Good evening," she said, "I'm 'Bama Smith. I understand you're looking for me."

"You're who?" Bart blurted while Gervais roared with laughter.

"It's a pleasure and a surprise to meet you, Miss Smith," Ben said. "I have to confess that you are not what I expected. Which only goes to prove again that one should very carefully reserve judgments. For example, I assumed from the conversation I had at breakfast that Mr. Gervais was a man without guile, a true southerner. I see I have been deliberately misled."

"You asked if I knew of a man called 'Bama Smith,'" Gervais said between laughs. "I don't. I thought you'd prefer a woman."

"It is, as I said, a pleasant surprise. Miss Smith, since Mr. Gervais has failed to show reasonable courtesy and has not introduced us, I'm Benjamin Gordyne."

His brother, recovering his voice, said, "I'm Bart Gordyne."

She gave Bart a prolonged look and smiled. That smile did what Gervais' gripping handshake had failed to do at the breakfast table. She held him in a spell. Her lips parted. He stared. Still looking at Bart, she said, "This is truly a double pleasure."

To some love never comes. Sometimes two people live

together for years and there comes that moment when one of them is about to slip out of reach forever. In the moment of death their eyes lock and, like light breaking through leaden clouds, the fact of love will wash their souls. Or love may come as the gradual budding of blossoms in a slow spring. It was none of these for 'Bama and Bart. She stood dressed neatly in green, her outfit harmonizing with the rich brown of laughing eyes and copper-tinted hair. He stood with rain water plastering the hair to his head and dripping puddles from the fringes of his buckskin jacket. Yet, the instant they caught each other's eyes, there was knowledge that said, "This is the one to whom I forever belong."

It was Ben who spoke first. "I regret, Miss Smith, that we meet when I am dripping wet and hardly presentable. If you will excuse me, I'll change and be back in twenty minutes,"

Finally finding his voice, Bart asked, "Would you have dinner with me tonight?"

"Please, hurry," she murmured.

The Gordyne brothers heard Jack laughing as they vaulted up the stairs. Ruby and Heather were not laughing though the men passed them on the first landing in such a hurry they hardly had time to say, "Hello."

Even the heavy rain did not affect business at Gervais Cafe. The brothers ushered 'Bama and Jack to a table. As Bart held 'Bama's chair, Ben was apologizing for keeping her waiting.

"You need not feel bad," she said as Bart lifted her off the floor pushing her seat under the table. "However, we're really going to have a problem if you keep calling me Miss Smith. I'm 'Bama to all my southern friends."

"Do your non-southern friends call you something else?" Ben asked as he took his seat. Heather came over with glasses of water and the question was not answered. As things slowed down, the conversation turned to the purpose of the meeting.

"Why did y'all put out the word that you were looking for me?" 'Bama asked.

"President Davis sent us out here on an assignment and told me that my contact would be 'Bama Smith," Ben said.

"We want to help you all we can, but we can't be much help if we don't know what we're doing," Jack said. "I think it's about time you tell us."

"Very simply, the Confederacy needs gold," Ben began. "About eighteen million dollars in gold is being shipped east every year. Our assignment is to find a way to divert some of that gold."

Briefly he outlined their positions in the army of Virginia and their trip across the continent. It took more time to explain the presence of Heather and Ruby.

"I assumed 'Bama Smith would be a man. I remember the president saying my contact would be about as honest as Judas Iscariot but he was southern. I guess he was right. Does Mr. Davis know you're a woman?"

"Probably not, but he does know me."

"Is that supposed to make sense?" Bart asked.

"He doesn't know a person named 'Bama Smith is a woman, but he does know me by another name. He probably does not know that he knows me at all, but he and Daddy went to school together. I met the president many times before he went to Washington as secretary of war. That was before Lincoln was elected. I came west with my brothers about the same time. He doesn't know me as 'Bama Smith and probably doesn't realize I may be part of the reason y'all are here."

"You?" they both asked and watched the grin on Jack's face.

"Tell them, Jack," she said and, while he talked, she stared at Bart Gordyne.

"We got us a little group trying to make things uncomfortable for the Yankees out here. We got the idea a while back that, with some support from Richmond, we might cause a little civil war here in California and take it away from the Union. One reason for doing that was to get our hands on all that gold."

They waited as Gervais forked a large piece of rare steak into his mouth. He didn't stop talking to chew.

"What better way to get someone in Richmond to listen to us than through a friend of the president? So 'Bama wrote to her daddy and suggested the president have someone get in touch with

'Bama Smith which is the name she uses in our group. When you asked for her by name, we knew you'd been sent by the president hisself."

Gervais stopped talking to signal for Heather. She came over and refilled his coffee mug. When she left, 'Bama said, "Now, tell us what you plan to do."

"Organizing a military campaign is a thought," said Ben, "but it's usually easier to walk around a mountain than to climb over. If people, North and South, hadn't been so all fired impatient, slavery would have expired like an untended fire. Because of the war, one way or another, it may go on for another hundred years. We don't want to make the same mistake here."

"We just got here," Bart pointed out. "We've spent some time reconnoitering. I might charge in and start a revolution, but, if you knew Ben, you'd know that he'll think on it a spell."

Ben was thinking as he used a piece of cornbread to mop the gravy in his plate.

"First thing I need to know is just what personnel do we have?" said Ben.

"We could probably muster two or three hundred in one week," Jack said, "and more if we've got a little time."

"That's not an army but it'd be about the right size for raiders," Ben observed. "Unless our raids were almost instantly successful, hit and run tactics would only alert the enemy to what we're after. What I meant by personnel is what can your people do? What skills do they have? You're a prospector now, Jack. What did you do before you came west?"

"I was a cabinetmaker in South Carolina. I don't know how that's goin' to help the Confederacy."

"I don't know either, but that's the kind of information we'll need to start with. When we get it together, we can draw up our blueprints and go to work. 'Bama, what do you do when you aren't plotting against the Union?"

"I help my brothers at the funeral home."

Bart nearly choked on his beans. "You what?"

"My brothers and I didn't come out here like most folks

169

hunting for gold. Daddy operated a funeral home in Mobile and we grew up learning the trade. We heard there were a lot of folks dying in the gold rush and very few people who knew anything about proper funeralizing. There was too much competition in Alabama so we packed up and came to San Francisco to provide a needed service."

"Profitable?" Ben asked.

"People are still dyin' and gettin' themselves killed," she said. "They pay well for a fittin' funeral."

"Who else?" Ben asked then held up his hand. Looking across the table behind 'Bama he saw Heather approaching with pound cake and coffee.

"Careful," he whispered. "Mrs. Wanderman, will you be so kind as to tell Mrs. Gervais that I really think she could not have found better help. The service has been excellent tonight."

"It would be my pleasure to pour this pot of coffee over your head, Colonel Gordyne," Heather snapped.

"Tell me, Ben, is that the way a southern lady would respond to a compliment?" Bart asked.

"I suppose this is one of those southern ladies to whom I have so often been unfavorably compared," Heather said.

"Oh, excuse me, Mrs. Wanderman," said Ben. "Allow me to introduce you to Mrs. Daniel Barnes of Philadelphia, I believe. Mrs. Barnes, Mrs. Warren Wanderman of Washington, D.C."

The two women looked at each other like knights of old measuring their opponents in combat.

"Pleased to meet you, Mrs. Barnes," said Heather.

"My pleasure, Mrs. Wanderman," said 'Bama.

"May I refill your cup, Mrs. Barnes?" Heather asked in a tone that said she'd rather pour the coffee in the woman's lap.

"Would you, please?" she challenged.

When Heather returned to the kitchen, Ben said, "I don't think we should discuss these matters anymore in public. We'll meet you at the mortuary in a couple of days."

They finished their coffee and the three men ushered 'Bama outside to her waiting carriage. There Bart put out his hand to

170

help her. She took it and pressed her fingers against his.

Turning to Ben, she said, "So now I am Mrs. Daniel Barnes. You think fast, Col. Benjamin Gordyne. Very fast."

"Mrs. Wanderman thinks fast as well," he said. "It did not seem wise to put you at risk by revealing even your special name."

13
SHADOW

The war divided San Francisco three ways - those for the Union, those for the Confederacy and those who did not want a war across the continent to interfere with the important business of making money. 'Bama's brothers were in this last group. Involvement on either side would have alienated half the city's population. All were going to need the services of an undertaker eventually, so they remained neutral. Still the mortality rate was very high. There were burials almost every day. This meant a constant stream of people, alive and dead. Some came for reasons unrelated to the disposition of dead bodies.

Being a woman and a younger sister had its advantages. It gave 'Bama Smith more freedom to put her convictions into actions. No one expected a young woman to have much judgment on political matters nor would it be held against her brothers if she acted like a fanatic. Besides she was an attractive women in a city made up mostly of men.

While exploring the streets, the Gordynes located the mint, the smelting company and the Harrington Brothers Mortuary.

Several days later, a tall young man in a business suit stepped out of a hack in front of the funeral home. As he opened the front door, one of the Harrington brothers met him.

"Good morning, sir," he said somberly. "How may I help

172

you?"

"I'm Ben L. Gordyne of the Richmond Post," Ben said. "I'm on assignment to interview successful southerners here in California. I've been told you are from Mobile and have a wide reputation for providing the best funeral services in this state. This would make a very interesting feature for my readers."

The mortician was skeptical.

"Why would the people of Richmond, surrounded by a war, be interested in a couple of businessmen in California?" he asked.

"Our readers tire of war reports," Ben replied. "We try to give them a variety of news."

Harrington was cautious.

"This will be printed only in Richmond?" he asked.

"Since you are from Mobile, the paper in that city might reprint it," Ben said. "I doubt that it will be printed anywhere else. Why do you ask?"

"I'm not sure it would be good for business if my southern ties were too widely publicized," he said. "It is not that I'm not sympathetic to the southern cause. It's just that I don't go around waving the Stars and Bars and singing 'Dixie' like some."

"I see," said Ben. "Well, I doubt that there would be any reason to reprint the story in San Francisco. Can you spare a few minutes for an interview?"

"Yes, we are not busy at the present time."

Ben took out a notepad and pencil.

"I assume you are one of the Harrington brothers, but I don't believe I caught your first name."

"I'm Howard. My brother is Henry."

"Is there anyone else involved in this enterprise?"

"Yes, our sister, Katherine. She prepares the bodies of our female clients for burial."

"If they are available, I would like to meet them, too."

"Of course. Right this way, if you please."

They stepped into an office. A man in a black suit was working at one desk. Ben could not see what 'Bama was doing at a drawing table in front of a large window. Her back was to him.

When the man looked up, Ben could see that Howard and Henry were twins.

"Henry, Kathy. I would like you to meet a correspondent from the Richmond Post, Mr. Ben L. Gordyne, I believe."

Henry stood. 'Bama sat motionless for a moment and then slowly turned. Ben showed no signs of recognizing her.

"I'm glad to meet you, Mr. Gordyne," said Henry. "What can we do for you?"

They shook hands.

"And I assume this is Miss Katherine Harrington," Ben said and stepped to the drawing board.

"It is a pleasure to know you, Miss Harrington," he said and, glancing at the work before her, asked, "What is this?"

"It's a special service we offer our patrons," Howard answered. "Brass is one of the longest lasting metals and our sister has considerable skill in engraving. She engraves a short epitaph and it is attached to the outside of the casket. People seem to like it. A brass plate will identify the remains for many years underground even if the tombstone is destroyed."

"Interesting," said Ben and wrote in his pad.

When he had finished he looked at the two men.

"I don't like to take you from your work," he said. "Perhaps Miss Harrington could spare the time to show me your facility. Then, if you are not too busy, we can complete the interview,"

For the next hour 'Bama Smith showed the "reporter" through the ornate and somber workings of the mortuary. She also told him a great deal more about the Confederate underground in San Francisco. Ben wrote everything in his notebook.

"What are you going to do with all this information?" 'Bama asked as they turned back to the office.

"I will write a report for the Richmond Post. If they print it, I may be able to encode some information for President Davis. At any rate my byline will let him know we've arrived in San Francisco."

For the next half hour he sat in the office and questioned the brothers. As he stood to leave, he asked, "By the way, can you

174

give me the names of some other successful people from the South? I would like to continue this series."

"Certainly," said Henry and they supplied him with an almost complete directory of the rebel underground.

"Ben" said Bart as they ate their dinner in the Gervais Cafe that night, "I think it's time I went to work."

"Right," Ben responded. "You've been spending too much time loafing around the city and wasting money in taverns. Before long you'll be wrestling mules again."

"I've about memorized the streets here and that ain't easy for a town of two hundred thousand."

"What you got in mind?"

"I'll get a wagon and a couple of mules to start a freight company."

"What do you propose to haul?"

"Anything the merchants and manufacturers want moved."

"You wouldn't have it in mind to concentrate on those who work with gold?"

"It did occur to me."

"When you starting?"

Ruby brought them plates piled high with beef stew and they were silent for a few minutes as they took to eating.

"By the way," said Ben. "I've been busy, too."

"Doin' what?"

Ben described his activities and Bart said, "If that don't beat all. We both went to The Citadel, but I'm haulin' freight and you're pushin' a pencil."

"Quality is what counts, my boy. Quality."

The Bartholomew Freight Co. was in operation by the afternoon of the next day and Ben spent the next two weeks interviewing some of the people whose names the Harringtons had given him. He also wrote and mailed his first dispatch. At the end of that time, he was discouraged.

"I've been all around the mint, but I can't get inside," he said as he sat with Bart and Jack Gervais in the lobby of the boarding house one night. "I've also explored the possibilities of the

175

smelting company. I don't feel any closer to that gold tonight than I was in Virginia. I need someone on the inside."

"Well, I'm gettin' closer," said Bart.

"How's that?"

"I've been hangin' out with a man who drives for Wells Fargo. He has carried some of the mint's cargo. He's hauled a shipment worth a few million to the wharf and watched them load it on a ship."

"How often do they go by sea?" Ben asked.

"Didn't say. But there's another route. Some gold goes by coach across the mountains. We intercepted one of those in Toledo."

"Does he know when the next batch will be moved?"

"No. That seems to be kept secret until moving day."

"That's what makes it difficult," said Ben. "It's hard to plan if you can't time it. We need someone inside."

A week later Ben rode into the livery stable after another interview. He dismounted and had started brushing down his horse when he heard a movement at the rear of the stall. Looking up he saw someone standing in the shadows.

"I hears you be lookin' fer a rebel what works in the mint." The female voice had an accent that reminded him of a southern hill country farmer.

Ben turned towards the door of the stable. Jack and 'Bama were standing in the dim twilight. They nodded and then walked away. Ben looked into the shadows at the back of the stall.

"Might be," he said as he started to brush his horse.

"I works there and I be's from the South."

"Is that so? What do you do in the mint?"

"I keeps the place clean. I sweeps the floor and empties the trash."

"What do they call you?"

"You don't need to know that, mister. You just tell me what to do, an' if'n I kin, I'll do it."

"How come they let a rebel work in the mint?"

"I married a Yankee. They don't know I's from Mississippi."

176

"You talk like that and anybody but a fool would know you ain't from the North."

"Sir, I don't have to talk like that," said the voice and the accent changed completely. "I'm really not sure which of my two ways of talking is my real tongue. I learned both of them while growing up."

"Have you got any children?" Ben asked. "You're getting into danger. I wouldn't want to take a child's mother from him."

"You really wants to know how old I is," she responded. "I's got five chil'ens, but they be all old 'nough to take kere o' theyselves. I be ol' 'nough to do what you wants."

"When did you come to California?"

"Mister, yo' sho' is full a' questions. My man heard abut the gold in '49 an' nothin' would do but he had to try fer it. He was all set to make a million. 'Nother of his dreams that never got nowhere. Liked to have killed us gettin' out here, an' then he found out diggin' is hard work an' low pay. He ain't never liked to do nothin' that'd make him sweat, but he was stuck out here with a wife an' two youn'uns and no way to get home. So he sold what we had and started servin' cheap whiskey to people followin' up to the gold fields."

"One more question, ma'am. Do you ever get near gold or finished gold coins in the mint?"

"Yes, mister, I does. They guards the place real good mos' times, but they gets a little kereless. I 'specks I could pick up a roll of money now and then. But I gatta change clothes and is searched when I leaves work."

There was silence for a minute as Ben pulled down some hay for his horse.

"Does I git the job?"

"You do."

"What does I do?"

"For now just keep your eyes open and keep me informed. I've got to come up with a plan. When I figure it out, I'll let you know. How can I get in touch with you?"

"I goes to work at three o'clock every afternoon. When yo'

wants me, yo' stand across the street from the mint. I'll see yo' an' meet yo' here when I gets off work after ten o'clock."

"Thank you, ma'am, I think you will do real well," Ben said. Tipping his hat into the shadows, he walked to the Gervais Cafe for supper.

That night Ben worked in the attic room he shared with Bart. He was seated at a table going over some papers by the light of a flickering coal oil lamp.

"What are you doing?" Bart asked.

"I've got all these names. I've interviewed most of them so I know what they can do. I'm just shifting them around to see if they won't slip into some kind of order."

"You go one way to recruit your troops," Bart said. "But I'm spending more time where people live and talk just bein' friends and I may muster as many brigands as you."

"We're doing our recruiting in different places, put them together and we ought to have a fair army." Ben laid his pencil down. "But right now they just don't fit. How do I get the gold out of the mint without it being missed? I'm too tired to think right now."

He stood, stripped down to his underwear, blew out the lamp and went to bed.

Gervais Cafe at breakfast was a noisy place filled with the heavy laughter and rumble of male voices mingling with the tinkle of steelware on china. There the next morning Ben found the answer to his problem. It all began with a roar from Jack Gervais that drowned out the other noise.

"Mrs. Wanderman," he shouted, "you've given me the wrong plate."

"That's the plate Mrs. Gervais told me to give you."

"This ain't what I eat for breakfast. She knows right well that every morning for twenty-two years I've eaten six fried eggs and a stack of hotcakes. Woman, what's the meaning of this?" His wife showed her face in the kitchen door.

"Heather, if he's gone to complainin' about my cookin', just you take his plate. Let him go hungry."

178

Heather reached down.

"Touch it an' you'll lose a hand," he said holding a knife over the dish. "What is it?"

"Any civilized person would know it's an omelet," Heather said. "All of you get omelets this morning."

"How come I don't get my six fried eggs?"

"Maybe it's time you got civilized," she said.

"Y'all will have to do with what you got this morning," Mrs. Gervais said. "Hens don't lay good in cold weather and we ran short of eggs. So, to spread 'em around, we chopped up some salt pork, onions and a few other things and mixed it in with scrambled eggs. Go ahead and try it. You might like it and you'll never miss your six fried. And I don't want to hear any more complainin', you hear?"

"Yes, ma'am," said Jack meekly and fell to eating.

Across the table Ben Gordyne lifted his fork to his mouth and stopped to look at the mixture of eggs, salt pork, onions and "a few other things" on its prong end. He took a bite. As he chewed it, he returned his fork to his plate and lifted another fork full of omelet.

"You know, Bart," he said quietly, "they'll never miss the six fried eggs."

"What's the matter?"

"They won't miss the bullion if we replace it every time we take some out."

"Yeah, but there ain't a whole lot of profit in that."

"There is if you replace eggs with salt pork and onions."

"How do you propose to do that?"

"Makin' an omelet is easy," said Ben.

"Jack," he said, turning to the big man across the table, "how would you like to go back to cabinet making?"

"What you want made?" Gervais asked with his mouth full.

"Coffins."

"Coffins? Who's fixin' to die?"

"Everybody's got to die and you got to have coffins ready ahead of time. The Harringtons are going to expand their business."

Gervais looked at him with a lifted eyebrow and said, "It's harder to figure you than a vein of gold. You tell me what you want made and I'll make it."

After breakfast Ben rode to the mortuary and asked Miss Harrington if she would have dinner with him that evening. Her brothers looked with favor on this proposal and Kathy accepted.

"Good," said Gordyne, "I'll pick you up at six."

During the day he could have been seen pacing off certain streets of San Francisco and making notes in his reporter's pad. About 2:45 that afternoon he was waiting in front of the mint to be seen by his inside contact. He waited until four o'clock and returned to the boarding house. When he left an hour later he was dressed as if he were going courting, a fact noted by Heather and Ruby. But romance was not the subject of conversation at dinner.

"I wonder how your brothers would like to enter into a new phase of your business?" Ben asked 'Bama as they ate.

"My brothers are always interested in new business," 'Bama said. "What have you got in mind?"

"People come to San Francisco from all over the world. A lot of them die here. It seems to me that a profitable business could be made out of offering people an opportunity to be buried in their hometowns anywhere in the world, payable in advance."

"Shipping bodies isn't as easy as shipping hides."

"It would be if you made air-tight, redwood coffins and packed the bodies in some kind of preservative."

Miss Harrington chewed on the thought for a few minutes as she chewed on a bit of filet mignon. Swallowing it, she asked, "What's your interest in this?"

"It may be I might want to ship something to Richmond," he said, "If your brothers already have some remains going when I'm ready to ship, another casket or two wouldn't draw attention."

When they had finished eating, Ben took 'Bama home and rode back to the boarding house. He walked his horse into the livery stable at ten o'clock.

"Good evening, Shadow," he said to the darkness. There was

180

a chuckle from the back of an empty stall.

"Good evenin', mister," said the voice. "Yo' got somethin' fer me ta do?"

"Maybe. But first I need some more information."

"Mo' questions?"

"I'm afraid so, but this time they're about the place you work. How does it operate? How is the gold accounted for as it is processed?"

"They weighs gold when it comes in the assayer's office an' the money comin' off a the stamping mill. That's gotta match 'n then Mr. Madrass or Mr. Woods counts the coins 'n puts 'em in boxes on scales in the vault. The weight added to the boxes hes gotta match the weight taken from the stampin' rooms. A tally sheet showin' the weight, the number of coins 'n the date is kept nailed ta the box 'n Mr. Madrass writes it down in a ledger book locked in his office. Since they knows how much each coin is supposed to weigh 'n how many is in each box, they kin know if it's all there.

"Mr. Madrass 'n Mr. Woods checks it all day 'n every night befo' they quits. They knows all the time what's in those boxes."

"Who are Mr. Madrass and Mr. Woods?" Ben asked.

"Mr. Madrass be the bossman. Mr. Woods bosses the mills."

"They can't watch the vault all the time if they're running a money factory. What do they do when they leave?"

"Locks the do's."

"Wouldn't it be easy to get in that vault?'

"Y'd hef' ta break through two locked do's ta do it. Every do' into the hall in front of the vault is kept locked except when it's being used, 'n there be a guard all the time."

It was a strange interview. Ben stood leaning against a back corner of a dark, unused stall. Shadow sat on a bale of hay. In the hour-long conversation, Ben learned the layout of the mint and how it operated.

"Tell me, Shadow, how do you clean the place?"

"I trim lamps, sweep flo's, empty ash trays, spittoons 'n trash cans. That kin'a thing. Mr. Madrass bees 'ticular. Wants ever'

181

thin' clean. He sends me out about once a week to pick up stuff people's throwed over the fence."

"What do you do with the trash?"

"After Mr. Madrass looks through it, I puts it in barrels outside the back gate 'n it's toted away once a week."

"Who carries off the trash?"

"Don' know. It's gone when I comes to work."

"Does Mr. Madrass inspect everything you take out?"

"Ever'thin' exceptin' the spittoons. I empties 'em ever' day in the outhouse in the corner of the back yard."

"Is there a spittoon near the vault?"

"One's by Mr. Madrass' do'. He won' let nobody in his office smokin' 'r chewin'."

"How does junk get into the back lot?"

"Drunks throw empties over the fence. I's found ol' shoes. Anything peoples don' want, they jes' throws it over the fence."

"Does Mr. Madrass inspect back lot trash?"

"No, I jes' takes it to the barrels."

Except for the sounds of horses at rest, there was silence as Ben paced the stall.

"Is we through?"

"Not yet, Shadow," Ben answered. "Who has keys to get into the vault?"

"Mr. Madrass, Mr. Woods an' the guard. They keeps 'em on their belts all the time. It takes two keys to git inta the vault. Mr. Madrass has the key to one lock, an' Mr. Woods and the guard hast the odder. When Mr. Woods ain't aroun', the guard use' his key."

"Do you ever use the guard's keys?"

"When I goes inta the other parts of the buildin' to clean up, he gives me his keys to unlock do's. But I cain't git inta the vault 'cause I don't ever have the odder key."

Ben walked the length of the stall and back.

"Is there ever a time when you are in the hall by yourself?"

"Mos' nights he asks me to watch while he goes to the outhouse."

"The back door is locked when he goes out?"

"If those do's ain't bein' used, they's locked."

There was silence in the dark stall.

"Is there anything else I ought to know?" Ben asked.

"Vault's almos' full," Shadow said. "They'll hafta fin' somethin' ta do with all those boxes of money 'fo' long."

"That does give me something to think about."

Again there was silence.

"Anything else, mister?"

"Not right now. We've got right smart work to do outside. Thank you, Shadow. You've been a big help."

Ben heard her laugh as he left. He went to his room, got out pencil and paper and drew a diagram of the mint. When Bart woke two hours later, he was still up.

"What you got there?" Bart asked.

"This is what the mint looks like. The vault's right here in the middle. The floors and walls are all concrete. Its door faces to the rear away from the public part of the building. Doors on each side of the hall open into the offices of Madrass and Woods. At the other end of the hall is another door which opens on a rear loading dock. In the hall are a chair, a spittoon and a lamp. We're going to make our omelet inside the vault."

"I don't see how you're going to do any cooking in there."

"My chef is a shadow who walks through walls." His brother laughed and went to bed.

"Jack," said Ben at breakfast the next morning, "who on our list knows anything about ceramics?"

"Ceramics? What's that?" Gervais forked another bite between his mustache and beard.

"The plate you're eating off of is ceramic. China. Do you have any friends who make china or ceramic ornaments?"

"No, don't think so. We import most of that stuff with the Chinese coolies."

"What about bricks? Anybody you know make bricks?"

"Buck Andrews over near Sacramento burns brick."

"You reckon he'd be interested in our little project?"

183

"Might be. He's from Atlanta."

"Even if he isn't, he might be able to make some plates for us and it might be best if he didn't know what they were for."

Bart stopped his coffee cup a few inches from his lips.

"Plates? What do you want with plates?" he asked.

Ben laughed and chewed a minute.

"A secret is like a bucket, the more seams you put in it the greater the chances are it will leak. The more parts you put in a plan, the greater the possibility of a breakdown. I hope you don't mind if I keep some things to myself."

"I do mind but I don't suppose it'll do me any good."

"Jack, could you build me a freight wagon in your spare time?"

"Spare time? I'm workin' harder for you than I ever did for myself diggin' gold. Why don't you use Bart's freight truck?"

"It isn't built for crossing the country. Here's what I need," Ben said and handed the cabinetmaker a drawing.

"What're these compartments for?"

"I may have to take some of your coffins to Missouri. To make it worthwhile, I'll have to take at least three of them. There isn't any way I can carry them and all our gear in a normal wagon."

"You don't want much, do you?"

"Can you do it?"

"If it can be done, I'll do it."

"Good." Ben drained the last of his coffee, put the cup down and leaned back his chair for a minute.

"Jack, I've discovered if I just mention I need a certain talent in your presence, somehow that talent shows up. All the people you've introduced me to so far have been high class, hardworking, honest citizens. But surely a man of your reputation and experience has come to know a few who don't fit that classification."

"Rarely do I associate with riffraff," Gervais said stiffly.

"Of course, all those scars you wear so proudly were caused by gentlemen of the highest caliber," Ben said. "Preachers probably. But that's not what I have in mind. I'm just wondering if, in this crime-free city, there isn't someone whose profession is assault and battery with intent to rob. It seems to me I've read of a few such happenings in your local newspapers."

He stood. "If you know of such a person, tell them I need his services. Right now, I've got to call on 'Bama Smith."

"Why can't I call on 'Bama and you stay here with Jack?" Bart asked.

"You don't know how bad things really are, brother. I've got to spend this day with that Alabama redhead and then tonight I'm going to be tortured by the company of Mrs. Wanderman at a Christmas concert. Terrible, isn't it?" He laughed.

"Oh, by the way, Bart, I'll need a couple of those double eagles you stole in Toledo."

"Why you mangy coyote, I ought to break you in two."

"Strictly business, dear brother, strictly business."

"I'd sure like some of that kind of business," Bart replied as he dug in his pocket and fished out two gold coins. Then they all laughed.

Ben took the double eagles to the mortuary. When he arrived, the brothers were at a cemetery. Their sister was preparing for the next funeral.

"Morning, Miss Harrington," he said. "Are you ready to translate yourself into 'Bama Smith?"

"What can I do for you?" she asked.

"Can you duplicate this in steel or brass?" He handed her one of the twenty-dollar gold pieces.

She examined it and then looked at him with a question in her eye. "Yes, I suppose I can. But why?"

"Before I answer that, can you duplicate it in reverse?"

"Reverse?"

"Yes, like a negative of a photograph."

"It will be harder, but I expect I can. But, again, why?"

"Right now, you are the only person I'm taking into my confidence. I need a template so that I can counterfeit them."

"What are you going to make the fakes out of?" she asked.

185

"Clay."

"Clay," she said looking at the disk in her hand. "You know, I think you just might get away with it."

She sat down at her bench by the window and picked up her engraving tools.

That night, as Ben ushered Heather into the opera house where the Christmas concert was to be held, a voice hailed him.

"Wait up," he heard his brother call. Turning, he saw Bart helping 'Bama Smith Harrington out of a carriage.

"I decided to make this a double, and 'Mrs. Barnes' very generously consented, " Bart said.

"How delightful," said Heather taking Kathy Harrington's hand. "My name's Heather."

"Please, call me Kathy." They walked into the opera house.

"I believe 'Barnes' is your last name," said Heather.

"Oh, yes, of course, and you are Mrs. Wanderman?"

"That is correct. It seems we have something in common."

"What is that?"

"We must both be widows."

"Yes, I'm afraid so," said Miss Harrington.

Three nights later Matthew Madrass left the mint in the rain. On his way home he stopped as usual at the Mother Lode Bar for one drink. Then he stepped out into the wet darkness of the deserted street and was assaulted. When he recovered consciousness, Madrass reported to police that his unknown assailant had taken all his money, his topcoat and his new felt hat. Nothing else seemed to be missing.

By the time the assault was reported in the newspaper, a tall stranger brought wax impressions of some keys to a locksmith whose accent indicated he was from Dixie. The locksmith reproduced the keys and asked no questions.

A week later, when no one was watching, the cleaning woman at the mint spent some time trying keys in Madrass' doors until she found those that fit. She hung those keys in her broom closet behind a dusting cloth.

It took Miss Harrington longer to produce a reverse of both

sides of a double eagle that would pass Ben's inspection. Finally, she gave him a pair which appeared identical to the original even under a magnifying glass.

"Jack," said Ben at breakfast the next morning, "I want to meet your friend in Sacramento. You ready for a boat ride?"

"Ain't got nothing better to do."

They finished their meal and caught a ferry to Sacramento. There Jack introduced him to Buck Andrews, a wiry old man with a Georgia cracker accent. Ben asked him if he made glazed bricks.

"I could if somebody asked for them."

"Are you equipped to make something smaller than a brick, say like a plate?" Ben asked.

"No, it would take a special kiln and special clay. I could put it together shortly. What you got in mind?"

Ben unwrapped the brass templates of the coin and said, "A merchant in San Francisco wants to give one to every customer who spends twenty dollars in his store. Spend a double eagle and get one back free."

"Seems like a good marketing idea," the brickmaker said.

"I wonder if you could make me a few thousand of them. We may need more later."

Andrews took the two pieces of brass and examined the intricate engraving. Then he looked at Jack and said, "I suppose this has something to do with Abraham Lincoln,"

"Could be," Ben answered. "You should make a profit selling what we don't need."

"You know, that just might happen if I can make them out of really fine potter's clay for ten for a penny and sell them for two cents each. That has real possibilities."

"It's also one way you can distance yourself from me. If you just sell them as clay copies, you've no control over how they're used if somebody wants to do something else with them."

"That's true."

"You'll do it then?"

"Glad to. Been waiting for a chance to get in this war."

187

"If you get started on it right away, we'll begin lining up customers for your surplus. We'll want thousands of them in circulation before we start cooking. We'll use them as salt pork and onions in our omelet."

"Salt pork and onions? What's he talkin' about?"

"He's a bit strange sometimes," Gervais said.

"We'll want our copies as near the weight of the originals as you can make them," Ben said before they left for the return trip down the river.

"Among all your friends do you have an alchemist?" asked Ben as they rode the sidewheeler home, "I need someone who can turn clay disks into gold."

The extra thousand in Buck Andrews' first delivery went to a jeweler who had learned his trade in Charleston. He gold-plated them.

14
CAPTAIN MIKE

Before Ben's "omelet" could be made operational, Bart cracked the eggs for "six fries" with the news he brought to the attic room one night before the new year had tarnished.

Pulling off his boots he asked,"Any word out of the mint?"

"No." Ben said. "Everything's waiting for exactly the right time."

"I don't know what you're waiting for, but the mint ain't awaitin' for you."

"What's up?"

"My friend who drives for Wells Fargo says they're preparing a shipment to go by sea day after tomorrow and I think we ought to try for it. He says it's going to be big."

"I don't want any of those working in our main offensive to be even remotely connected with what has got to be a completely separate operation," Ben said.

"Since you're the only one who knows what's going on, I don't think you ought to be involved in this," Bart said.

"Let's reconnoiter a bit," Ben said. "I know from other sources that the vault is about full. I agree with your friend. They're ready to make a shipment and since snow has all the passes blocked, this one will go by sea. Now, do you have an idea on how we can divert that shipment?"

"I think so. They've got some real good taverns in this town and I've been busy cultivating a few bandits."

"Fine. This one's yours, Bart. Good hunting. It's my advice that you pick the best troops to lead the charge."

Bart blew out the light and went to bed. He was up before daylight the next morning.

"Be careful," Ben said as Bart opened the door to leave. "You're the only brother I've got and I don't want to have to tell Mama you ain't comin' home."

Bart grinned as he started down the stairs to Mrs. Gervais' pantry where he helped himself to some ham, eggs and coffee. Fortified with this he rode to a rundown area called Sidney Town and found the shack of a man named Mike who had helped him load his freight wagon one time. Mike was doing what he usually did in the morning, sleeping off a drunk. Bart built a fire, made some coffee and started ham and eggs frying. Then he shook the snoring man who looked like a bum.

"Mike.. Mike..wake up. I need you to do some work for me."

The man let out a snort, belched and reached for the bottle sitting nearby. Draining the last drop of home-brewed whiskey, he sat up. Bart handed him a cup of black coffee. Mike's hand shook as he held it. He drank and Bart filled his cup again. It took a little longer to empty the second.

By the time Bart had ham and eggs ready, Mike had worked himself over to a crate that served as a table and, sitting on a smaller box, began to eat.

"To what do I owe this hospitality?" he asked.

"I'm giving you an advance on a little job I want done."

"Can I have a drink first?"

"Now, Mike, you know you won't get any work done if you start drinking first. You do the work first and maybe, if you keep real busy, you'll make it through the day without drinking."

"Ya reckon?"

"Maybe."

"What kind of work do you have in mind?"

"How long has it been since you were cashiered from the U.S.

army?" Bart asked.

"Three, four years. Why?"

"How would you like to sign up for Confederate duty?"

"I might go sober for that."

"That's what I thought. Can you recruit me four other men of similar sentiments?"

"Like recruiting for free drinks. What you want done?"

"I need five men who'll ride guard on a Wells Fargo wagon while we relieve the Yankees of some of their gold."

While Mike finished his breakfast, Bart outlined his plan.

"Timing is the important thing," he ended. "Everything's got to be done exactly on time."

"You really mean to take that gold to Jeff Davis?"

"I do if it can be done."

"I'm ready."

"You and your men be ready tomorrow morning when the wagon driven by Pigeon Platt leaves the Fargo livery. Follow it but not too close until it stops. When Pigeon gets down, y'all move in and take your places. Do it right and I'll put thirty dollars worth of grub on your shelf."

"That's about what I got in the U.S. Army for a whole month.We'll be there."

Bart went to find the talkative driver of a Wells Fargo rig.

"You really think you know where that vein of gold is up in the Sierra Nevada?" Bart asked as they ate plates of stew at Irish Nell's Cafe.

Pigeon got his name from the fact that he was a short man with bowed legs whose rear swayed like a walking chicken.

"Positive," said Pigeon. "The only thing keeping me from it is a grub stake. I'd have to move a lot of dirt to find it and would take perty near a whole summer of diggin' jest to git to it. It's there all right. Trouble is I need a better than average grub stake. I been savin' to go. Then the bank went bust. My time is runnin' out, because others know about that vein."

"Pigeon, would you like a partner in this?"

"Not really, but I might if the terms was right. What you got in mind?"

"I could grub stake you and you could chuck your job and go work your claim while I stay here. My freight line would keep us both in beans until you find that gold. I'm willing to gamble on it if you'll pay me back with interest when you find it. "

Pigeon did not stop to think about it.

"It's a deal," he said and they shook hands on it.

"You tell me what you need and I'll have it ready for you tomorrow," Bart said. They made up lists while eating.

Pigeon Platt was already in the seat of his Wells Fargo wagon when Bart showed up and asked him in an off-handed manner, "Have you heard any more about the mint's shipment?"

"Not d'rectly, but I've been assigned to pick up somethin' there about ten o'clock tomorrow morning."

"You be there by nine. I'll have your grub stake ready, and you can be on your way to the gold fields before dark."

Ben stood outside the mint at three that afternoon. He met Shadow in the livery stable at ten as usual.

"I've got just one question." Ben said, "Do you have any idea when they're going to empty the vault?"

"Yea, mister. Cain't be sure, but somethin's goin' t'morroa'."

"Thanks, Shadow."

"Y'er welcome, mister."

Pigeon Platt started his run to the mint early the next morning. Three blocks from the stable where the two horses had been hitched to his boxed wagon, he found Bart standing beside a burro loaded down with supplies needed for prospecting. The man beside Bart was holding a horse. Platt stopped.

"Hi, Pigeon," Bart greeted him. "Here's your grub stake. Are you ready to go?"

"I ought to finish this run first," Pigeon said.

"Somebody may beat you to that gold."

Pigeon hesitated.

"Get down, give me your keys, mount up, ride out and don't look back."

Pigeon jumped off his seat and the stranger holding the horse took his place. Before he had settled in the saddle, the Wells Fargo freight wagon began to move. Mike, shaved, armed with a rifle and looking like Army, climbed up beside the driver. Two armed horsemen took positions ahead of the wagon's team and two more dropped in place behind. Pigeon Platt looked around. Bart was gone. Platt rode towards Sacramento.

The procession arrived at the delivery door of the mint about nine o'clock. A vault of blue sky covered the city though the streets were muddy from recent rains.

"You're early," remarked Madrass as the wagon pulled into the alley.

"We have received intelligence that someone has learned of this shipment and is planning to rob it on the way to the ship," Mike said. "Wells Fargo feels it would be better if we moved it early before the raid is set up."

"But my security people aren't here yet," Madrass protested.

"Our informant tells us one of your guards may be part of the plot so we've got our own men. Wells Fargo is responsible for this shipment. We'll get it to the ship."

"Where's Pigeon?" Madrass asked.

"He was sent off on another run to mislead the highwaymen. Listen, Mr. Madrass, I've got a Wells Fargo wagon, the key to unlock it and the shipping orders. If you don't mind, let's get it loaded so that we can be on our way before they get set up to rob us."

"Yes, of course," said Madrass and opened the vault.

Under the watchful eyes of Madrass and Woods, fifteen boxes of gold bullion were transferred from the vault to the wagon which was then carefully locked. Mike drove out and Madrass and Woods walked to their buggies in the back lot.

"You wait here for the security guard and bring them along as soon as they're ready," Madrass told Woods. "I'm going to follow that wagon to see that nothing happens to it."

He got in his carriage, turned the horse in the narrow lot behind the mint and started for the street. Blocking the entrance to the alley was a large freight wagon.

"Where is the driver of this rig?" Madrass screamed.

"Here he comes," said a young woman standing nearby. She wore a black dress and coal bucket bonnet. Bart, carrying a large crate on his back, struggled across the muddy street.

"Move it! Move it!" Madrass shouted.

"Delivered this to the wrong address," Bart said as he set the box down in front of Madrass' horse.

"If that is your wagon, move it. I'm in a hurry."

"Certainly, sir. Right away." Bart took his seat and whipped the mules into motion. "The box, you idiot. The box," screamed Madrass. "Get that box out of the way!"

"Come back! Come back!" shouted the young woman.

Seeing Bart's wagon disappearing around a corner, Madrass jumped from his buggy and tried to move the box himself. It weighed about three hundred pounds. Running into the mint, he rounded up several men and they ran to help him move the crate. Bart was back when they reached the street.

"Stupid of me to go off and leave the box sitting there," he told Madrass as he unlocked the back of his wagon, "but you were in such a hurry to get out, it just slipped my mind."

The four men from the mint struggled to lift the crate into Bart's wagon.

"Here, let me give you a hand," Bart said and stepped around to take one end. His fingers slipped as he tried to slide the thing into the back of the wagon.

The crate jerked out of the hands of the other men and fell to the street where it slowly sank six inches in thick mud.

Madrass' men wrestled with it for a few minutes. The mud produced a strong suction holding it down. In a few minutes they were above their ankles in thick ooze.

"Have you got a rope?" Bart asked.

"Get a rope," Madrass screamed at a mint employee who had come out to watch. When the rope arrived, Bart tossed the middle of it to one of the men wading in the muddy street.

"Circle this under one end of the box," he ordered. When this was done, he tied the two loose ends together, looped the knotted

194

ends over his right shoulder and pulled. Slowly the mud released its grip and the crate began to stand on end.

The mint's security guard chose this moment to ride up. Bart's feet slipped. The rope jerked. The box, which was almost upright, twisted and slammed back into the muck at the feet of the two lead horses. They reared against the horses behind them. The rope slipped and became entangled in the legs of a skittish mare. One of the riders fell into the mud. Bart reached to help him, got him about to his feet and then appeared to slip. He released his hold on the guard, stumbled a couple of steps and came up under the chest of another horse. In a move that was almost too quick for any to see, he straightened his back and legs and lifted the mustang and his rider off the ground. The horse fell on his side in the middle of the street, tossing the astonished rider into the mud. The horse jumped to his feet and bolted down the thoroughfare.

"I'm truly sorry about all this," said Bart as he helped one of the men to his feet.

"Move it! Move it!" screamed Woods from the seat of his buggy.

"Clear the street. Clear the street. Get out of my way!" shouted Madrass from the boardwalk, while the laughter from the gathered crowd and cursing from the mud-splattered men echoed among the buildings. The woman in black stood watching.

Once again the men looped the rope around the end of the box. Once again Bart strained as he pulled. This time he got the crate standing on end against the opened door of his wagon and two men helped him lift it inside.

"I'm really very sorry to have delayed you," Bart said as he climbed onto the seat and then carefully shifted the crate to balance his load. "I do hope it hasn't caused you any inconvenience."

Madrass was dancing on the boardwalk.

"Move it! Move it!" he screamed.

Bart locked the doors of his vehicle, walked to the boardwalk to retrieve his hat and climbed back up.

"Good day to you." He tipped his hat and whipped the mules

into motion, proceeding only enough to clear the alley. Madrass bolted out and passed Bart. The woman who had been watching walked to the freight wagon and climbed up to the seat beside Bart.

"You are impossible. Still I loved it, so I reckon I'm impossible, too," said 'Bama Smith and they laughed until they hurt as Bart steered his mules after Madrass.

Meanwhile, the Wells Fargo wagon made an unscheduled stop at the loading dock behind Collier's Construction Co. In not more than fifteen minutes the lids were pried off seven boxes of coins, the gold was dumped into three coffins and replaced with a dry mixture of sand and cement.

"I wish we'd had more cement," said Collier to Mike.

"Too bad," Mike said as he and the driver got back in their seats, "but we could not have spent much more time here anyway. Thanks."

As it was they were barely on the street again when Madrass,Woods and the mud-covered security guard caught up with them and doubled the escort to the Market Street Wharf.

Arriving at the waterfront, they all stood guard as the wagon was opened and stevedores began transferring fifteen boxes into the hold of the ship.

When the Wells Fargo wagon was empty, the driver turned it around and started back towards the city. His "guard" began to disperse. Mike was riding the wagon. A half a block from the wharf he heard his name called. He looked into an alley and saw Bart standing in the shadows. Dismounting from the shotgun seat, he walked over to Bart. The wagon rolled on.

"Somethin' the matter?" he asked.

"No, sir, you handled it so well I've got you another job."

"Not for me, you ain't. I'm headin' for the nearest bar. I gotta have me a drink," said Mike and turned to leave.

"Captain," said Bart, "how would you like to serve with General Lee?"

Mike turned back.

"How are you ever going to arrange that?"

"Take this coat and get on board that ship."

"That all?" said Mike suspiciously, taking the coat.

"Pretty much but not quite. This coat has two things in it, a wallet in one pocket and an envelope sewed into its lining. The wallet has a passage to New York and enough spending money to keep you. The envelope has instructions to President Jefferson Davis on how he is to get the gold you just helped requisition. I want you to get on board that ship and deliver the envelope to the president."

"Just like that?"

"You tell the guard you have a message from Col.Ben Gordyne and the president will be right glad to see you."

"How's that going to get me a commission with Lee?"

"That envelope also contains a recommendation that you be given the commission."

"You think he'll do it?"

"Yes, if you stay sober enough to deliver that envelope."

Mike looked long at Bart.

"You think I can do it?" he asked.

"I'm trusting you, Mike."

"Thanks, pal." Mike shook Bart's hand and marched towards the ship.

An hour later three water-tight coffins arrived at the wharf in a Harrington Brothers Mortuary service wagon. They were consigned to Wilson's Funeral Home, Richmond, Va., by way of Pastorman's Mortuary in Washington. D.C. The invoice said they would be picked up on arrival.

The coffins were loaded on board and two hours later the Panama Steamer took the tide through the Golden Gate. During the sea voyage, the sand-cement mix was supposed to absorb water and very rapidly harden into hundred pound blocks of concrete.

Wells Fargo found its wagon parked in the regular place. Pinned on the seat was a note. "I quit. Gone to the diggings. Pigeon Platt." Since everyone knew of Platt's dream, this was not unexpected.The Panama Steamer would take three weeks to make

197

the trip south to Central America. There the ship's cargo would be loaded on railroad cars belonging to the line built by Cornelius Vanderbilt between the oceans. At Colon on the Atlantic side, the fifteen crates and three coffins would wait about a week for another ship that would stop at Cuba before moving north to New York.

15

HUNTERS

Legs Pharson was backtracking.

After two months of prowling through Denver and visiting mining towns spread over the eastern slope of the Rockies, the Pinkerton agent realized he had gone up a box canyon in his search for Mrs. Heather D. Wanderman. He decided that she had never been in Denver so like a good hound he returned to the last place with a clear scent, the arroyo on the bank of the North Platte in Wyoming. He went to Fort Laramie, a bustling settlement. In addition to the military post the town had a stage stop for the Oregon Trail and served as a supply center for Wyoming and western Nebraska.

Legs passed around Heather's picture and asked questions of everyone who came into the trading post. He found no tracks.

"Somewhere," he complained to the proprietor, "there must be someone who saw four riders go through."

"Junk DuBris would know," said the trader.

"Who's Junk DuBris?"

"He watches the trail like a vulture. Ain't nobody goes through these parts that he don't see. He and his partner are half-outlaw. They live in a shanty between here and Fort Kearney and they picks the droppings of the wagon trains moving through. They's worse 'n crows when it comes to stealing. Real slick and real mean. He'd kill for a woman that pretty and I ain't saying what he'd do with her when he got her."

"Is it possible nobody's seen them go through because Dubris got to them first?"

"I'd say it's likely."

The next morning Pharson saddled his mustang and rode east.

Usually Junk wasn't easily found, but as summer faded the wagon trains stopped coming through. It was time for DuBris and Scythe to pack up their gleanings for the journey to the Missouri River. Legs found them moving a heavily loaded wagon east along the Mormon Trail.

"Good afternoon," said Pharson, touching the brim of his hat.

"Same to you." DuBris slowed down.

"Would you be Junk DuBris?" asked the detective.

"Might be."

"Have you seen this woman?" He handed over the picture of Heather.

DuBris examined it carefully.

"What if I have?"

"It could be worth a thousand dollars to you if you can help me locate her."

"One thousand? Ruby said her parents would pay fifty thousand to anyone bringing her home, and you want to cut me in for only one thousand?"

"I don't know what Miss Hunsford told you, but the Pinkerton Detective Agency is only authorized to give a one thousand reward for information leading to the recovery of Mrs. Wanderman."

"I aim to hold 'em to fifty thousand if I ever find her. They owe me that much. But, before I do that, I'm gonna kill that black-headed heifer and the two lizards with them."

"So you have seen them."

"Oh, yeah, I more'n seen 'em. I rescued the women from Indians what were takin' them off for their own pleasure. We killed two of them Indians and wounded two others. For our trouble they treat us like a couple of buffalo chips."

200

"So the two men were with them?"

"Not when we took them away from the Indians. They rode off by themselves in the middle of the night and the two men caught up with them after we'd finished off the Indians. That's when all the trouble started."

"Which way were the women riding when they were by themselves?" Legs asked.

"West."

"West?" Pharson muttered. "But they didn't go into Fort Laramie. Why west? What's west of here?"

"Not much exceptin' Indians and mountains between here and Oregon."

"What about California?"

"Nobody goes this way to California anymore. Since the Army put in Fort Douglas near Salt Lake City and the Overland Stage cut through south of the Great Salt Lake, everybody going to California goes by way of Denver."

"If you wanted to hide your trail, you could still go this way," the detective said.

"Yeah, I suppose so."

"California. Always California, Why? What are they going to do in California?" Pharson said, returning the picture to his wallet. "So I'll go to San Francisco and find out."

"Not before spring you ain't," Junk told him.

"Pinkerton kin be our bird dog," he said to Sonny as he watched Legs ride off to Fort Laramie. "He'll find them and after we get rid of this load in St. Joe we're headin' for San Francisco and maybe pick us up fifty thousand and enjoy ourselves while doin' it."

Legs rode back to Denver where he learned all the passes were closed. It was April when he finally took a room in a boarding house near the Overland Stage's western terminal and began searching San Francisco for Heather Wanderman. DuBris and Scythe were not far behind. However, they spent little time looking for Heather. It was easier to find the detective.

A few days later Jack approached the table where Ben and

Bart were having their evening meal in the Gervais Cafe.

"Somebody tall and thin as a light pole is flashin' a picture of our house guest around the police station askin' questions," he said.

"Pinkerton?" asked Bart.

"Yeah."

"What did the police tell him?" Ben asked.

"Too many rebels on the police force for him to get any information there. They sent him on a snipe hunt to Monterey."

"He'll be back and he's trouble," Bart said. "That man has trailed us all the way from Toledo, Ohio. He's better'n any trail dog I ever had and I've had some good ones."

"You want I should have him dropped in the bay?" Gervais said. "Even a good hound can't follow a trail under water."

"Might not be a bad idea," Bart said.

"Sometimes it's better to go around a mountain than to try to climb over," said Ben.

"Does he always talk in riddles?" Gervais asked.

"Usually," answered Bart. "You wait a minute or two and he'll say, 'There are three ways to handle the Pinkerton Agent. One...'"

He stopped talking as Heather approached them.

"There are three ways to handle the man who is hunting Mrs. Wanderman," said Ben in a confidential tone that only spurred Heather's curiosity. "One, we could follow Jack's suggestion and dispose of him. Two, we could have Mrs. Wanderman locked up in a jail which has a sympathetic jailer. But I have a better idea."

"What's that?" Bart asked.

"Jack, isn't it about time you went back to the mine?"

"I hadn't planned on going back. I'm too old for that kind of work and the gold fever ain't as hot as it once was."

"Would it make panning gold more attractive if you took Mrs. Wanderman into the mountains with you?" Ben asked.

"It might, but I doubt if Liza would approve."

"What kind of conspiracy are you rebels hatching now?" Heather asked as she filled Ben's cup with coffee.

"I had it in my mind that you might be gettin' tired of being cooped up here. You're looking poorly. It'd be good for your health to get out in the open air for a while."

"What are you talking about?"

"The man from Pinkerton is in San Francisco."

"He is?"

"Yep. He's showing your picture all over town. I figure we'll have to move you. So what I want Mr. Gervais to do is take you prospecting in the Sierra Nevada Mountains for a few months. I hear it's beautiful in the mountains during the summer. You'll make a real nice gold miner's daughter."

"I've got a daddy and he isn't Jack Gervais."

"What do you think, Jack? With some help, do you reckon you could keep a couple of women out of sight until fall?"

"Both of 'em?" Gervais asked.

"Yeah, it would be mean to send her up there alone with an ugly rascal like you. Besides I don't think Liza would let you go with just one."

"I see what you mean, though I'm enjoying my work in the cabinet shop and there's considerable demand for it right now, if you know what I mean. But I've got a couple of partners to work my claim this year. They'd sure like a good cook."

"Well, I ain't heard nobody say she's a good cook," Bart said. "She's just passing. A little help from Ruby would improve it some."

"A caveman wouldn't know good cooking from the leftovers of a vulture," Heather responded to their laughter.

"Can your partners be trusted?' Ben asked.

"Sure," Gervais answered. "I'd trust Spook Haynes and Paul Painter with anything I've got."

"Seein' as you ain't got much, that ain't saying much," said Ben. "What I want to know is can they be trusted with Confederate secrets and two fair-to-middlin' pretty Yankee women?"

"Paul and Spook is both from Dixie. Between the two of them they's nigh unto a hundred and fifty years old and spent most of that time in the mountains to git shed of women. They'll do."

"Can they leave tomorrow?" Ben asked.

"It'll take some doin', but I think so if I can find them tonight. If I'm gonna do that, I'd better get started."

Gervais pushed away from the table and left.

"Colonel Gordyne, I hate you," Heather said.

Ben stood and stared at her standing very close to him.

"Do you really, Heather?" he asked.

She looked up at him and did not answer. He read her face. The fire went out of her. The tautness of her cheeks relaxed. The thin line of her clenched lips widened as they parted slightly.

"I'm sorry, Heather," he said. "It won't be for long. When we finish our work here, I'll send for you and I'll take you home."

"You called me Heather," she whispered.

The city was still sleeping when the Gordynes and Liza Gervais watched a party of four prospectors mounting up outside the boarding house. Heather's foot was in the stirrup as she turned to look at Ben standing on the porch.

"Heather," he said, "I'd like a word with you."

She gave her head an angry toss and tensed her muscles to saddle up. Turning her head, she looked at him again. A beam from the dying moon brushed over his lean face. She took her foot from the stirrup and stepped towards him. He came down the steps to meet her, reached out a hand and drew her to him.

"Heather," he said softly, "when this is all over, win or lose, will you marry me?"

"Oh, Ben. Yes, Ben. I'll marry you now if you're of a mind."

His left arm circled her waist. She tilted her face to him and her arms circled his neck. His right hand touched her cheek. The kiss was tender and prolonged.

"I'm of a mind," he said as he released her, "but you have a duty and I have a duty. When that's done, I'll ask you again."

"I may not say 'yes' again, Colonel Gordyne." But she laughed when she said it and turned back to her horse.

"Spook Haynes. Paul Painter," Ben called to the prospectors who were already on their horses.

"Yes, Colonel Gordyne," they answered.

"You take good care of her, y'hear?"

"Yes, sir."

The party of four horses and two burros moved east towards the mountains.

A few days later, Legs stopped looking directly for Heather. He received a wire instructing him to drop that case and start trying to find out what alchemy was used to transform seven boxes of gold coins into blocks of concrete. He was advised that the transformation could have taken place anywhere during the three-month sea and land voyage from San Francisco to New York. He was to start looking at the point of origin.

Legs had other ideas. As he stepped out of the Western Union office he met Junk DuBris and Sonny Scythe. These encounters happened frequently and the detective knew they were not coincidental.

"Found any trace of Mrs. Wanderman?" DuBris asked.

"You'll have to find her yourself. I just got orders to discontinue that investigation."

"We ain't about to quit looking for fifty thousand dollars."

"One thousand," Legs reminded him, "and she may not be around here any more. Several million dollars in gold is missing and I've been instructed to find it. From what they tell me it looks like the rebels who have Mrs. Wanderman are the magicians who made the gold disappear."

"You mean if we find her, we'll find all that gold?" Sonny asked in astonishment.

"Could be, but if they've got that much gold, would there be any reason for them to stay in San Francisco? It seems likely they took the same ship east with the gold. They're probably spending it in New York."

He said the last to divert their attention because another thought trickled into his mind as he turned away from them.

Nope, he said to himself. If they've gone east, Mrs. Wanderman would be safe home in Washington by now. Those scoundrels are still here some place and Mrs. Wanderman is with them. If I can find that gold, I'll find her.

He set out to investigate and started by getting acquainted with the people who patronized the taverns around the mint. It wasn't long before the detective discovered a number of men who remembered the time a teamster tipped a horse over in the mud on the street in front of the U.S.Mint. They were still laughing about it.

Then one day a fellow who shared his table was retelling the story to a newcomer and casually added, "That were the strongest man I ever seen. He just lifted that horse and rider clean off the ground. It was the day of the last big shipment. Mr. Madrass near exploded."

"What?" Legs said.

"Madrass almost exploded."

"Who is Madrass?"

"He manages the mint. He was trying to get his buggy out of that alley to follow that gold shipment to the dock and this guy had the alley blocked."

"How long was the alley blocked?"

"I don't know. Fifteen or twenty minutes I reckon. So much was goin' on, it's hard to say."

"Maybe a half hour?"

"Maybe. Why?"

Pharson did not answer. He picked up his hat and left as fast as the long legs for which he was named could take him. Those same legs took him immediately to the mint where he introduced himself to Madrass and asked, "May I have a few minutes of your time?"

"Really not now. I'm far too busy."

"Too busy to talk about seven crates of your gold that turned into cement some place between your shipping dock and New York? It may have disappeared before it left your vault."

"That's impossible."

"I'm sure you are right, but do you want to talk about it?"

"Yes, yes, of course."

They went into the office.

206

"I watched them load those boxes on board the ship at the Market Street Wharf myself. Every one of them was there and none of them had been switched. I'm sure of it."

"Tell me about that morning," Pharson said, and got the story as far as Matthew Madrass remembered it.

Then he went to Wells Fargo to try to interview the driver assigned to the wagon that day and was told that he had turned in his vehicle and gone prospecting.

"May I guess that he left the day he took a gold shipment from the mint to the wharf?" Pharson asked.

"Yes, I believe you're right. Why?" The supervisor looked surprised.

"Seven boxes turned up in New York filled with cement."

"So Pigeon Platt did his prospecting right here in San Francisco."

"It's possible, but I don't think so."

"Where is that gold?"

"I'd guess it's in Richmond helping Jeff Davis buy guns."

"You don't mean it."

Legs nodded and stood to leave. He walked the route from the mint to the wharf asking every storekeeper along the way if they had noticed anything unusual the day of the shipment and got only negative answers. One thing he noticed was that a lot of the people he questioned had southern accents.

That night Shadow was waiting for Ben at the stable. She told him of the detective's visit to the mint.

"What's he lookin' fer?" she asked.

"Somebody took part of that last shipment after it left the mint," Ben told her. "He's looking for it."

"Should I hold up what I's doin'?"

"I don't think what he is doing has any connection with our operation. In fact it might throw him off. But, Shadow, it's entirely up to you. You're in a dangerous position and I don't want you to get hurt. You can stop if you wish."

"Why'd you say what he's doin' might he'p what we's doin'?"

"He knows that gold was taken after it left the mint, so it's not

207

likely that he'll expect we're doin' something inside the mint too. He may think that we work outside because we can't get in. You can be sure they're going to be guarding every dollar that goes out. Unless you see them begin to tighten things up inside, I don't think you're in any more danger now than you were before."

Legs mailed his report to the New York office. He concluded it by saying, "The gold has probably been spent to help finance the Confederate Army. I know how it was stolen, but I doubt if you could prove any of it. That's two shipments they have diverted. Somebody had better be watching the next. In the meantime, I will continue to look for Mrs. Wanderman, Miss Hunsford and the two rebels who masterminded this operation. I am convinced they are around here some place waiting for the next shipment to go out."

While he watched, DuBris and Scythe watched him.

"He may say they've left town," Junk told Sonny, "but I've a notion that as long as he stays in San Francisco, he's pretty sure they're still somewhere about."

16
THE DIGGIN'S

Gervais' caskets were built in two styles. On the outside they looked identical. What he called the regular kind were large, copper-lined boxes to hold bodies. The second version had an interior that was divided into five chambers. At each end and in the middle were smaller sections separated from each other by two larger spaces. When the three smaller sections were filled with gold packed in straw, the box would be evenly balanced and the approximately two hundred pounds of coins each box could hold would not slide around or rattle when the casket was moved.

Lids were not hinged. When a casket was ready for use, a bead of beeswax was run around the lip. The lid was put on like the lid of a boiler and bolted down with wingnuts. The wax sealed it and made it air-tight.

Before Heather and Ruby were sent off to the diggings, Jack had finished seven coffins. Three of them were stored under boards in the workshop where the special sections gradually filled with gold. During the winter and spring Shadow continued to exchange the plated ceramic disks for gold coins in the boxes on the scales in the mint's vault.

She wasn't searched when she entered the building. Every day she carried in a few clay coins. She left her work clothes in the broom closet and never had money, real or counterfeit, on her when the guard searched her before she went home. The guard let her use his keys to get into the other parts of the building to do her work. In this way, when Madrass' keys were duplicated, a key from the guard's ring was also copied.

At least once every night the guard left his post. As he went to the corner of the back lot, he would invariably say to Shadow, "Keep an eye on things. I need to check on Johnny's house." The back door could only be opened from the inside. If the other guard was not present, Shadow had to let him in. While he went outside, she opened the vault and made Ben's omelet, substituting gold-plated clay disks for twenty-dollar gold pieces.

The synthetic weighed less than the originals, but the geometric fact that groups of circles always leave spaces between them supplied the answer to that problem. To make up the difference in weight, Shadow simply filtered sand into the space between stacks of counterfeit double eagles until the reading on the scale exactly matched the tally sheet.

She dropped the gold pieces into the spittoon near the entrance to Madrass' office. When the guard knocked, she opened the door for him. The coins stayed in the spittoon all night and most of the next day. About the first thing Shadow did each afternoon when she came to work was change the water in the spittoon. She dumped the contents into an old boot hidden under weeds in the corner of the back lot. Once a week she picked up the trash in that area and added it to the contents of a barrel parked outside for the trash wagon.

While she worked on the inside, a great deal of junk collected in the alley behind the mint. Bart was in charge of littering the back lot so that there would always be an old boot or shoe for Shadow to use. To his amusement, Ben got the job of hauling off the trash thrown over the fence because Madrass might remember Bart as the fellow who blocked his alley.

Slowly, the caskets in Gervais' workshop gradually accumulated a substantial amount of bullion and the vault at the mint collected an equal number of clay disks.

Ben had other duties besides collecting trash. One of them

was to watch the Pinkerton agent. He discovered that Junk DuBris and Sonny Scythe were also watching Legs.

"I knew we should have hung them," Bart said, when Ben told him.

"There's no question in my mind what they're looking for and they want Pinkerton to do their finding for them." Ben agreed with his brother. It had been a mistake to let the junkmen go free.

"They're thinking murder. Remember what Junk swore when we turned them loose to walk barefoot to Fort Laramie?"

"Yes. I'm glad Heather and Ruby are in the mountains. They're safer with grizzly bears than with DuBris and Scythe."

Ben had not reckoned on the news network of sparsely settled country. It was one of those rare days when San Francisco sweated under a hot sun. Junk retired early to Drake's Saloon, leaving Sonny to lounge around with his eye on Pharson. He moved to the bar, standing next to a couple of tough-looking, bearded prospectors.

"Ol' Jack Gervais done struck it rich this time," said one of them. He had a broken nose. "Ain't even there to work it and he's makin' a mint."

"That a fact?" asked the other man. He had a face like an Indian and hair the color of pinestraw.

"Yeah, he may have sent that light-haired woman to the mountains to cook and keep house for his two partners, but it be my notion she brought more luck than bacon. His partners don't talk much but if'n what I saw be jest a sample of what they're pulling outa thet hole, her name oughta be 'Lady Luck' 'steada 'Heather.'"

Junk almost spilled his drink.

"She's pretty, but the blackheaded one looks more like luck to me," said the other fellow.

"Her name wouldn't be Ruby, would it?" asked DuBris.

The two miners looked at him for the first time.

"Could be," said the man with the nose scar. "You know her?"

"We've met," said Junk. "Been a long time. I've been wondering what ever happened to those two. You say they're workin' the mining camps now? That's a long way down from the docks of St. Louis."

"They ain't doin' nothin' in the mountains 'ceptin' helpin' Jack Gervais' partners work that claim," said the man with the molasses-colored hair. "And, mister, if you want to stay healthy, I'd give you some advice. Watch what you say about those two. You may be short, but there are men that'd kill you for what you just said."

Junk's eyes narrowed. Better to be careful, he thought. "Maybe I got the wrong women."

"You sure has," said Scarface. Junk put his drink down and backed away. The two prospectors watched him go. Outside he found Sonny.

"We don't need Pinkerton no more," he said. "I've found that fifty thousand by myself. It's prospecting in the mountains and from what I hear we may be able to pick up a good bit more than that while we make the four of them bleed."

The next morning they mounted up and rode out. What they did not notice was that Legs Pharson was watching them from the upstairs window of his boarding house. He kept shaking his head. Junk and Sonny were taking trail gear with them. Something was up.

The two took the ferry over San Francisco Bay and rode on into Sacramento. There, while moving around hangouts where prospectors seemed to gather, they picked up rumors of a big strike to the northeast. At the federal building where mining claims were filed, they found on a map the location for Gervais diggings. It took them two weeks to reach the site on the slopes of a mountain.

****

In San Francisco Ben conferred with 'Bama Smith, Bart and Gervais.

"Any of you seen Dubris or Scythe recently?" he asked.

"No," said 'Bama. The others shook their heads.

"That bothers me more than somewhat," Ben said.

"Why?" asked 'Bama.

"Pinkerton is still around and they're gone," Ben answered. "As long as I could keep my eye on them, I figured I knew what they're doing. They smelled bad enough when I could see them. When they can't be found, I smell trouble. One evening Junk and Sonny bought trail supplies. The next day they vanished. Y'all scatter out and see if you can get a scent of them. I think it's time I talked to Mr. P. League Pharson."

That night, as Legs approached his lodgings after a day spent investigating the same matter that troubled Ben, a man's voice called out of the darkness between two buildings. "Mr. Pharson, may I have a word with you?"

The detective tried to see down the alley.

"You don't know me, but you've followed me all the way from Toledo," said Ben. "You're good. Now, maybe you can help me."

"Why should I help you?"

"I know where Mrs. Warren Wanderman is and you've spent a year looking for her."

"That's true. How may I help you?"

"Do you know where Junk DuBris went?"

"As a matter of fact, I think I do, and if you value Mrs. Wanderman's life, I think you'd better get to her in a hurry."

"Why?" asked Ben. Sudden fear squeezed his throat.

"I saw DuBris and Scythe ride out of here early four days ago. They didn't return, and I began to wonder why. I spoke to them the day before. They told me that as long as I was around Junk was certain I was staying here because of Mrs. Wanderman, and they'd stay, too. The next day they rode out with trail gear. I suspected that somehow they'd found out something about her whereabouts. That bothered me because those two think they can hold her for a fifty thousand ransom. I expect they have other things in mind for both women. So I started asking questions. Today I visited Drake's Saloon which they frequent. The proprietor remembered Junk's visit five days ago. He also remembered that Junk was talking to two prospectors."

Legs was trying to see Ben. But there was only a shadow.

"I located the two men. From what they told me, I think Junk is on the way to get Mrs. Wanderman. I assumed the two men they said were working the mine were friends of yours. It was my intention to head up there in the morning. I hope we're not too late."

"Thank you, Mr. Pharson," said Ben. "I hope so too."

Gordyne started to push by the detective.

"Just a minute, sir," said Legs. "Do you know where that mine is?"

"I don't, but I know who does."

"Who?"

"That you don't need to know."

"May I go with you?"

"I'd like to have you, Mr. Pharson, but I'm afraid it would conflict with my duty."

In a few steps he was across the street. He freed his horse from the hitching post, jumped into the saddle and raced for the Gervais boarding house. In less than an hour, he, Bart and Jack were on their way to the mountains.

****

Ten days later Paul Painter pushed a loaded wheelbarrow out of the Gervais mine and dumped the contents into the crusher. Turning back, he found two strangers barring his way. One of men pointed a gun at his chest. The other held a knife by the blade. They both looked surprised.

"You're not the pig who made us walk a hundred miles in our bare feet," said DuBris.

"Where're the lizards who took those two bitches from us?" Scythe spat out the words.

214

"Who are you?" asked Painter. He was shaking.

"Kill him," said Junk.

Sonny flipped his knife. It arched through the air. Painter dropped the wheelbarrow and jerked his hands upward. He was too slow. The knife stabbed into his neck just above the collarbone. It went through his windpipe, cutting off a shout that would have alerted Spook Haynes in the mine and the two women in the cabin. It also cut the artery to Painter's brain.

The dead man pitched forward into the wheelbarrow. It toppled over and rolled down a small grade with a crash.

"What happened?" Spook Haynes stepped out into the sunlight to see. What he saw was the blaze of a six-shooter and an explosion in his head. He fell dead. The women in the cabin heard the shot and rushed to a window.

"It's Junk DuBris," Heather gasped.

Ruby saw Paul and Spook on the ground and screamed.

"Quick, get a rifle," Heather said. She jumped for the holstered gun hanging from a peg by the door. Back at the window, Ruby raised the rifle and fired without aiming. There was nothing to shoot at the second time. Junk and Sonny had rolled out of view.

Wind sighed in the tall trees. Birds continued chattering. A chipmunk scampered for cover as the shadow of a hawk floated over the clearing.

"All right, Heather, come on out and we'll go easy on you," Junk yelled.

There was no answer. He lifted his head to look and nearly lost it as a bullet bounced off a rock inches from his face.

"Damn, that woman can shoot," he muttered. "Give us the gold and you can go," he called and got no response.

Junk, tired of waiting, figured darkness wasn't far off. The cabin had one window and one door.

"I'll stay here and keep'm busy at the window," he told Sonny. "You circle the cabin and git to the door. You're bigger than me. I'll be shootin' at the window while you try the door."

When Sonny was ready, Junk fired a shot which shattered a

pane. Ruby screamed. He fired four more times. While the women watched at the window, Sonny charged the door. The lock broke.

"Drop those guns," he commanded. "Come on, Junk, I got 'em. Now the fun begins."

"Where's the gold?" DuBris stalked into the room.

"Find it," challenged Heather.

"It's easier and more fun to make you tell us," he said. "Tie them up, Sonny, and lay 'em on the floor."

"How we gonna make them talk?" Scythe asked.

"I still got scars from the rope that black-headed heifer used to whip me," DuBris said. "I think a brand would give her some scars she'd keep a while."

Ruby began to cry.

"Quit bawling, y'pig," he ordered kicking at her. "You won't have the brand long 'cause you ain't got long to live, but we're gonna be very careful to keep this other sow alive. Her friend says she's worth fifty thousand on the hoof. I ain't sure her daddy will think so after the hard ridin' we're going give' her for three thousand miles, but he'll pay before he knows that.

"First you're gonna tell us two things, Mrs. Wanderman.Where's the gold hid and where are the two buffalo chips you were riding with in Wyoming, 'cause I aim to lengthen their dyin' and shorten their livin'."

Junk grinned. Sonny laughed. Neither of the women spoke.

"Do you think, Sonny, that a brandin' iron might open their mouths?"

"Even if it don't, a couple of cows like that ought to be branded," Sonny laughed.

"Build a fire while I find a piece of iron we can use,"

Scythe went to the fireplace and set to work while DuBris scrounged around outside looking for a piece of metal. In a few minutes he returned with a long bolt used to hold timbers together in mines.

"Roll that red hot across their flanks a time or two, and I'll bet you my share of the gold they'll talk," he said.

Scythe got the fire burning and his partner was setting the

bolt in it to heat when Heather said, "It's getting late. You must be hungry. After you've had your fun, we won't be in any condition to cook your dinner. Why don't you put these games off until we've had something to eat?"

"A cool one, ain't she?" Sonny said.

"Yeah, and she's probably thinkin' of a way to break out of here while she's cookin'," Junk snorted. "Still we ain't eaten since sunup and I'm hungry."

"A noose'd hold her while she cooks," Sonny said. "Put a rope around her neck, and if she starts actin' funny, I'll just pull it tight."

"That'd work. Go to it."

The line was looped on a slip knot around Heather's throat and her hands and feet were untied.

"You got an hour," DuBris said. "Start cookin'."

Heather went to the kitchen corner of the room and began fixing potatoes, cabbage and steaks. She put a pot of coffee on to boil and mixed up a batch of biscuits. Scythe kept his hands on the rope. DuBris checked his branding iron in the fire. Ruby lay on the floor where they had dumped her. Her eyes were large with fear.

In a little more than the allotted hour, there were four plates on the table, four cups of hot coffee, the necessary utensils and bowls of food.

"Eat," Heather commanded and the two men drew up chairs.

"Looks good," said Junk.

"Sure does," said Sonny.

"Aren't you going to let Ruby eat?" Heather asked.

"No. Why should she? She ain't gonna live long enough to enjoy it." Junk loaded up his plate. "I promised you back in Wyoming I was gonna to kill her. A man's only as good as his word. She's goin' to die tonight, but only after you tell me where that gold is hid."

"Are you going to brand her before or after you do the other things you've got in your minds for us tonight?" she asked.

"Heather, what are you suggesting?" Ruby screamed.

"Now that's somethin' to think about," said Sonny with his mouth full and gravy trickling from his lips.

"She'd be a lot more fun if she were well fed," said Heather. "Besides they always give a condemned man a last meal before they hang him."

"She's right, Sonny," said Junk. "Put the other end of your rope around her neck and let her eat."

The four of them sat at the square table. Sonny's sharp throwing knife lay near his right hand. DuBris' handgun was by his plate.

"Sonny, if this is a sample of her cookin', we're going to eat well on our ride to Washington," said Junk. "I'm really gonna enjoy this trip, I am."

Heather stood.

"Where you going?" demanded Junk.

"Your coffee cup's empty. I thought I'd fill it," she said walking to the wood stove.

"Now ain't that nice?" DuBris grinned.

"Yes, sir. If this is the kinda service we're gonna get, I'm sure gonna enjoy the trip."

They drank their coffee and wiped up the gravy with biscuits.

"Fun time begins," said DuBris pushing back his chair. He carefully picked up his gun and slipped it in his holster as he went to the fireplace to inspect the bolt.

"Red hot and ready to burn," he said.

"Me, too," said Scythe standing. "Red hot and ready for action. That can wait. Com'ere, woman."

He pulled the end of the rope that was around Ruby's neck.She screamed again and started to cry.

"You don't have to do that," Heather said. "We'll tell you where the gold is."

"Where?" demanded Junk.

"There's a trap door under the cupboard."

The two men moved towards the pineboard cupboard. Junk stopped, looked at Heather and grinned.

"Smart, ain't you? Watch her, Sonny, while I look."

The two women sat at the table. Scythe stood, holding the rope in one hand and a knife in the other. DuBris went to the cupboard. Pulling it away from the wall, he found a trap door. He knelt down, hooked his fingers under the lip of the door and lifted it back against the wall. Then he reached down and strained to bring up a small box.

"Heavy," he said, grinning over his shoulder at Sonny. The box was locked. Junk pulled his gun and fired one shot shattering the padlock. He laid his pistol on the floor, opened the box and lifted out two deerskin bags. One was rounded-out full. The other seemed to be about half full. They were tied at the neck with rawhide cords. Holding them over his head, he said, "Look at that, we're rich."

"Whoooeee!" Sonny shouted.

Bringing the bags to the table, Junk said, "Get me a clean dish." Heather obeyed.

He moved the lamp to one side and swept the dirty dishes with a crash to the floor, pausing to stare first at Sonny, then at Ruby and finally at Heather. He opened the full bag and poured a mound of gold dust and nuggets into the dish.

"Whooooee!" shouted Sonny again, " Ain't it purty?"

Junk handed him the other bag. Sonny pulled at the knot with his teeth. It yielded and he poured the contents of that poke on top of the mound already in the center of the table.

In fifteen years, gold had drawn a million men from around the world. To many it was a madness. That madness was in three pairs of eyes as they stared at the shining little pile before them. While they were thus occupied, Heather began tugging at the slip-knot on her throat. The noose was almost big enough to slide over her head when DuBris looked up and grabbed for a gun that was lying on the floor by the open trap door.

"Pull the rope," he screamed.

Sonny looked up first at Junk and then at Heather.The noose was almost off. He reached for the rope which, in his excitement, he had laid aside. He jerked it with such force that it closed the noose and pulled Heather, choking, to her knees.

Junk stepped to her and gave her a push. She tumbled to the floor, still clawing to loosen the rope so she could breathe.

"Nice try, sow," DuBris said, "but no woman's got brains enough to outthink Joshua K. DuBris. If you weren't worth fifty thousand on the hoof, I'd tell Sonny to keep the rope tight until you strangle." She finally loosened the knot and lay gasping for breath.

"Junk, you can't trust these heifers," Sonny said. "They can't do much if I string 'em up from a rafter so's their feet just barely touch the floor."

"Once in a while you surprise me, Sonny," Junk answered. "Go ahead, then we'll see how the smart Mrs. Wanderman figures her way out of that."

Sonny jerked Heather to her feet and dragged the two women under a rafter. Then he tossed the middle of his rope over the beam. Pulling it tight, he knotted it in such a way that Ruby and Heather, suspended back to back, were forced to raise themselves on their tiptoes from time to time to take the pressure off their throats.

"There," said Sonny stepping back to survey his work, "it won't hang 'em as long as their legs hold out."

He turned to look at DuBris, expecting a word of commendation. Instead what he saw was Junk's back as the little man carefully brushed the gold back into the buckskin bags. Sonny stood silent for a moment. Then he looked around at the women and licked his lips. Next he looked again at Junk DuBris. He pulled his knife. Heather held her breath. He lifted his knife and was on the point of throwing it at DuBris' spine.

"You finished?" said DuBris. The knife flashed into its holder as Junk straightened and turned towards them.

"Yeah, almost," said Sonny.

"Good. Now I've got to figure out what we're gonna to do with them. How would you like to die, Miss Hunsford? I've thought of that many times since you used that rope on me. I've dreamed up some wonderfully, painfully slow ways to kill a bitch. Trouble is I don't have the time. I've got fifty thousand dollars waiting in Washington. So you get to die faster. One more night's all you got. Would you like to spend tonight with Sonny?"

"Junk," said Sonny. "we got all that gold. Who needs to go three thousand miles for a little bit more?"

Junk laughed. "Things sure can be funny sometimes. This morning, fifty thousand dollars sounded like all the money in the world. Tonight it's a little bit more and I'm not sure there is fifty thousand at the end of the rainbow."

He turned to Heather and said "Your parents were willing to hire Pinkerton to look for you, yet he tells me they only offered a thousand dollar reward. Ruby says they'd pay fifty thousand. Do your folks really have that kind of money?"

Heather hesitated. If she said "Yes," it would have been a lie. She had invented twenty-five thousand to appeal to Ruby's greed, but she knew even this was more than her father could put together. She also knew that the only reason Junk was going to keep her alive was to collect the ransom. A movement at the dark window behind DuBris was another reason for her hesitation. It was enough to give DuBris his answer.

"Tomorrow we'll plan their future," he said. "Tonight, well, tonight we'll teach them how to love."

"I know more about lovin' than you'll ever know," Heather challenged.

"Heather," cried Ruby, "I'm surprised at you."

"Yeah, I'm a mite surprised, too," Junk said.

"Oh, come on, Ruby. Let's entertain these two gentlemen for awhile."

"I wouldn't even think of it."

"It might be enough to make them think we're worth keeping alive."

"I doubt it, but you can go ahead and try," said Junk.

"Yes, siree," sang Sonny, "and it'll sure make the night a whole lot more fun."

Heather raised her hands to brush her hair as the two men stepped close.

"These aren't men," Ruby hissed. "They're not even animals.

They're monsters. They're devils."

She screamed as Sonny pulled her face towards him to kiss her. She turned her head away and bit her lip. His hands were rough and his fingers hurt as he pulled her to him.

"No," she sobbed. "Please, no."

His left arm circled her waist.

"Shut up, you bitch," he growled as he kissed her.

Junk reached to touch Heather's face. With one hand she coyly played with her hair. With the other, she held the hand that touched her face. Suddenly she clutched the rope above her head with both hands, lifted her right foot off the floor and, with all her force, kneed him in the groin. DuBris groaned, staggered back and stumbled over a chair.

Sonny turned to see what had happened. The furious little man on the floor drew his gun, and, using the table for support, was in the process of pulling himself up when Bart Gordyne crashed through the door followed by Ben and Jack Gervais.

DuBris spun and fired across the table. His bullet smashed into Bart's abdomen, clawed a raw hole through him. Bart, staggering, fired and missed. DuBris turned the gun on Ben. He was slow. The colonel fired once. His bullet drew blood above Junk's right ear and DuBris tripped on the chair, smashed his head hard on the floor and lay still near the table.

Sonny drew his gun as Ben fired again. Scythe was too late. He was already falling as he pulled the trigger and his bullet splintered a board in the wall over Ben's head. Ruby screamed.

Heather said, "Bart's been hurt." Ben, calling out "Heather," rushed to untie her.

"Where's Painter? Where's Spook?" Gervais shouted. Bart leaned against the wall clutching at his side and began to fall. Gervais caught him and eased him to the floor. With one arm, Ben lifted Heather off her feet. With his other hand he took the noose from around her neck.

"Are you all right?" he asked.

"I am now," she said clinging to him. He kissed her. She was trembling.

Gervais was busy cutting away Bart's shirt to get at the wound.

"Will somebody, please, let me down?" Ruby asked.

"Oh, sorry," said Ben and turned his attention to her.

When she was released, Ruby picked up the guns Junk and Sonny had dropped and put them on the washstand near the stove. Ben and Heather were helping Gervais with Bart. Ruby joined them.

Ignored on the table were two bags of gold.

17
PANAMA STEAMER

Bart had passed out and was bleeding profusely. Ruby tried to staunch the flow with some toweling. He was so heavy that they could not move him to a bunk so they made a pad for him on the floor.

"Bart, Bart, can you hear me?" Ben tried to remain calm, but he feared the worst.

Ruby boiled water and Heather bathed the wound. Gervais found a blanket and some medication. When his brother needed him most Ben felt helpless. He stood at the shattered window staring into the darkness. Ignored in the effort to take care of Bart were the two men sprawled on the floor. No one saw DuBris open his eyes and quickly close them. Nor, a few minutes later, did anyone see a hand snake over the edge of the table and snatch two bags of gold. Junk hid them in his shirt.

Several minutes later Ben turned his attention to Junk and Sonny. He dragged them both outside and closed the door as Gervais again asked his question, "Where are Painter and Spook?"

"They're both dead, They were ambushed as they came out of the mine," said Ruby. Heather explained what had happened in the cabin.

"Just as Junk asked me if my folks could pay a fifty thousand dollars ransom I glanced at the window and thought I saw someone. I wasn't sure, but I decided I had to cause a diversion just in case."

"So that's why you started playing up to them, "Ruby said. "Colonel Gordyne, you'd better watch her. She's shameless."

"Maybe, but that brazen diversion gave us the cover we needed to break the door down," Ben said.

"How come you came sneaking in like thieves?" Heather asked.

"We were ridin' up bold as brass," said Gervais, "We'd been ridin' hard ever since we left San Francisco. Scared near crazy that those two had found you. When we topped the ridge across the valley, we saw the light in the window. Everything looked fine and peaceful. Then we heard a shot. We got off'n our hosses and came in on foot. What were they shootin' at?"

"They shot the lock off your strongbox," Heather said.

"Some man started hollering like he was drunk and we were really worried then. What was all the shoutin' about?"

"Sonny went crazy when he saw the gold," Heather said.

"How did they find my gold?" Gervais asked.

"She told them," Ruby said indignantly. "They hadn't done nothin' to us yet and she just politely told them. First, she fixed them a mighty fine supper and then she told them where to find the gold. Heather Wanderman, I don't understand you at all."

"I've heard it said that God put 'thou shalt not covet' at the end of the ten commandments because it covers everything," Heather said. "You can learn a lot at an old timey country church. I spent summers at granddaddy's farm and watched a sow nursing little pigs. I went to church and heard that people were born sucking and never stopped. Gluttony, drunkenness, thievery, greed, lust."

Now that it was all over and Bart was as comfortable as they could make him, Heather felt the need for nervous talk.

"Humans may not always want the same things, but they're all wanting something. All you got to do to please a person is find the right teat. Living with politicians in Washington, I listened to a lot of dull man talk. Once one of them said no economic system is ever going to work that doesn't stand on the universal law of increasing wants. Ben, isn't that law consistent with human nature?"

"I reckon," he answered, his mind more on his brother.

"I thought if I could tap that law in Junk, I'd trap him. People like those two aren't different from pigs. So I went down into their dark souls and stirred up some good old-fashioned lust. I fed them and I told them where the gold was hidden. It almost worked, too. Sonny was within a fractured second of killing Junk so he could have all that gold to himself."

"Yeah, and us, too," Ruby said. "Don't forget that. Sonny wasn't all that much in favor of Junk's plan to kill us. He had other ideas."

Heather smiled. "That was the lust that finally sprung the trap."

"A woman that smart is dangerous," Jack said. "And, talkin' about greed, isn't there anything around here to eat? We haven't et since breakfast. I'm hungry."

Bart groaned and opened his eyes. Ben knelt beside him, whispering, "He's awake." The others gathered around.

"How's it feel, Bart?" Ben asked.

"It hurts worse'n gettin' snagged with a fishhook, Ben. How am I goin' to do?"

"Can't tell, son," said Jack. "You got a bad one. Real bad."

Bart looked around at their solemn faces and grinned.

"Don't worry, I'll make it." He could barely speak.

"Sure you will, Bart." Ben took his hand, "Mama wouldn't like it if you didn't come home."

Heather started putting together the makings of a second dinner. Ben, worried about his brother's high fever, prayed and kept watch.

Gervais headed for the door, saying he wanted to see about the bodies of his friends. Ruby started to set the table, then stopped and yelled out, "Where's the gold?"

Jack turned around and stared at the table.

226

"It's gone," he yelled.

They rushed to the door. Down in the ravine a horse galloped into the night.

"DuBris wasn't dead," Heather said.

"While we was busy with Bart, that skunk stole my gold." Jack was furious.

"That bullet must have grazed his head," Ben said. "Or he was knocked out when his head hit the floor. He was playing 'possum when I carried him out. Thank you, Miss Hunsford."

"What for?"

"For picking up their guns. If he'd gotten his hands on them, we'd all be dead."

Bart's fever was burning high and he was delirious.

"We've got to get him to a doctor," Ben decided.

"We'll kill him if we move him," said Heather.

"Nevertheless, it has to be done."

Jack went outdoors and began putting together a device made of saplings and rope to be suspended between the rear of one horse and the chest of another. They would put Bart on the stretcher and the horses going single file would carry him over the mountains. Before sunup they were ready to move. They pulled Bart's pad out the door and lifted him to his traveling bed. After strapping him into it, they set out for the nearest doctor. Jack stayed behind to work his claim and bury the dead.

It was a slow trip out of the trackless mountains. On the way they asked about Junk DuBris and were told he'd been seen riding south towards Monterey. They made better time when they finally reached a stage road. Bart's fever broke and when they reached Sacramento, he was past needing medical aid.

"This guy ought to be dead," the doctor said. "Shoulda waited around a few days and buried him. Instead you drag him half way across California, which is enough to kill a healthy man, and he comes in here ready to take solid food. This man must be made of shoe leather and railroad tracks."

"Naw," Ben said, "he's just too dumb to know he's dead."

"Shucks," Bart sniffed. "It ain't nothin' for a Citadel man."

227

"You two." Heather turned away to hide her tears.

"Mind you," the doctor said, "he ain't reached the end of the river yet. Rebel or not, it's going to take you a spell to get back into your saddle. If you try to do anything inside of six weeks, I personally will come and shoot you.

"Ma'am," he turned to Heather, "you look like the only one of this bunch that's got more sense than a grasshopper. I'm putting you in charge of this patient. It's your job to see that he gets plenty of rest, lots of water, and vegetables...especially vegetables.

"That'll be five dollars."

"Yes, doctor," said Heather.

"Five dollars?" Bart tried to rise from his stretcher. "What have you done to earn five dollars?"

"My fee goes to ten if I've got to answer more questions."

"Pay the bandit," Bart said.

They reached San Francisco in two days and put Bart up on the ground floor of Mrs. Gervais' boarding house. 'Bama Smith was at his bedside in half an hour and took over nursing duties. She told Ben that Shadow needed to see him so he went to the livery after dark.

"Mister," Shadow told him, "they's ready ta take 'nother load t' the boat."

"Is it our stuff?"

"No, sir. It be the makin's of the smelter. Talk around the mint has it thet they's movin' 'bout 'nough t'sink a ship. Gold bars headin' out t' New York."

"What about our clay disks? Is the mint ready to move them?

"Won't be long. They's got six boxes waitin' an' they don' much like to have thet much aroun'. California banks don't need all we's made. So they'll ship it east soon."

"Well, Shadow, I think it's about time we closed up shop and moved out of here. The way things are going back home, Jeff Davis will need our production right soon. Sherman is moving on Atlanta. If it's to do the Confederacy any good, we've got to get it east right away."

228

"Mister?"

"Yes, Shadow."

"What's goin' heppen to me when they finds them clay disks in New York? I's the onliest person what coulda made the switch."

"That's right, Shadow. I hadn't thought of that."

"Should I disappear?"

"No, Shadow, that would draw attention to you and they will hunt you down. We'll just have to make sure that those clay disks don't get east, won't we?"

"Yes, sir. Kin yo do thet?"

"I'll have to, won't I?"

"I'd sho' 'preciate it."

"Good night, Shadow."

"'Night, Mister."

'Bama was standing by Bart's bed when Ben returned to the boarding house.

"Lots of water and vegetables is what the doctor ordered," she said, "especially vegetables."

"I've eaten more vegetables in the last week than I've eaten in my whole life before and if I ever escape from you I'll never eat another the rest of my life," Bart said. "They couldn't kill me with bullets, so you are going to do it with this diet."

"Stop complaining and eat." 'Bama pushed the plate at him.

"I think what Bart needs is a sea voyage," Ben said.

"Sea voyage?" they both exclaimed.

He told them what he had learned from Shadow.

"When that shipment leaves the smelter it's going to be so well-guarded, Lee himself couldn't get to it with his entire army." Ben shook his head. "From what Shadow says, I may have to leave here in a hurry and you aren't ready for an overland trip. Besides, I want you on that ship. If there is any way to divert that gold between here and New York, I want you to find it."

Bart grinned. "You put a few of our special coffins on board and I'll find a way,"

"My idea, exactly," said Ben. "I'm sending Heather along to keep you on your diet and I hope I can maneuver Legs on board to get him out of my way for our other operation.'

"Pinkerton might complicate things for me."

"I'm sending him along to make sure Heather gets home," Ben said. "Somewhere along the way, you may have to make a choice between that gold and her. Your assignment is the gold. The detective has a special interest in Heather. He'll take care of her for me."

"What about me?" asked 'Bama. She did not get an answer because Heather knocked on the door and walked in.

"Come in," said Bart. "We were just talking about you. Ben tells me you're going on a sea voyage."

"What?"

"Yes, Heather, I'm sending you home. You won't be able to contact anyone for about four months. And, since Bart's land travel is limited, I'm going to send him with you. Just to make everything nice and cozy, I'm going to get rid of that pesky Pinkerton agent the same way."

"And what are you going to be doing while we're enjoying the luxuries of an ocean cruise?" Heather asked.

"Oh, Ruby and I are going to take a leisurely trip east by wagon. Just the two of us."

"You're going to send me around the horn to nursemaid your brother while you travel to Washington with Ruby?" Heather demanded. "Ben Gordyne, I'll kill you first."

"Oh, you'll not be going around the horn. Just to Panama City. There you'll take a train to the Atlantic and catch another ship to New York."

"While you and Ruby take the land route to New York?"

"Oh, no. I'll drop Ruby off in Ohio."

"I'm going to go home?" Heather asked.

"Yes."

"You promise to meet me in Washington?"

"When this war is over, Heather, I've a question to ask you. I'll meet you in Washington."

'Bama slipped out the door without speaking.

"I'm going to miss her," Bart said.

"Does she know that?" Heather asked.

"I hope so."

Ben stationed himself near the smelting company early two mornings in a row. On the third day the plant was surrounded by mounted troops. He also noticed the Pinkerton agent standing in the crowd watching the activities and strolled over to stand beside him.

"It's a long way to New York," he said.

Legs recognized the voice.

"You," he said.

"Yep, it's me."

"Did you find Mrs. Wanderman safe?"

"She wasn't safe but we found her. She's safe now. Sonny's dead and Junk ain't been seen around lately. It's a long way to New York." Ben tipped his hat and strolled away.

A freight wagon loaded with several hundred pounds of gold ingots pulled out of the smelter's yard and a battalion of troopers fell in around it. The parade made its way through the streets of San Francisco to the Market Street Wharf and the gold was loaded on board the Panama Steamer.

They haven't got that shipment, Legs told himself as he watched the loading, but it's a long way to New York.

He was still watching when a hearse and a funeral home utility wagon rolled to the dock. Three heavy caskets were taken out of the vehicles and loaded on board. Turning to leave, he saw a wagon driven onto the wharf by a man with a badly scarred face and a heavy beard. A sick man lay in the bed of the wagon. Seated with the driver were two young women. There were only two trunks in the wagon. From this he deduced that the injured man and one woman were to be passengers. The other woman probably was there to bid them bon voyage.

He turned to leave again, stopped, looked again. It was the woman in his photograph, the one he'd been hunting for more than a year. She was getting on the ship with the other woman. He did not recognize the emaciated man who was carried aboard. Stevedores brought the leather-bound steamer trunks after them.

231

The driver of the wagon was turning his vehicle around when Pharson approached him.

"Where is Mrs. Wanderman bound?" he asked.

"I understand the young lady is going home to Washington," said the driver.

"Who was the man on the stretcher?"

"I wasn't told. I think he is the young lady's brother. He was shot when somebody tried to rob their mine."

"Do steamer trunks usually weigh that much?" Legs asked.

"Your curiosity ain't healthy," said the wagoneer. "You got any reason to know?'

"I'm a Pinkerton agent," Legs said. "The case I'm working on involves gold stolen from the U.S. mint."

"Mister, lots of people takes gold out of California that they worked hard for. I expects there's gold in those trunks, but that don't mean it's stolen," said Jack and whipped his horse into motion.

Legs raced for the nearest telegraph office. The message he sent read, "Mrs. Wanderman sails today on Panama Steamer for New York. Cargo includes gold. Am following."

He hired a hack to take him to his rooming house.

"Wait," he told the driver and hurried inside to pack his bag.

The crew was about to pull up the gangplank when his long legs carried him back to the dock. Ben chuckled as he watched the detective board. Then he waited in a buggy for 'Bama Smith to come off the ship.

"A soldier's duty often hurts others more than the soldier," Ben said as they rode away from the wharf.

"Like you and me," said 'Bama. "Oh, Ben, I already miss him so much."

She was crying. Ben put his arm around her shoulder and said, "You're woman enough to bring him back."

After taking her home, Ben went to the yard behind the Gervais boarding house where the specially built delivery wagon was parked. It was painted black. Wood ashes had been spread over it while the paint was wet. Now Ben beat it with a crowbar until it looked well used. Stacked under the driver's seat were two coffins. Another was built into the floor inside. Each one contained about two hundred pounds in gold coins. Ben built a bed on the casket inside the wagon. When this was finished, he stocked the wagon with all the supplies and gear two people would need for a trip to the Missouri River.

The next day Ben hitched two draft horses to the wagon and left for Sacramento. There he backed the vehicle into the warehouse at Buck Andrews' brick plant, stabled the horses nearby and returned to San Francisco.

18
SEA SOUTH

The Panama Steamer was a hybrid: a sidewheeler with sails, possessing neither the racehorse beauty of a sailing ship nor the draft horse slugging power of later steamers. But as far as passengers were concerned, the hybrid was an improvement over sailing ships because she was spacious and luxuriously furnished.

Although the Gold Rush had played out, more people were still entering California than leaving. All shipboard space was needed on northbound trips. Often bunks were rented in shifts to accommodate swarms of immigrants. Headed south the situation was much different. Private staterooms were available for each passenger.

Two Chinese coolies had carried Bart to his cabin on the boat deck. Heather and 'Bama watched as they shifted him to his bed. He appeared exhausted. 'Bama stayed until a crewman walked down the companionway shouting, "All ashore that's going ashore."

On an impulse, she bent over Bart and kissed him. A smile of surprised joy spread over his face as he opened his eyes.

"That ought to heal me real quick," he said taking her hand.

"You come back, y'hear."

She had tried to make him understand how she felt. Did he?

"Yes, ma'am, I surely will." Bart squeezed her hand. She

realized he meant it and smiled.

"'Bye," Heather said.

"Bye, Heather. This one's mine. You can have Ben."

They did not laugh as 'Bama left. Legs passed her as she walked down the gangplank.

When the cabin door closed, Heather turned to Bart. His face was to the wall.

"Are you all right?"

"Yeah, I'll be fine," he answered, burrowing in the pillow to hide his tears. "Just need some rest."

"I'll get settled in my room. It's next door. If you need anything, just call."

After she left Bart sat up and spoke to the closed door. "I hate to trick you like this, but right now I think it best if you keep on playing nurse."

He paced the length of the small cabin once, turned and repeated the exercise. It exhausted him.

"I'm still weaker than I thought," he muttered, "but I sure hope I can make them believe I'm weaker than I am."

Shore swells were still rocking the ship when an orderly brought his evening meal. Heather helped the crewman get four pillows behind his back so he could sit up to eat.

"More vegetables," he grumbled as she placed the tray before him. "How do you expect a grown man to live on rabbit food?"

"You hush, Bart Gordyne, and eat," she commanded. "If you don't stop complaining, I'll make you get your own meals."

The banter continued as Bart cleaned up his plate.

"Sure isn't anything wrong with your appetite." Heather picked up the tray.

Bart slipped off the piled pillows, closed his eyes and lay still. As Heather closed the door behind her, she caught a glimpse of a tall man in a dark suit leaning against the bulkhead.

An hour later Bart rolled his feet to the floor and stood. Again he paced the room until he felt his knees about to buckle. Every two hours, he repeated this exercise. Before the ship berthed at Monterey, Bart felt strong enough to venture a short distance outside his stateroom late at night. After that he walked a little farther until he was spending most after-midnight hours wandering through the darkened ship. He slept during the days.

At Monterey the Panama Steamer took on fifty bales of hides and more passengers. Among these were a well-dressed man named Manuel Morenda and Junk DuBris who was wanted by San Francisco police for two murders and robbery. When DuBris saw Pharson leaning on a railing, he hurried to secrete himself in his cabin. Two bags of gold were not enough; perhaps the detective could lead him to more.

One evening Heather came out of Bart's stateroom after bringing his dinner. The ship's doctor had put him on a more substantial diet. Still his continued weakness troubled her. She walked to the promenade deck and leaned on the rail, looking towards the sun resting like a great rose in a bed of grey-black clouds on the far horizon. A light breeze wrinkled the ocean like iridescent tissue paper. Ground swells had died away. The twilight air was cool. Several minutes later a tall man in a black suit and bowler hat came and stood by her.

"Magnificent," he said.

"Yes," she replied, a little upset by his interruption.

There was silence for a time and she was beginning to think he had joined her just to look at the setting sun.

"Mrs. Duncan Wanderman?"

She looked at him, surprised that he knew her name and asked, "Do I know you?"

In answer he handed her a photograph and she found herself looking at a worn copy of her own wedding picture.

"You must be the Pinkerton agent. I've been expecting you."

"You have been hard to find, Mrs. Wanderman."

"That's because the Gordyne brothers took considerable care to keep me hidden. In fact, I doubt you would have found me now, if Col. Ben Gordyne had not wished it."

"You mean I've been set up?"

"I wouldn't be surprised, but Ben Gordyne has been very careful to keep me uninformed."

"I assume Ben Gordyne is one of the two men you have been traveling with."

"Correct."

"Is he on this ship?"

"No, but his brother is."

"I know. Bart Gordyne is the man they carried aboard on a stretcher. Recovering from a gunshot wound, I believe?"

"Correct again. How did you know that?"

"I talked to the man who brought you to the dock. If I have it right, he was wounded rescuing you from Junk DuBris."

"I have to say you are correct again. You seem to be very good at deducing things after they happen, Mr. Pharson. I've known you were around for a long time, but wondered when we'd finally meet. Now, I suppose, it's too late."

"Why?"

"I'm on my way home so my parents no longer need your services."

"But I have another assignment," he said.

"What is that?"

"How were seven hundred pounds of gold coins transformed into cement on an ocean trip from San Francisco to New York?"

Heather giggled. "They did that?"

"Your friends are real magicians. I'm on this ship to see they don't repeat the trick." He drummed his fingers nervously on the rail.

"Mrs. Wanderman, I understand you were working as a Union informant when you were captured by the Gordyne brothers. Do you still consider yourself employed in that capacity?"

Heather hesitated as she asked herself one question: What would Ben want me to do? She remembered him saying, "You have a duty..."

"I do," she said.

"Can you tell me where Ben Gordyne is?"

"He's probably on his way east over the mountains with a load of Union gold while you play around on this ship."

"I can't believe that. The gold is on this ship."

"It is?"

"Does that surprise you? A wagonload of gold bars is locked in the ship's vault."

"Are you sure?"

"I watched them take it from the smelting company under heavy guard and load it on board. The Gordynes did not divert it the way they did the last shipment. It's on board."

"Are you sure it's gold?"

"How could it be anything else? The ingots were taken directly from the smelter to the ship."

"If it is, you may be sure that Ben Gordyne does not intend for it to get to New York."

"Perhaps Bart Gordyne ..."

"If Bart were his normal self, he could tuck a barrel of it under each arm and swim ashore, but Bart's too weak to walk across the room. How could he do anything?"

She paused a minute and then said, "Maybe he doesn't have to do anything."

"What do you mean?"

"Is it possible that another shipment of gold is going east overland and Ben Gordyne has put the three of us on this ship to get us out of the way while he waylays it? He told me he was putting you and me on this ship to get us out of his way for four months."

"The mint," hissed Pharson banging his fist on the rail.

"What's that?"

"The San Francisco Mint was about ready to send another shipment east. This is just a diversion."

"Very likely," she said, "But I wouldn't put it past Ben Gordyne to gamble on both sides of the table. I'd advise the Union to keep a careful eye on both shipments."

"We could have Bart Gordyne arrested. That would put a stop to any plans they have to transfer the gold on board this ship to the rebels."

"How could we have him arrested?"

"The captain would arrest him if you tell him your story."

"Could he do that?"

"The captain is an officer of the United States. He has authority to arrest criminals on his ship."

Heather looked across the darkening ocean. The orange sun had been quenched in its black waves and only streaks of light fanned out across the heavens. A few stars were coming out.

"Will you do it, Mrs. Wanderman?"

"Bart Gordyne was almost killed saving my life," she said. "and when this war is over I expect to marry his brother."

"The war is not over and the conclusion of it may be locked in this ship's vault. Think it over, Mrs. Wanderman. I will wait until morning for your answer. Good night."

"Good night, Mr. Pharson."

Heather went to her cabin, but she did not sleep. She spent the hours trying to make up her mind. The sound of a door opening and closing decided for her. She threw off the sheet and hurried to peek into the hall. By the faint light of a bulkhead lantern, she saw Bart walking down the companionway.

"Judas Iscariot himself," she muttered as she returned to her bed. "He's not even using a cane."

That night Bart made a discovery. One of the passengers who had boarded the ship at Monterey also seemed to be searching for something. He watched from the shadow of a stairwell as a well-dressed man with the features and coloring of a Spaniard explored the same passages he was investigating. He decided the only thing on board that could excite such curiosity was gold.

The next day Bart's morning nap was interrupted by a knock on his door.

"Come in," he said.

Two men holding revolvers pushed in. Behind them was the ship's officer, Capt. Andrew Waters. Behind him was Legs.

"This is hardly the way to say 'good morning,'" Bart said.

"Mr. Gordyne, can you tell me why you were wandering around my ship in the early hours of the morning?"

"Captain, is there some regulation I do not know about

prohibiting such a venture?"

"No, but it seems unusual when you appear to be attempting to convince everyone on board, including the ship's doctor, that you're incapacitated by a serious wound. So, answer my question."

It was then that Heather stepped into the doorway.

"So that's it," Bart said. "Has my lady friend been telling stories again?"

"This gentleman is P. League Pharson, a detective with Pinkerton. I must say that he and Mrs. Wanderman have been telling me some strange tales about you and, unless you can provide a reasonable rebuttal, I'm afraid I shall have to place you under arrest."

"What am I charged with?"

"Stealing a million dollars in gold in Toledo to start with. Attempting to divert it to the rebels among other things. Wrecking a train. Robbing the San Francisco Mint. They have also led me to believe that you may be on board my ship with a plan to steal the gold in the ship's vault."

Bart laughed and sat up.

"Does that really seem reasonable, Captain Waters? Your ship's doctor knows I am recovering from a wound that is usually fatal. How could I break into your vault? And, if I succeeded, do I appear to have strength enough to carry the gold away? How do they say I carried off a million dollars in gold in Toledo? Am I Samson? Do any of you know how much that weighs? Really, captain, you flatter me. I was wounded, nearly killed, by men who kidnapped her.

"Mrs. Wanderman is a very beautiful woman."

He turned to look at Heather. The four men followed his lead.

"Unfortunately, she also has a wild imagination. Her parents have offered a reward for her return and I am taking her home to get it. For reasons of her own, she does not want to go home."

Looking then at Legs, he said, "Is it possible Mr. Pharson wants that reward and part of that gold for himself? It might be advisable for you to see if there isn't a connection between Mr.

Pharson and another passenger who was searching through your ship last night. The three of them might break into your vault. Not I. Go away and let me rest." Bart lay back down.

"You raise some interesting questions, Mr. Gordyne, but you do not answer mine," the captain said. "I am not here to conduct a trial. I am here to make sure that the passengers and cargo of the Panama Steamer arrive safely at their destination. Mrs. Wanderman and Mr. Pharson have made a strong case against you and I see no reason why they should have invented the story. Therefore, Mr. Gordyne, I'm placing you under arrest."

Startled, Bart sat up in bed.

"A guard will be assigned to your cabin until we get to Panama City," the captain continued. "There I'll let the United States consul decide what to do with you. You have the freedom of the ship, but if you ever try to get out of sight of your guard, I will confine you to the brig. Is that clear?"

"Yes, sir, but there are others who covet your gold."

"Coveting and getting are two different things. You are my concern just now, and you will not leave this ship until an officer of the United States comes on board to get you."

Turning to a seaman holding a gun, he said, "Mr. O'Dune."

"Yes, sir?"

"You are assigned to this gentleman for the duration of this voyage. See that he is never out of your sight. You will sleep so that he'll have to move you to open the door."

"Yes, sir." O'Dune appeared too heavy to be moved unwillingly.

"Mr. Derino?"

"Yes, sir," replied the other seaman.

"Double the guard on the vault."

"Yes, sir."

Captain Waters took Heather's arm to usher her from the cabin. She looked at Bart and said, "I'm sorry, Bart."

He grinned. "Nothin' to be sorry about, Heather. Ben would be mighty proud. There are a few more rivers before we get to New York and there be more'n one way to catch catfish."

19
THE TRAP

With Bart, Heather and Legs at sea, Ben was playing a waiting game.

Three days after they sailed, he was awakened early one morning by a knock on his attic door. He heard someone whispering his name.

"Who is it?" He struggled into his pants.

"It's me, 'Bama."

He opened the door. Standing in the narrow hall were 'Bama Smith, Liza Gervais and an older woman he did not recognize.

"This is Shadow," 'Bama said. "Something's going on at the mint she thinks you ought to know about."

"Hello, Shadow," Ben said.

"Good morning, Colonel Gordyne," said the woman who had spoken to him before only from the dark in the accent of a backwoods settler. "They've moved it."

"Tonight?"

"Yes, colonel. While I was at work this evening they brought an Overland Stage Coach into the lot behind the mint. It was there when I left. Mr. Madrass was still in his office, so I waited behind the fence and watched. Not too long after, two night guards, a driver, Mr. Madrass and Mr. Woods carried boxes out of the vault. They put them in the boot and covered them with canvas.

Then they drove the coach out.

"I followed. They took it to the dock and drove it right on board the Apache of the Sacramento River Steamship Line. I went to find 'Bama and she brought me here."

"They'll take it to Sacramento," Ben said, "pick up some passengers and head east. Are the guards still with the coach?"

"Not mint guards. Five well-armed civilians were standing around trying to look like they weren't Army. One of them with a shotgun rode beside the driver. The others got inside."

"They'll move it out before the first snow in the passes," Ben said. "and I've got to be ahead of them."

"Colonel Gordyne, do you have a plan to sidetrack those boxes before they are opened?"

"I think so, Shadow."

"I can still disappear?"

"Not yet. If my plan doesn't work, I'll get word to you."

The door across the hall opened and Ruby joined them.

"What's all this about?" she asked.

"I was about to sneak back to Ohio and leave you here, Ruby," Ben said. "But you caught me, so I reckon I've got to take you with me. Pack your bags. We're leaving."

"In the middle of the night?"

"Just as soon as you can be ready, and, if you have anything you don't want to leave behind, that'd better be half an hour."

"Can we do anything?" Mrs. Gervais asked.

"You can help Ruby pack," he said and looked at 'Bama and Shadow. "You ladies have been outstanding. Our job isn't finished yet. Yours is. We could not have done any of this without you. I don't know how to thank you."

"I do," said 'Bama.

"How's that?"

"Send Bart back to me."

"He's mine," said Ruby and they all laughed.

"You can thank me by making sure those boxes don't get to New York," Shadow said.

"Yes, ma'am," said Ben and returned to his room to pack.

Within an hour Ruby and Ben were on board the ferry heading for the eastern side of San Francisco Bay. They rode hard to Andrews' warehouse in Sacramento where they picked up the draft horses and Gervais' specially designed freight wagon. Ruby climbed in the back and went to sleep. Ben mounted the driver's seat and steered for the mountains.

The Overland Stage pulled out of Sacramento about noon the next day. Its passengers included a couple of worn-out prospectors and four men who looked military though they were dressed in civilian clothes. The driver and shotgun guard made up the crew.

When she woke, Ruby joined Ben on the high driver's seat.

"Well, I've got it," she announced after an half hour of unusual silence. Ben had his mind on something else and only the last words registered.

"What?" he asked.

"I've been trying to figure out what's going on ever since Heather and Bart vanished without a word. Then, this morning you rush me out of San Francisco. And now we're heading east. I think I've solved all the mystery."

"You have? Tell me."

"Bart was hurt too bad to make this trip over the mountains and you knew it was about time for someone to ship out a load of gold. So you sent Bart on ahead with Heather to look out for him. Those women brought you word that the gold was going to be shipped today and you rushed out to be ahead of the shipment. Some place up there in the mountains you're going to waylay it and transfer it to this wagon. Isn't that right?"

"You're closer to that gold than you think," he said.

"So we're going to get it," she cried out. "You and I are going to get all of it, right?"

"We could."

"Oh, Ben, I'm so glad you brought me with you."

She was silent again. Something troubled her.

"Why did you bring me along?" she asked.

He was slow to answer.

244

"We've been through a lot together, Ruby," he finally said, "and you're a beautiful woman. I wish I could say I brought you with me because of that, but you're old enough to hear the truth."

He paused and cleared his throat. "So here it is. What would you have done if I ran off with the gold without you?"

She did not answer so he answered for her.

"You'd have the Union Army on my trail in two hours. There would have been a posse waiting for me in Sacramento. You joined up with us in Ohio because you thought we had gold and you still hope there is gold someplace. Well, Ruby, there is, but it's not mine and it's not yours."

"I'll get it if I can," she said angrily.

"Yes, I know."

They rode through the still afternoon. The mountains before them reared up and the shadows of the horses and wagon stretched ahead of them. Neither spoke for several minutes.

"How much gold is there on that coach?" Ruby asked.

"Not enough to make you happy."

"What do you mean by that?" she snapped.

"How much would make you happy, Ruby?"

"Oh, I don't know. I'd like to have lots of it, but I'd be satisfied with just a few pounds."

"I know how much would make you happy, Ruby."

"You do? How much?"

"Just a little bit more and no matter how much you got the answer would always be the same. 'The horseleach hath four daughters that say not enough,'" he quoted.

"What are you talking about?"

"Nothing. Nothing."

The coach stopped for the night at a stage station, but Ben and Ruby fixed their evening meal by the side of the trail. Ruby slept inside the wagon. Ben made his bed on the ground between the wagon's wheels. He stretched out and looked up at the boards above him. For a few minutes there was silence. Then Ben laughed.

"What's funny?" Ruby asked.

"Nothing," he said, but he was wondering how Ruby would act if she knew she was sleeping on a coffin and what she would do if she found out the "body" in the casket was made of gold.

As they switched back and forth on the steep grades, Ben carefully searched the sides of the trail. He was looking for something he had noticed many times on the trip west. At the top of each long climb, he stopped, stood on top of the wagon and searched the back trail for the coach behind them.

"They are making better time than we are," he told Ruby after one of these stops. "We can't let them catch us."

"Why?"

"Somewhere up the road a piece I've got to set a trap. We must be far enough ahead to have time to get it ready."

The coach was getting uncomfortably close when Ben found the place. They were approaching Donner Pass in a driving rain, traveling along the summit of a ridge. The narrow road ahead dropped away down the face of a precipice. The horses started and within a minute, Ben began struggling with the brakes. He was so busy he almost missed what he had been looking for.

Where the road leveled off he pulled the horses to a stop and dismounted. As he started walking up the slope, he heard Ruby call out, "Where you going?"

"I want to check on something." He shouted so he could be heard above the storm. "You stay dry. I'll be right back."

He walked up the trail to a wooden bridge over the back end of a deep cut in the face of the precipice. It was a sheer drop of several hundred feet to a river below. Most of the fir trees above the trail stood tall. Others leaned outward, their roots evidently exposed by those who had dug the road and also by years of erosion.

Just a little bit of help would make that one tree fall, Ben told himself. It's so near gone, a good wind would do it.

He inspected the bridge, walked a bit down the road, turned around and paced back to the bridge.

Might work, he thought, and returned to the wagon.

"Are we camping here?" Ruby asked.

"No, just setting a trap."

He took an axe, shovel and a coil of rope back up the trail. Thinking that now he could use Bart's strong arms, he started setting up his trap. To work, it had to look natural.

Using a sapling as a lever, he broke lateral roots until the tree fell taking a ball of roots and earth into the middle of the road below. Its branches came to rest over the edge nearly parallel to the trail. The top was over space about ten feet out from the bridge. With a rope he tied the tree to the outside log spanning the cut. It was one of three supporting beams for the bridge. The road was blocked.

Ben examined his work and made sure the rope was well hidden in branches of the tree and in the brush by the side of the road. Picking up his tools, he whistled and walked back to the wagon.

"Give me some dry clothes, Ruby." He stuck his head inside the door.

"What have you been doing?" She rummaged around in his bag.

"I wish I could wait and watch the fun," he said. "I'd like to tell you about it, but we've got to get on out of here."

"Why?"

"There's going to be some powerfully unhappy gentlemen up that road in a bit. If I was them, I'd shoot me."

He took the clothes she handed him. After he changed, he covered himself with a slicker and climbed back into the driver's seat.

"Move it," he shouted at the horses and lifted up his voice to laugh.

It was near dark and still raining when Ben pulled up at a home stage station.

"We'll spend the night here," he told Ruby. "Maybe we'll find out what happened at the bridge. This might be our last trail break before the Missouri."

He escorted her into the smoky log hovel that served as a layover point on the Overland Stage route.

"You go ahead and eat while I take care of the horses," Ben told her at the door.

When he returned Ruby was seated at a greasy table feeding on rancid bacon and corn dodgers and arranging with the station keeper's wife to share her bed for the night. Passengers in such places usually slept on the floor. Only crew members got bunks. Ben looked around the dirty quarters and decided he would rather eat a cold meal and sleep on top of a coffin.

"I'm going to spend the night in the wagon," he said. "You get some sleep, Ruby, and be ready to move out early."

Some time during the night it stopped raining. At first light Ben was up. He had finished hitching the horses to the singletree when seven wet and weary men rode bareback in from the west. He grinned. The trap had worked. He followed them inside.

"What happened, Corn?" the station keeper asked.

"We brought the stage along Carson's Ridge," one of the men said. "It were raining fit to turn the road into a river. Luke here turned the team off'n the ridge down the face of that mountain. I could see he were havin' trouble holdin' her back."

"Yeah," said a heavyset man with a full beard covering most of his round face. "Up there on the ridge the wind near blew us off'n the mountain. But I started on down because the wind was comin' from the other side and there wasn't a whole lot of wind on her face."

Ruby came from the kitchen with steaming coffee. The men stopped talking to warm themselves with a hot drink.

"What I didn't figure on," the one called Luke said, "was what that wind and rain had done to those trees. About the time we come up on the bridge over Carson's Cut, we saw this tree had been blown down and its roots and a ball of dirt near as big as a wagon was lyin' in the middle of the trail on the other side of the bridge. The horses near ran into it before they stopped."

He paused to sip coffee. "When we stopped, the coach was sitting on the bridge and the lead horses were in the branches of the tree. The rest of the tree was hanging out over the gorge.

"The thing was so neat we thought it might'a been a holdup.

Corn here stood up and looked around. When we didn't see nothin', I walked over to the root to see what we could do to get it out of the way." Luke paused to take a drink.

"He hollered back at me," Corn said, "and told me to shake out the passengers to help roll the tree over the side. They joined us,we put our shoulders to the root, and over it went. Trouble is it took the bridge with it."

"I ain't sure what happened next," said Luke, "but I figure that the top of the tree whipped back, caught the underside of the bridge and flipped it and the stage on top of it right off'n the face of that mountain. If the singletree hadn't snapped, it would have pulled the horses after it. The whole thing went spinnin' down to the river fallin' to pieces as it bounced."

"Was there anything of value on the stage?" Ben asked.

"You might say so," said one of the men who looked as if he could have been Army. "Four of us were riding the stage to guard a shipment of six cases of gold coins from the mint."

"Is that so?"

"Yep," said the military-looking fellow. "There's ways to fight robbers, but there's no way to guard against that kind of accident."

"Will any effort be made to salvage the gold?" Ben asked.

"Don't hardly think so," said Luke. "I saw one of those boxes bounce off the face of the cliff. It shattered and spread those coins like sowing wheat in a tornado. The river's got the rest of them and it drops over four or five waterfalls in twenty miles."

"That's a serious loss," said Ben.

He looked up. Ruby was staring at him.

"Come on, Ruby, we've got a ways to go before dark."

He held the door for her as she picked up her bag and coat. She said not a word as he helped her up to a place on the driver's seat.

"That's for Shadow," he said as he whipped the horses into motion and they started the climb up to Donner Pass.

"I don't understand," Ruby said at last. "I thought our gold was on that coach."

"That is exactly what I want everybody to think. To do that, I had to get rid of that coach, but I didn't want to kill those men and horses doing it."

"But what about our gold?" Ruby demanded."Where is our gold?"

"Maybe I sent it on ahead with Bart and Heather."

"Where are they?" she demanded, almost screaming.

"On a ship somewhere off the coast of Mexico by this time, I reckon."

"And they have my gold?"

"I said 'maybe.'"

20
RUBY'S CHOICE

The war reports Ben picked up in Denver were mixed. The South had won some battles of strategic importance, but even this could not stop the rising tide of the Union sweep.

The news turned the trip across eastern Colorado and Kansas into a race to get his cargo to the Confederacy in time. Ruby, still hostile, spent most of the journey sulking in the wagon.

When they arrived at the bend of the Missouri River Ben heard that Sherman had started his march from Atlanta to the sea. His military training told him that this maneuver could be catastrophic, severing the Confederacy. The rampaging Union army would wreck all in sight. He knew the war was headed for a climax.

Driven by this urgency, he very nearly killed his horses sprinting to the railhead. There he demolished the wagon to get at the three caskets hidden in its frame.

"What are those?" Ruby demanded when she saw them.

"Coffins," he said.

Ruby's face brightened.

"My gold," she said. "It's been in the wagon all the time."

"You're part right," Ben said. "The gold was in the wagon. But it isn't your gold, Ruby. I've got to get it to Richmond."

"Why don't you forget the stupid war?" she demanded

angrily."It's all but over and the South can't win."

"I don't know if there's enough gold in those coffins to buy victory for Dixie, Ruby, but I must try."

"What will you do with it if you can't get it to Richmond in time?"

"I have not even considered that alternative."

"You and I could live very well with all that gold." Ruby spoke softly.

Ben looked at her. "Smoldering" was the word that passed through his mind. Boldly she searched his face and he remembered the black Franklin wood stove used to warm his bedroom on cold days in South Carolina. How many times as a boy had he risen in the dark of a frosty morning to build the fire? Often he would open the grated door and look into the darkness within to see, glowing like cat's eyes, remnants of the last fire smoldering in dark ashes, waiting for a little fuel and a little breath to start burning again.

Smoldering, he thought. Somehow those full lips, those glistening, dark eyes behind long, black lashes, that face framed in a cloud of black hair took him back to that Franklin stove and those smoldering brands.

What he saw was desirable and beautiful. This did not stop with her face. Every feature, from her ivory throat and full figure to her tiny feet, said, "I'm a woman" and every delicate motion she made repeated the refrain.

That woman and that gold, well.

Her statement, "the war is all but over," echoed in Ben's mind as he looked at her and he knew she spoke the truth but he jerked his eyes away from her.

"I must get that gold south," he said.

"What will you do with me?"

"When you are no longer a threat to our mission, I'll put you on a train to your uncle in St. Louis."

"I go where the gold goes," she said.

The next morning they took a train rushing east. The three coffins were in the baggage car.

Ben's spirits rose when he reached St. Louis where he heard that Gen. Hood was leading an army of fifty thousand Confederate troops into Tennessee. Perhaps he could intercept that army and transfer the caskets to the southern forces. But Sherman was cutting Georgia in half with a fifty-mile wide belt of total destruction.

With this in mind, he had their tickets changed to go through Indianapolis. There they stood on the platform beside the three coffins and the large valise, watching the train pull out towards Washington.

"What are we doing here?" Ruby asked.

"Turning south," he said. "Let's find transportation."

"What are we going to do with this gold?"

"It isn't going any place."

"You mean you're going to just let it sit there by itself?"

"Who's going to steal three filled coffins? Come on."

At that moment a newsboy came by shouting, "Read all about it! Rebel invasion stopped. Hood withdraws towards Nashville."

Ben bought a paper, sat on one of the caskets and read the account of the battle of Franklin, Tennessee, where Hood's effort to draw Sherman away from Georgia was stopped by Schofield's Union army. Ruby read over his shoulder.

When he had finished, Ben carefully folded the paper, swatted it in frustration over his right knee. Ruby leaned close to him.

"Ben," she said softly, "the war's over. You can't get this gold to President Davis in time to change that. Please, take the gold and me and let's go some place together."

For a long moment he sat very still looking away into the distance where the track branched out. Ruby pressed close and held her breath. Suddenly Ben pushed her away and jumped to his feet and stood looking down at her.

"You're a whole lot different than I thought Satan was supposed to be," he said.

"Ben, why not? I know it hurts, but you can't make any difference. Why not enjoy what you've got?"

"There are three reasons which I don't think you would

understand."

"Tell me and see if I understand."

"Honor, Bart and Heather."

"Yes, and what are Bart and Heather doing about honor on a romantic cruise in southern seas while you work yourself into a Union trap?"

He paused again before answering.

"Just like Satan, you go too far," he said.

"I'm not much on demonology."

"You have insulted my brother and the woman I will marry after this war. If you were a man, I'd whip you for it."

"But I'm not a man," she said standing. "Look at me. There's gold and here I am. Aren't I more of a woman than that...widow?" A locomotive roared in from the east making conversation impossible until it hissed and screamed to a stop. Ben spent the time inspecting her from the raven hair to the tiny black shoes.

When he could be heard again, he said, "You're pretty enough I guess, but again like the devil, you don't understand reality."

"What's that supposed to mean?"

"When you grow up, you may be half the woman Heather is today."

She slapped him.

"Come on, we've got to find us transportation to Nashville," he said and turned to leave. She started to follow him, stopped and gasped, "Ben."

He turned and looked at her. She slumped to sit down on one of the caskets.

"Ben, I..."

"What's the trouble?"

"I'm not well."

"What?"

"I got dizzy. I thought I was going to faint."

"Oh, don't tell me that. Let's go."

"I'm sorry, Ben. Really I am, but I think I'd better just sit here for a spell."

"What's the matter?"

"Just one of those female things we can't talk about."

"Oh."

"Please, just leave me here a few minutes. You go arrange transportation and come back. I'll be all right."

"You sure?"

"Yes, yes. I just need to sit a while."

He started to leave.

"I'd like to read the newspaper while you're gone," she said.

Handing it to her, he turned again towards the ticket window in the waiting room. She began immediately to hunt through her handbag until she found a pencil. Once he was out of her sight, she scribbled around the margin of the newspaper.

The line at the ticket window was long. The military had taken over some trains so civilian passengers had to make other arrangements. His turn finally came. He looked over his shoulder and saw Ruby busy with the newspaper.

"May I exchange these tickets for two to Nashville?" he asked the clerk.

"Sorry. The army has commandeered all trains to move troops to Nashville. Sheridan is out to destroy Hood there and he wants every man he can get. There'll be no civilian traffic until late tomorrow."

"Tomorrow?"

"Yes, sir. I'm sorry, but there's a war on."

"How am I going to get to Nashville?"

"By horse if you're traveling light. If not, by coach. Then, with a battle going on, I ain't so sure you'd make it."

Gordyne moved away from the counter. Through a window he saw Ruby talking to the newsboy. He left by another door and went to find a wagon and a horse with enough stamina to pull them and their load to Nashville. It took him some time. When he returned, Ruby was standing before the steps of one of the passenger coaches. The coffins were about twenty feet away.

"Ready to go south?" he asked.

"I don't think so," she said.

"Ready or not it's time to go."

"You may go east, and I may go west, but neither of us are going south."

"What makes you so sure?"

"I'm sure because like Satan you have overestimated your cunning. Any fifteen-year-old girl is more devious than you. And, just in case you don't think of it, any reference to the contents of those coffins will be a guilty plea."

"What are you talking about?"

Instead of an answer, a male voice behind him asked, "Col. Benjamin L. Gordyne?"

For just a micro-second Ben went rigid. Then he said, "We're wasting time, Ruby. Let's get on the road."

"Col. Benjamin L. Gordyne?" the male voice asked again.

"I believe the sheriff wants to talk to you," Ruby said.

Ben turned. There were five men behind him. One wore a star. They all had guns. The sheriff appeared solid and competent. The other four wore deputy shields. They looked as if they had spent too much time drinking beer.

"Were you speaking to me?" Ben asked.

"I am if you are Col. Benjamin L. Gordyne of the Confederate Army," said the sheriff.

"I'm afraid you've made some mistake, sir. My name is Jim Jackson."

"This young lady says you are Col. Benjamin L. Gordyne and that you are responsible for robbing a gold shipment in Toledo, wrecking a train in Ohio, robbing the San Francisco Mint and wrecking a stagecoach near Donner Pass. She also says you have been holding an agent of the United States against her will. Those are serious charges and, except for the fact that she seems to knows an awful lot about cases we have been trying to solve for a long time, I wouldn't be inclined to believe her, but, you see, I do. I believe you are Col. Benjamin L. Gordyne, and, unless you can convince me otherwise, I'm going to have to hold you."

"If your mind is already made up, how can I convince you?"

"Where are you from, Mr. Jackson?"

"Upstate New York."

"Upstate?" the sheriff asked as an amused smile played over his face. "The way you say state sounds more like Charleston than Buffalo, Mr. Jackson. Where is Mrs. Warren Wanderman?"

"Who?"

"Mrs. Wanderman, the United States agent who was abducted by Confederate spies in Washington."

"Am I supposed to know?"

"Miss Hunsford says she is on a ship with your brother and a great deal of California gold and your plans are to divert that gold to the Confederacy."

"Since she knows so much, why don't you arrest her?"

"Mr. Jackson, this young man brought me this paper," the sheriff said pointing to the newsboy. "He said Miss Hunsford told him there was a thousand dollar reward if you were captured. Now how did she know about that reward?"

"What reward? Why should there be a reward for my arrest?"

"Around the margin of this newspaper Miss Hunsford wrote a message suggesting she had information concerning a Confederate agent and asked me to come. She knows so much about these unsolved cases. She knows Mrs. Wanderman's name, even her father's name. And she described her perfectly. She knows about the robbery and the train wreck. How, Mr. Jackson?"

Ben did not answer.

"I thought it wise to investigate further," the sheriff said. "While we were waiting for you to return, I talked to the ticket agent. May I see your ticket, Mr. Jackson?"

"The ticket agent would not sell me one."

"I'm referring to the ticket you used to come to Indianapolis. Miss Hunsford said you came by train."

"What if I say she lies?"

"Tell me, does this young lady really look like a liar, Mr. Jackson?"

"She doesn't look like the demon who took the form of Bathsheba," said Ben as he fished the tickets out of his inside coat pocket. The lawman inspected them.

"Tell me, Mr. Jackson, why you bought tickets to Washington

in St. Louis, then got off the train in Indianapolis and tried to exchange them for passage to Nashville?"

"Is it a crime to change my mind?" Ben asked.

"No, Mr. Jackson, but Miss Hunsford said you changed your mind because you hoped to slip back to Dixie by joining General Hood's forces. I'm afraid, Colonel Gordyne, I'm going to have to hold you while we investigate these charges further."

He nodded to the officers who closed in around Ben. "Where can we get in touch with you, Miss Hunsford?" he asked.

"Can you put me up in a hotel?"

"We usually use the Berliner for witnesses and jurors. It's only two blocks north."

"I'll be there if you need me, Sheriff Aston."

"Come along, Mr. Jackson," the lawman said to Ben who studied the four deputies. They appeared ready to kill a Confederate spy.

He followed the sheriff. When they reached the end of the station platform, Ben looked back. Ruby had already talked a squad of soldiers into putting the caskets in the train's baggage car.

Ben and his guards were about to descend to the street when the newsboy shouted, "There he is! There's the Confederate spy!"

A young fellow with a notebook rushed up. "Sheriff Aston, is this really the man who wrecked the train in Ohio last year?"

How would he know that, Ben wondered and then decided he worked for the sheriff. Or he might be a reporter.

The man never got an answer. Two things were happening at one time. A regiment of troops began marching onto the platform to take up positions alongside the train and a mob of those who had heard the newsboy's shout began gathering. Suddenly the station was jammed with people, swarming like bees towards Ben.

"Sheriff, is he really a rebel spy?" someone shouted.

Aston faced the crowd.

"We don't know yet. I'm only taking him in for questioning."

"Dirty rebels cost me my leg," one man yelled.

"A leg? I got a brother buried in Chattanooga."

"Hang him," someone else called and this cry was picked up throughout the growing mob. Ben glanced over towards the train. Ruby was boarding one of the passenger cars oblivious to the commotion she had created.

"Hang him," shouted the mob.

Sheriff Aston raised his hands.

"Quiet," he ordered. The noise died down.

"Now listen, this man has not been charged or convicted. Hear me. You will not lay hands on him. If he's guilty, I'll be glad to hang him myself, but until he has been convicted, he's innocent."

"Hang him," a loud voice cried out. "Let's show slave masters what we think of them." Many others started yelling again.

The police officers pulled their guns and faced the crowd. This action diverted attention from Ben for just a moment. He dropped off the edge of the platform, ducked under a freight wagon and pulled loose the reins of a saddled horse standing by a hitching post. A bullet from the mob sang over his head as he vaulted into the saddle. The row of freight wagons shielded him from more bullets and by the time the angry crowd flooded out into the street he was half a block away. He turned a corner into a street between warehouses. Riding two blocks as fast as the good horse would take him, he slipped off at the entrance of an alley, slapped the horse into motion and ran for four blocks parallel to the tracks. Then he circled back, determined to get in that baggage car. The train was pulling away as he looked cautiously out of an alley.

Ruby was standing on the platform watching the train as it gathered speed. There was no sign of the coffins. The valise was at her feet.

A ragged boy walked by kicking a rock ahead of him. Ben fished in his pocket and found a coin.

"Here, young fellow," he said. "If you go tell that young lady over there that Mr. Jackson wants to see her, I'll give you two bits."

The boy looked at the coin and ran. He spoke to Ruby. She

259

turned and saw Ben. He slipped into a lunch room, sat down and watched as Ruby picked up the valise and made her way to him.

"They got my gold." She had been crying.

"So fly the wages of deceit," said Ben. "What happened?"

"I was on the train ready to ride to St. Louis when the conductor came and said I had to get off. He said the army had taken over the train and there would be no civilian passengers. He made me get off. I tried to get them to understand that I had some things in the baggage car, but all those soldiers were loading up and nobody would listen to me. The train pulled off with my gold. Oh, Ben, what am I going to do?"

She began to bawl again. He handed her a handkerchief and ordered two cups of coffee. She stopped sniffling when they arrived.

"What are you doing here?" Ruby asked.

"Know a better place? They'll be looking all over the city and half the country. The last place they'll look is at the depot where it all started. I've got a wagon and a good horse across the street. Shall we head for Nashville and see if we can get the gold back?"

"When?"

"Now."

"Let's eat first."

They placed their orders and ate in silence for a while.

"Something bothers me," Ruby said. "Why did you send that boy to get me? After what I did, why didn't you just let me go. I thought you were caught."

"You had all my money in that valise."

"That's not very flattering, Colonel Gordyne."

"No, but it's true, Miss Hunsford."

They finished their meal and rode out of town. As a half moon came up, Ruby moved close to him. He felt the heat of her soft body.

"I'm cold," she said. "You could get me warm."

"There's a jacket in the suitcase."

Life with Ruby is like walking on a broken foot, Ben thought. I'd shed her, but she'd have the sheriff on my tail before morning.

260

21
MISTY GRAVES

Sheriff Alston sent telegrams in all directions trying to find Ben. No one reported seeing him. He even alerted authorities in Nashville. Then, seeking more information, he went to the Berliner Hotel and found that Ruby had not checked in.

Though Ben stopped only long enough to rest his horse, the Battle of Nashville was over before he arrived. Hood had been defeated. His army was never again a threat. Ben and Ruby began searching for three misplaced caskets. Their questions were greeted with grisly laughter.

"Coffins? Sure I remember coffins," the freight master told them. "Hundreds of them. A graves detail went over the battlefield and put all the dead in coffins. A baggage car and four freight cars were near full."

"What became of them?" Ben asked.

"What else do you do with coffins? You bury them."

"Where?"

"In the military cemetery."

They drove in a misty rain to the burial ground and found hundreds of new, unmarked graves. Ruby sobbed in wretched despair. Ben looked over the field in awful silence. For a full half hour, they stared as the cold rain dribbled over them. Then without a word, Ben pulled the horse around.

Returning to the city, they took rooms near the railroad station and silently climbed the stairs to the third floor. Ben carried the valise. Neither spoke as they walked down the dingy hall. Their steps echoed on the wooden floor. They stopped before Ruby's door. She put her key in the lock, turned and looked at Ben. He set the valise on the floor. Opening it, he took out a small reticule.

"Here are your things," he said.

"Thank you," she said, taking it.

"Hungry?"

"A little."

"Change into something dry and I'll be back to get you in a bit."

Later they ate in silence in the nearly empty hotel dining room. Ben drank the last of his coffee.

"Well, Ruby," he said, "we can go home now. I reckon it's all over. Maybe Bart will make it."

"You mean Bart has some gold, too."

"I said 'maybe.'"

There was silence again. Ruby played with her food.

"What are you going to do, Ben?"

"First light, I'll take the horse and wagon and head for Atlanta. Maybe I can catch General Johnston before Sherman does."

"What about me?"

He felt around in the inside pocket of his black coat. Extracting an envelope, he handed it to her.

"What's this?" she asked.

"It's the money I took from you in San Francisco. Remember? Here's a little bit more. It ain't much but it ought to get you to St. Louis."

Ben watched her as she slipped the envelope into her bodice. Ruby took another small bite and sipped her drink. He leaned back in the ladderback chair. She put down her glass.

"Ben?'

"Yes?"

"May I have my ticket to Washington?"

"What for?'

"Keepsake, I guess. A reminder of the time we've had."

He took both tickets out of his pocket and gave them to her.

"Thank you, Ben."

Laying her napkin on the table, she said, "I'm tired."

They went upstairs to their rooms.

"Goodbye, Miss Hunsford," he said as she opened her door.

"Goodbye, Colonel Gordyne."

It was after midnight when Ruby slipped barefooted down to the hotel lobby. There was no one at the desk. A note under a bell read, "Ring for service." On this card she printed, "Col. Benjamin L. Gordyne, Rebel spy, is in Room 304," and returned to her room.

Light was just beginning to erase the night when Ruby heard the door across the hall open and close. She went to her window and looked down as Ben stepped from the hotel. Flanking him were four Union soldiers.

Ruby took her bag and made her exit through the rear of the hotel. She went to the livery where Ben had left the horse and wagon. In a few minutes it was hooked up.

First to St. Louis to pick up Daddy's strong box, she thought as she rode away. Then I'll use the ticket to Washington. Maybe Bart has some gold.

22

STRANGE ALLIANCE

When Bart and Heather arrived in Panama City, that settlement hardly deserved to be called a city. Temporary housing of tents and shacks indicated few of its inhabitants planned to make the town a permanent home. It was a staging camp on the way to the gold fields of California. A constant stream of people coveting a bit of the golden dream poured in to wait for the next ship north. The stampede had slowed, but there were always more people waiting for passage than the ships could carry. The surplus became the city's semi-permanent population.

The Panama Steamer stood offshore. Small boats came out to pick up her passengers and cargo. The tide, sun, temperature and humidity were high when Bart and Heather leaned on the rail looking down on the "schooling" boats below and the swarming people on the shore.

Captain Waters had ordered Bart confined to the ship until the American consul in Panama City could be notified of the charges against him. Heather had to stay to tell her story again. O'Dune, Bart's guard, stood in the cooler shadows nearby.

Stevedores wrestled the ship's cargo of cowhides and furs into rope nets. The vessel's cranes lifted the loaded nets and, swinging them over the side, lowered them to the boats below. Passengers stepped carefully down the steep gangway into other boats for the short journey to shore.

Bart turned his attention to others leaning on the rail. The Pinkerton agent near the stern was watching him. At the prow, his face shadowed by a broad-brimmed white hat, stood a tall, thin man with a smoky complexion.

"As a Union agent, you might be interested in that Spanish-American aristocrat," he told Heather, nodding forward.

Heather looked and asked, "Why?"

"He's the curious explorer I discovered wandering around in the early morning when I had some degree of freedom. He doesn't seem to be in a hurry to get ashore."

He turned his attention back to the land. A fine black carriage drawn by two handsome horses stopped at a point near the end of the railroad siding. The slender woman who stepped out captured Bart's eye. Her pale face was set off by rich, black hair. She was elegantly clothed in a full-skirted, red dress and carried a matching veiled bonnet.

"There's Spain in her," Bart said to Heather.

"Ben wouldn't like it if you looked at me like that," she answered with a touch of envy in her voice.

The woman stood by the side of the carriage and waved her hat in the direction of the ship. On board, Bart saw the man at the prow lift his hat in response, but he made no move to disembark.

Bart turned his eyes back to the woman. She was beautiful enough to catch any man's attention. A fat man in baggy clothing was talking with her. Then he strolled towards a small rowboat, got in and pushed off.

A switch engine backed a boxcar into view. It stopped as close to the water as possible and a squad of troops jumped out to take guard positions between it and the shore. On board the line of debarking passengers was stopped. The water around the ship was cleared of boats. A skiff, somewhat larger than those used to ferry freight and passengers, set out from the land and tied up at the foot of the gangplank.

Immediately members of the crew, under the watchful eye of Captain Waters and a ship's guard, began carrying ingots of gold from the ship's vault to the smaller craft below.

"How much is it worth?" Heather asked as the last bar was stacked.

"I'd guess about five million," Bart said.

"How do you plan to steal that?"

"An interesting challenge," he said. "You got any ideas?"

"If I had, I wouldn't tell you."

"Neither will I tell you. I'll bet you one of those ingots our friend over there has a plan."

"You mean he's going to try to steal that gold, too?"

"Yes, and if he succeeds, guess who'll get blamed."

"You?"

"Right. So, if I'm going to get the blame anyway, I might just was well do the stealing, don't you think?"

"You can't get away with it."

"We'll see. You just might tell your friend from Pinkerton that he'd do his country a favor if he'd watch those other thieves as closely as he's watching me."

"Why?"

"He isn't staying on board because he likes this ship. I'd sure like to know what he's got on his mind. Between here and shore is the only place unguarded. How? I don't like to be suspicious of beautiful women, but I know she's part of it."

As the lighter below was being prepared to cast off, another small boat put out from shore. In it were two men in black suits and pith helmets and two men in uniform. Bart nodded in its direction and said, "The American consul comes to greet me."

"Look," said Heather, excitement making her whisper sound like a shout. "That man's waving his hat."

On shore the woman lifted her hat. Then a movement under the shadow of the prow of the Panama Steamer flickered in the corner of Bart's eye. A sail was being raised on one of the flotilla of small crafts waiting to resume the task of transferring cargo and passengers. In the bottom of the boat was some kind of cargo hidden by a canvas. What set Bart in motion was the fat man raising the sail. He was the same one who had spoken to the

266

woman on shore.

"There's the fox," he barked and turned to run behind the people lining the ship's rail.

"Where you going?" called O'Dune and jumped at his prisoner.

"Sorry, ol' buddy," said Bart and hit him just below the ribs. The momentum of his charge and the power of the blow, dropped the seaman to the deck. Bart raced forward, knocking down several men who tried to stop him. As he ran he pulled off his shirt. The boat below him was underway when Bart reached the bow. He paused long enough to take off his shoes. Then he leaped up on to the rail, balanced briefly and dove for the top of the mast. He missed, but caught the sail. The jerk of his weight on the cloth pulled the rope out of the hands of the fat man below and he was enveloped in sailcloth.

Bart fished around under the canvas. Pulling the cursing man out, he threw him overboard. Out from under the tarps covering the cargo on the deck came eight armed men. Bart dove over the side and started swimming to meet the boat carrying the American consul. The men he had left behind took aim at him.

"Hold it," shouted Captain Waters from the deck of the Panama Steamer. Beside him stood armed crew members pointing guns. The men below in the small boat put down their rifles.

The two soldiers in the consul's boat fished Bart out of the bay.

"What is the meaning of this?" demanded the American who Bart figured must be the consul.

"Those men were going to steal the gold," Bart gasped as they neared the gangplank. He stayed on the boat after it pulled up to the ship's landing platform and the consul, his aide and the two uniformed men went on board. Heather came and sat beside him. Bart glanced up and grinned.

"Now I'm a hero," he said and looked towards the shore. The boat with the gold was docked. They could see troops transferring its cargo to the boxcar. The Spanish-looking woman had disappeared.

The tall, thin man was no longer leaning on the rail.

In a few minutes the consul and his party returned, bringing Captain Waters with them.

"Mr. Gordyne?" the consul asked.

"Yes, sir."

"I must say what you have just done is rather remarkable."

"It's the least I can do for my country," said Bart.

"The charges brought against you appear to be preposterous in the extreme and since you have just saved the United States about five million dollars in gold, I think we can forget them."

"Thank you, sir."

"As for you, young lady," said the consul, turning to Heather, "I don't know what your game is, but I suggest you find some other way to play it."

"Yes, sir."

Bart looked at her and grinned.

"You polecat," she whispered.

23
ROSITTA

Bart and Heather spent the night in the official residence of the American consul. The not so fortunate Legs sweated in the heavy tropical heat while curled up on a pile of hides near the loaded boxcar. His uncomfortable sleep was disturbed every time the military detachment changed guard.

Morning was sudden, like a jump from darkness into the steambath of daylight. Shortly after the new day arrived, a rickety steam engine backed a mix of passenger and freight cars onto a siding. A sleepy brakeman disengaged the engine from the cars and a switch was made to pick up the guarded boxcar.

Legs walked alongside as it was pulled on to the main line and then backed into the siding where the rest of the train waited. When the attachment was complete, the engineer yanked twice on a whistle cord and pushed the throttle. Drive wheels spun briefly on rails and the train puffed inland, slowly picking up speed. Pharson jumped for the steps of a coach, grabbed a hand rail and swung aboard.

Several minutes later the engineer applied the brakes and the train stopped at a makeshift passenger terminal. Pharson glanced out a window to see Heather and Bart saying goodbye to the consul.

A first class rebel eel, slick as buttered corn, Legs said to himself and scrunched down into his seat to try to catch some sleep.

On the platform, Bart watched as four men loaded three wooden caskets into the baggage car. When this was done, he took Heather's arm and assisted her onto the train. They found seats across the aisle and four rows in front of Legs. The train rolled out of the city into a canyon of green created by sky-touching trees of the thick jungle. As speed increased, a current of air moved through the coach's open windows relieving the oppressive heat. Heather and Bart laughed as they talked over what had happened.

"Look," Bart said, clutching Heather's arm. "That woman coming in the door. She gave the signal to start the attempt to steal the gold yesterday in Panama City."

"Are you sure?"

A man followed the woman into the car.

"Certain as daylight. She was standing on the dock. I was watching her, wonderin' what a beautiful woman like that was doing in all that mob of sweaty workmen."

"I remember," Heather interrupted. "You were talking to me and eyeing another woman."

"Yeah, do you blame me? Anyway, I was wondering what she was doin' there. She was standin' with a big hat in her hand watchin' the barge carryin' the gold move away from the Panama Steamer. All of a sudden she lifted her hat and waved it. I looked around and saw our friend there lift his hat. They were both signaling the fat man on the sloop. When he got their signals, he started moving out to intercept the gold. That's when I figured out what was going on."

"You mean that woman is part of the robbery attempt?"

"As near as I can figure it out."

The woman and her companion made their way slowly down the aisle.

"They're lookin' for someone," Bart said.

"Do you suppose they're looking for you?"

"Me? Why?"

270

"You didn't do them any favors yesterday."

"That's so, but I don't have anything they want now."

"If I were them, I'd want your head and if I had further plans for the gold in the boxcar I'd want to be sure you weren't around to spoil my game a second time."

The pair stopped in front of Bart.

"Hello, my friend," said Bart. "Weren't you on the Panama Steamer out of Monterey?"

"No," the man said. "I think you must be mistaken."

"Neither was I. Must have been two other guys."

The couple continued on to the next car.

"That's the man who was exploring the ship's corridors in the middle of the night," Bart said.

"I never saw him."

"He must have stayed in his cabin during the day."

"Is it possible that a mutual interest gave you opportunities honest people don't have?"

"Now what could you possibly mean by that?"

"You were wandering around in the middle of the night when everybody thought you were too weak to walk."

"Just getting my exercise," he said and they laughed.

"I need exercise now so I'm going after them," Bart said.

"I'm going with you."

"Mrs. Wanderman, Ben gave me orders to watch out for you, and I'm telling you to wait right here."

"You could get killed."

"It's a possibility. It's also possible that I might save that gold from falling into the wrong hands."

"That is among the funniest things I've ever heard."

Bart walked through the train looking for the dark-haired woman. He found her on the rear observation platform. She stood alone looking back over the long tracks. He stepped beside her and she glanced up at him.

"So, Senor Gordyne, we meet," she said.

Her English was excellent with only a slight Latin accent.

"You know me?'

271

"No, but Senor Morenda told me of you."

"He is the one who was not on the Panama Steamer?"

She laughed.

"He did not tell me your name."

"I am his sister, Rositta Morenda."

"The beauty of the name fits the beauty of the named."

She looked up at him and smiled.

"I would not want them to kill you," she said.

"Does someone want me dead?"

"There are several in the council who are very angry for what you did yesterday. Why did you do it?"

"It may be that I have other plans for the gold."

"So I understand. Manuel tells me you were confined to your cabin for attempting to steal it."

"That's not quite right. I was put under guard because there was a suspicion that I might try to steal it.'

"Yes. Why would they be so suspicious of you?"

"Someone said I was working for the Confederacy."

"Are you?"

"I am now taking Mrs. Wanderman home to Washington. There is a reward for her return."

"The detective could take her and you did not answer my question. I will assume the answer is yes. So I will tell you that the Council of Ten is a group of revolutionaries who will restore liberty to our country."

She turned to him.

"You see, Senor Gordyne, you and I have the same motives. We need that gold to pay for our revolution as you need it to pay for your Civil War. We do not want any more competition in our efforts to get it. Therefore, the council is prepared to share it with you if you will help us. Or, if you would join us we could make you a man of considerable influence in our country."

"How can I be of service to you?'

She moved closer to him.

"For one, you could divert the man from Pinkerton. If he had not been watching the railroad car last night, we would have tried again to get that shipment."

She said this and stopped. They were standing face to face. She looked boldly into his eyes and said, "Personally, I would like very much to work with you."

Startled by the statement, Bart looked into her mischievous dark eyes. It was tempting. Then he thought of 'Bama.

"Miss Morenda," he said, "your beauty is not the only attraction I am discovering in you. Getting to know you would be quite an experience. I hope I shall have that opportunity. All this just makes it more difficult to turn down your offer. The gold isn't yours and it isn't mine."

"Then they will kill you," she said quietly, stepping away.

Bart, looking after her, discovered that three men had come unnoticed onto the platform. They rushed him in an attempt to push him over the side. His hands gripped the rail and their initial effort failed. One man pushed hard on his head while each of the others grabbed a leg, lifting his feet off the floor to hurl him head first onto the railroad ties rushing beneath them.

He bent his knees and let his legs go limp, depriving them of leverage. Then he straightened his legs with a sudden kick and hurled them back against the wall of the car. He felt one man's rib crack under the force of his foot and he heard the man's cry of pain. By twisting his body, he freed his head from the hands of the man who was pushing on it. Swinging around, he hit that man with his forearm, knocking him against the side railing. Before he could regain his balance, Bart caught his foot and pushed. The man went over the rail. He hung on with one hand for a short time, trying to find something to stand on and dropped away, tumbling down the embankment into the jungle below. Bart turned to his other attackers. One of them was huddled in the corner of the observation platform. The other was slicing at him with a knife. He feinted a retreat, backstepping. Then he leaped at the man, stopping just short of the stabbing blade. Turning in close, he caught the slashing arm in both hands and broke a bone. The man screamed and the knife flew into the jungle.

Bart looked down the track to see the one he had thrown off

the train crawl up out of the swamp trailing a crushed leg.

Stepping inside, he stood a minute examining the passengers. Even the back of her head made Rositta stand out. He went to her and bowed.

"Some citizens of your country back there need medical attention," he said.

"You peeg," she hissed reverting to a more natural accent.

Bart laughed and strolled towards the front of the train. He met Heather in the next car. She was coming to find him.

"You're right," he told her. "Those people don't like me."

"What happened?"

"Had a right nice chat with Miss Rositta Morenda. Beautiful woman. I think she loves me. She called me a 'peeg.'"

"Did they hurt you?'

"Me? No. They did try to throw me off the train. One man landed in the swamp. I think he's got a broken leg. Another's gonna have trouble with his arm for a while. It'll hurt the third to breathe for a week or two."

"She's right, you know?"

"What?"

"You are a 'peeg.'"

The train rocked on across the isthmus carrying them into the Atlantic port of Colon. They went by carriage to the port where The Islands, one of Cornelius Vanderbilt's glistening new steamships, was preparing for her run to New York. In addition to the cargo of gold, lumber, hides, furs and three caskets, the vessel took on about fifty barrels of sugar and some mahogany. Passengers were not allowed aboard until the gold had been stowed away. Then they were ushered to their cabins by crew members.

At the top of the gangplank, Heather and Bart looked back at the bustling crowd on the dock below. Suddenly, Heather gasped and grabbed Bart's arm.

"Oh, no! It can't be." She leaned over the rail.

"What?" Bart asked.

"I thought I saw Junk DuBris by that wagon."

274

"Don't see how that could be. The varmint here in Panama?"

They both kept looking at the shifting mass of people below, but spotted no one resembling DuBris.

"You're imagining things, Heather. He's long gone,"Bart said. They went below.

DuBris snickered as he saw them leave the railing. He had been watching when the gold went on board and managed to keep out of sight behind some barrels. His plan was working, all right. He had followed Pharson on to the Panama Steamer, believing Legs was after the gold shipments too. He was still on his trail and also watching that Gordyne fellow and the woman called Heather. He would take care of them later. Meanwhile, more good luck. The sign by the shipping line's office here read, "Able Bodied Seamen Wanted." He could smell it. A few more weeks and more gold. He was going to be rich!

Like a magnet, California's gold still made it easier to muster a full crew going south and west than one going east and north. It was always necessary in Colon to hire replacements for those who jumped ship. Junk signed on for night duty.

While The Islands was in port, the areas below deck were stifling. Most of the passengers went below only after sunset. Bart was already prowling the ship. He watched as stevedores stored the three coffins in a baggage room with trunks, bags and other personal items the passengers were not likely to need during the voyage. The purser stood at the door checking a list as each piece was brought in. Next to him were two armed marines.

Of particular interest to Bart was a corner of the baggage room set aside by steel bars like a jail cell. He could see what looked like two canvas-covered mounds on the floor at the back of this cage. Rope cargo nets spread on top of them were fastened to rings in the bulkhead and the floor. Must be the gold, he thought.

Bart went to his cabin and tore a leg off a pair of pants. Knotting one end, he created a canvas bag. With this he went strolling through the ship. Conveniently located in the corridors and public rooms of the ornate vessel were standing receptacles where smokers were expected to dispose of cigar stubs and

275

cigarette butts. These were filled with wet sand. About twenty pounds of this went into the bag. As he moved about, Bart also took some of the candles which graced the tables in the deserted dining room. He returned to his cabin, tied up the other end of his bag and printed his name in wax on it. Then he returned to the baggage room.

"Excuse me, sir" he said to the purser.

"What is it?"

Bart appeared slightly embarrassed.

"Well, you see, sir," he said, "I've something here that's somewhat more valuable than the usual items carried on board. I don't like to think it wouldn't be safe in my cabin, but, well, sir, I was wondering if there isn't some place it could be locked up that would be a little safer?"

"Certainly. I'll be glad to lock it up in the security section of the baggage room. It'll be behind bars over there."

Bart hesitated.

"I don't mean to question your honesty, sir," he said, "but who has the key?"

"You will notice that the cell door has two locks. When we get everything loaded, each will be locked. The ship's captain has a key to one lock, and the captain of the marine guard has a key to the other. I have a key to this door. It takes all three keys to get in there."

"Does it take three keys to lock it?"

"The others will lock it before we sail, but right now we are in the process of loading and it's only locked with one lock. I have the key. I can put your...ah, package in there."

Bart appeared to hesitate. "I see," he said and started to move away. Then he turned back.

"Would you be so kind as to let me put my package in your security cell?"

"Of course." The purser found the key on his ring and led Bart to the barred cell. He opened the door and Bart entered, looked around briefly and set his bundle of sand on the floor between the two canvas-covered piles.

"It won't roll around there," he told the purser as he stepped out.

The ship sailed at dusk, heading for Havana where more cargo would be loaded. During the two-day voyage Bart explored The Islands, especially the section near the baggage room. At night he worked on a drawing of the area and lay in his bunk trying to figure a way to transfer the gold from inside a locked cell to three caskets outside.

On one of his strolls through the ship, he discovered that Rositta Morenda and her brother were on board. Several times he met them and figured they were exploring, still trying to get at that gold. The Islands stayed in Havana about a week. During this time some of its hides and lumber were exchanged for barrels of rum and more sugar. Bart took Heather on a tour of the city, but he did not leave the ship most days. He kept a close watch on the cell, figuring the Morendas might try to steal the gold while they were in port. Nothing happened.

The trip north started in balmy weather. Sun rays bounced off the clean whiteness of the sleek vessel as she steamed toward Florida cutting like a sword through the silken surface of the sea. If there was any wind, it stood to the stern, making the ship a place of suffocating heat.

Finally, high, thin clouds moved in as she rounded the Florida keys. Capt. Bowman's passengers sighed with relief. They woke the next morning to see a fine mist of cold rain washing the ship's polished decks. The rigging whistled in the wind.

Moving up the coast the ship leaped as great breaking waves rushed under her. She shuddered as she plunged. Deep torrents of green water swept over the decks.

"At this time of year it's not likely to be a hurricane," Bowman said to the few passengers who sat with him at the captain's table that night. "But the Atlantic can kick up some mean storms at any time. There is no danger. My ship can weather anything the sea can throw at her. She's the best ship afloat."

That was encouraging. Still most of his passengers kept to

their cabins. Bart used the early darkness and deserted decks to advantage. With a small carpetbag in hand, he stumbled along the swinging companionways. On previous walks he had discovered the shop where the shipwright kept his tools. In this room, he lit a candle and by its light selected a large wrench, a brace and bit, a keyhole saw and a handsaw. He blew out the light and with the borrowed tools in his bag walked to a room filled with rope, nail kegs, sailcloth and other ship stores.

He shut the door, lit his candle once more, rolled up his sleeves and grinned. This storeroom shared a common bulkhead with the baggage room. Rows of deck-to-ceiling shelves divided the area into eight neat aisles, each ending at the common wall. Roped to the wall at the end of each aisle was a barrel of tar.

Bart walked down three of these before he found the heads of six bolts forming a vertical line on the bulkhead.

Those bolts hold the cell to the wall, he told himself and grinned again.

He untied the rope that lashed the tar barrel to the bulkhead and moved it out three feet from the wall where he secured it to the shelves on either side of the aisle.

It'll be tight, but I believe I can work there, he thought as he laid a bolt of sailcloth on top of the barrel and fastened the end of this to the wall.

Nice tent, he decided, crawling in with the bag of tools.

Bart blew out the light, sat down next to the bulkhead and began the job of making a door. The ship's noise as it plowed through the storm covered the sound of his work.

He drilled through the wooden bulkhead about two feet from the floor near the lowest bolt. Then, taking the keyhole saw, he pushed it through the hole he had drilled and began sawing. Not easy. The bulkhead was made of double planked oak and he deliberately made the push-pull of his sawing irregular to conceal the sound within the other noises of the bucking ship.

But the noises also covered other sounds. Regularly throughout the night a watchman made his rounds and, as the ship growled and groaned, Bart could not hear him coming.

278

Once on these rounds the watchman thought he heard something in the storeroom. He stopped at the door and listened. It came again. He opened the door. A beam from his hurricane lantern shot into the room before the door was fully opened. Light filtered around the edge of the canvas. Bart stopped the pull of the saw.

He sat motionless as the watchman held his lantern high and let the beam sweep between each row of shelves. Then the man backed out and shut the door.

Bart waited a few minutes and continued to work. Morning was near by the time he pushed at the plank he had been sawing. It cracked. He forced it again and a piece broke away, falling back to the darkness beyond. He had a hole in the wall.

Laying aside the tools, Bart spat on his hands, rubbed them together and reached through the opening. He felt around inside the cell. His finger touched cloth, then a metallic surface. Had to be it! The thing felt like an ingot and was heavy enough. He pulled it through the hole, laid it on his thigh and struck a match.

The bar was gold!

He grinned. Then the match burned his fingers.

It was tempting, but he knew the night was about over and in a short time people would be moving about the ship.

Bart returned the ingot to its place, put his tools through the hole and laid them behind the stacked gold in the baggage room. Reluctantly, he came out from under his cover. He lighted the candle, set it on a shelf, moved the barrel back into its place to hide the opening and spread canvas over the top.

After searching the room one more time to make sure everything was in place, he blew out the candle. His hand was on the doorknob when he noticed a thin line of light under the door. Someone holding a lantern was on the other side. He put his ear to a panel and heard voices but could not understand what they were saying. He waited through what sounded like an agitated conversation.

Bart was beginning to fear daylight would bring some of the crew to the storeroom, but eventually the light began to move away. He opened the door slowly and looked at the disappearing backs of two men. One looked like Manual Morenda, he thought. The clothes were familiar. The other carried the lantern.

Bart followed. As they turned the corner in the corridor, he saw the other man's face. It was Junk DuBris! Heather had been right. He must have come aboard at Panama.

The two went to a cargo bay and descended a ladder to the hold where casks of rum and sugar were stored. Bart stopped at the head of the opening to watch and listen.

"We could mix gold with the sugar in a few of those barrels," Morenda said. "Stealing sugar in New York will be easier than stealing gold."

His English isn't nearly as good as Rositta's, Bart thought.

"Yeah," said Junk, "but first we've got to get it out of the vault. I wish I knew how Gordyne plans to do it."

"Si, Senor DuBris," said Morenda. "We should watch him, but I do not think it will be any easier to take it from him than to get it out of the vault."

Bart could not hear any more of the conversation as the two below him moved out of sight among the barrels. When they returned to the ladder he heard Morenda say, "Good night, Senor DuBris."

He watched from the shadows of a companionway as they headed down the corridor. Something was afoot. They had made plans, he decided.

Though he was a veteran skipper, Capt. Bowman could not break his ship out of the storm's grip. On the second night, as the winds continued to mount, Bart enlarged the hole in the vault's wall making it large enough to crawl through. On the third night he unbolted the barred cage in the baggage room from the plank wall and exchanged clay bricks from the coffins for gold ingots. When this was done, he pulled the barred cell back in place and rebolted it to the bulkhead. He left the drill and saws in the cell, but tucked the wrench onto his belt inside his shirt. He also removed his pants-leg bag of sand.

When they find my opening, he thought, they'll find the saws and drill but nothing to take off those nuts. That may make them think the gold was taken out through the storage room. Since my bag is also missing, they may not think I stole their gold.

As he walked back to his cabin, Bart let the sand dribble out of the pants-leg bag as far as Morenda's door.

Fingers of gray light were pushing through the running rain when he tossed the wrench and his bag over the side. A quick walk back to his cabin and soon he was fast asleep.

About noon hunger woke him. The Islands was still leaping before the storm. He finished his meal in the dining room and strolled around the deck enjoying the blasts of wind and talking to a few other persons brave enough to face the gale.

In the gaming room he watched a card artist take gold away from a couple of bearded prospectors.

Returning to his cabin, he found the door open. Inside, under the personal supervision of Captain Bowman, two marines were searching his belongings. Heather and Legs stood watching.

"Looking for something?" Bart asked as he stepped through the door.

"Where is the gold?" the captain demanded.

"Gold? What gold?"

"Mr. Gordyne, this gentleman is an agent of the Pinkerton Detective Agency."

"Yes, captain, I know him. We shipped out of San Francisco together."

"This morning he discovered a hole cut in a bulkhead of the baggage room. He reported this to me. We investigated and discovered that someone has removed about seven hundred pounds of gold from the security cell."

"Did they get my package?" Bart asked anxiously.

"Your package?" Captain Bowman asked.

"Yes, sir. The purser was kind enough to lock up a package for me when we sailed from Colon."

"I don't know. We are not looking for a package. I asked you where you put the gold and, Mr. Gordyne, I demand an answer."

"There are two hundred people on board. Why search my

281

cabin?"

"Because, Mr. Gordyne, Mrs. Wanderman says you are a secret agent of the Confederate Army on a mission to divert Union gold to the Confederacy. You were observed returning to your room early this morning."

"Was I seen carrying seven hundred pounds of gold?"

"Let me talk," said Legs.

"No, you were not carrying gold, but on two nights Mrs. Wanderman saw you leave your cabin about ten o'clock. I followed you to the deck and lost you in the darkness. You did not return to your cabin until morning."

Bart looked at Heather. She would not face him.

"I have difficulty sleeping," he said. "A trait I inherited from my father. Rather than lie abed all night, I get up and walk around. Does that make me a Confederate spy and a thief?"

"Mr. Gordyne," Captain Bowman said, "I cannot believe that you walked the passageways of my ship for eight hours for two nights and never once passed the bridge, never once met a watch, never once spoke to the marine guards. I insist that you tell me where you spent those nights."

"This has to be in confidence, of course?"

"I shall be the judge of that. If you do not tell me, I shall confine you to the brig until we find that gold, and if I find that you did take it I shall have you hung. Now, where did you spend sixteen hours of darkness?"

"I must first assure you, Captain Bowman, that Mrs. Wanderman is not involved in this in any way. She is engaged to my brother," Bart said.

"All right, all right. Where did you spend those nights?"

"First, Captain Bowman, please, check to see if the thieves got my package. If it's missing, it's not likely that I'd steal my own valuables."

"All right. I still demand to know where you spent two nights on my ship."

"May I ask you to consider something else. If I were the thief, do you know what I would do after I removed your missing gold?"

"I have a ship in a dangerous storm. I cannot play riddles with you. Where did you spend the nights?"

"Let me answer my riddle, then I'll answer yours. I would pretend to discover the hole I cut and report it to you. Now Captain Bowman, your question. The West is very hard on men. Many of them die. I notice some of your passengers are widows going home to families in the East. The storm frightens them. Some of them are very attractive. One of them particularly needed comforting. Jealousy has accused more than one innocent person."

The captain looked at the detective. The marines grinned at each other. Heather put her hand over her mouth. At that moment the ship rolled far over on its starboard side and hesitated while they all held their breaths. Somewhere a woman screamed. The Islands pulled herself upright.

"It's not the gold I'm worried about right now," Captain Bowman said. "It's this storm. Excuse me, Mr. Gordyne. I've got to take care of my ship."

"No problem, captain. Perhaps I can help you find the gold."

"I could use some help. I can assure you, I'll find it before it gets off this ship, and when I do the person who has it will hang."

Turning to the guards, the captain said, "Whoever stole that gold had to take it out through the storeroom. They could not have gotten it out of that cage, through a locked door and past a guard. We know two places it is not. It's not in Mr. Gordyne's cabin and it's not in the baggage room. I want this ship searched. Start in the storeroom. It may be hidden in one of those barrels."

At the door, Legs turned to face Bart and said, "You are too smooth, Mr. Gordyne. I'm going to enjoy watching you try to slip your head through a noose."

During the night, tons of water battered the ship's superstructure. Several ventilators were torn out and water poured into the holds. The engines were flooded and the helpless vessel ran before the wind towards land. Time after time the prow climbed to the summit of mountainous waves. When it passed over a peak the ship would reach a point of uncertain balance and then the bow would come crashing down into a trough, sending columns of water shooting towards the low-hanging clouds. As she fell waves filled the foredeck. The angry water raged and churned in its close confinement until, its anger spent, it streamed through the narrow scuppers.

Parts of the superstructure were torn away. More water cascaded into the ship's compartments. Her seams began to crack.

Captain Bowman ordered everyone to bring life rings to the ballroom. It was still dark.

Bowman raised his hand for silence. The groaning of the floundering ship and the pounding of the waves were the only sounds.

"We are not far from the coast," he assured his frightened passengers.

"Which coast?" someone shouted.

"Of that, I cannot be certain. It's been four days since we could take a reading and we do not know how fast we have been moving. However, I am sure we are near Georgia or the Carolinas. Cape Hatteras may be our biggest hazard. We'll try to find a bay. We may have to beach the ship."

The passengers clung together. Someone screamed, "We're going to sink."

"There is no reason to panic," Bowman said. "You know your lifeboats. If the order to abandon ship is given, go to your boat. There's plenty of room for everyone. Just be calm. The greatest danger we face is panic."

Someone began to pray.

"What we need is a panic," DuBris whispered to Morenda. "If we had an empty ship, we'd have the gold to ourselves." He stepped out the door and waited for Captain Bowman.

Heather was watching Bart. Then she looked for the Morendas. When she turned again to Bart, he was gone. Legs was standing beside her.

"Where did he go?" Heather asked.

"I don't know, but I'm not about to let him get too far away," Legs said and started pushing his way through the crowd toward

284

the door. Heather followed. It took them some time to locate Bart on the stern deck where barrels of rum were roped to the hand rail on the bulkhead. He was busy opening these and emptying them into the gutter.

"What on earth are you doing?" Heather demanded.

Bart looked up, rubbed his chin, thought a moment and said, "A full barrel serves no useful purpose on a sinking ship. But empty, they'll float real good. Come on, give me a hand."

"Why do you want them to float?" the Pinkerton agent asked skeptically.

"If the ship sinks suddenly, there may be a lot of people floating around in the ocean. If they can grab hold of a barrel, they might be able to ride it ashore. Come on, Heather, give me a hand. Mr. Pharson, will you see if you can find rope? We'll need to tie it around these barrels to give people something to hang onto."

Legs took off his hat and scratched his head as if his instincts were telling him Bart had something less than saving lives in mind. But he went off looking for rope.

Junk DuBris followed Captain Bowman out of the ballroom. The ship's officer started down a ladder. As an experienced seaman, he descended facing out like someone going down steps. Junk looked around. No one was in sight. As the captain's shoulders came level with the deck, Junk kicked him in the back of his neck. Without a sound, he tumbled to the deck below. His neck was broken.

Several minutes later when the body was discovered the news of his death swept through the ship. Before the passengers recovered from this shock, Junk ran through the passageways shouting, "Abandon ship! The captain's dead! Abandon ship!"

In an instant the corridors filled with frightened people clawing their way to the boat deck. Efforts by the first mate and the ship's crew to restore order were useless.

"If it wasn't going to sink before, it is now," said the first mate to a seaman. "It'll be a disaster if we don't get them into the boats."

As daylight began to brighten the cloudy skies, passengers piled into lifeboats. Some were on the verge of launching themselves into the wild ocean.Water streamed over the deck, pouring into the ship through hatches and stairway doors left open by panicked passengers.

"Come on," Bart said, grabbing Heather's arm. Followed by Legs they scrambled back to the crowded main deck. Some lifeboats had already been launched. Bart passed Heather into one. Legs jumped aboard and then turned around.

"Take care of her," Bart shouted above the roar of the wind.

"Where are you going?" Heather cried.

"I've got a job to do," he called and turned away.

She started to follow. Pharson caught her arm and pulled her down to the seat. They watched as Bart ran to a hatch and disappeared into the ship.

The lifeboats rode chaotic waves as they slowly drifted from The Islands.

"There he is," someone shouted.

Heather looked. Bart came on deck dragging a large crated object.

"The gold!" Heather said. "It's in the coffin!"

They watched Bart tie three empty barrels to the casket and lash it to the rail.

"What's he doing?" the first mate asked.

"If that casket is filled with gold," Legs said, "it would sink. Looks like he hopes to use empty barrels to float it ashore."

"We helped him tie those ropes," Heather said in disgust. "We helped him steal that gold."

"It isn't stolen gold now," the first mate shouted. "It's salvage from an abandoned ship, but he's crazy if he thinks he can get it ashore in this storm."

Bart went below again and then three people appeared on deck.

"Who are they?" Legs asked.

"Rositta and Manuel Morenda," Heather said. "What is he doing with them?"

286

The third person wore the uniform of a seaman.

"Junk DuBris!" said Legs."How did he get on board?"

"Some of our crew jumps ship when we get to Panama and we hire whoever we can get. He came on there," said the first mate as the lifeboat dipped between waves. When it reached the top of the next wave and they could see again, The Islands looked farther away and the deck was deserted.

"Bart? Where's Bart?" Heather cried out. As if in answer, Bart appeared pulling another casket through the hatch. Once again he lashed it to three empty barrels. Then he went below deck. The Morendas and DuBris came out of hiding and examined his work.

"What are they doing?" Legs asked.

"Looks like they plan to take the gold away from him," Heather said.

The next time they came over a wave, The Islands, listing badly, was riding much lower so the watchers had a clear view of the deck. The storm seemed to be losing its punch.

"Look!" Heather screamed. "Junk's got a gun."

DuBris aimed the revolver at Manuel Morenda who was bending over a barrel. They heard no shot, but saw Morenda straighten stiffly and stagger against the rail. He slid into the gutter and rolled lifeless as the ship rocked.

Rositta rushed to help her brother but Junk yanked her away. He put his arm around her waist and laughed when she kicked at him. The Islands lurched under their feet and, staggering, he loosened his grip.

Rositta tried to run towards the hatch where Bart had gone. Junk reached out and threw her to the deck just as Bart reappeared, backing through the door, pulling a third casket. Junk leveled his gun at Bart's back. Rositta screamed something. Bart ducked back inside just before the gun spat. Rositta started to run. DuBris turned to her and fired. She staggered, fell and seemed to be trying to crawl to her brother.

Bart stepped into the doorway to face Junk's revolver with a life preserver in his hand. Rositta lunged at the gunman's leg and the shot went wild. As Junk struggled to regain his footing on the sloping deck, Bart pulled back his arm and hurled the life preserver at Junk. He missed. As Junk ducked his second shot went wild. Bart stooped behind the third casket and prepared to push it across the sloping deck at the gunman. Junk gripped the rail with his left arm and aimed the revolver in his right hand at Bart. Rositta fumbled in her brother's coat and pulled out a handgun.

The storm moved in again. A curtain of rain came down between the ship and the watchers in the lifeboat. They saw The Islands no more.

"He's gone?" asked Heather.

"I can give you no hope," said the first mate. "If they get away from DuBris, this storm will take them."

24

KOETEE PLANTATION

The last thing Rositta Morenda remembered was the pistol jumping in her hand. Then pain in her side exploded and there was darkness.

She awakened to find herself afloat in the ocean. She could hear surf breaking on the shore. How had she been able to get off the ship? Then she noticed that her hands were tied to a barrel and Bart was with her. Gasping and sputtering as pulsing pain raced through her body, she tried to speak but failed.

"You're a tough one," she heard Bart say.

As they rode a tall wave, she saw a beach lined with trees bending before the gale.

"This is going to be rough," Bart warned a few minutes later as they entered the breakers. "Hang on tight."

With both hands she gripped the rope that fastened her to a barrel. He was behind her. His arms were under hers. One of his hands was folded over the rope next to hers. The other arm was between her head and the barrel as a cushion. There were other barrels tethered to the one they were using.

One of the waves lifted them high and dropped them into still water behind a sandbar. The breaking sea continued to pour over them. "Water," she murmured, wondering why she had no strength to reach down for a drink.

"Looks like home." Bart muttered a prayer of thanks and untied her hands from the barrel.

He picked Rositta up and carried her out of the reach of the waves, laying her down in a bed of seagrass where the rootball of a fallen tree provided shelter from the cutting wind. Taking off his shirt, he wrung the sea water out of it and held it up to catch the rain. He pressed it to her lips and she drank. Refreshed, she slept.

It was night when she opened her eyes. The air was cold but the wind had died down and a crescent moon hung over the ocean. Bart stood over her. Wet sand clung to his hands and arms.

"Senor Gordyne, where are we?"

"Good question. Another is, if I leave, can I find this place again? Lot of palmetto trees. They kinda thin out north of Georgetown and don't grow natural above Little River."

Rositta had drifted back to sleep. He carried her inland and towards morning came to an inlet with oyster beds. He gathered some, opened them with a knife and wakened her.

"Thank you, senor," she whispered. The oysters were easy to swallow. She thanked him again in Spanish.

He dressed the wound in her side with a piece of her linen skirt and, picking her up again, walked along a tidal creek.

"More of these streams here than I'd find to the north, so I expect we're south of Charleston," he told her as they crossed one of them. He used broken branches to float her over several creeks. Finally, they reached a broad river. Its water was brackish but drinkable. They were very thirsty.

"Ain't but two or three rivers south of Charleston this big until you get to the Savannah," he said. "I don't think we're that far south. Since there's no fort or any building in sight like near Beaufort, unless I'm way off course, this must be the Edisto."

Rositta, listening, nodded her head. She did not understand what he was saying but she felt safe in his care.

Bart followed the waterway for a mile or two and came to a plowed field. Beyond this was a slave's cottage, small and abandoned.

"Probably gone to join Sherman," he said.

Standing by the shack was a weathered wagon. Honeysuckle had not yet climbed into the spokes indicating it had been moved since summer. Bart could see the harness hanging under the eaves of the shed.

"Usable but I sure wish they'd left a mule."

Inside the hut he found a bunk with one worn blanket. He laid Rositta down. Someone had left matches, a tin of cornmeal, molasses, shortening and salt pork. In the field were collards. With these he made a meal. Rositta woke the next morning to find Bart preparing to leave. A jug of water and a hoecake had been placed on a stool by her bed.

"I'm going to the beach," he told her. "I'll be back before dark."

Rositta lay on the hard bunk all day watching the shifting shadows move by the door. It was getting dark when she heard him returning. That night she could sit up to eat. They had oysters, collards and hoecakes.

In the morning Bart placed Rositta in the wagon on a bed of grass covered with the tattered blanket. He put food and the water jug next to her. Rositta was barely aware of this.

I sure wish they'd left the mule, Bart thought again as he got between the wagon's shafts. Putting the harness over his left shoulder and under his right arm, he started pulling the wagon inland up a two-track, sandy loam road.

The day was getting on towards dark when they heard a dog barking and a man cursing. There was the crack of a whip and the dog yelped in pain. This was followed by a woman's shout.

"Don't you dare hit Snuff again," she commanded.

"Miserable rebel hound," the man shouted. "Doesn't know when he's licked. Quiet that mutt or I'll shoot him."

"Down, Snuff," the woman called out and the barking stopped.

Leaving Rositta in the wagon hidden in a grove of trees, Bart walked carefully through underbrush to the edge of a clearing. What he saw made him take cover behind some bushes.

Two women and two girls stood in the yard of a large

plantation house. Three of them were weeping. The oldest gripped a gnarled cane in her right hand. It was raised as a weapon. An old hound lay growling at her feet.

A group of black women and children looked on. Three Union soldiers were carrying clothes and furnishings out of the house. Two armed men stood watch at the foot of the steps leading up to the broad front porch. A sergeant wearing a sidearm and puffing a cigar leaned against an old oak near the driveway.

"Mrs. Sanders," the sergeant said, "it ain't my wish to burn your home, but General Sherman says there's no other way to make you rebels quit fightin', so we're doin' what we're told to do."

"Burnin' our home won't make us quit fightin'," the gray haired woman said.

"Well, maybe not, but still we've got to try."

Carefully Bart backed away through the underbrush and made his way to the rear door of the house. Inside he watched two Union troopers carrying a table to the yard. From a window in a front room he saw them set it in a pile near the women. The sergeant pushed himself away from the tree and walked towards the house.

"That ought to be all they'll need to set up housekeeping in the barn and I don't see anything else that'll do us much good," he said. "You keep your eyes on these ladies while I go inside and build a little fire. I don't want them interfering."

As he spoke he mounted the steps to the front door. Those in the yard waited. They waited longer than they expected. They waited long enough to get concerned.

"What's keeping Sergeant Bayles?" a soldier asked.

"Let's go see," said another and two men headed for the front door.

They were about to put their feet on the first step when a window on the third floor shattered. Looking up they saw their sergeant being pushed through the casement. Bart's hand gripped the man's belt and held him suspended out the window. A rope was around the soldier's neck.

"Howdy," said Bart.

Two of the soldiers aimed their rifles at the man in the window.

"I'd be careful with them guns if I was you," Bart said. "Shoot me and you'll hang your good buddy here. I'm sure you don't want that to happen. Now I suggest you lay those weapons down real careful."

The soldiers hesitated. The man in Bart's grip gave them no command, but Mrs. Sanders stepped forward and took a rifle from the nearest man. The second woman ran to the other guard and snatched his gun away. The other rifles were stacked out of convenient reach. "All right, ladies, put a gun on them," Bart said. "If one of them moves, shoot him."

Then, turning his attention to the man in his grip, he said, "If you don't want to hang, put your hands inside the noose around your neck."

The sergeant complied, and, using his free hand, Bart pulled the noose tight until the man's weight was on the rope. Hand over hand, Bart lowered him to the ground. Then he slid down the rope and joined the group in the front yard.

"You got us. Now what are you going to do with us?" Sergeant Bayles asked. "Kill us and you'll have the whole Union Army on you. Turn us loose and we'll be right back."

"That may take some thinking," Bart said, "and I'll think a whole lot better when y'all are tied tight."

"Coral and Rachel, find us some more rope," Mrs. Sanders commanded and the girls hurried away.

Bart stood by with the sergeant's revolver in his hand.

"I'm Mrs. Kale Sanders, sir," said the older woman as the girls returned and started tying the sergeant's hands. "This is my son's wife, Katie, and these are her girls."

"Pleased to meet you," said Bart. "Ma'am, I think you'd better send someone to burn one of your barns."

"Why?" she asked.

"If there are any more Yankees around, they'll see the smoke and think our friends here have done their job. Maybe they won't come looking for them tonight."

"Rachel, go burn the empty slave quarters. We won't be needing them anymore anyway."

"Yes, Gran'mama," said a girl Bart judged to be about thirteen. She ran towards the rear of the mansion. Within a few minutes a column of black smoke billowed above the trees.

"March," Bart commanded when all the hands were tied.

"Where to?" the sergeant asked.

"To the smokehouse," he said.

Inside the windowless, log building, the bound men were tied to heavy timbers. Then the door was barred. Twilight settled over the countryside. While the women were moving their goods back into the house, Bart disappeared. He returned carrying Rositta.

Bart introduced her and said, "She'll need a doctor."

Rachel was dispatched to find one. After Rositta was put to bed, Bart sat in the dining room eating cold fried chicken and drinking wine.

"Where are the men?" he asked.

"Sherman has crossed the Savannah and is marching towards Columbia. An army is gathering on the Salkehatchie River to try to stop him there. Mr. Sanders and Kale have gone off to see if they can help." Mrs. Sanders sighed. "But what I want to know is who are you and where did you come from?"

"It's best that you don't know," Bart said. "If Sherman finds out what I've done here and learns of my identity, it won't go easy for my family. It may also jeopardize my mission. Right now we need to figure out what we're going to do with the men in the smokehouse."

"We could burn the barn around them," Katie said.

Mrs. Sanders stood up abruptly and left the room. In a few minutes she was back wearing a cape and holding a cane.

"Where you going?" asked Katie.

"To negotiate a prisoner exchange."

"What?"

"I've asked Paul to bring my carriage around. I'm going to look for the commanding officer of the men we've taken and tell

294

him we'll return his men to him, if he'll promise not to burn our home. If I'm not back by sun-up, burn the smokehouse." Turning to Ben she said, "Mister, I don't know who you are, but I can tell you we are mighty grateful for your help. We'd like you to spend the night in our house. However, I don't think that would be wise, so I'm saying goodbye now. I hope you'll return some day. Is there anything at all we can do for you?"

"There are a couple of things," Bart said.

"Name them."

"I sure would appreciate it if Miss Morenda could stay with you until she's able to travel."

"What else you need?"

"A mule, if you don't mind."

"A mule? You can have a horse."

"Mule'll be better if I run into Sherman's troops."

"Anything else?"

"Directions to St. Stephens."

Mrs. Sanders drove off while Katie got Bart a mule. He was gone when the doctor arrived.

25
COMING HOME

February in Indiana was cold. Heavy snow covered the land outside the stockade where Col. Benjamin L. Gordyne was confined.

Ruby Hunsford could not be found. While military investigators and civilian lawmen searched for her, Ben paced the stockade and answered questions at almost daily interrogation sessions. He soon learned several things. They did not know for certain that Ruby had gone to Nashville with him or who had left the note for them under the bell on the hotel desk. Their only witness was missing. Without her, they had no evidence against him.

"Captain Flayze," he said one morning after a long hour of confrontation. "I think we have had more than enough of this.I have told you repeatedly that I was hoping to return to my home in South Carolina after an unsuccessful venture in California. I am needed at home. You are delaying my journey."

The officer bundled up a file of papers on the table before him and tied it with a ribbon. Pointing the packet at Ben, he said, "These are copies of reports by military and civilian investigators of things that happened from Ohio to California, and I'm as sure as sunrise that you, Mr. Benjamin Gordyne, are involved, but I'm done with you. This whole thing started in Washington and

Washington has ordered me to send this file and you back to them for action. I'll put you on a train this afternoon with a military guard."

A month later Ben Gordyne was again called before a military interrogator. Col. Eli Payne sat behind an unfinished table. The flag of the United States stood to his right. President Lincoln's picture adorned the plank wall behind him. Ben was in a ladderback chair in the center of the room warmed by a fire crackling in the stove behind him. Two guards stood by the door to his right.

The questions covered the same ground as those he had answered in Indiana.

"Sir," Ben said after almost two hours, "I think I have been very patient and cooperative. I have listened to all of this before in Tennessee and Indiana. There was nothing then and there is nothing now to tie me into any of these strange events. Where is your evidence? You cannot even tie all these isolated things together. Do you really believe it possible for one man to do all you accuse me of? Where is the woman who brought these charges against me? Where is the mysterious Mrs. Wanderman? Colonel Payne, produce your witnesses or let me go."

The door on his right opened and Ben turned to look. Heather stepped into the room. Ben stood. There was silence as they embraced each other with their eyes. Colonel Payne, observing, smiled and changed his line of questioning.

"Madam," he asked. "are you Mrs. Heather D. Wanderman?"

"Yes, sir," she answered in a small voice.

"Thank you for coming over, Mrs. Wanderman. I am Col. Eli Payne. I regret that it was necessary to ask you to help in a rather unpleasant duty. Please, be seated."

Heather looked at Ben. He bowed and showed her the chair he had been occupying.

"I believe you recently survived a shipwreck off the coast of Carolina," Colonel Payne said.

"That is correct," she answered.

"Where did you reach land?"

"I believe it was around Cape Fear in North Carolina. Near Wilmington."

"Is Washington your home, Mrs. Wanderman?"

"It is."

"Was a man named Bartholomew Gordyne on the ship with you?"

"Yes, sir."

"What happened to him?"

"I do not know. He was on the ship when I last saw him. I'm afraid he went down with her."

"How did you get home from Wilmington?"

"I went by train to Richmond. Arrangements were made there to pass the civilian survivors through Confederate lines. We rode a stage to Washington."

"Did anyone in Richmond know that you were once an undercover agent for the United States?"

"No, sir."

"Perhaps you should have told them."

"Why, sir?"

"You would not now be facing a rather difficult situation.Tell me, Mrs. Wanderman, why didn't you stay in Richmond?"

"Why should I, sir? Washington is my home."

"Ah, yes, but is the United States still your country?"

"Are you questioning my loyalty, sir?"

"The possibility did occur to me that in two years you might have found a higher loyalty. Mrs. Wanderman, what was the name of the ship you were on?"

"The Islands."

"Where did you board The Islands?"

"Why are you asking me these questions?"

"I'm trying to find out where you have been for the last two years and who you have been with. Perhaps we have two defendants in this case."

Payne stood and paced the floor in front of Lincoln's portrait. He stopped and turned sharply towards Heather.

"Mrs. Wanderman, you were on your way home from

California, were you not?"

"Yes."

"What were you doing in California?"

"I worked in a coffeehouse."

"How did you get there? Why did you go there?" He did not give her an opportunity to answer. "Is this the man who abducted you in Washington and took you to California?"

Heather jumped to her feet.

"Colonel Payne," she said, "this is the man to whom I am engaged to be married and I refuse to answer any more questions."

Ben faced the Union officer.

"Colonel Payne," he said quietly, "there is no need to involve Mrs. Wanderman any further. I admit all the charges."

"No!" Heather cried clutching his arm. "No, Ben, please, no."

"Col. Gordyne, you realize you could be shot for this?"

"Yes, sir, I do."

There was a brief silence. Heather sat again and covered her face with her hands. Payne wrote a few lines on a piece of paper and signed his name.

"Take him away," the officer commanded and the two guards stepped forward and took Ben's arms.

"Wait," Heather said as they opened the door.

"Yes, Mrs. Wanderman?" Colonel Payne said.

"I have a suggestion which may shorten this war."

"What would that be?" he asked in a tone that indicated skepticism.

"This man was commissioned by General Lee and President Davis to attempt to bring gold to the Confederacy. The South is in desperate need of that gold to continue the war. If Davis is told by his own agent that there is no hope of getting that gold, it may encourage him to accept defeat."

Payne looked at Heather in surprise. Standing, he walked to the front of his desk before speaking.

"Mrs. Wanderman, you may have a point. Executing Colonel Gordyne will cost a bullet. If he can shorten this war, he may save us thousands of dollars and hundreds of lives. Colonel Gordyne is an impressive man and an outstanding soldier. We will gain nothing by hanging him and probably punish him more by requiring him to personally admit failure to General Lee.

"Mrs. Wanderman, I will recommend your suggestion to my commander."

"You may hold me to make sure he obeys your instructions," Heather said.

"That will not be necessary," Ben said.

Col. Payne looked at Gordyne. Heather stood and her eyes sought Ben's. He did not turn to look at her. The guards led Gordyne through the door. Heather collapsed into the chair and covered her mouth to stifle her sobs.

At dawn ten days later, Payne gave Ben a horse on the Virginia side of the Potomac River.

"Colonel Gordyne," Payne said, "Richmond has been taken. Jefferson Davis is moving his staff south by rail. You will not be able to reach him. The war may already be over. I have talked this over with my commanding officer. He has discussed it with others. We agree too many people have already died in this war and that, if turning you loose will save one soldier's life, then shooting you would be a mistake. Your mission is to find Lee and tell him that you have failed. Mrs. Wanderman is being held on suspicion of treason. If you fail in your mission, if you make any attempt to come back north and retrieve that gold, she will be tried. I'm sure you do not want that to happen. Now ride."

Ben mounted the grey filly. The two officers exchanged salutes and Ben rode south.

Six days later he intercepted the Army of Northern Virginia at Appomattox, Va. It was April 7, 1865.

****

Dogwood and azalea blooms were falling at Gordyne

Plantation when Ben rode up to the door of Bonmaison. A blue tick hound greeted him with a tired wag of her tail as he dismounted. The warm spring sun filtered gently through the great oaks. Spanish moss waved its welcome in a light breeze. The place appeared deserted. Inside, everything seemed to be in order. Floors were swept, furniture, dusted. The breeze tossed a diaphanous curtain in the parlor. But all was still.

The smell of home cooking floated in the cool air indicating that someone had recently prepared a meal. Ben went to the dining room. A candle burned in an ornate holder near one end of the massive oak table spread with a white lace cloth. Fresh-cut flowers were arranged in a crystal bowl. His mother slumped at her place at the end of the table nearest the kitchen.

Eunice Gordyne was dressed for the evening. Her long white hair was combed and coiled in a neat roll on the top of her head. She wore a freshly ironed black skirt and a lacy white blouse. She did not move.

She had dined and stacked the dishes neatly to take them to the kitchen for washing. She had started to stand when pain slashed through her head. Sorrow and strain touched her tired heart and a blood vessel burst in her brain.

Her son leaped to her side. She lifted her head and looked at him.

"Benjy, you're home." Her tired eyes stared at him with love and then she slumped over.

Ben picked her up and searched in vain for a pulse as he laid her on the carpet.

"Oh, Mama," he sobbed and cradled her in his arms. There was no heartbeat. She was gone.

The candle melted down. The flame died. Darkness filled the big house. The blue tick hound bayed at the moonless sky. Across the swamp another hound answered. Sometime during the night, Ben carried his mother's body to her bed. Then he lay down and slept.

In the morning he walked around the plantation. It was deserted but everything seemed to be in order. He made a box out

301

of cypress boards, lined it with a feather quilt and loaded it into a wagon. Carrying his mother downstairs, he laid her in the box and nailed the lid tight. He hitched up a mule and rode to the family cemetery on the bluff overlooking the Santee River. There he saw the new stone slab over a grave. It gave him the news of his father's death. Nearby was a new grave marked by a cypress slab with the inscription, "Bartholomew J. Gordyne." Thus he learned that his brother had come home, too. Ben had no more tears. He dug a grave next to his father's and there he buried his mother.

Kneeling between the two mounds of earth, he laid a hand on each and said, "I swear Gordyne Plantation will live again."

He rolled down his sleeves, put on his coat and hat, threw the shovel back in the wagon and turned the mule toward home. As he rode away he noticed a new grave in the area outside the wrought iron fence where slaves were buried. Its inscription said simply "Nida." Beside it someone had planted a magnolia seedling.

"My second mother. There's one who would never run away," Ben muttered and headed back to the big house.

After fixing himself a meal, he found a hoe and went to the vegetable garden. Spring planting had been done, but the soil needed tilling. He worked until dark.

As the weeks went by, Ben did not try to keep the whole plantation running by himself. He selected a field in which cotton had already been planted and worked it carefully. He transplanted some tobacco into another ten acres. He milked two cows morning and evening.

He kept a half a dozen laying hens and a rooster, a sow with a litter of five, a boar, a mare and two mules and one good riding horse. The rest of the animals were turned loose to run wild in the fields he did not intend to cultivate.

Ben looked up from milking one evening about a month later to find a familiar black face peering at him through the barn door.

"Taylor Jack, you old scoundrel," he shouted jumping up and spilling a bucket of milk in his excitement. "Where in creation have you been?"

"Us's been lookin' fer work, Mr. Ben."

"'Us'? Who else you got with you?"

"Dora. You remember Dora? She's my wife now."

A young Negro woman with three small children clinging to her skirt stepped into view.

"These be's our chil'n," Taylor Jack said. "Rose, Rando and Laddy."

"Dora. Sure I remember Dora. We used to play down to the river together. Where y'all been?"

"We went off with everybody when General Sherman went through. Mr. Lincoln said we was free, but free without food don't help a man with a family too much. We couldn't find no work no place, Mr. Ben. So we's come back to see if there be's somethin' we could do around Gordyne Plantation."

Pausing, he stepped into the bright sunlight slanting through the barn door, straightened his shoulders and looked boldly into Ben's eyes. "But, Mr. Ben, we ain't workin' for nobody unlessen we be's free."

"You're free, Taylor Jack. You're free, and if you work around Gordyne Plantation, you'll work like a free man. I can't pay you much, but you'll have food for your family and a place to sleep until we get back in production. You can have some of the livestock that's running loose and you can work a piece of land for yourself."

"We kin stay?" Dora asked.

"Sure you can stay, Dora, and I'm powerfully glad to have you back."

"When is we goin' fishin' agin, Mr. Ben?" Taylor Jack asked.

"Maybe Saturday, Taylor Jack. Maybe Saturday. Until then there's a sight of work to do."

"Let me go fix supper," Dora said and headed for the house with the children running excitedly ahead.

Taylor Jack picked up a pitchfork and started throwing down some hay while Ben went back to his milk stool.

****

The virgin dogwoods of the spring had turned to the scarlet women of the fall. Ben, Taylor Jack and Dora were breaking corn in the late afternoon of a sunny day. The children played in the field. Dora saw her first. The black buggy was pulled by a white mare.

"Who's that comin'?" she asked and the men straightened to look. The children ran to their mother.

The buggy stopped at the edge of the field. The woman who stepped down wore a gray traveling dress with white lace at her throat and a white sash around her narrow waist. A small gray felt hat perched among her golden curls.

"Heather," Ben said to Taylor Jack. "It's Heather Wanderman."

"Who that be?" Dora asked, but Gordyne was striding across the field to the pole fence.

"Heather," Ben called. "What are you doing here?"

She waited. Ben vaulted the fence.

"What are you doing here?' he asked again.

"I had a promise from a man in San Francisco and I came to see if Ben Gordyne keeps his promises."

Ben looked down at his rough worn clothes and shoes that were about to come apart on his feet.

"I'm not the man who made the promise, Mrs. Wanderman."

"What is that supposed to mean?"

"The man who made that promise was a plantation owner who could offer a woman something. I'm a hardscrabble, dirt farmer who's wondering how I'm going to pay his taxes. I haven't a thing to offer you."

"I didn't say I'd marry a plantation, Ben Gordyne. I thought you asked me to be your wife."

"Heather, do you ..."

"Kiss me."

He threw his hat to the ground, circled her waist with his right arm and drew her to him. She tilted her head back and his lips

304

found hers.

"I've waited a long time for that," she said when at last he released her.

"Well, I reckon we knows now who that be," said Dora.

"Yeah, we sho' do," said Taylor Jack.

"Dora. Jack," Ben called. "Come here, I want you to meet somebody."

Taylor Jack's family came over to the fence.

"Heather, I want you to meet my friends, Mr. Jack Taylor and his wife, Mrs. Dora Taylor. These are their children, Rose Taylor, Rando Taylor and Laddy Taylor. This is Heather Wanderman who is soon to be my wife."

"Pleased to meet you, Miss Wanderman," said Taylor Jack.

Dora beamed at her children.

"Did you hear that?" she asked. "Us's got a las' name like proper folks. I's Mrs. Dora Taylor."

A month later Mrs. Heather Duncan Wanderman became Mrs. Benjamin L. Gordyne III in the little white church in St. Stephens. Among the well-wishers who filled the pews and spilled out into the churchyard were Heather's parents and her brother, Arthur.

There was more news a week later when a thin man wearing a stovepipe hat and a black suit came calling.

"Legs," Ben shouted as he opened the door. "Legs Pharson. What in tarnation are you doing in South Carolina?"

"I haven't finished my investigation yet," Legs said as he stepped into the hall of Bonmaison.

That night they sat around the fireplace in the parlor and talked about Toledo, Maumee Crossing, St. Louis, Fort Laramie and San Francisco.

"I'm not telling you about my trip east," Ben said. "I can't be hung for something the Feds don't know about. But, Bart, well, he's gone and they can't hang him either."

"Last I saw him he was on deck with Junk DuBris," Legs said as he and Heather told the story of the sinking again.

"Our lifeboat dipped between two waves and when we came

305

back up, he was gone," Pharson said. "Never saw him again."

"Well, at any rate, he got home," Ben said. "His grave is out there in the cemetery. Taylor Jack, tell him what happened."

"Mr. Bart came home all right," Taylor said. "He walked in one evening."

"Did he bring anything with him?" Pharson asked.

"No, sir. Jes' walk in empty-handed."

"What then?" Pharson prompted.

"He stays 'round two, three days, en was gone. Said he had to git back to the war. When he comes back, well, when he comes back, I helps bury Mr. Bart."

"Did anybody ever hear my mother say anything about what Bart brought with him?" Ben asked.

"If she did, weren't none of us but Nida around to hear it," Dora said. "Mr. Lincoln says we is free and General Sherman seen to it that we was. So, one night we jes' lef'."

"This is not just a friendly call," Legs said. "It has been reported to the owners of the gold that Bart got off that ship with some of it. They have retained Pinkerton to investigate and since I was on the case from the beginning, I've been assigned to it. You certainly aren't spending any of it and you say Bart was killed in battle. I'll check on his grave tomorrow and report the gold apparently went down with the ship."

"That's the way it looks," Ben said. "We could sure use some of it, but it isn't here."

****

Next spring on a bright April day Ben was working in the fields when a man who said he was Kale Sanders came by with his wife Katie. They asked for Bart Gordyne.

"He isn't here," Heather told them.

"Can you tell us how we might find him? We've come to thank him for saving our home from Sherman's raiders last year."

306

"I'm sorry to tell you this, but we believe Bart was killed at the Battle of River's Bridge. His body was brought home and is buried in the family cemetery."

The visitors looked at each other.

"He asked for directions to St. Stephens when he left our house," Katie said. "How did he get to Erhart where the battle was fought?"

They were silent for a spell waiting for someone to give an answer.

"Please, wait a few minutes until we get Mr. Gordyne," Heather said and asked Dora to send one of the children to tell Ben they had visitors.

When he came in from the field, Heather said, "These people say that Bart was at their home about the time of the Battle of River's Bridge."

Ben stared at the couple, turned away, laid his hat carefully on the sideboard and looked back.

"Who are you?" he demanded. He was angry and suspicious.

"This is Mr. and Mrs. Kale Sanders of Keotee Plantation, down by the Edisto. They say they came by to thank Bart for saving their home from Sherman's raiders."

Ben looked at the couple again and said, "If you are after the gold, it's at the bottom of the Atlantic."

"I don't know about any gold," Mrs. Sanders said and there was a touch of anger in her voice, "but I assure you that Bart Gordyne was at our home after the shipwreck."

Ben sat down.

"I share your sorrow," Sanders said. "We owe him a great deal. I was at the Battle of River's Bridge when your brother did a rather remarkable thing for us and I wanted to thank him."

"Tell us about it," Ben said.

"Six Union soldiers came to our door about noon that day," Mrs. Sanders began. "Kale's mother, our two daughters and I were alone in the house. Most of the hands had run off by that time.

"The soldiers sat at our dining room table and we served them

307

our food and our wine. They ordered us out of our home and started stripping it of things they wanted."

She told her story which became a part of the legend.

"He came to our house a few days before the actual battle at River's Bridge," Kale said ending their account. "Some of the younger men harassed Sherman all the way to Columbia. Maybe he joined them. If so he could have been killed anywhere in that hundred miles."

"Yes, I suppose so," Ben said. "Bart was like that."

"What happened to the Miss Morenda?" Heather asked.

"After the war was over, Miss Morenda thought it would be safe to tell us about Bart Gordyne of St. Stephens."

"Did she say why she was shot?"

"No. She never told us what they were fighting over," Sanders said. "Perhaps she was the prize. Miss Morenda said she didn't remember much after she was shot and only came to as they neared the shore. I don't know how she lived to reach our home. I've thought your brother fought to keep her alive."

"Did she ever mention bringing anything to land with them?" Ben asked.

"No. If Bart brought anything with him, she didn't know about it. It was only by the grace of God that they got themselves ashore."

"Then what?" Heather asked.

"Nothing, really. She stayed with us about three months until she had recovered enough to travel. One Sunday, when we returned from church, we found a note saying 'Thank you,' and 'Goodbye.'"

"What do you think?" Ben asked Heather that night as they prepared for bed.

"I think he had to make a choice between the woman and the gold and did the only thing a real gentleman could do."

Ben threw a pillow at her.

SHADOWS MEET

1979

According to the Gordyne family history, Heather persuaded Ben to build them a cottage near the road. In it Benjamin L. Gordyne IV was born, followed in due time by the fifth and sixth to carry that name. Bonmaison, the mansion on the bluff overlooking the Santee River, stood empty. There was never enough money to keep it up.

More than a century after the simple funeral of Mrs. Eunice J. Gordyne, Bull finished reading her notes on the Civil War as the rest of us concluded the evening meal. It was the day after we had opened and closed the grave of a woman buried under the tombstone of Bart Gordyne.

I took the manuscript from him and was still reading long after all the others had gone to bed. It was a straight report by skeptical woman. She had not been sentimental.

"Clay brought Benjamin home from Charleston today," she wrote of her husband's death on January 3, 1864. "Said he had a heart attack. I know better. Bad women, bad liquor and bad oratory finally killed him.

"Jan. 5. Pastor Craig said some mighty nice things about Benjamin at the funeral today. Made me wonder if we were burying the right man."

That was the tone of her reports on religion, society, politics and the war. From the account it was evident that she was having more and more difficulty managing the plantation.

"Jan. 28. Wrote to Jeff Davis today asking him to send one of my boys home to help me here. Clay works hard but Lincoln sure didn't help. I can't hardly get the field hands to do anything."

"Feb. 12. Wonder where Benjy and Bart are. Haven't heard from them in over a year."

In this way she kept a record of events around the plantation: purchases and sales of tobacco, cotton and corn; plantings and harvestings; births and deaths among the neighbors and in the slave quarters.

"Jan. 13, 1865. Nida is real sick. High fever and coughs all the time. Can hardly get her to eat anything."

"Jan. 19. Katie Joyner came by. Said we'd better hide our valuables because Sherman has crossed into South Carolina."

"Feb. 26. Nida died today. Clay found her. 'Mama's dead,' he said. Never seen Clay cry before. She helped deliver all my babies. Treated Benjy and Bart as if they were her own. Been with me near forty years. I'll miss her. She was my servant but we were friends. I'll bury her near the gate."

"Feb. 27. Sad day. Woe-be-gone darky brought Bart home this morning. Said he was killed in battle near Salkehatchie River. Put his casket in parlor and helped prepare Nida for burial tomorrow."

"March 3. Clay's gone. Said he had nothing at Gordyne Plantation since Nida died. Did he ever know he was Bart's half-brother? Most hands left with him."

Several more straightforward accounts until: "April 19. War's over! Boys should be home by now."

Boys? I thought. Then she knew Bart was not dead.

That was the last entry. The date on her tombstone says she died the next day and that was the day Col. Benjamin L. Gordyne came home.

The kitchen clock said it was 2:15 a.m. The calendar said June 17, 1979. My eyes blurred with weariness, I closed the aged notebook and tried to focus on the strange bit of calligraphy on the front cover.

> "Death's words even down
> The other side.
> Tis won. Do rest till
> Three shadows meet.
> Or eat Juanitta's tone."

I nodded over the kitchen table and jerked my head up. Once more I glanced at the book's ornate cover, walked towards the stairs and stopped. What had my tired eyes seen? I returned to the table and picked up the manuscript. Did that last line really say, "Or eat Juanitta's tone?" In the last blurred look at the cover, the words ran together, and I read; "Ore at Juanitta's stone."

Excitedly I tore a page out of the back of the notebook, found a pencil and began to scribble. Half an hour later I had:

> "Death sword seven down
> the other side.
> Tis won. Do rest till
> Three shadows meet.
> Ore at Juanitta stone."

Only the last line made any sense. I was sure now the poem was not part of the original cover. The old lady scripted it there and meant it for a clue which might have been plain enough to Bart or Ben Gordyne coming home from the war. But what could it possibly mean to anyone a century later? I went to bed taking my scribble sheet with me.

I was the last one up the next morning and went down to find Bull on the telephone talking to a real estate broker about selling Gordyne plantation. Santee was at the table reading the notebook.

"How do you read the old lady's poem?" I poured a cup of coffee and sat down.

"What poem? This woman would have made a good CEO for an oil company. She didn't have a poem in her."

"Here, let me show you." I closed the book and pointed to the verse on the cover.

Santee read it and frowned. "Bad poetry."

"Now read this version of it," I said, handing her my scribble sheet.

"You're saying the old biddy left a clue to the legendary Gordyne gold."

"Could be." I went over to the counter and broke a couple of eggs into a skillet.

"'Ore at Juanitta's stone' seems to have some kind of meaning. Who's Juanitta? And I certainly don't see either rhyme or reason in the rest of it."

Bull came to the kitchen. He could not contain his excitement.

"Martin thinks he's got a buyer who may pay up to a thousand dollars an acre for the land," he said. "That's five million."

"Five million?" shrieked Santee jumping from her chair and dancing around the kitchen with her brother.

"Easy, Sis," he said. "Remember taxes and brokerage fees. There are a lot of maybes in this. Mama won't get that much."

"Who cares? Who cares? What's a million more or less?"

The notebook was forgotten as Rain and Martha hurried in to find why Santee was shouting. We spent most of the day talking about selling Bonmaison. The last time I saw the notebook it was on top of the refrigerator.

The next morning Santee and I had to catch a plane for Illinois. Five minutes before leaving for the Charleston airport, she remembered the notebook.

"I'd like to read it on the plane," she said. I brought it from the kitchen and we broke the speed limit down the highway to make our flight. In the air, Santee started talking to a woman next to her and ignored the book. It was still unread three months later when she received a telephone call from Bull telling us that their mother was to sign the contract for the sale of Gordyne Plantation at four o'clock the next afternoon in Charleston.

Sometime in the early morning, Santee woke and remembered the notebook. When I went down for breakfast, she was curled in a recliner reading it. I got a cup of coffee and a ham biscuit at a fast food place on the way to the newspaper office. As I walked in the door, Edna, the secretary of the editorial writers turned me around and said, "Don't sit down. Santee phoned. She says to meet her at the airport in forty-five minutes."

"What?"

"She says there's an emergency in St. Stephens. She'll tell you about it on the plane."

"But I've got to finish that editorial for Sunday's paper."

"The first draft is all right. Santee told me you would not be back until Monday."

My wife can do some unpredictable things. I called home. No answer, so I gave it to Edna, hoping it wouldn't upset the publisher's blood pressure, and took a cab to the airport.

"What's this all about?" I asked Santee when I found her in the terminal.

"Our plane is loading," she said. "Let's go."

We boarded and were barely strapped in before it started rolling down the runway.

"Now you're going to tell me what's going on," I growled.

"We've got to stop Mama from signing that contract."

"Why?"

"I've solved the riddle."

"What riddle?"

"Eunice Jamison Gordyne's riddle of the Gordyne gold."

"You know where it is?"

"Not exactly, but I know it's there."

"Where?"

"Under Juanitta's stone."

"Except for the poem on the cover, Juanitta wasn't mentioned in that whole manuscript. How can you possibly know where Juanitta's stone is?"

"Juanitta was a very important character in the legend and in Miss Eunice's record, but I wouldn't expect a man to notice."

"You are making me angry."

"Remember Nida? She was the midwife for both Benjamin and Bart. 'Nida' is the way a baby just learning to talk might say 'Nitta,' which is short for 'Juanitta.'"

313

"Nida? She was Miss Eunice's personal maid. She died just before Bart's coffin came home. She was buried that same day. Miss Eunice switched coffins!"

"Now you're getting it. The woman in the coffin we dug up in Bart Gordyne's grave was Juanitta. So the gold is where Nida's grave is."

"Where's that?"

"No, no. For that you'll have to wait. The clues are locked in the baggage compartment."

"I'll kill you," I muttered and we both laughed.

"That clears my family's name of murder."

"Murder maybe. But what about Clay's family tree?"

"Clay? You mean Nida's son?"

"We don't know that, do we?"

"It says Clay was Bart's half-brother."

"Yeah, but Clay had two parents and we don't really know which woman was his mother."

"Oh, I hadn't thought of that."

"Gender bias. Women always assume it's the man's fault."

The plane landed at 2:30 p.m. Somehow we managed to reach Broad Street before four. Santee raced into the law offices of Clarrison, Parnell and Simms while I paid the driver and took out our bags. From inside I heard Santee scream, "Mama, don't sign anything!"

The receptionist would not let her go back to where the closing was in process. My entry created a distraction and Santee scampered down the hall calling, "Mama, Mrs. Rain Gordyne, don't sign those papers!"

Bull stuck his head out a door.

"For heaven's sake, Santee, what in the world has gotten into you?"

"Please, Bull, don't let Mama sign those papers."

"Why?" he whispered.

"I know where the Gordyne gold is buried. I deciphered Miss Eunice's code."

I had gotten past the receptionist and joined them. Bull looked

314

quizzically at me.

"I think she has," I said.

"We're getting five and a half million for the land." He frowned. "I hate to risk a deal like that."

"Will the buyer wait a day while we check this out?" I asked.

"He's here from Seattle for this. He may not be able to stay."

"Let's see," Santee said and we went into the board room where papers were spread ready for Mrs. Gordyne's signature.

Seated around the table were six well-dressed men, probably the attorneys, real estate brokers and the buyer. They were watching us as we went over to Martha and Rain Gordyne. Bull made a quick introduction.

"Bull, what's going on?" asked John Parnell.

"I'm afraid we will have to delay the signing one day," Bull answered.

"Why?"

"My sister has uncovered some information which may make the sale inappropriate at this time. We need one day to investigate this information."

"I have business to attend to in Seattle," said Randolph S. McCurry. He looked like a business tycoon anxious to expand his west coast lumber empire to the Atlantic. "I cannot wait around here."

Parnell turned to Mama.

"Mrs. Gordyne, it's up to you."

"Mr. McCurry," Bull said, "I have a proposition. If you'll postpone this until Monday, we'll all fly out to Seattle to complete the deal should we determine that the information my sister has uncovered is not valid."

"I suggest that it would be inappropriate to consider another offer at this stage of negotiations," McCurry said.

"Sir," Bull said. "Yours is the only offer we are considering. Mrs. Gordyne and all the heirs have agreed to that. We have discovered something that may be of historical significance which we really feel compelled to investigate."

Mama hesitated, her eyes moving from Santee to Bull and

finally to me.

"That's the only arrangement we can make right now, Mr. McCurry," she said, gathering up her pocketbook and umbrella. "I'm sorry, but I cannot sign this contract until I know what my daughter has discovered."

"I'll wait one day," said McCurry. "If you want to sell, you'd better be prepared to do it tomorrow."

We walked out with Mama leading the way, got into Bull's battered station wagon and drove to the plantation. On the way Santee reviewed as much as she had told me and no more.

"When we get home," she insisted, "we'll get Mark's scribble sheet and a couple of shovels and go the cemetery. Then I'll interpret the rest of the code."

"And if you don't we may bury you out there," said Bull.

"And I'll help shovel dirt on you," I promised.

"And I'll take five and a half million dollars out of your skin before they do," said Mama.

It was after six when we got home, but the long summer evening gave us an extra hour of daylight. We changed into work clothes and packed the makings of sandwiches and some cold drinks in a cooler. Santee took the notes out of the suitcase while Bull and I got shovels. Then we drove to the graveyard.

The sky overhead darkened as we approached the cemetery and a stiff wind tossed the tree tops. Lightning ripped through the clouds to the east. Though vibrations of thunder shook the air, the western sky was clear and the setting sun probed beneath the canopy of clouds.

"Shall we wait until the storm passes?" Martha asked.

"It'll be dark then and we've got to have an answer for McCurry tomorrow," Bull said as Santee began reading.

"'Death sword seven down the other side.' Death points us to the cemetery. Are there any swords around here?"

"Sure. The wrought iron pickets on the fence look like swords," Martha said.

"So we count seven of them," Santee decided.

"Starting where?" Bull asked. "And does the account tell us

where Miss Eunice buried Nida?"

"The day Nida died, Miss Eunice wrote she'd bury her near the gate," I said. "Which gate? There are two gates, one in the cypress rail fence around the whole cemetery and one gate through the wrought iron fence."

"I'd say it's this iron gate because of the sword reference," Bull said.

"You're on the green," Santee said. "Want to try for a birdie? Which side of the gate?"

"The next word is 'down,'" Martha reminded us. "The graveyard slopes to the river. On the down side of the gate."

"'The other side' has me stumped," Santee said. "Anybody have an idea what that means?"

"Members of the Gordyne family are buried inside the fence. Slaves were buried on the other side. Nida was a slave." Mama said.

I was counting seven "swords" down from the gate.

"What's the rest of the poem mean?" Bull asked.

"'Tis won' spelled backwards is 'Sit now,'" Santee prompted. "Is there any place to sit around here?"

The wind was up and Martha had to shout, "The bench!"

A path paved with brick bisected the Gordyne plot from its gate to the back fence. Against this fence was an ornately carved, granite bench.

A gust of wind twisted the trees into a wild dance.

"It's fixin' to storm, y'all," said Mama, but ignoring the wind I paced the way to the bench and sat.

"Look," I called, pointing. "What does the poem say about shadows?"

"'Rest till three shadows meet,'" Santee read.

The evening sun sitting on the western horizon behind me traced my long shadow across the graves to the far fence intersecting it at picket thirteen.

"That isn't sword seven," Bull said.

"No, but this isn't February either," Santee noted. "In February the end of the shadow of a person sitting there might have met the beginning of the shadow of the seventh sword. Shall we wait until February?"

"Now what?" Martha shouted above the roaring wind.

"I'm looking straight over the top of sword seven," I shouted back. "If the end of my shadow intersected with the beginning of sword seven, then the end of sword seven's shadow would ... it would touch the shade of the magnolia tree by the cypress gate."

"Three shadows meet," Santee shouted. "I'll bet you half a coffin of gold, that's where we'll find Nida's stone."

Under the low branches of the oldest magnolia tree I had ever seen, we found an uncut boulder. It resembled a meteorite or a large irregular piece of lava. It looked natural but it was certainly out of place resting on the sandy soil of the South Carolina Low Country. I stood on it and looked through the branches of the magnolia tree towards the setting sun. It was a direct line across sword seven to the granite bench.

"Three shadows meet at Juanitta's stone," I quoted. "The third shadow was not the shadow of the tree, but this boulder."

Near it was a sunken rectangle which marked the outline of an old grave. If there had ever been a cypress marker, it was gone.

"Nida's stone," said Rain.

Bull and I picked up our shovels and started digging.

"Where do you suppose Bart went?" Santee asked.

"If I had the chance, I'd take the woman and the gold and run off to South America," I said, throwing a shovel of dirt at her feet.

"And I'd claw your eyes out."

"I wonder if he had better luck with her war than he did with his own?" Bull was working at top speed. We had a good-sized hole started.

Lightning cracked over our heads and a curtain of rain rolled in from the swamp. It splashed in the puddles and pushed a soggy mist into the branches. The sound of the storm drowned out conversation and the pounding rain slowed our shovels, but it did not stop our digging. We were wet yet it didn't seem to matter.

The summer storm moved north after about fifteen minutes leaving us in the afterglow of sunset. Minutes passed. No one spoke.

After a half hour, Bull and I looked at each other. I knew he was thinking that we should give it up, but we went back to shoveling.

The wet dirt was heavy and we'd dug about four feet when Bull's shovel hit something metallic.

"What's that?" whispered Santee in the silence that followed.

Bull stopped, felt under the dirt with his hand and pulled up a three-sided bar about eight inches long.

It was gold! Even in the dim light we could see the shine through the dirt.

"We found it," Bull said calmly, as if he had located a lost button.

"We found it!" screamed Santee. She and Martha hugged each other and started dancing. Bull handed the bar to his mother, who brushed off the dirt and held it up in the fading light.

"Well," she said, "we won't be selling the plantation."

The two of us in the grave were on our knees digging with our hands. The pine coffin had rotted away. We scratched around until we had uncovered twenty bars. It was now too dark to continue and four of those heavy ingots were about all we wanted to carry for the present.

"There's always tomorrow," said Martha.

Bull laid his shovel aside and started to climb out of the grave. I was still searching when my hand found a soft packet in the sandy soil.

"What's this?" I asked handing it to him.

"Too dark to tell," he said."Let's take it home."

We threw a few shovels of dirt back into the hole to cover any bars that might have been exposed by our digging and left.

Mama and the girls laughed and cried all the way home. I didn't blame them at all. The end of the story. Ben, Bart, Heather and even Legs and Ruby seemed more real to me. It was all true.

Hard to believe!

We stacked the ingots on the kitchen table and sat around to inspect the packet. Sealed in tar was a layer of oilcloth. Inside

319

that was a wrapping of brown paper. In that was an envelope containing several sheets of notepaper which Bull unfolded with agonizing slowness.

"What is it?" demanded Santee.

"Obviously, it's a letter," said her brother.

"Yes, but who's it to and who wrote it?"

"It starts, 'Hello, Ben,' and it ends," he said, shuffling the pages to look at the bottom of the last page, 'Bart.' Mama, you read it."

Rain took the letter and adjusted her glasses.

The letter went:

"Hello, Ben. You know I'm not much for writing, but you need to know what's happened. I'm in an abandoned farmhouse on Two Notch Road north of Columbia. The city is on fire. I can see it burning. Sherman's troops are moving this way.

"I've tried to get to General Johnston to tell him about our assignment. Nobody at headquarters believes the farfetched yarn. He won't see me. I should have brought a bar of gold as proof. Johnston has started moving his troops to North Carolina to make a stand there. He couldn't stop Sherman in Georgia or South Carolina. I don't think he can do it there. So I am going back to Edisto Island.

"If Heather got ashore, I expect she's already told you about the storm. Mama can tell you how I made it to shore. I buried three coffins behind the sand dunes on Edisto Island. To mark them, I cut a "G" in the bark of three pine trees. I left Rositta with the Sanders.

"Now my plans. After this war is over, the government or somebody may come looking for the gold. Nobody but Mama knows I got it ashore. I figure it's salvage from an abandoned ship and belongs to us. I think if lawyers get into this, it'll be years before anyone knows who owns it and by that time the lawyers will have all of it. It's best if they think it went down with the ship. So I'm going to disappear. I don't want to get you in trouble.

"However, I did decide to bring one coffin home. To keep it from Yankees, lawyers and other robbers, Mama has agreed to

320

bury it in my grave until you get back. You'll need it to rebuild the plantation so don't spend it all in one tavern. You know the BIG TROUBLE we found at Rebel Flag.

"I will take Rositta to Charleston and ship her home to Colombia, South America. She wants me to go with her. Can't say as I blame her, but I've had enough of civil war. I'll grubstake her. She did shoot Junk Dubris for me. And now? Since I don't like lawyers and I don't want to be arrested nor cause you any trouble, I'm going to Alabama with a banjo on my knee. Love, Bart."

"Why Alabama?" I asked.

"Oh, Mark," answered my wife in disgust, "how can you be so unromantic? Let me spell it out for you. B. A. M. A. Smith."

"Oh," I said.

#

ABOUT THE AUTHOR

Carlton W. Truax is the son of missionary parents and spent most of the first 22 years of his life in China, Burma and Hong Kong. As a youth he ran telephone lines through the Burmese jungle for the U.S. Army during World War II.

After graduation from Bob Jones University, he worked as a staff writer for newspapers in Columbia, S.C. He was also in public relations and was managing editor of the South Carolina Insurance News Service before retirement.

He has been a part-time pastor of a number of small rural congregations and teaches regularly in South Carolina and Georgia churches.

He and his wife, Georgianna, live in Lexington, S.C. They have five children and 12 grandchildren. This is his first novel.

Daniel Defoe

BANJO ON MY KNEE is one of a series of novels being published by Senior Press which was established in 1993 to promote creative writing by mature authors.

Senior Press seeks fictional works by those 50 years of age and older. Novelists who have never had a book published are given priority.

Daniel Defoe, pictured above, is a symbol of achievement for all senior writers. He is considered by many to be the father of modern journalism and was 60 in 1719 when he completed his first novel, LIFE AND STRANGE SURPRISING ADVENTURES OF ROBINSON CRUSOE.

For further information on forthcoming books write

SENIOR PRESS
P.O. Box 21362
Hilton Head Island, SC 29925